Thaw

NICOLE LUNDRIGAN

NICOLE LUNDRIGAN

Jesperson Publishing

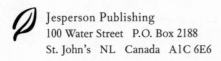 Jesperson Publishing
100 Water Street   P.O. Box 2188
St. John's   NL   Canada   A1C 6E6

Library and Archives Canada Cataloguing in Publication

Lundrigan, Nicole
        Thaw / Nicole Lundrigan.

ISBN 1-894377-11-7
        I. Title.

PS8573.U5436T43 2005   C813'.6   C2005-900804-0

Interior Design: Rhonda Molloy
Cover Design: Adam Freake
Editor: Tamara Reynish

Printed in Canada.

This is a work of fiction. Any resemblance to actual events or persons
is entirely coincidental.

For my sister,
Cyndi

And my brothers,
Steven, Peter, Davey, and *Robbie*

With much love and appreciation.

prologue

uring a blinding blizzard on Christmas Eve in 1898, a young woman heavy with child pushed her way down a snow-covered lane. Her husband trudged along beside her, his head bowed against the shards of ice cutting into his face. Both wore long steely-grey woollen coats, and the woman had a black scarf tied over a mound of ginger hair that was braided and pinned at the nape of her neck. They were lost and had been wandering for two hours. And now, the woman's mittened hands quivered uncontrollably as she traced a peeling white picket fence that could have been any one of a dozen.

"Ain't never seen nothin' like this in all me years, maid," the husband hollered, wind shaving away his words. "Come up like crazy. Can't see the nose in front of me face. Should've stayed to Mudder's."

At once the woman stopped, and leaned her full weight against the fence. Her eyes were glossy with fear and rapid blinks scattered the snowflakes that were settling on her lashes. Without speaking, she gripped her husband's wrists, and brought his palms to her abdomen, hard and smooth like a massive beach rock. She dreaded to let go of him, for she knew if he took a step backwards, just one single step, the swirling storm would swallow him and she would be alone.

Crouching against the fence, she reached up under her skirts with one hand, and tugged down her long underclothes. Tight bands of heat seized her abdomen as she screamed her agony out into the howling sheets of snow. Her husband inched backwards to remove his coat, and she shrieked again, clawed for him, knocked away his fur hat, and clutched his reddened ears.

"Ye got hold to me, maid," he cried in pain. "Now let me be, for the love of God."

He pushed his coat underneath her, blanketing the drift of snow where she lay. Reaching behind her, she grabbed the fence. As she birthed the baby, she tore away the two wooden slats she had been holding. Her husband plucked a crimped pin from her hair, clamped the slippery cord with three swift twists, and severed the connection with his shiny pocket knife. Then, he bundled the crying child in his fisherman's knit sweater and tucked it inside his soiled coat, while his wife squat to discharge the afterbirth.

"C'mon, maid. Lest the wee one catches her death."

"Her?" The woman's heart swelled inside her chest.

"Yes," he said. "Beautiful hazel eyes, she got. Right like her mudder."

The woman stood slowly, her knees like the tide. She pointed to the placenta, a bloody, gelatinous mound that steamed next to her snow angel impression, and said, "We can't go leavin' that."

"Don't be so foolish, me duck."

"We got to bury it." The woman wavered as blackness pressed in around her eyes and she rolled her palms over the sharp points on the pickets to steady herself. "Where we lives. The lilac tree. Beside our window."

"What? In this kind of storm?"

"Keep it," she said. "'Til the earth softens."

Her husband's head was bare as his hat had scampered away, and the wind whipped his white shirt into a flag. "Maid…" he said, shaking his head.

Then, in a brief moment of silence when the blizzard inhaled, sheep bleated somewhere off in the distance.

"I knows where we're to," he yelped. "Heavenly Fadder has shown us the way. 'Tis good fortune."

"'Tis?" she asked as she began to weep. "But. But if we leaves it, she'll go astray. Won't never know where her home is to. Where she belongs."

The husband tugged at his wife's arm and she conceded. She was too weak to persist. As they pressed onwards through the blizzard, the wind grew weary and the night calmed. The woman stole rapid breaths through damp mittens that were pressed over her deadened nose. Surrounding her, the air was blissfully aglow as moonlight bounced off every fat flake. Might be a certain beauty to it, she imagined, if only she could step aside, somehow manage to distance herself and get a decent look. *Then again*, she pondered as she stopped to rest just outside her saltbox home, *the beauty itself might only reside inside this fleeting blindness*.

Within moments, three shorthaired dogs, feral and emaciated, happened upon the warm placenta. They tore it apart with throaty growls, gulped down every bite through bloody muzzles, and licked the soiled snow clean. Bellies satiated, they frolicked and danced, rolled around in the drifts, and finally curled into tight balls to sleep. They never whimpered once as the temperature dropped and ice crystals cloaked their bodies.

The morning after the storm, a farmer walking his property line noticed the broken fence and the dead dogs. He hammered the two slats back in place, then loaded the dogs into old flour sacks, and dragged them to the edge of the cliff. With a swing of his strong arm, he tossed them in a great arc up and out towards the famished sea.

one

When Tilley Gover turned eleven, his mother, Maureen, gave him a clock radio that projected the time onto his bedroom ceiling in hypnotic blue numbers. Though it was equipped with an alarm, in the three years he had owned it, he never once used it. Instead, every morning, except Sundays, at precisely seven o'clock, the porch door woke him up. At this early hour, his father, Earl, arrived home from a night shift at the local fish plant. When the weather was warm, Earl stretched the screen door beyond its natural limit and let it snap shut with a rousing, tinny clang. In winter, after frost settled in and the left side of the house had hunkered down beneath the snow, Earl kicked the ill-fitting main door closed with his slushy work boot. The earsplitting "Christ, Jaysus" that followed was always enough to drag Tilley from his clammy, teenaged slumber.

In 1977, summer descended on Cupboard Cove like a damp

dishcloth, as constant drizzle seeped from the steely sky. In his muggy room, Tilley awoke with the standard screen door special, the complaint of a distended spring, then the door barking back. When he consulted the fading numbers on his ceiling, they revealed his father had returned home ten minutes early. From experience, Tilley knew that whenever his father's bowed legs carted him home faster than usual, there was a piece of news, some thread of local gossip that he was dying to share. This was not uncommon. At the fish plant, workers blathered constantly while they split open bellies or tore out guts with rubber-gloved hands.

Sounds trickled in from the kitchen. Tilley heard a chair being drawn out, the settling of a heavy load, and pipes groaning as someone ran the tap. Detangling himself from his sweaty sheets, he hung his stubby legs over the side of the bed. Stretching, his toes barely graced the tan, shag carpet. When he focused on his newly hung wallpaper, with its big game pattern and stately conifers, Tilley breathed deeply and straightened his back.

"First off, I's starved, starved, starved." His father's voice was aggravated, gruff. "Got a hole rotted right through me gut, maid. C'mon with a cuppa tea." Then came a slish of slippers across the linoleum, the kettle being dropped onto a burner.

As he did every morning, Tilley wandered out into the kitchen in his brother's striped, hand-me-down pyjama bottoms and a soft, cotton T-shirt. Taking the stool nearest to the window, he waited for his breakfast.

"How's me little man this marnin'," his mother said to him.

"I's good," Tilley said, plucking sleep from his eyes. "Tired, I s'pose."

"That's cause yer a growin' b'y, is all," she replied.

Seated at the rounded end of the counter, Earl let out a snort. "Soon be time for him, then."

Tilley propped his elbow on the counter and leaned hard on his fist.

"Never ye mind, me son," Maureen said, as she stood by the wood stove, melting margarine in a pan. "Ye'll sprout right through the roof one of these days."

She cracked a single egg and blinded the yolk with one stab. Slipping a generous slice of homemade bread into the left compartment on the toaster, she hovered like a honeybee until it was slightly crisp. She pushed the plate into the narrow space between Tilley's elbows and said, "Down the hatch, honey." His egg on toast was already cut into nine neat squares. They needed only the jab of a fork, then for him to shovel it in.

Earl ran his rough hands over his face and wiped his leaking nose onto his shirtsleeve. Then without looking at anyone, he lifted his copy of the local newspaper, the *Full Bucket*, to eye-level and let it sail down. It landed on the countertop with the noise of an open-handed slap. On the front page, bold type and photos announced an arrival.

"Well, now then. Ye's not goin' to believe this," he said, thumbnail mining his left nostril. "Our little Cupboard Cove ain't gettin' her hotel after all. Ye knows that big house up on the hill? Some good for nothin' painter and his mangy brood are movin' in."

"Well, ain't that somet'ing'," Maureen said. "Never thought no one could make that kind of fortune paintin'." She ran her fingers along the wall behind the sink. "Could use a new coat in here, that's for sure."

"Yer that daft," Earl said, shaking his head. "Not paintin' houses. Pictures, maid. Pictures."

Earl Gover considered himself to be a sharp man with a keen sense of observation. No doubt about it, he had been the first to notice the city man wandering down by the post office. Walking home from the fish plant earlier this spring, he'd spied this gentleman (that seemed the appropriate word for him) pacing back and forth. The man wore trousers creased to cut, a robin's egg blue sweater, and was walking with another man who clomped in unlaced boots, a heavily scarred hard hat atop his head. The worker pointed towards the mountain, wagged his finger back and forth, and then made notes on a bright yellow legal pad that was attached to a sturdy clipboard.

"Somet'ing's up," Earl had said to Tilley one morning over breakfast. "I can tell ye that. I seen a government man in town."

Within weeks, machines chewed through the trees and wound a smooth road up the mountain. Power lines were erected. "That's some kind of top class operation goin' on," Earl said, as he followed the progress from his vantage-point at the kitchen window. He made mention of the number of loads of crushed stone, the pouring of the cement foundation, and the shiny newness of the trunks that carted up supplies. "Winse t'inks 'tis a hotel goin' in," he said. "And I reckons he got the mystery cracked wide open." Soon, the frame went up, leather-skinned men crawled over it like termites and Earl said to Maureen, "Tourism, maid. That's the way, girl, that's the way." By mid-June, windows were installed, board and batten hammered in place, and the entire structure painted a regal red. Earl sucked tea from his cup, stuck out his pinky, and said, "'Tis lovely grand, ducky. Lovely grand."

When the exterior was finally completed with its towering cupolas, gently sloping roofs, and tar black shingles, Earl remarked, "Now that brings a touch of class to ol' Cupboard Cove, don't ye t'ink? Though, for the life of me, I don't know what to Christ Premier Moores t'inks we needs a hotel for."

But that midsummer morning, the *Full Bucket* spread out on the counter before him, Earl's tune was decidedly less merry.

"Pull the curtain to, Maureen," he said. "I can't stand the sight of it." He rapped the front page of paper with his knuckles, ink blurring underneath the pressure. "Winse showed me. Wish to God now that I had gone and made a bet with him on it."

With the words now smeared like a bruise, the front page still managed to announce: 'Renowned Painter Comes Home.' "'Tis some rich arsehole instead," Earl continued. "T'inkin' he'll come to the Cupboard, hoist up a massive eyesore, build his own top shelf to the place. He now, ridin' 'round on the pig's back, makin' a damn fool out of us hard-workin' men livin' here all our lives." He drew hot tea past his lips, into his dry mouth. "He now, got hisself the highest house in the harbour. Udder than that crazy ol' hermit's place, but that's only a tinderbox, no bigger than a shithouse, so that don't count." Shifting his weight back onto the stool, he folded his arms across his chest, and pushed icy fingers into his armpits.

"But how do ye know there's somet'ing off 'bout him?" Maureen said, placing toast near Earl. "He might be the nicest kind."

"Oh, I knows, me dear. Ye don't be makin' stuff like he do without bein' queer in the head."

"Yes, now. A cutter from the plant is sure to be a real authority on that sort of t'ing."

"I's as much a bloody authority as I wants to be, missus, I'll tell ye that."

Earl had never forgotten the time he'd seen one of Boone's paintings. Not that he had sought it out. His idea of art never moved beyond the glory of a moose head, antlers and all, showcased above a fireplace. It was two years earlier when he'd had a devil of a time passing his water. Although he told Dr. Richards things got fooled up from spending too many hours in his hip waders without going, the good doctor was convinced the trouble had something to do with a temperamental gland in his backside. "Yer Fadder died with it," Dr. Richards had said, "Best we haves ye checked." So Earl was sent to the Good Hopes

Hospital across the Bay to see a specialist named Dr. Butt—a man with a lopsided grin and a slippery glove.

As Earl leaned over, johnny coat hanging open, his eyes travelled to the painting displayed just above the examining table. In fat swipes, with thick globs of oil, children sledding had come to life against the backdrop of a brilliant mountainside. One youngster, though, stood frozen in the foreground, mouth opened slightly, entirely naked from the waist up. He seemed to be gawking straight at Earl, as if Earl's forced examination was some sort of imposition on the boy.

Amidst the gaiety of the scene, that slack-jawed child with the bluish barrel chest and hungry ribs grated on Earl's nerves. The boy made him sense something he couldn't quite identify. At a glance, the face was bland, even boring, a dim-witted boy who might slip through childhood unnoticed, overlooked by his peers. But upon closer inspection, and Earl's position offered this very opportunity, a stroke here, a shadow there had created tension. It was the eyes, Earl realised, wanting but unable to give himself a proud slap on the back. Those eyes didn't fit the child. The bulging cheeks flushed from cold, soft lips, a smatter of freckles—yes—they all belonged on the young. But those eyes were aged, not innocent at all: those of a tainted man.

Dr. Butt placed his dry hand on Earl's hip, or maybe just an inch lower, not more. "'Tis a Boone, ye knows. A print is all, mind ye. His 'Window' series. A gift from a patient."

"Window?" Earl groaned. He started to hold his breath, then stopped himself.

"I knows," Dr. Butt said, working swiftly. "Nar window in sight. But, I reckons he meant the eyes. Windows to yer soul and all that stuff. Not the most pleasant, I s'pose, but I haves it there as a distraction."

Earl lurched forward, or was pressed forward, he couldn't be certain. He stared up at the painting, the boy's face only an inch away. While Earl's hindquarters scorched from the probing, it was then that he noticed a muted reflection disguised in the smoky swirls of the child's left iris, a reedy woman in a gauzy dress, barefoot, arms reaching out towards him.

"There now," Dr. Butt said as he withdrew his finger. "Not a t'ing wrong. She's top rate."

Something vile snuck up the back of Earl's throat and burned the back of his tongue. He wasn't sure which way to move. Both ends were so hot. How could anyone dare call any section of his body 'she,' most especially his backside? He reached behind, bunched the gown in a fist, stared hard at the mismatched grey socks he was wearing. Lucky for Dr. Butt. If Earl hadn't been freezing, standing in a draughty office with a dress on, with a mammoth need to use a toilet, he would have taken a rock to the man's head. Though, of course, he didn't. He said, "Thanks, Doc," instead.

Even today, Earl shuddered at the memory of it. He didn't know what disgusted him more, having been tapped like a maple tree, or having been so close to that disturbing boy in the painting. While Earl's sleep generally led him down into a soggy cavern, that night he had dreamt in full colour: diapered babies, rolling hulahoops, a sweet cherry square stuffed into someone else's warm pink mouth.

"And just whatd'ye t'ink of it all, me son?" Earl said to Tilley.

Tilley shrugged, kept his elbow on the table, cheek still cupped in his palm. His father was fond of asking questions, answers not required. "Nothin', I s'pose."

"Listen to him, Maureen," Earl said, pressing crumbs into his thumb, licking them off. "I thought teenagers knew it all. He now, fourteen, and don't know a damn t'ing."

"Leave the b'y alone, Earl," Maureen said, scouring the sudsy egg pan with fervour. "It'd be nice to get a breakfast down without havin' ye climbin' all over him every second."

Tilley kept his mouth closed, teeth busy, working the toughened toast, cutting through the soft white of the egg. He was nearly finished, swallowing the last bite with a mouthful of watery orange juice, when a heavy drumbeat rattled the floorboards, and sent a rush up through the legs of his stool. Three swift bangs of Earl's boot on the linoleum brought it to an instant end. Then, Tilley's older brother, Boyd, appeared in the basement doorway with bushy hair and painted on denims that were dull along the crotch.

"Good to see ye up early for once, Boyd," Maureen said. She lifted the tin foil cover off of a ceramic bowl, smoothed and folded it, then tucked it into a drawer.

"Up, ye says?" Boyd replied, his body shaking in a wet dog fashion. "I ain't been down yet, Mudder." He scratched the faded front of his jeans. "What a night I had. Have I told ye 'bout it already?"

"That'd be a trick, me son," Earl said. "I don't know when ye'd be tellin' us. I was to the plant, yer Mudder was to her bingo."

While raking the spotty stubble on his chin, Boyd said, "Uh, yeah. Right on. Well, I was over to Boyle's Billiards and this couple of b'ys comes rollin' in from McGinty's Gut. Blackie Tripe and some udder feller. I knowed they was up to no good, right? Martin was there, playin' a bit of pool, doin' nothin' wrong, right? Then Blackie and his crony wants a game, and Martin says to them, 'As soon as I's finished, b'ys. Wait yer turn.' Neither bit lippy or nothin'. Well, ye can be sure they didn't want to be waitin', cause next t'ing I sees, Blackie is takin' a potshot at Martin, knockin' clear his wind, while the udder one gives him a good root square in the nuts."

"Mind yer tongue b'y, 'round yer mudder," Earl said.

Boyd nodded swiftly, hands coursing through the air as he spoke. "Right on. And then Martin's down for the count, gruntin' like some wild pig on the floor. So, I steps up to the plate, and I says to Blackie, 'ye caused enough trouble already, buddy. Ye best be headin' on out.' Well, the udder one with the rat face, ye knows how they grows them in the Gut, right, starts comin' at me and I spins him 'round, grabs him by the belt, and heaves him that hard through the door, he rolls right down into the mucky ditch. Cussin' left and right and left again, mess he's in. Blackie, now, was that pussified, he hauls his ass outta there, tail stuck so far between his legs, he could take a bite off the tip."

Earl frowned. "Don't know what ye expect me to say 'bout that, Boyd. Almost got yer teeth knocked in by two bits of trash."

"'Almost' nothin', Fadder," Boyd said, on his toes, fists formed, jabbing the air near Earl's head. "After they's gone, I's back over talkin' with Teena, and Billy Boyle hisself comes up to me, he was watchin' the whole t'ing. And he asks me if I'd mind keepin' an eye on the place, now that Angie's havin' her baby, he won't be 'round as much."

Maureen glanced up from the bowl, spiced raisin cookie dough in her grip. "Ye means he offered ye a job?"

"That's what I's been sayin', Mudder, if ye hasn't been listenin'. I got meself a job at Boyle's Billiards. Gettin' change for the pinball machines, makin' sure no one rips off the eight ball, keepin' out the rowdies, and the like."

Earl was up from his stool again. "I'll be damned," he said, a solid clap to Boyd's back. "That's really somet'ing. Whatd'ye t'ink, Maureen?"

"That's wunnerful news, Boyd," Maureen said, palms rolling, fingers not missing a beat. "Wunnerful news."

"Didn't t'ink I could do it, did ye? No, b'y. Well, that I can. I'll be the best b'y Boyle's Billiards ever seen. No time, I's apt to be takin' that operation right over. Knock the 'l', 'e' right off his sign, change her to a 'd', and I'll be in business."

"Yes, by Christ, ye never knows. Out of high school for no time and look at ye. Yer on yer way, me son, yer on yer way. Why, I remembers when I was yer age. Me first real job." Earl laughed, a memory simmering. "I was taggin' beavers, traipsin' through the woods in me rubber boots, alongside the ponds. As long as I lives, I'll never forget that gargeous sound of a beaver whackin' his tail on the water. Caught them in a trap, I did, lovely creatures, then I pierced their ears like I'd been doin' it since the day I dropped out of me Mudder. By Jaysus, I was the best tagger me supervisor ever seen, he says to me. I was right proud. Never made much of a dollar, mind ye, but 'tis all 'bout experience me son, and I was only startin' out. This is a real opportunity for ye, now Boyd. Yer takin' yer first step into the real world. Responsibility, b'y. 'Tis all 'bout experience and responsibility. Take heed now, Tilley. Get yer head out of yer runny eggs and take a gander 'round the kitchen. We got a young man in the room here, a young man. Yes, me son."

Reaching around Maureen's waist, Boyd grabbed formed cookies from the pan. "Hey numbnuts," he murmured to Tilley as dough melted in his mouth. "If ye wants, ye can come 'round before I opens up. I can let ye have a game or two for nothin'."

Tilley slid off his stool, smacking his sweaty bare feet on the linoleum. He stole a rapid glance at his father, wondering if the slapping sound would instinctively send him running in search of watery rodents. Not a budge. "That'd be alright, Boyd."

"Listen to him," Earl said, delivering a swift clout to Tilley's head. "'That'd be alright,' he says. Couldn't ask for more, me son. Ye couldn't ask yer brudder for nothin' more."

Tilley's hand sprung to the hot spot on his scalp. "I meant, cool, Boyd. That'd be real cool."

"No sweat, dickhead," Boyd said through a lion's yawn.

"Boyd! Watch that lip." Maureen clinked dirty beaters and

measuring cups into the sink, louder than necessary. "And Earl, go on to bed out of it. Ye've been up all night. But for the love of God, get yerself a wash. Ye reeks to the high heavens."

With the *Full Bucket* snug in his grip, Tilley made his way down the hallway, several paces behind his father. When Earl closed the bathroom door and started the shower, Tilley tugged open the linen closet, hefted himself up to the highest platform, and crinkled his body in order to fit in. After he had located his flashlight along the edge of the plywood, Tilley dragged the door to with his fingertips. Hidden atop the pilled bedclothes, bath sheets tough from line drying, he was completely out of sight. His father, who has never made a bed, who preferred to dry himself with a mouldy bathmat rather than seek out a fresh towel, would never find him there.

Tilley flicked on the flashlight, held it in his teeth, and unrolled the paper.

Renowned Painter Comes Home

Cupboard Cove residents welcome the return of internationally renowned painter, David Patrick Boone. Made famous for his distinct style best demonstrated in his oil scenes of children at play, Mr. Boone was born and partly raised in this very community by his parents, Mr. and Mrs. Harvey Boone.

Displayed in galleries across both Canada and the United States, his acclaimed work has been described as 'hauntingly original' and 'sinister, but satisfying.' Since hearing of the move, local

bank manager, Harold Gullage, has purchased a
number of prints and will be displaying them in
the coming weeks for all his valued customers.
For complete story, see headline: 'Famous
Painter Moves Back', page 2.

Tilley folded the paper once, twice, let it drop down the thin
crack between the shelf and closet door. Reaching behind his
head, he found a tattered exercise book, the chewed pencil tucked
inside a pillowcase. Carefully, he sharpened it, and as the shavings
dropped into a sandwich bag, he heard a low whine just outside
the door. Peering through the slats, Tilley saw Clipper, their
arthritic dog, crouching, healthy tail flicking at lightening speed.
Gradually, while Tilley's eyes drifted and his thoughts shifted
from one side of his head to the other, the image of Clipper's face
disintegrated, turned from a living dog into a series of lines and
tones, shadows and light. He opened to a blank page; let his
pencil glide over the paper. From its pointed tip emerged a
dripping grey tongue, limp spotted ears, eager black eyes. Then,
almost before he knew what was happening, it was there.
Transferred perfectly. All the pieces of Clipper's face were
present, though interrupted by the dust-coated wooden slats of
the linen closet door.

two

On Sunday mornings, most people in Cupboard Cove gathered at St. Peter's, a greying clapboard church at the very base of Main Road. No matter the season, drafts wafted through the old building like cold ghosts, dankness eternal. Having much to say, the affable Reverend Grimes managed to speak and sing in monotone for a full ninety minutes. But during that time, attention never wavered, tongues remained still.

Mid-sermon, the reek of takeout unfailingly replaced the smell of lemon polish and ancient, leatherbound prayer books. Next door to the rectory was Tubby Gould's 'Chicken Deelicken,' which he proudly owned and operated. Shrewd businessman and self-proclaimed doubter of all things, 'save a good feed,' he would crank up the heat on his deep fat fryers every morning at 11:15, drop in frozen, breadcrumb-coated chicken bits, and angle his exhaust fan accordingly. After worship, mouths were watering so badly that handfuls couldn't make it home to their cooked dinners. Eager patrons landed on his steps, tore into Tubby's offerings, and, not wanting to get a single stain on their Sunday best, licked their greasy fingers clean.

Seated in the fourth row from the front, Tilley shivered slightly and tried to focus on the two-dollar bill folded in the back pocket of his dress pants. Even though his mother had a pot roast simmering, he would stop for a quick plate of fries, nothing more. As rich gravy dribbled in his mind, an elbow came up and knocked his head back against the wooden pew.

"Hey, watch it!" Tilley said.

"Sorry, Till." The roving elbow belonged to Walter Payne, Tilley's best friend.

"And squish over," Tilley said. "I can't even see from where I is."

Walter tilted his head towards Tilley, said, "B'y, I ain't got much room meself. Mudder's almost on top of me here. Don't know why we all got to poke ourselves into the same row."

Tilley looked up at his friend, eyed his oak-coloured freckles, coarse orange hair that was like a rusted mop still flattened from a motionless sleep. Just above Walter's left temple, there was a white patch as though a cabbage moth had lit upon his head and refused to move. While Tilley wore a short sleeve, cotton shirt, Walter's skin shone at the edges of his nubbed sweater and wool slacks. Trying to shrink himself, Walter drew his elbows together, causing the fat on his trunk to relocate and creating an unfortunate mound of cleavage in the 'V' of his sweater.

A flash of white calf must have caught Penny Payne's eye, as she leaned out over the pew, gripped the bottom of her son's church pants, and said, "Did ye grow again me son, or what?" Then to Maureen, who sat on Tilley's other side, "I swears to the Lard I can't keep this b'y in clothes. If I lets them trousers out anudder time, 'tis just as well I don't sew them back up t'all."

Tilley watched the colour in Walter's cheeks drop into his sweater and rise again, leaving his skin blotchy, berry stained. Then came the smell, an emission that always followed any comment on Walter's mushrooming weight. Oozing out of Walter's pores, it reminded Tilley of something smothered, like leaf lettuce forgotten in a grocery bag. But Tilley didn't mind. They had known each other far too long for an odour to do anything more than crinkle his nose.

Maureen and Penny were best friends, so Tilley and Walter had been together since birth, napping in the same crib, tumbling out of the same playpen. Often they would play in Walter's backyard, Tilley roaming free through the weedy grass, climbing over stumps, catching ants in his cupped hands. Walter's adventuring was curtailed, for Penny kept him tethered to the clothesline, a harness crisscrossing his chest and attached to a reasonable length of string. Not once did Tilley try to tempt Walter into a game of tag, for he knew Walter would surely sever himself if he ran to catch Tilley, or at the very least displace his wind. Most often, Tilley stayed within Walter's well-worn circle of space.

"Lindy Tuck had her very last yesterday," Penny said to Maureen. "T'was a section." She leaned hard against Walter, once again drowning Tilley in flesh and wool.

"Me Lard. How many is she up to now?" Maureen asked.

"Believes 'tis seven or eight in almost as many years."

"That's a lot in this day and age."

"No doubt. 'Round seven or eight too many, if ye asks me," Penny said. "She got Dr. Eric to tie her tubes right tight while he was in and around. Double-knot, she says."

"Just as well."

"'Fore she goes under, she makes us swear not to say a word. She don't want Ed to know. He don't believe in that, she tells us.

That's all good and well for him, I says to her. But if he finds out, tell him Nurse Penny says those varicose veins in yer legs got their own notions 'bout it."

Penny opened her mouth to continue, but with a gentle tap of his wooden cane on the floorboards, Reverend Grimes urged her back to attention. "Heavenly Fadder," he said, "Please grant me the small mercy of a few moments of silence in yer good house."

His soft voice flowing out from the altar quieted the shuffling, the Sunday morning pre-service gossip, and the talk of a cold beer after dinner. When he moved to the pulpit, he gripped the sides firmly, the dull ache in his hip a guarantee of afternoon rain.

"I sees we got a break in the drizzle. 'Tis a gargeous marnin' the Lard has given us," he began. "A samplin' of His gracious nature. Let us appreciate it while it lasts."

"While what lasts?" Wilf Tippet hollered from the eighth row. "The fine weather or His gracious nature?"

Another tap of the cane silenced the ripple of easy laughter.

"If ye don't mind, Mr. Tippet, I'll carry on."

As Reverend Grimes began discussing the origin of the hymn, "Abide With Me," a gust of wind rippled up from the back of the church, rustling papers, scattering the Reverend's notes across the expanse of plush burgundy carpet.

"Ah, Mr. Boone," Reverend Grimes said, when he peered through the spectacles pinched on the end of his nose. "Welcome to our humble church. I knows in the city, they starts at 11:00, but here we likes to spend a bit more time with the Lard and haves our service at 10:30 sharp."

Penny whipped her head around, joints cracking. Leaning back against the pew, her saluting chest liberated her blouse from the band of her skirt. "Will ye take a gander," she whispered to Maureen, her mouth working a piece of chewing gum at an increasing speed. "I'd take he over a chocolate bar any day, maid."

At the back of the church, a wafer-thin man in a double-breasted suit and red satiny tie stood in a shaft of sunlight. Beside him was a woman in a jigsaw puzzle dress and polished shoes. She whispered something to the teenaged girl at her side, who then glanced back towards the door as someone from the last pew stepped up to close it. The young girl gripped the arm of an elderly woman who had translucent eyes and a dried fruit face.

"Please, please," said Reverend Grimes. "Come forward. There's plenty of space up here." As the group walked up the aisle, he said, "The congregation and meself would like to extend a warm welcome to ye, Mr. and Missus Boone, to both yerselves, yer lovely daughter, and of course, the senior Missus Boone."

David Boone nodded, then proceeded with his family to the front of the church, everyone turning to follow except for Tilley who was lost behind both his mother's upper arm and a fold of Walter's sweater. When they reached the front pew, Reverend Grimes' mother shifted down from her regular place, and twisted her head as though she had detected something of great interest just beyond the narrow stained glass window. With one hand, her gaze steady, she felt for her handbag underneath the pew. Though the service was just beginning, Flossie Grimes clutched the handle of her purse with pale doll hands, appeared as ready to spring as an eighty-two year old possibly could.

"Will ye look at that?" Penny said, as she tucked her blouse into the honey-coloured rim of her control-top hose. "Flossie up and moves. Now that's an odd t'ing."

"Yes, 'tis an odd t'ing, is right," Maureen said.

"Front row," Earl whispered to Maureen. "We's been comin' here now since we was married and we only managed to make fourth."

"Yet anudder good reason to get yer back up," Maureen said.

Earl clenched his jaw, spread his legs a little wider.

"Seein' now as me papers have flown hither and to," Reverend Grimes said, "I's goin' to fly by the seat of me pants." For the next hour, he preached about loving your neighbour, though only out in the open, about lending your hand, though not handling, about living in harmony, though keeping late night whiskey swilling raucous music-making to a minimum. "And now, before we heads out into this fine, fine day," Reverend Grimes continued, "I's got one community announcement. We all knows Clint Morris, the janitorial custodian at Cupboard Collegiate. For those who don't," he nodded at David Boone, "Clint is right famous 'round here at Christmastime. He sells the best turkeys this side of the island. Well, Clint and Janet are expandin' their farm, and he'll be takin' a year away from his scrubbin' to see if they can make a real go of it. Clint tells me that he's already got an order squared away with Samson's Grocery, and of course, he'd like to thank the congregation in advance for yer patronage. Yer all welcome to pass by anytime ye wants a turkey or a cuppa hot tea."

Reverend Grimes grimaced as he stepped down from the pulpit, white sneakers poking out from underneath his robes. "We wishes ye well, Janet and Clint. Now, as always, we'll close with 'Our Fadder.'"

As they finished mouthing the word "Amen," Flossie Grimes slid off her seat, and with legs like two potato wedges, shuffled down the side aisle. Knowing convention stated he should be the first to walk through the church, Reverend Grimes bit his tongue, lest some remark about his mother escape into the microphone and reverberate off the wooden beams overhead.

Exiting the building, Tilley slowed, waiting for Reverend Grimes' moist palm to muss his muddy brown hair. But when the throng dawdled, lingering on the wooden steps, Tilley was left bewildered in a swish of dresses, suits, perfumes, and cologne. Ahead, in a crack of daylight at the door he noticed a pair of impossibly thin ankles uplifted in sling-back shoes, the toe of one foot pinching the toe of the other.

"Where's she off to in that kind of rush, I wonders," Margie Bugle yelled out.

"Is there a fire we don't know 'bout?" Wilf Tippet said with a snicker.

"She ain't herself," Reverend Grimes said, apologetically. "Not herself these past days."

"Gettin' on is all," Margie said though she was no baby bird herself.

"Yes," Reverend Grimes replied. Still, he wondered. "Yer likely right, thank you Missus Bugle. Gettin' on is all."

"P'raps she caught a whiff of Tubby's," Wilf suggested, patting his medicine ball belly.

"P'raps," Reverend Grimes said, nodding thoughtfully. "P'raps that's all there is to it."

Tilley could not see the Reverend's mother as she motored towards the rectory across the freshly trimmed grass. Instead, as he was nudged and kneaded by the crowd, he closed his eyes wanting more than anything to commit to memory those pale ankles, those delicate shoes.

"'Twas a lovely cut of meat," Penny said as she shoved the emptied bag of frozen carrots, the severed lid and can of sugar peas into a garbage bag. "Thanks for havin' us, maid."

"Don't be talkin', Penny," Maureen said, rinsing plates in the sink. "Yes. Tender as a boil, 'twas."

From the living room couch, thick snores sedate from pot roast Sunday dinners rolled out from phlegmy throats.

"Earl and Winse," Penny said. "They's two of a kind, all right."

Maureen smiled slightly. "Tea? Or coffee?"

"A mug of coffee'd be right nice." Penny hoisted five-year old Missy onto a stool, slid a book of nursery rhymes before her, and said, "Read without movin' yer lips, now. Not one peep."

"But I can't," she whimpered.

"Didn't ye hear me? I said not one peep, young lady."

From the cupboard, Maureen took down two ceramic mugs, smooth brown on the inside, miniature orange explosions decorating the outside.

"Every time I goes into that church," Penny said as she eased her ample backside down into the vinyl backed chair, "I t'inks 'bout our weddin'. How gargeous we was, those floppy hats with the baby blue ribbon. Right stylish. Dress off the shoulder. Mudder had her say 'bout that, I can tell ye. But, I paid her no mind. And the men, how they was lookin'. Dapper as can be. Winse. Earl, too. I thought to meself, yer gettin' yer wish, maid, yer gettin' yer wish."

"Hmmm," said Maureen, scooping instant coffee crystals into her mug.

"Didn't we t'ink we had it all?" Penny said, wistfully. "I should've known. Me with a name like Penny, married off to a man with a name like Payne. Any fool could tell I wasn't headed for riches and relaxin'."

"Why is ye goin' on 'bout that for?" Maureen said. She emptied the kettle, letting the steam from the mugs billow up onto her open neck and over her chin. "Those days is long over."

"Oh, I don't know, maid." Penny said. "We got two near grown. I got me work. Winse now, I could take him or leave him, but I got he nonetheless. 'Tis just I'd like a change, I 'spose. Somet'ing different. 'Tis all a bit dreary."

Maureen carried the mugs, the carton of milk, and the sugar bowl with the chipped lid to the table. Penny may have wished to have Winse, she thought, but she never once wished for Earl. She liked him well enough, wanted him even, like a girl wants a pretty dress. For years, she could admit to the wanting, but wishing was something else altogether different. A wish she might've saved for someone just beyond the bend in the road, someone who could've skulked in during the dead of night and lured her away.

No. Earl just made the first offer when she was finally old enough to accept one. He had pulled up onto the shoulder of the road in his truck, passenger side door hanging open, tempting heat pouring out into a wintry night when bitter winds were planting spikes in her cheeks. She climbed aboard that evening, and the next evening too. And when the icy crystals that were snagged in her hair and on her mittens melted in that cab every night for three weeks, she knew the deal of a lifetime had been solidified.

Maureen braced herself for her father's reaction, so she was entirely unprepared for his acceptance, his welcoming of Earl. For twenty-one years, she had toiled for her father's love. And all Earl had to do was hoist himself on top of the roof by way of a rickety ladder, shove a stiff broom down the chimney a dozen times, and shovel out the filth that collected on the hearth. In two short hours, he became the son her father never had. "Ye got me blessin', me son," he had said to Earl. "Not that ye needs it. A real man will do his own t'ing, needs neither blessin' from no one." If only Maureen had have known it could be that easy.

"Ye could have an affair, I s'pose," Maureen said, peering at Penny over the rim of her mug.

Penny choked. "Yes, now. Who'd ye have in mind?"

"Buddy Clickett up the lane is single. Eileen's been passed on now a year, so that's fair, I figures."

"Ye might be on to somet'ing," Penny said, a faint blush on her cheeks.

"Though the parts of interest might be that wrinkled, ye'd be itchin' to pass an iron over him."

They snickered.

"That's right. Though, on the other hand, wouldn't have to worry 'bout Winse knockin' his teeth out if he caught us. Don't s'pose Bud Clickett got nar tooth left in his head."

Maureen smirked, blew steam, and slurped her coffee.

"Did I tell ye 'bout Hazel Boone?" Penny said.

"That one's mudder?"

"The very one. She was over to the hospital this week. Sittin' there in the waitin' room. Calls me over, sizes up me nametag, and says in a hush, 'Nurse Penny, can ye help me? I's sure to God I's in the family way.' I nearly pissed meself when I heard the words spill out from the ol' woman's lips. Me Lard," Penny whispered, "I believes she's near eighty. 'Can I do a check on her,' she says. A check? That woman. She's a few ribs short of a rack. Her son now, that David feller, in church this marnin'. He ain't too rough on the eyes, I can tell ye that. Bit on the skinny side, but I'd love the job of fattenin' him right up." Penny put her hand on her chest, cleared her throat, then she reached over and yanked Missy down to her lap, pushed forkfuls of iced chocolate cake into her gaping mouth. "The poor mudder, though. Someone shoot me if I ever gets like her."

David Boone walked through his new house, reaching out to feel the coolness of a doorknob, the silky smooth texture of a painted spindle, the woven fabric on his armchair where he often sat and smoked. Though beautiful, the home was much more than he ever wanted. He would have preferred to return without the ostentatious display of wealth. Although he selected the location, the style of shelter made little difference. It had nothing to do with his reasons for coming back. His wife, Annette, had demanded it, and concession was not an option.

"If you're going to be moving us somewhere left of nowhere," she had said to David when he announced the news, "where I'll likely have to catch my own dinner with a length of wire, then I'll be expecting some level of luxury."

"Whatever you want," he had replied. He was not one for arguing. "You shall have it."

Funny how she was in tune with such things as thread count and diamond clarity, but she seemed blind to David himself. Over the past year, his body had melted away, slowly, of course, but inch by inch his reserves had slipped discretely off somewhere more appealing and decided not to return. Now his suits dangled on him, his shoulders like a wire rack, and a rapid shift in movement made him flinch, parts inside grinding when they should have been still. When Annette gazed at him, her plaster smile had not changed. But when David was honest with himself, he acknowledged that his wife was exactly as he had wanted her to be.

Before he climbed the main stairs, David paused to watch his mother in the parlour. Hazel was perched on the edge of her high backed chair, the wheat-coloured material so worn that the armrests shone from years of contact with her skin. On her lap, two thin legs of polyester, she balanced a porcelain plate of purple grapes. After popping one into her mouth, she chewed deliberately for several moments, then puckered her lips, and shot a spray of wet seeds onto the hand tied Persian rug.

David looked down, slightly embarrassed. He would ask his daughter, Marnie, to clean up the mess later. Annette was still angry after finding a soft bun complete with slices of ham hidden away in one of her new zippered black leather boots. That had sparked the now recurring conversation about placing his mother in an old age home.

"Really, David," Annette had said, holding up a foot streaked with curried zucchini pickles. "That's where she belongs."

"Absolutely not," David replied. "I gave —."

"You gave what, David?" she interrupted, each word spoken with surgical precision. "Your promise? Your word? To whom did you give it? Because if it was to your mother, if you gave your word to her, I can tell you with confidence, my dear husband, she has no memory of it. So, once and for all, you can just go ahead and absolve yourself. Completely. Here. Now."

Annette hoisted her skirt to her waist and, with an exaggerated hip-swivel, peeled off her pantyhose and tossed them high in the air. They arched above David's head and hitched onto the side of the wicker trashcan.

"It's still no, Annette."

"Is it guilt, David? Is that it?" she said, her voice had softened, like a cube of butter melting in a pan over low heat. She slid her skirt back into place and sashayed two steps towards him. "You've got nothing to feel guilty about, my love." Her hand touched his soft cotton shirt. "She's been with you forever, you've cared for her, given it your all. But, right now she needs to be someplace where she can get the attention she so richly deserves. Think about it. Just please think about it."

David turned away from his mother, climbed the steps of the main stairway to his conservatory. The room had two solid walls of floor to ceiling windows: a room he had requested be constructed on the northwest side of the house. Poised and ready, a telescope waited patiently. But it was only a prop. David had little intention of ever viewing the stars or scanning the grooves on the surface of the moon. Instead, he opened the bottom drawer of his mahogany desk, removed a set of brand new binoculars, and drew a leather ottoman toward the windows.

Hunching over, he steadied his elbows on the window ledge. When he saw nothing but a mass of leafy treetops through the binoculars, he began to question why he had come back at all. What or who was he hoping to find? When he made the decision to leave his home in St. John's, return to Cupboard Cove, he was confident he would discover what he needed, the oil to grease those awkward hinges and finally seal that door permanently. Now, he wasn't so certain, thought of himself as silly. Maybe the stroke had muddled his brain more than his doctors would admit.

He was about to put the binoculars away, when he noticed something—just a thin wisp of smoke, no more than a whisker, winding its way through a clump of spruce trees and silver birch in full foliage. David's knees buckled. He collapsed onto the ottoman, binoculars still locked in his rake-like grip. The closeness of the hermit's shack surprised him. Only ten short minutes of swift strides through the underbrush, and he could be right there.

three

hile Tilley waited outside the bingo hall for his mother, he watched people coming and going from Boyle's Billiards just up the hill. Built several yards back, away from prying streetlights, it throbbed with a life of its own, music heaved into the night, pool balls crackled. A couple swaggered out through the door, moved along the side of the wooden building, then lingered in the shadows. Lean bodied, the boy propped himself up against the wall, let his girlfriend tuck herself neatly into the curve of his torso, her hands disappearing inside his jean jacket. They remained so perfectly still, Tilley wondered if perhaps they had fallen asleep.

The crowd in and around Boyle's Billiards were Boyd's friends. The boys Tilley knew from the Cove were nowhere in sight with the exception of Walter, of course, who was perpetually by his side. Instead, they were off hiding in the woods, sipping stolen beer, and trying to convince the few wayward girls who joined them for a feel up their shirts, down their shirts, even through their shirts—it didn't matter. Neither Tilley nor Walter had ever been invited into the woods, where low fires burned and high-pitched giggles ricocheted off the trees like the cackle of crows. And not once had either of them even gotten close to a girl's shirt, except for Walter's cousin Ida's, who liked to push her scrawny chest up against anything: Tilley, Walter too, a bare wall, even the side of a cold woodstove.

"Wouldn't go there even if I was asked," Walter said as he leaned with Tilley against the brick bingo hall.

"Me neither," Tilley said. "Not a chance."

"I can just picture the size of black flies in the woods this time of night, all the rain we've been gettin'."

"Yes, b'y. Like wasps."

"Try dragonflies comin' at ye."

"Bound to get bit to pieces."

Walter dropped his cigarette in the dirt, crushed it with a muddy sneaker. "I hopes they do. Eyes so swoll up, they can't find their way out of the woods."

Tilley smirked. "Yeah. End up at the ol' hermit's shack, wonderin' where their mudders is to." Tilley flicked his cigarette butt several yards away, watched it smoulder, then walked over to crush it.

From the open doors, he heard Dickie Price call out, "Here we goes, ladies and gents. Beee14…we got a Beee14. Alrighty, then. Let's take her home folks, with a Gee 47…we got a Gee 47."

Three nights of the week, Maureen worked as a 'ticket girl' for Dickie Price who organised the evening bingo. When Tilley was younger, Maureen had offered Boyd a generous raise in allowance to baby-sit him. That first night, Boyd made Tilley peanut butter crackers, read him Stone Soup, and had him tucked into bed on time. Two nights later, he stuffed Tilley into the clothes dryer, turned it on for a count of five before he'd let

Tilley have a much-wanted slurp of Mountain Dew. After a week, Maureen strolled through the door to find Tilley's mouth bloody, his front tooth chipped. Boyd had helped Tilley bob for apples (that is, shoved his head down) in the soap scum coated bathtub. And on Boyd's last night, two months into the job, Maureen returned home during a winter storm to find every window open, Tilley huddled under a blanket on the couch. On top of the stove, she noticed the scorched tips of two butter knives, and close by, Boyd sat cross-legged on the linoleum gulping down blueberry pie filling with the flattened end of a can-opener. Before leaving the following night, Maureen tore open a bag of Oreos, turned on "Loony Tunes," and told Boyd that his services were no longer required.

When Tilley became sick of gouging out creamy centres, bored with "Roadrunner," he snuck down the lane, along the shoreline, past Farmer Vickers' expansive property, and up onto Main Road where the bingo hall rollicked, windows glowing. His mother was stunned to see him that first night, but soon, she began to feign surprise when she emerged through those double doors. And gradually, he knew, she expected him to be there.

Tilley heard a shrill voice cry, "BEEEEEENGO," followed by the sharp scrape of chairs across a wooden floor.

"They's clueing up," Walter said. "I best be gettin' on home. Mudder'll take a slice outta me if I's late for her rerun of "The Incredible Hulk." She goes all dizzy over that Lou Ferrigno feller. Makes me hold on to the rabbit ears so she gets the best reception."

"Why don't she fix it herself?"

"We's talkin' 'bout Mudder here," Walter said, then lowered his voice. "Don't get me angry, she says to me. You won't like me when I's angry."

Tilley laughed. "Watch yer back, b'y. If ye spies either tinge of green comin' out on her…"

"Yeah. That'd be a sight," Walter said as he turned, lifting a hand goodbye.

Ambling up Main Road, Walter drove his fists deep into the pockets of his corduroys, shoulders hunched as though an icy tongue had licked him. Watching Walter leave, oversized and overdressed, Tilley remembered the very last time he'd seen the milky skin on Walter's chubby legs.

During the spring when Tilley was eight, Walter's baby sister, Missy, had roseola. Her soft back was hot with a spiking fever and a mottled rash had begun to spread along her froggie belly, up towards an invisible neck. Normally, he and Walter never spent time with Boyd or Walter's older brother, Martin. But that day was a muggy blanket, and the four boys had collected in the Payne kitchen, trying to cool off by resting against the appliances.

"Go on outdoors, will ye's?" Penny had hollered from the living room as she positioned Missy in the crook of the couch. "Get out from underfoot."

"And do what?" Martin asked. "We's bored out of our skulls."

"Ye got me completely aggravated," she said as she tucked an afghan around the baby's body, sat back on the melamine coffee table. "Missy's that sick, I can't hear meself t'ink. Just get outta me hair."

"I knows," Walter said, caterpillar eyebrows raised. "I seen some kittens in a box down the lane behind Snook's Drugs. How's 'bout we go and grab one? Bring it on home to Missy?"

"Yes, now," Martin said. "We's lucky enough to be 'llowed in the house ourselves, let alone with an animal in tow."

"Ah, yer right," Walter said. "I'll be an old man before I ever sees a pet."

"What about gettin' somet'ing in a cage?" Boyd said. "Like a gerbil."

"Nah," Martin said. "Mudder'd set a mousetrap, hove it right in through the cage door."

"How 'bout a fish," Tilley said. "A fish ain't no trouble. And babies likes to watch fish. Can't see why they would mind that."

"No good neither," Martin said. "Fadder'll be drunk one night, hear a rumble down below, swallow the t'ing whole."

Walter grimaced.

"That I might," Walter's father called out. "Ye knows I likes me fish right fresh out of the water." Two steps down into the family room, Winse had been listening from his olive-green chair. His feet were planted on the matching humpty, a Black Horse beer bottle lodged between his thighs. He stood, stumbled into the kitchen, laid the empty bottle beside the garbage container. "I'll tell ye what b'ys," he said as his finger ducked between his shirt buttons, delved into hidden places. "What ye needs is a real animal. A man's animal. Not messin' 'round with some pissy-assed cat or a wee bite just waitin' to happen. I'll make ye a promise, b'ys." His hand moved up under his shirt, scratches audible. "Ye knows those giant horses runnin' wild down to Button's Field? Ye builds me a stable, and I's talkin' 'bout a real good stable here, and I'll thieve one of those, bring her 'round for ye. How's that for a promise, b'ys?"

"Is ye serious, Fadder?" Martin said.

"Yes, me son." Winse cocked his head. "As serious as serious gets. Now go on. Get crackin' at it."

Simultaneously, the four boys glanced over at Penny, but she hadn't heard what Winse said. Instead, she was taking advantage of Missy's baby-aspirin-drowsing to paint the infant's tiny fingernails with an overripe tangerine polish.

They moved outside. Yes, they agreed, he had said it. They all heard it. And a promise is a promise. Yes, siree. They just needed a few supplies to get them started.

Martin went to the shed and returned with a wheelbarrow and pump. He inflated the tire while Boyd headlocked first Tilley, then Walter, knuckling their heads. With war whooping and arm punching, the small group headed into the woods tracing the Payne property line. There was little need for actual discussion here; they already knew that when provisions were required, there was no more reliable bet than a visit to the old hermit's junkyard.

"Maybe he ain't even home," Walter whispered when they emerged from the path.

"Don't be a tit, Walter," Martin said. "He's a bloody hermit."

Crouched on the edge of the yard underneath a flowering dogwood, the three turned to Tilley. Boyd said, "Go on, b'y. Yer the smallest."

After scanning the torn curtains that framed the empty shack's windows, Tilley vaulted into the open yard, kept low to the ground, and returned dragging lengths of lumber behind him. He did this over and over again, varying his route, until the wheelbarrow was filled to unsteadiness. Boyd and Walter made the first trip back, while Martin and Tilley waited, leaning against a tree. "No need to kill ourselves, right?" Martin said. After three trips, they agreed they had collected enough to make a good start on the stable's foundation.

While Tilley was making a dash for a final piece of two-by-four, the door of the shack burst open. The old hermit lunged out, thin, bare feet, a shotgun already pressed against the shoulder of his disintegrating shirt.

"Run, Till—," Boyd yelled, but the crack of the gun stole the final syllable. Pellets of salt sprayed out from the barrel of the hermit's gun, showering Tilley's back, his hair, the bare skin on his legs. A pea-sized chunk stung Tilley's behind, making him drop the wood.

"Don't let me catch ye back here again, ye scoundrels," the hermit yelled after them. "Or 'twon't be salt ye'll be feelin' come 'cross yer arseholes."

They tore down the trail, Martin pushing the load, the others grabbing the lumber that spilled out left and right. Finally they stopped, peels of laughter rising up into the budding canopy. "I's goin' to piss me pants," Walter said, dancing and pinching. He lurched towards a tree and left a dark triangular stain on the bark.

When they returned to the yard, dumped out their load, Martin tossed shovels and a pitchfork from the shed onto the grass. Winse was on the back stoop with a beer bottle in each hand.

"Whatd'ye t'ink, Fadder?" Martin said from the middle of the garden, soil already turned.

"'Tis as good a place as any, me son," he said with a nod of his head.

"Here to here, then," Martin said as he indicated where to dig. "That still should leave plenty of room for Mudder's spuds."

"What're those bluish leaves?" Walter said. He nudged a plant with his sneaker.

"Weeds, b'y," Martin said.

"Is ye sure?" Walter said, bending down for a closer look. "They's weeds?"

"Yeah, I's sure. Now get diggin' or get out of it altogether."

Two hours later, Martin said, "Keep at it, b'ys. If he'll get one, I figures he can catch two of them." Suddenly, he was an authority. "Horses are the sort that fancies a bit of company."

"Might not be ready before the baby gets better," Boyd said. "But I reckon Missy won't know the difference anyways."

"Nah," Martin said. "Might take all summer to build her up. And then we'll paint her candied-apple red. That'll be right on."

"Yeah," Boyd said, "and we can fix on one of those doors that splits in two. So Polly'll stick her head out."

"Polly?" Tilley said.

"Sounds good enough to me," Walter said.

"Can ye imagine Maxine and Teena wanderin' by, seein' us

slavin' away puttin' on the roof?" Boyd said.

Martin smiled and threw a handful of dirt at Boyd, "Next t'ing they'll be wantin' a stable of their own. We'll be openin' up our own construction business."

Boyd rested his thin elbow on the end of the shovel handle, squinted into the sunlight, and grinned back at Martin. He felt a rush of youthful pride, a plan of such magnitude, and two thirteen-year olds hatched it.

"Well, I can tell ye this," Tilley said, rubbing his backside. "I won't be supplyin' yer lumber, that's for darn sure."

A loud banging on the screen door brought everyone to attention—all, that was, except for Winse. He had fallen asleep on the back porch, wedged himself in the corner, half his body blocking the screen door.

"Winse!" Penny's shrill voice stabbed at Winse's ears, jolted his legs upright before his head could wake up. "What is they doin'?"

Winse teetered on the top step, left side of his sunburned face like a peeled beet. He rubbed his eyes and began to chuckle. "A horse, maid," Winse slurred. "I's on me way to lasso a wild horse." His laughter came fast and furious now, boulder stomach jiggling, straining the buttons on his shirt. "Keep her in yer garden. Yes, me dear."

"Walter!" Penny roared, his name fat on her tongue. "Ah Christ, me cabbages." She shifted her weight from one foot to the other and back again, face scowling. "I just gone and sowed them last week. They's ruint. Right ruint." She pierced the air with a pink shoe she was holding in her left hand. "For the love of the Lard, get on with ye's."

Walter let his shovel drop into a clump of the soft mud.

"Get on with ye, I said." With a quick flick of her wrist, Penny launched the shoe; the thick heel striking Walter square in the face before it dropped down into the hole right next to his spade. Bright red liquid exploded from his nose, travelled all the way to Tilley where it spattered in bear claw marks across his hand. Blood began to course out of Walter's nostrils, sliding down over his quivering lips, dripping from his chin. At first Walter did not budge, then slowly he brought his fingers to the coarse white hairs of the moth near his temple.

Penny shook her fist. "Wipe that gawk off yer face, b'y. Yer lucky I's not handy to me udder shoe." Turning to her husband, she said, "And Winse, I's that poisoned with ye, I can't even get a word out." She stomped back into the house.

"Women," Winse said. "Ain't worth a pinch of shit. I was only tryin' to do her a favour. Get all ye little beggars out of her business." The wooden steps groaned as he made his way to the gravel drive. He stopped in front of Walter, shook his head. "Face on ye, ye poor beggar. Cheer up, me son. And Martin, if she's wonderin' where I's off to, tell the ol' bag I's gone on to Nips-n-Bites for a drop with Earl."

No one budged until Winse wobbled down the road and disappeared around the corner of Billy Boyle's split-level.

"C'mon, me son," Martin finally said, putting his hand on Walter's back. "Don't pay them no mind. Bunch of losers, they is."

"That's right," Boyd said. "We'd a made a fine stable. Just got the spot wrong."

Martin walked Walter into the house. "Let's get ye cleaned up."

Boyd lumbered off but Tilley waited there in the pile of dirt, blue leaves jutting out here and there, the occasional mass of knotted bleached roots. There came the cry of a sick baby and when the howling moved deeper into the house, Tilley left the garden and climbed the back stairs. Through the screen door, he could see Walter seated at a chair in the shadows of the kitchen. On the table before him was a tub of orange pineapple ice cream, and Walter was digging in with a soupspoon, dumping mounds into a plastic bowl. Sometimes the mound never made it. Walter's fingers pulled it off the scoop, his mouth denied no longer.

Peeking through swollen eyes, he motioned to Tilley. Then he attempted a smile, and with a strangled voice, nasally like a boxer's, said, "Martin told me I could eat meself happy. Do ye want some?"

Tilley shook his head, tore off down the stairs, followed the gravel road all the way home.

The next day, even though warm spring had surrendered to hot summer, Walter wore long trousers, a velour sweatshirt, and complained of being chilled through. From a cardboard box in the basement, he'd located Martin's old winter clothes and layered them on.

Somehow, during the previous afternoon in the vegetable garden, Walter's internal furnace had completely shut down. Though Walter could not explain why he was feeling cold, it made perfect sense to Tilley. During those moments of planning, stealing, and digging, the four boys had forged a union of sorts. Their minds had raced with the infinite possibilities, their cores fiery with self-admiration. Then, a callous laugh, a pink-shoe-turned-projectile dropped like a torrential downpour. And Tilley knew, whenever something was running on bust, instead of slowing, it's much more likely to simply stop.

$\maltese$

"Well, now. Yer lost in thought."

Glancing up, Tilley saw his mother standing beside him. He hadn't noticed her emerge from the double doors of the bingo hall, though she would have been easy enough to spot in a crowd. During the spring and summer months, Maureen preferred to dress only in white: white pants, still-whiter shirts, once-white shoes or sandals. Under a full moon, she resembled a flame during that split second before pursed lips extinguished it.

Leaning in, close enough to kiss him, she said, "Is that smoke I smells on ye?"

"No Mudder," he said, eyeing his sneakers.

"I wants the truth, Tilley. Let me smell yer hands."

She gripped his wrists, lifted his fingers to her nose.

"Ah," she said after sniffing. "Me own son is a black-arsed liar. Gets that from yer fadder's side, ye do." Then, after a moment, "Just as well ye loans me one, seein' as ye got them on ye. I's runned out." She lit the cigarette with a white lighter, and after taking several quick inhales, like sips of water, said, "Don't be goin' all smug on me now, cause I don't condone ye one little bit, that smokin'. No, I don't condone ye."

She wound her arm through Tilley's, his head barely reaching her shoulder. That had been her fault, his height. He was four, playing on the linoleum in the kitchen, and she was leaning over the sink, pulling feathers from the stiff body of a turr. She even remembered the resistance of the feathers, how stubborn they were at first when she tugged, then the sudden release, and she eased them out. Smoke came out of nowhere, draped across her face, smelling like toast about to catch fire. Bread in the oven— she had forgotten it. She rushed to the billowing source, stepping over Tilley on the way. The upshot of her actions never even crossed her mind, until she heard Earl screech from the kitchen doorway.

"What've ye gone and done, woman?" he had said. "Steppin' over the b'y. Anyone with a grain of salt knows steppin' over a child'll stunt his growth."

Maureen was bent over the stove pulling out the double-humped loaves, blackened beyond recovery.

"That's ol' foolishness," she had replied. But shortly after that, the nicks Maureen drew on the wall just inside Tilley's bedroom door started getting closer and closer together. And within a few years, he went from being an average child to not a midget by any means, but the runt, the cow's tail, or, as Earl called him, "the horse's dowdy arse."

Maureen never believed it at first, that she could have caused it. Her pregnancy had been uneventful, she'd quit smoking, ate the best food she could find. As a toddler, he was not a finicky eater, loved a drop of turkey soup, and sucked the spoon clean. He had plenty of energy; skipped, and ran, had nearly ruined the mattress on her bed with all his jumping. And then one day, he simply stopped sprouting, as though a fist came down hard on a wooden table, shocked Tilley with the noise and said, "No more." Dr. Richards offered no explanation, other than diagnosing him with "failure to thrive." So, in the end, Maureen had to relent. Her action was the only cause for it.

Strolling beside Tilley, she drew him in closer, took a deep breath from the night. Somewhere, a lawn had been freshly mowed and the sweetness of cut grass and gasoline lingered. She could hear crickets or grasshoppers, maybe some other insect, she wasn't sure, but the sound was pleasing nevertheless. Even the dampness had a freshness that made her want to breathe deeper. It was such a stark contrast to the inside of the bingo hall. In there, smoke hung like a low fog, blotters squelched incessantly, and the bins near the front stage churned and tumbled and tumbled and churned. Everywhere she turned, hands beckoned, "Tickets here, maid," and when she handed over a paper chance to them, their pinched faces transformed into an uncomfortable blend of desperation and thrill.

"I hates it," she said to her son. "I honestly hates it."

"Hates what?"

"Me job," she said. "'Tis the most horrible t'ing. Sellin' those peel tickets to the poor folks 'round here, they now t'inkin' they'll strike it rich when I knows bloody well even if they do win either dollar, they'll waste it just as fast on more tickets."

"Not much ye can do 'bout that, Mudder," Tilley said.

"Just seems a real shame, is all," Maureen replied. "'Tis the first Wednesday of the month, and the crowd on the pogey got their cheques, so the hall was jam-packed, right blocked. Some of them'll spend every penny and have nothin' to show for it when they goes home. A dozen mouths to feed, and nothin' to show."

"Well, someone's winnin', or else I imagines no one'd be goin'."

"Yes, yer right on that. Ye knows, I t'inks I've heard Wilf Tippet roar out 'BINGO' more times than I can remember. I has to escort him up to the stage so Dickie can run through his numbers. And I swears, no matter which way I moves, somehow Wilf's hand manages to find me backside. Then for the rest of the night, I has his filthy inky prints on me good, white pants and I got to wash them right when I gets through the door. Don't t'ink yer fadder'd be too pleased seein' those kinda marks on me rear end."

Tilley stared at the pavement as they walked, kicked an empty can into the ditch, a persistently muddy gouge that lined the edge of the road.

"I 'spose I shouldn't be tellin' me son that sort of t'ing," she continued.

Maureen walked faster, the exposed nail on the sole of her white pumps clicking with each drop of her foot. Tilley pictured the heels of her shoes, the missing rubber pads, and the claw marks from being repeatedly thrust down through crushed stone. He flinched slightly with every metal tick.

"Why don't ye just quit?"

"Can't do that."

"Ye could," Tilley said. "If ye wants."

"Not a chance," she said. "Money don't grow on trees, me son. Long as Dickie'll keep me on, I'll be workin' me three nights a week. Maybe one day if ye strikes it rich, I can give it all up."

Tilley shifted away and moved just ahead of her. "Ah,

Mudder. Don't be countin' on that."

"Ye never knows," she said. "So. High school for ye this year. That's a big t'ing."

"Yeah," he said. "Not that big, though."

"Whatd'ye mean?" she said. "'Not that big'. 'Tis big, alright. This is the time, Tilley me son, when the biggest of big decisions is made."

"Don't t'ink I got much to be decidin' on. Me classes is already picked for me. Only choice I gets is between gym and art, and we all knows I ain't goin' in for gym."

From within Tilley's shadow cast by the streetlights, Maureen smiled weakly. "That's not what I means. I means after. What ye wants to do with yer life."

"Mudder, ye needn't be gettin' any thoughts of shippin' me off to college. Ye knows I barely made it through grade eight math and I can barely read me own writin'."

"I blames meself for that, ye knows. I never should have stood for it. Some lady from the city came 'round, taught the kindergarten that year. Lush was her last name, don't even recall her first. Ye always wanted to be writin' with yer left hand, but she had some kind of silly thought that there was a wickedness 'bout that, so she bound yer left hand behind yer back, forced ye to work with yer right. I never should've allowed it. I knows now that's what set ye back."

"Doubts it," Tilley said. "Just I don't got the mind for that stuff, is all."

Maureen sighed, tried to tuck a lock of hair behind her ear, though it was much too short and resisted.

"Well, one t'ing's for sure. Ye got a real talent for that drawin' business."

"And I knows that'll take me a fat far distance."

"That it won't if ye don't make a plan for yerself. Ye got to have some kind of plan, Tilley Gover."

"As much as I figures, when I turns sixteen, Art Knuckle'll take me on at the fish plant. Fadder might put a word in for me. I figures that'd make him right proud."

At once, the clicking heel stopped. Two paces ahead, Tilley turned around to see what had caught his mother's attention. She was standing on the side of the road, her clothes radiant. On the opposite side of the ditch, a slate fence marked the frontage of Arthur Vickers' land, and an enormous crab-apple tree sprawled up and over, its branches sagging with developing fruit.

"Mudder?"

After a moment, she said, "I remembers when this fence was built. Me own Fadder helped Mr. Vickers tear away the rotted picket one, light up a grand fire in the yard. Then they worked together pilin' up the slate, piece after piece after piece, like some sort of sharp-edged puzzle."

"Yeah," Tilley said, taking a step towards his mother. "'Tis a nice fence."

Maureen continued to stare.

"And this tree. Me Lard, it's been here these years. Older than I is. After the fence was built up, me and Penny came 'round with buckets, filled them with the hardest apples we could yank down. Then we hid. Right there." She pointed to the gate opening. "'Round back of the fence. We must've waited 'bout an hour, but sure enough, Earl and Winse comes up the lane. And by God, did we pelt them with the whole load in our buckets. Never knocked neither bit of sense into them, but still, we pelted them some good. They was cussing like ye never heard, and we was beside ourselves laughin'." Her eyes glistened and she turned to look straight at Tilley. "I was close on yer age at the time and believe you me, I was likin' meself very much. Earl Gover was all there was. I couldn't t'ink of nothin' else."

Tilley nudged his mother and chuckled lightly. "That's somet'ing I can't imagine. No ma'am."

"Well now," she said. "That was it." The heel click resumed, and after several moments, it settled into a regular pace. Then, just before they reached home, Maureen said, "Ye knows, I never did trust Mr. Vickers. Had neither wife as long as I knowed and kept a load sheep pent up in his barn. I t'inks that's a good policy. Not puttin' much stock in a man who lives by hisself and locks up his sheep. Anyone, I figures, would likely t'ink the same."

Tilley climbed the steps first, opened the screen door to let her through.

"Thanks," she said. "For meetin' me."

"No trouble," he said. "I's goin' to see if either show's on before I crawls in."

She tapped her cheek, and Tilley planted a quick kiss, barely a kiss at all.

"Okay," she said. "Goodnight, me love. See ye in the marnin'."

Maureen reached up to touch her cheek, the dampness already dried. There. Another walk over. These past two weeks, he had been hurrying along, taking swift strides while she lingered, wanting to talk. She was worried that any day now, she would emerge from the bingo hall and he wouldn't be there. When only last summer, or maybe the one before, he had held her cold hand all the way home.

"I'm going out," David called down the hallway. He tugged a cable-knit cardigan from the coat rack while reaching for the brass knob.

Placing a dry hand in between the pages, Annette closed her book. She had been reading Nin's, *A Spy in the House of Love*. Not reading exactly, it was such a slender volume, reading would have led her to ingest it too rapidly. Instead, she merely sampled, took a moment to pause, then sampled again.

How she envied Sabina, her frequent dalliances, how she sought…sought…. Just what was she seeking? Something, to be sure, though Annette was unable to define it. A feeling more so than a word, she decided. A charge. Yes, a charge. A connection.

As the youngest of the Belty sisters from St. John's, she had imagined so much more for herself than a house, a child, a husband (not having imagined the mother-in-law at all). She could have married any man, but she chose David. Although he was an acquaintance of her father's, David first came into their house as a miniature photo on the back of a Christmas card, one of his paintings printed on the front. The card rested on the mantle for mere hours before Annette plucked it up, tucked it inside her blouse, pressed it onto her skin as she carried it to her bedroom. After tracing every line of his solemn face with her fingernail, she re-examined the photo using a metal frog with a magnifying glass belly. He was perfect, his solemn face much older, but perfect. She always loved a challenge and in the weeks to follow, she had insisted that she and her oldest sister, Judy, have soup and sandwiches at The Clever Battalion, where David Boone was known to lunch.

And now, here he was, all sluggish arms and nubby cardigan, a flat soda when she craved something entirely fizzy. Though unlike Sabina, Annette was determined never to permit her body to stray. But in recent years, she had given her mind the occasional day pass.

"Enjoy yourself," she said, as she cracked the spine of her book, wanting to give each phrase, each word, equal illumination.

"A breath of fresh air is all," he said, buttoning.

"Yes, yes," she said, as her eyes scanned for their proper place among twisted legs, heated sheets. "Whatever else at this hour?"

David closed the door quietly. With crushed stone crunching under his feet, he moved down his steep driveway. It remained unfamiliar, even though he had directed and paid for its carving.

Up over a short rise, the sound of his steps softened as he came upon a dirt road riddled with potholes, treacherous craters in the dark. The street was vacant and he could hear his mouth draw air like a winded animal.

He passed Flossie Grimes' house on the left and recalled the moment when he had stepped into her porch. Glancing around he was surprised to see only the bones of her home remained the same and unshared years of living had grown up around them. They had exchanged warm letters over the years, and his heart banged against his ribs as he anticipated her welcome. But he was never invited in. Instead, she met him with a pinched expression and her harsh words hitched at her throat like snagged threads.

"Ye knows ye could've come home either time 'tall," she managed to say. "But why'd ye go and bring that one with ye?"

"That one." David required no clarification. "That one" had meant his mother.

He continued down the lane several long paces past the Grimes' house, then slowed. Memory still ingrained within his two feet; they sensed when to stop.

No path led to the front stairs of the saltbox house that stood before him. Instead, the bottom step ended in a patch of substantial grass that rolled down into the ditch where its ragged edge was torn, rinsed away.

A different colour coated the clapboard, yes, but the house was still very much the same. Though now, street and porch light enhanced the moon's illumination. All the crannies where he hid as a child were lost. The scalloping was also missing. Years ago, his own father had cut out the lacy pattern, painted it white, and nailed it on to the edges of the roof as a surprise for David's mother. Likely, it had disintegrated, fallen off from decades of brackish winds ripping off the sea.

David frowned when he saw a small black figure perched on the front step, straw hat, legs crossed at the ankles. With his metal fishing rod poised and ready, the joyful boy maintained a perpetually tilted head and wide grin, his painted teeth electric-shock white.

Then, as David watched, someone drew back the sheers in the square window to the right of the front door. A small boy. He appeared no bigger than a five or six year old, and he placed his palm against the glass, gazed out into the night. David felt a blast of air around his body, throwing strands of hair into his watering eyes, making the legs of his trousers flap like pegged laundry. He had a powerful urge to remove his shoes and socks, to tear over the cool damp grass towards that window. How he wanted to press his face against it, remember the instances of weightlessness when he counted foamy crests and nose-diving gulls. But he resisted, and leaned back into the palpable gust.

When he noticed the alien glow of a television set flickering in the background, the impulse diminished. He chastised himself. And he knew that surrounded by darkness in a deafening gale, his imagination had grown livelier than ever.

The curtain drifted back, and the boy disappeared. David turned away. Such a long, long time ago, he tried to tell himself. *Why can't I just let it be?*

four

"Best get yerselves ready," Earl said one hot afternoon when the sun was splitting the rocks. "We's leavin' in an hour."

"Leavin'?" Maureen said as she dumped a steaming teabag into the sink. "Where do ye t'ink we's goin' to?"

"Talkin' to Winse earlier. Mentioned to me he and Penny was headin' up to the pit for the night. Wants us to tag along." Earl clapped his hands once. "We needs steaks and beer, ducky. Can't go showin' up empty handed, now can we?"

"Christ Earl," Maureen said through colourless lips. "Ye knows I can't stand it up there. Besides, Tilley's got stuff to do. Right Tilley?"

Tilley was seated on a stool at the counter, where he was underlining his viewing choices in a recent issue of the Newfoundland Herald. Without glancing up, he mumbled, "Not really, Mudder. Not much on far as I can see."

Maureen scowled.

"What's wrong with ye, maid? Ye too good for sleepin' in a bus?"

A bus was right.

Two summers ago, Winse Payne announced he had finally scrimped and saved enough to realise his dream. He purchased a school bus that was on its last legs, gutted it, scraped the gobs of bubblegum off the floor, walls, ceiling, and drove the wreck to Henderson's gravel pit. Near the edge of the pit, he parked his rusty, barren bus, and with the help of Earl, Wilf Tippet (who owned the neighbouring bus), and Dickie Price, they secured it with concrete blocks. There, Winse's orange camper, a deluxe model, outfitted with a pot-bellied stove and bunk beds, became a permanent fixture.

"That's not it," Maureen said. "And ye knows it. I'se never been one for campin' is all. Can't stand all the drinkin' and don't much care for the black flies."

"Well, yer goin' and that's that." Then, to Tilley, he said, "And ye can wipe that sour look off yer puss, me son. Walter'll be there, and so will yer little friend, Ida."

Huffing, Maureen showcased her overbite. "Tilley's got no interest in Ida Payne. I tell ye that girl's been bad since the day she was born. Like her guts is too hot. Heat comin' off her like a Coleman lamp. If ye asks me, she needs to be put 'cross someone's knee and have her ass reddened."

Earl closed his eyes for a moment, tongue darting out between smiling lips.

"And it ain't yer lap I's talkin' 'bout," Maureen said, splashing the hot tea down the drain. "Yer mind's that far down in the gutter, I prays to Jaysus for a hellish storm, wash it right out to sea."

"A mind's a terrible t'ing to lose, me lovey." His meaty hand sprung up, planted one on her behind. "What would ye do then?"

Maureen jerked her hip, spun away. "Ye can be sure I'd t'ink of somet'ing, Earl. Somet'ing real good."

As Maureen strolled across the paved parking lot of Samson's Grocery, she caught sight of herself reflected in the Plexiglas. Her distorted image rippled past sale flyers and a help-wanted sign. Adorned in white, she appeared larger than life, shoulders uneven as her vinyl, kitchen-sink purse weighed down her left side. She had to admit her thin belt was too tight, its metal buckle hidden under a generous fold of fat. Sunlight found its unfortunate way through her sheer shirt. Beneath it, she could easily see her beige bra, a mass of thick bands, plenty of fabric straining with the burden, and sliding up her back. Maureen tried to shift her focus, identify the specials, but it was difficult. Her mirrored twin mimicked every awkward move.

Just inside the door, she fumbled in her handbag for her list. Bananas. Tilley loved bananas. Most mornings around eleven, she'd snap the neck on one, peel it midway, bring it to the linen closet, and hand it up. How long had he been hiding in there? She wasn't sure. She had discovered him quite by accident when she was putting away an armload of towels.

Once, when she had pulled open the closet door, a drawing drifted out, fluttered, and dipped, landing on her slippers. She bent to retrieve it and saw it was a picture of herself sketched on lined exercise paper with a standard school pencil. Her heart skipped a beat as her eyes traced those lines that created a soft youthful face. Gone were the deep creases around her mouth, the slight crack in her front left tooth, that slack skin underneath her chin. Even the birthmark beside her nose looked purposeful, lovely, not like a splotch of mud in need of a wiping.

"I wants it," she said, clutching the image to her chest.

"Alright then," he said from his high post. "Ye can keep it."

Edges folded neatly, she tucked it somewhere Earl would likely never see it—inside the pages of her Bible. Many nights, when Earl had left for his shift without so much as a "goodnight," she would slip her portrait from the Old Testament, feel soothed by the awareness that this is how Tilley saw her. By his hand, she had become wholly beautiful, entirely alive.

With bananas in her rickety cart, she moved onto the meat selection, plucked up a family pack of sirloin. After checking her flyer for beef specials, she confirmed the sale, and went to ask Jimmy O'Toole why the meat was not marked down.

At the packing counter, Maureen waited behind Mrs. Boone, the painter's wife, who stood straight-backed in a knee length, lavender dress, drinkable cream-coloured shoes.

"Bird Balls," Mrs. Boone said to Jimmy, holding up the weighty, rectangular, Styrofoam dish. "I've never seen this before."

"They's a lovely set, missus," Jimmy said with a flashy smile, wink. "Don't ye t'ink?"

Her face was stern, even her curls stood at attention, afraid to relax. "Something local, I take it?"

"Yer right on that, ma'am. Made just out back by young Terry Clancy." He nodded towards a man with a flattened face, eyes like slits. "They says he caught a bad case of the Down's 'fore he was born. But I tell ye, he's a real wizard with those bird balls."

She glanced at Terry, "Is he fit to prepare food?"

"Sorry, ma'am? Don't t'ink I's catchin' ye?"

"I mean is he clean?"

"Of course he's clean. Downright spotless. Sure, ye could eat right off him. His mudder gives him a good scrub behind the ears everyday 'fore he comes to work." Jimmy winked again but when Mrs. Boone's face remained like stone, he coughed lightly and said, "Yes ma'am. We follows all the proper procedures that we knows."

"Right." Tapping the package of Bird Balls with a pearly fingernail, she said. "And how do you cook these?"

"Cook? Is ye havin' me on?"

"No, sir," she said, nose lifting slightly. "I'm perfectly serious. I'm from the city and no one sells this sort of thing there."

"From the city, ye says."

"Yes." Her toe began tapping. "St. John's."

"Ah, yes," he said. "I've heard of St. John's, though I don't know nothin' 'bout cookin'. If ye can hang on for a sec, I'll have to call me missus on that one."

She waited while his chunky fingers dialled the numbers, lots of eights and nines taking their time rolling back to position.

A moment later, Jimmy returned to the counter and said, "Moderate oven in a roaster, lid on tight 'til ye smells them. Ye'll know, she said. Ye'll know."

"Thank you," she said, dropping the package of suet and seeds into her cart. "You would do your customers a service by offering some cooking instructions on the packaging. Not everyone is familiar with the preparation of Bird Balls."

"Right," Jimmy said, shoulders square. "I'll carry yer comments into me advisement."

As Mrs. Boone turned to walk away, he leaned out over the counter and called, "Oh yes, Missus. I almost forgot. Me wife says to make sure ye has a thick slice of bread to sop up all the goodness yer goin' to find in yer roaster."

Maureen stepped up, meat in one hand, grocery flyer in the other. "Well now, Jimmy O'Toole. I never seen the like. Yer the very Devil in the flesh. Sendin' her off with that in her head."

"Ye might be right," Jimmy said, as he took Maureen's sirloin, slashed back the price by one dollar. "Though as me wise ol' mudder always used to say, ye get what's comin' to ye. Some time or anudder. It all comes 'round."

Ⅺⅇ

When they arrived at the bus, Winse was standing beside a smoking hibachi, pressing down on several fatty burgers with a metal spatula. Flames licked up, singeing every hair off the back of his right hand.

Earl slapped Winse on the back. "Just in time, we is. I's starved." He handed Winse a grocery bag.

"That's some grand bit of meat b'y," Winse said, as he tore off the wrap, held the bloody steak in one hand. He sprinkled it with table salt directly from the box, dropped it on the grill. "Grab yerself a beer, ol' man. Can of pop for the b'y."

"Hi Tilley." A bird's song rang out from the entrance of the bus. There was Ida holding the metal rail and hanging out through the bi-folding doors. She wore a pair of child's shorts, ill fitting in every direction, and a gathered halter-top fastened with strings at the tops of her pale bony shoulders. Beside the strings were the thin straps of an unnecessary pink bra.

"Yeah, hi," Tilley said, the fringe at the base of his jean shorts suddenly of great interest.

Jumping from the bottom step arms stretching to the sky, she posed for a moment in the shape of a flattened 's'. "Haven't seen ye since last summer. Have I grown or what?"

Tilley plucked loose fibres away from the jean material when Earl nudged him, said, "Go on, b'y. Say somet'ing nice to the young lassie."

When Ida stood beside Tilley in her wooden clogs, she was a full six inches taller.

"I guess," Tilley managed. "Ye've grown some."

"Sweet Lard have mercy," Maureen said under her breath.

"I knows, I knows," Penny said, handing Maureen wine in an emptied peanut butter glass. "Me own girl's off to her friend's house and I gets stuck with the Queen of Sheba here."

"'Tis disgustin' the way she gets on. A twist tie's got more shape," Maureen said.

"Had to bring her," Penny said. "Not much choice 'bout it. Winse's sister calls last minute. Somet'ing real important, she says. Out on the prowl again is more like it. A real slag, that one."

"Look at her stickin' her chest out like she's Dolly friggin' Parton," Maureen said. "When there's nothin' more there than the two ends off a Q-Tip."

Walter's head jutted out from an open window of the bus. "Mudder, where's me Popsicles to? I don't see no Popsicles in the cooler. Ye said ye was buyin' Popsicles."

"How to Christ he remembers every word I says is beyond me," Penny said to Maureen. Then to Walter, "There's none, me son. Ye can wait for yer supper."

"Aw, Mudder," he said. "Then why'd ye go and tell me for?"

"I can't wait 'til he's growed up and gone," Penny said to Maureen. "Give me head some peace." She sipped from a near-empty glass, then raised it towards Maureen. "Give it a try, maid. 'Tis right lovely for a screw-top."

$\cdot$

"I loves butter," Walter announced as he poked spoonfuls of margarine into a baked potato.

They ate at a picnic table inside an area built onto the bus. Wooden posts had been hammered into the ground, heavy-duty plastic was draped and staple gunned to create what Winse called his "sunroom;" three sides see through, one side solid bus.

Walter scraped every scrap from the skin on his potato, then tore into a sesame bun like a rabid dog, while Ida nibbled, stopping frequently to reapply shimmering lip gloss. Tilley felt her watching him as he chewed and he was grateful for the earlier nights of late summer that disguised the powerful blush scalding his cheeks, burning his hair right to the follicles. Under her watchful eye he ate gingerly, all around the edges of his hamburger first, and then slowly consuming the very centre made up of soft, raw beef.

"This is the life," Walter said, margarine dribbling down his chin. "When I gets older, I's goin' to get married and get a bus of me own."

"Bit young to be t'inkin' 'bout gettin' married, ain't ye?" Penny tugged beige tissues from a box, handed them around.

"Not really," Earl said, nodding at Walter. "Sure 'twas on me own mind when I weren't much older than the b'ys here."

"Really?" Maureen asked, her voice sounding shriller than she'd intended.

"Well," Earl said, lifting his hands and knotting them behind his head, sweat stains on full display. "Not actually marryin', I guess."

Winse poked Earl in the ribs. "I 'llows."

"Yeah," Earl said. "I might've been fifteen goin' to dances over to the Gut." He gulped the remainder of his beer, took a mint-flavoured toothpick and jammed it between his teeth. "Ah, the girls in those days was plentiful. I could've had me pick."

Maureen squinted, eyes trying to guide her hand towards the wine bottle. "Don't mean nothin'," she slurred. "Somet'ing from the Gut'd snap at their uncle's corpse, warm or cold."

"So long as 'twas stiff," Penny said, twittering. She took the wine bottle from Maureen, filled the glass to overflowing, and slurped up a mouthful from the pool on the plastic tablecloth.

Maureen pushed a dried piece of steak around her plate and stared down at Mr. Peanut painted on her glass. With his gleaming smile, faded bow-tie, waffle shell, she thought him rather handsome. Normally she didn't drink, a half-bottle of beer maybe, but no more. Somehow tonight, she had made her way through five or six tumblers of cheap red wine on an empty stomach. She didn't feel as giddy as she'd hoped. Instead, when she moved her head left or right, her blinking eyes took their sweet time catching up.

"Lovely barbecue," someone said. Maureen was surprised to realise that it was her own voice, wavering at the end of a watery tunnel. "Winse."

"What is ye talkin' 'bout?" Penny wailed. "'T'was as salty as the brine."

"Next time, do it yerself," Winse said, teeth gnawing through a generous bite.

Maureen rose from her lawn chair, knocking it back into the dirt. "I t'inks I needs a moment," she said, and stumbled out through the door made from a section of rolled up plastic.

After twenty minutes had passed, Earl spit out his toothpick, said to Tilley, "Yer mudder's gone to have a piss in the woods. Only woman I knows can get lost havin' a piss in the woods. Go on and find her, me son."

She wasn't hard to spot. A fat new moon suspended in the sky illuminated her white clothes. Crouched by the side of a spruce tree, mouth agape, pants at her ankles, she was fast asleep.

"Mudder," Tilley said as he tugged at her, relieved to see she had managed the underwear before dozing off. "Get yerself up."

"Huh? What?"

"Get up, I says."

He helped to pull her pants up, though refused to zip.

"Oh me lover," she rasped.

They made their way back to the bus, he with his hand around her waist, she with relative steadiness. She said, "Don't even go t'inkin' 'bout it. She's ain't yer type."

"Who ain't?"

"That Ida Payne girl."

"Never knew I even had a type, Mudder. 'Tis news to me."

"I sees it now. Gettin' yerself mixed up with the likes of her."

"Ye don't need to be worryin' yerself 'bout that."

"Shorts now, that tight."

"Shh, now. Mudder."

"'Tis like she got a hare lip 'tween her legs."

"Shit, Mudder. I ain't even lookin' at her."

"Well, yer Fadder can't say the same. Got me right turned. Right turned."

Tilley clenched his teeth, pressed his tongue against the roof of his mouth, as his mother put much of her weight on him, let her cheek rest on the very top of his head. Once she stopped to retch, clasping Tilley's shoulder, nails dug in, but the effort was unsuccessful.

He led his mother to the bus, helped her up the thin steps meant for single file. As she slid into the bottom bunk, her skin greasy, roller curls sticky with turpentine, she whispered, "Don't ye go fussin' in the mornin', me son. I'll have yer egg on toast ready when ye opens yer eyes."

"I knows how to kiss." Ida said in her musical voice as wind made the plastic room suck in air, then exhale sharply.

"Like I cares," Walter said.

"Maybe Tilley do," Ida said, licking her lips. "Do ye want a kiss, Tilley?"

"No thanks," Tilley said.

"Is ye sure?" She puckered.

"That's alright," he said. He was kneeling on the ground of the plastic room trying to untie the multiple knots that bound his sleeping bag. He could hear a ruckus inside the bus, and every so often, Winse or Earl knocked against the windows causing the plastic to crinkle.

"Fuck ye then," Ida said, "Ye don't know what yer missin'."

"Saucy as a black, she is." Walter sat on the picnic table, slurped mouthfuls of grape Kool-Aid, mouth stained.

Ida stood in the very middle of the room, swaying to her own internal tune. Over her halter-top she had pulled on a cotton cardigan for warmth, though her skinny legs, complete with bruised knees, were still bare. "I still knows how. Been practisin'."

"On the back of yer hand no doubt," Walter said.

"No, shithead. With Chester."

"Not our cousin, Chester," Walter said.

"That's he."

"Christ, Ida. Yer sick. He's only three years old."

"So? He's a b'y ain't he? Don't do him no harm. Besides, he's almost as big as yer dumbtit friend over there."

The wet knot released, Tilley's sleeping bag unfurled like an awakening fiddlehead on the pebbly floor. "Ah, shut yer traps the two of ye," he said. "I's goin' to sleep out of it." He snuggled down into his makeshift bed, his pyjama legs rubbing against the pictures of alert elks, soaring pines that lined the army green shell. He looked upwards before dozing off. Just beyond the plastic roof, filmy from all the hot breath and never-ending chatter, the stars were like smears, the moon a spotlight.

❧

Night had settled in when Tilley rolled over onto a sharp piece of shale. Even through the sleeping bag, it drove into his hip, the jab rushing through him, shutting down his dream. As he inched backwards into his cocoon, felt sleep fluttering towards him once again, he heard something—a sound so faint, his body registered it before his ears did. A throaty groan. Again. And then again.

At first, Tilley had the unpleasant notion that the noises were coming from Walter and Ida. But when he turned his head, Ida was a breath away, tucked into her sleeping bag. As he listened to the distant moaning, he watched Ida and felt a warmth moving, fog of sleep burning off. She appeared much softer as she dozed, the baby blue eye shadow not as glaring, and underneath the layers of gloss, her lips visibly chapped. Delicate hairs framing her face were damp and her thumb was held firmly in her mouth. As he watched her mouth work the thumb, Tilley felt his drowsy blood perk, ignoring limbs and brain, pumping brazenly downward. Several buttons were undone on Ida's nightshirt and while Tilley's eyes lingered, he permitted himself to count them. One. Two. Three. Tiny buttons. Just inside those, he had to arch his neck back an inch, he could see she was still wearing a bra, pale pink, tufts of tissue sticking out.

Shoes crunched just yards away. Tilley whipped his hands up from inside the sleeping bag, bunched the material in his sweating fists, his body like a storage-room mannequin. Beside him, Winse Payne's converted school bus gripped as someone stepped aboard. When he looked under the bus, near the concrete blocks by the front tire, Tilley glimpsed a familiar pair of men's shoes.

Then, a voice. Barely audible amongst the rustling trees, the repeated questioning of a tired owl, but Tilley's ear seized the sentence, funnelled it through.

"Yer one busy beaver, missus."

And when Tilley heard his father words, the sweat coating his torso and the back of his neck transformed into an instant, sobering chill.

High on the hill in Cupboard Cove, Annette Boone carried the black, speckled roaster to the table, her hands safe inside elbow-length oven mitts. Next, she brought a plate piled high with corn on the cob, the kernels shrunken, grieving for the can. She slid her hand into a damp bag of Mammie's Bread, layered the slices gently in a basket. At the grocery store, she always checked for moisture inside the bag, believing that meant the bread was fresh, still warm when Missus Mammie wrapped it.

Waiting for dinner, Hazel Boone had been seated at the dining-room table since four that afternoon. And also waiting for bedtime, she wore her nightgown on over her elastic-waist burgundy pants and lemon yellow blouse.

"I'm trying something new," Annette said as she lifted the lid. Heat slapped her and her smiling face melted. "Well, that's not quite what I expected." She looked around the table. "I don't suppose…Anyone?"

Inside the pot, a mess of seeds floated on two inches of clear, hot grease.

"Ewww. What is it?" Marnie said.

"The package said, 'Bird Balls,'" Annette said. "Mr. O'Toole at Samson's informed me they were a local delicacy."

"Did they, by any chance, have a ribbon pinned in the top?" Marnie asked.

"Yes," she said. "For easier handling, I assumed."

"Mom. I think you were supposed to hang those from a tree. Just maybe, for the birds?"

Annette let the lid, still firmly grasped in the oven mitt, clink back onto the roaster. "Well, I won't be going back there any time soon."

"Not sure you have much choice," David said. "The next grocery shop is thirty minutes away."

"I don't care if it's two hours away. He won't get the best of me."

"Perhaps it was an honest mistake," David said.

"I doubt that very much," Annette said. "More like an amusement at my expense."

"What'll we have for dinner?" Marnie asked.

"Don't you worry," she said, taking the basket of bread. "I've got leftover potato in the fridge. I'll put together some sandwiches lickety-split."

Marnie groaned. "Your speciality."

"What was that, young lady?" Annette said as she opened the fridge door, pulled out hard mashed potato in a metal bowl and a bottle of ketchup. "It's not my fault, you can be sure of that. If your father hadn't have moved us to this little hole in the wall to satisfy whatever it is he needs satisfied, then we would still have Agnes preparing our meals. A much finer gourmet than myself I admit, but we certainly couldn't expect her to leave her husband and come with us."

Annette returned to the table with sandwiches, a peel-back package of ham, and a jar of sweet hotdog relish. Hazel nibbled without a word. After several bites, she reached out with a shaky hand, stripped off a slice of lunchmeat, brought it to her chest, then discreetly let it drop to the floor.

"Nan," Marnie said. "You dropped your meat on the rug."

"I never did no such t'ing," Hazel snapped.

"Yes, you did. I saw you. Nan, c'mon."

"That I didn't lassie, and don't go sayin' I did."

"Mother," Annette said, taking a full breath of air. "If I've said it once, I've said it a million times, food is for your plate, not the floor." Then to her husband, "David, there has to be a woman in the cove who will come and clean. I simply can't keep up after her. She's worse than a newborn."

"Please Mom," David said. "Don't throw your food on the ground."

"Alright. Alright," Hazel said, pouting. "I was just tryin' to sneak a morsel to the poor dog."

"Dog?" David asked, eyebrows lifted.

"No one pays her no mind these days. Poor t'ing."

"Mother," Annette said, "we do not have a dog and under absolutely no circumstance, do not even think that we ever might."

"Tell her, David," Hazel said, her eyes glassy, chin like jelly. "Tell that woman."

"Mom—."

"Ye've had her since ye was not even one," Hazel said, pleading. "And we can't give her up. Popcorn's just a wee crackie, she don't make no trouble for no one."

David jaws stopped mid-chew and his hand dropped back to the table. Mouth suddenly dry, he could not swallow and was forced to spit the mouthful into a paper napkin.

Popcorn. His childhood dog.

He pinched the bridge of his nose as old memories were rooted out, dusty, dusty. His mind suddenly felt like a mouth full of new fillings, the surrounding molars unacquainted and aching. Short legs and hair, a black patch over the dog's left eye. On the beach, when he skimmed stones, she would race along the cliff's edge like a blur. This very instant, David could hear her nails clipping across the wooden floor as she pranced on her back paws for a morsel of meat, his mother crooning, "Oh, ain't she a pretty little girlie?"

David stood up from the table. "Excuse me," he said to his wife. "I don't think I can eat."

five

As soon as Tilley was old enough to grip something in his fist, he started to draw and colour. Not once did he teethe on a crayon or pencil, he instinctively knew what to do with it. Often while Maureen mixed bread or peeled vegetables, she would strap Tilley into his highchair, piece of brown paper taped to the kitchen table, and let him draw: first he drew lines, then shapes, then stick-figures. By the time he was three and a half, Tilley could sketch a whole face, cat's eye glasses and all.

Earl didn't like it.

"B'ys that age ought to be racin' 'round, playin' with guns and tanks, haulin' in a bit of wood, for God's sake. Not drawin' flowers to the table. That's for queers and pussies."

When Earl came home with a miniature toy rifle that cranked and popped, Tilley didn't protest when Boyd ripped it from his hands. For days, Boyd shot up everyone and everything, including Clipper the dog, who huddled by the radiator, teeth bared, a powerless growl rumbling in his throat.

"I loves shootin' me head off," he would announce before he shoved the muzzle in his mouth, cranked and popped, then puddled to the floor, eyes rolling, body twitching in mock death.

Late one Saturday afternoon, Earl strolled into the kitchen to find Tilley seated on a stool sketching the face of a porcelain doll planted on the counter before him. Tilley's tongue protruded slightly as leaned left and right, caressing the doll's cheek. Maureen hummed while she sliced partially frozen moose meat on a wooden cutting board next to the sink.

"Don't tell me ye got him messin' 'round with dolls?" Earl grabbed Maureen's upper arm, swung her around, knife thrust mid-air. "Tell me that's not what I's seein' through me own bleary eyes."

"Don't get yer knickers in a knot, me son," she said, pulling free. "He's only lookin' at the t'ing." She wiped the blood in a dishcloth, touched Earl's back. "Why don't ye go see what he's doin'? I never seen nothin' like it. That b'ys got somet'ing. Somet'ing right special."

Earl's fist came down on the counter with such force, dishes in the sink rattled. At the sound, Tilley started, his pencil crayon scratching a navy streak across the page.

"I don't give a rat's hairy arse what he's got." Earl's face was beet red, nearing explosion. "Next t'ing ye'll have him in a dress. The b'ys like a sheet. Underbelly of a slug got more colour than he. Only friend he got is the biggest kind of dough ball. That Walter character's too fat to get out of his own way. Hear me now," he said, as his broad hands came down on Tilley's pad. "That's enough of this. I don't want to see it again. Hide nor hair of it."

With one scrunch, Earl grabbed up the drawings, lifted the burner on the wood stove, plunged his arm down in the fire, and decimated Tilley's drawings. Second swipe, Earl grabbed a margarine container full of crayons, tossed them in. The stench of melted wax poured out from the hole, saturated the room.

"There's no need for——," Maureen began.

"Don't cross me, maid," he said, one foot forward, leaning hard.

Eyes shining, Tilley was down from his stool running at his father full speed, fists clenched, ready to pound.

"Ye, ye," was all he could muster. His face was contorted, eyes blinking back what felt like girl's tears, as he rammed against the wall of Earl, tumbled backwards onto the linoleum. "Ye, ye. Ye."

"'Tis 'you', not 'ye', ye spoiled rotten little twat," Earl yelled. Then he put both hands on his wide belt, his fingers worked rapidly to release the tongue. With a firm grip on the buckle, he was ready to yank and hollered, "Take hold to him, Maureen, or I'll give him somet'ing to really bawl over."

Maureen cradled Tilley in her arms and brought a paper bag to his hyperventilating lips while Earl forced his feet into laced boots and stomped out the door.

"Shh, me lovey," she crooned. "Yer Mudder'll buy ye a new pack. Better than the last. Ye'll see." And slowly as she said, "Yer mudder loves ye," over and over again into his teacup of an ear, his breathing calmed.

❧

The next morning, Maureen awoke to find Earl in bed beside her. Lifting the sheets when she arose, she smelled his body, gases from a hot chicken dinner, rich gravy, gliding out and lingering in the room. Not her cooking. Last night, she had saved the moose in the refrigerator, fed Tilley and Boyd grilled cheese sandwiches instead.

Thaw

As Maureen raised her flowery nightgown over her head, Earl opened a watery eye, stared.

"Ye didn't do yer shift last night," she said.

"No," he answered, tongue thick from sleep. "Art says he's hit a lull. Take a few days for meself." Earl ran his fingers through the curly hair peppering his chest, then rolled onto his side, and tugged the spread up over his shoulder.

Never mind, Maureen thought as she folded her nightgown, slid it underneath her foam pillow. Everything will come 'round. Tough times can't last forever.

six

id-September, Tilley made his way down over the hill towards Cupboard Collegiate. After days of drizzle, sunlight managed to burn a small hole through the clouds, and as he walked a straight line, his left side was clouded, right side warmed. Nearing the beach, he met a girl as she struggled to push her newborn along the shoulder. Mud flecked up on the underside of the stroller, errant rocks testing the thin wheels. Looking twice he thought how much the shiny baby resembled a plastic doll, the mother a dreamy child.

"Hey!" Walter's voice.

Tilley glanced towards the shoreline to see Walter waving, rushing up the grassy path towards him. Against the horizon, Walter nearly vanished in his prison-grey coat.

"Don't tell me yer ready for winter already," Tilley said.

Walter scratched the fabric. "I hates bein' cold."

"No chance of that," Tilley said. "Let's get a move on, else we'll be written up tardy."

"Hold up," Walter said. Then, in a flat tone, "Gotta wait for Ida."

"Ida?"

Walter rolled his eyes, hollered down towards the water, "C'mon, will ye?"

Ida skipped up the path, jacketless, her altered kilt a length that made boys reevaluate the benefits of a gusty day.

"Hiya, Tilley," she chirped.

"Yeah, hi."

"From now on, I won't be standin' 'round waitin' for ye," Walter said to Ida as he trod out onto the road. Sparks of the coat's orange quilted liner flashed with each rub of his thighs.

"Do whatever ye wants, ye jerk-off," she spat back, middle finger at attention. "I can find me own way. I don't need no help from no one."

Ida kept pace with Tilley, spoke peanut butter scented words into his ear. "Mudder's got a job in Tronto. Some scout, she said, came into the club where she was workin', told her she got the glow of a star 'bout her."

"Wow."

"Yeah. Gonna make her famous, he was sayin'."

"That's good, I s'pose."

"Yeah, and when she gets it all straightened out, she'll be sendin' for me. Yes, she will."

"Sounds right on."

Ida twisted up her hair, dropped it. "Got a smoke?"

"Not for someone yer age, I don't. Yer too young for that."

"Give it here. I wants one." She mock-punched him in the shoulder.

"Alright, alright," he said, fishing into his back pocket.

After she lit the flattened cigarette, she knocked him on top of the head with a fist. "Too young, he says. Christ, ye must've been smokin' since ye was three by the size of ye."

"Yer real funny, Ida. I could laugh so hard me head'ed drop off."

As they neared the chain link fence that ran up the centre of the school parking lot, Ida leaned her head towards Tilley and murmured, "Meet me back to the beach after school and I'll give ye a blow job ye'll never forget."

Tilley's face flushed instantly even though he commanded it to do otherwise. He choked slightly and managed to utter, "I got afterschool sports."

"Like what? Basketball?" she said, smirking. Smoke rings drifted out from her open mouth. "C'mon, b'y. I'll pump ye right up like a balloon."

A few steps ahead, Walter turned. "I hears yer dirty mouth, Ida. Don't t'ink I don't. Watch what yer sayin', me dear, or I'll go back and tell Mudder and Fadder'll ship ye off right quick to a foster home where ye belongs."

Ida scowled, kicked a pebble with her buckle shoe, then flounced down one side of the chain link fence while Tilley and Walter went down the other. Even though Ida was in junior high, she shared the same building as the high schoolers, but occupied the east side and was not permitted past that imaginary line drawn in the central hallway.

Three minutes into recess, Ida had already established an entourage. Leaning up against the fence her skirt askew, she offered up herself as entertainment. Her white panties pressed into the chain links and with what little padding her rump provided, created a half-dozen diamond shaped, raisinless buns.

Like feral animals, the boys sniffed around her. Some were coyotes on the ground, howling as though Ida's underwear was the fullest, most mesmerizing moon. Others, chest-beating baboons, clung to the fence, rattled it in and out with such force, Ida was flung forward onto her knees. When a heady squall upped the ante, Ida on all fours, the baboons went wild, threatened to rip the metal posts from their cement blocks.

"Christ," Walter said. "Will ye look at the show she's puttin' on?"

"No shortage of attention that's for sure," Tilley said though he averted his eyes, searched the eaves of the school for evidence of abandoned birds' nests.

The ruckus caught the attention of Miss Priddle's scouring, beady eye and she soon arrived on the scene, blouse buttoned up to her earlobes, heavy-duty stapler behind her back.

"Ye t'ink I haven't seen yer kind before?" she said to Ida, marching around her like an army corporal.

"And what kind is that?" Ida said as she stood up, scraped shards of shale from her palms.

"And she's saucy, too," Miss Priddle said to whoever was listening and everyone was. "We gets one or two like ye every year. Not one ounce of class. T'inkin' ye'll get a free ride, hussyin' yerself up like a bit of trash."

Hands on her hips, Ida leaned forward with squinted eyes. "Least I's not dressed like a dried up ol' prune."

"Oh, me lovey," Miss Priddle said now tapping the stapler against her thigh. "Ye needn't imagine I cares one iota what ye t'inks of me outfit. 'Tis young minds I's got to be bothered 'bout." She held out the stapler to Ida. "Now fix yerself."

"What?" Ida said stepping back.

"At Cupboard Collegiate, we has a rule or two 'bout how our students bodies' has to be presented and that's got nothin' to do with brazen girls presentin' their bodies." Snickers from the crowd. "Skirts not permitted above the knee. Now turn that scrap of fabric into a pair of shorts or I'll be callin' yer aunt in jig time to take ye home for makin' a holy disgrace of yerself."

Ida's face melted, defiance burned off. Grabbing the stapler from Miss Priddle's outstretched hand, Ida hunched over legs buckled, clipped together inch after inch of tartan fabric.

"Good and tight now," Miss Priddle said with supremacy like liner on her curling lips. "Right across, me dearie. See that there's nar gap."

There was no graceful exit here. An attraction amid a sea of spectators, Ida returned the stapler and bound her arms tightly across her chest. Walking towards the building she tried not to blink as exposed ends of the staples pricked her inner thighs. With her thumb and forefinger, she formed a vice grip on the tender skin underneath her arm. It worked. Her mind wrapped itself around that cutting pain, neglected the well inside her that yearned to rise up and gush over.

In the hours that followed, Ida earned herself a nickname for her display of arched back, budding chest, lean bottom. Despite its length, it still managed to take hold: "Fried-Egg-Ida-Side-Order-o'-Ham."

As the crowds tumbled out during lunch hour, Tilley could see Ida, skirt gathered in a poof, sulking in the dim entranceway of the junior high. She stared at the spot where she'd been reprimanded; another girl had taken her place, though she was on the opposite side of the fence. While Ida was a mess of gangly limbs, snarled hair, the new girl sat with her legs crossed neatly, wearing flared jeans and laced-up shoes. From a Tupperware container, she rapidly speared leftover Kraft Dinner, brought forkfuls up inside the hood of her jacket.

Tilley did not recognise the lime green rain slicker or the twisting vine of embroidered flowers that grew up the leg of her jeans. But he did remember the ankles. From the church door. He was certain. Beyond pale. They were bleached. Bones like white buttons he longed to press, activate.

As he gazed, his palms grew sweaty, even his thoughts began to stutter. All for the sake of an ankle. Boyd had once said to him, "I's a tit n' ass man, meself" and Tilley wondered if he could simply be an ankles man. Perhaps, even a leg man, an extremely-lower-leg-sort-of-man.

"Hey Marnie," one of the coyotes yelled out.

<u>Marnie</u>.

"Would ye kiss a rabbit between the ears?"

She looked up, hood falling away to reveal pleasant rounded cheeks, blunt shoulder-length hair.

"Yeah, sure. I guess."

The coyote's tongue stretched to touch the tip of his nose and he grunted as he reached deep into the front pockets of his jeans. Tugging the white liner as far out as it would go he motioned to his crotch, said with sizzle, "Come on, then. I's waitin'."

Wearing a stained-tooth grin, he bucked his hips and his cotton ears lolled back and forth. She half-smiled, eyes darting, and tugged her hood back over her head, a turtle easing back into its shell.

Uncertain of how his feet found courage when his mind hesitated, Tilley's small frame now hovered just inside the coyote's shadow. "Leave her alone, arsehole," he said, wondering who owned the plucky tongue living under his words.

"Go suck yerself off, ye faggot," the coyote said, jamming his pockets back into place. "If ye weren't Boyd's brudder, I'd flatten ye into a pancake." Then, he rattled phlegm in his throat and spat near Tilley's sneaker before lumbering off.

Looking up again she squinted slightly towards Tilley.

He stood before her wearing foolishness like a second skin while his feet held firm, tongue dormant and his mind beckoned him to speak or leave.

She reached deep into her book bag, retrieved a packet of wax paper, and brought it to her lap. When she unfolded it, Tilley could see three shiny peeled eggs nestled together.

"Want one?" She held them out to Tilley.

Even without the help of the wind he could smell the vinegar stench and frowned. "Not for me."

"I'll have one," Walter said, at once standing beside Tilley. His hand shot out, seized a slippery orb. "I loves pickled eggs. Always gets one when I goes to Nips-n-Bites to fetch Fadder."

"Me too," she said, taking bites with perfect small teeth. "Love them, that is. When it comes to my mother's cooking, I've developed a taste for anything in a box, can, or jar."

"Maybe then," Tilley said, leaning down to pluck up the last egg. He chewed slowly trying not to breathe and remembering to keep his puckered mouth closed.

seven

In early October, Maureen and Tilley made their way along one of the overgrown paths that crisscrossed the forest behind their house. Maureen strode in front carrying a plastic grocery bag that contained four warm bottles of jelly—two raspberry and two squashberry. Each one was wrapped carefully in a double-page from an old issue of the *Full Bucket*.

"I just don't feel safe comin' through these woods on me own no more," Maureen said over her shoulder. "Not since those two young fellers from the Gut hauled that poor Mercer girl up here. Done what they done."

"Well, I don't mind comin'. Nothin' better to do."

Maureen came to a thin stream, waited for Tilley.

"Not much older than yerself now, if ye can believe it," she continued as she stepped onto a flat wet rock, water frothing around it. "Guess that's what comes when yer mudder is also yer sister, and yer fadder, who's likely yer brudder t'inks incest is somet'ing with a half-dozen legs livin' under a rotten log in yer yard."

"Can't we talk 'bout somet'ing else?" Tilley asked, skipping across the stream.

"Alright," she said. The path was wider now, and they were able to continue side by side. "How's school goin'?"

"'Tis good, I guess. Got Mr. Chuckle for homeroom. So, that's cool. He don't give no one a hard time."

"Chuckle? Me Lard. I had him for a class when I went there. Young'uns used to call him, 'Huckleberry Chuckle.' But for the life of me, I can't remember why. I's surprised he's still there."

"Same one," Tilley said, smiling. "Hey, did ye know Ida is livin' over to Walter's?"

"Yes." Mouth taunt. "Penny told me."

"She says her mudder's busy with some modellin' job."

"Modellin' what?"

"Didn't say."

"Modellin', me backside. The mudder served a drink to some young feller, and if Penny's tellin' it straight, she served somet'ing else to him too. And then next t'ing ye knows, she drivin' 'cross the rock, drivin' straight through to Hawaii, she says. Left Ida with some udder floozy barmaid, workin' all kinds of hours, bringin' home all kinds of men. Comes home, finds Ida sleepin' on the kitchen floor. Downed a whole bottle of spearmint cough syrup, she did, and they couldn't rouse her. 'Tis a lovely taste I knows, but ye got to mind yerself. Her and some b'y from the bar carts Ida to the Good Hopes Hospital where they calls the Welfare or the Child's Services or whoever it is that they calls. And one of them gets hold of Winse."

"Oh. I never knowed."

"No. And 'tis a good t'ing ye don't. Next t'ing ye'll be pityin' her, and I tell ye, she'll sniff that on ye like a shark sniffs a thread of blood in the water."

After walking several minutes in silence, they passed the clearing known as Busty Bend, where spruce trees displayed an impressive array of swollen burls. Someone had dragged a threadbare mattress up through the woods. Nearby a half-empty box of tissues was disintegrating from the heavy rainfall.

"Disgustin'," Maureen snarled. "Young crowd these days no better than a pack of animals. Who in their right mind would go and haul in a dirty ol' t'ing like that. When we was yer age, we used to picnic here. Good and simple. No thoughts of picnics nowadays, I reckons."

Tilley coughed, tugged down the sweatshirt that was riding up his hips. And though he couldn't help but envision the mattress occupied, a cheap blanket heaving, he said, "'Tis only ol' garbage, Mudder. Don't mean nothin'."

"Yes. Yer right. It don't." She scratched at her throat with rounded nails. "So, is ye goin' with yer Fadder on Saturday?"

"Don't want to."

"Ye got to, I's guessin'."

"Don't see why I got to have a hand in it, is all."

"Just the way 'tis, Tilley. Earl took Boyd when he was 'round yer age and now 'tis yer turn. That's what fadders do; show their b'ys how to hunt."

"Don't see why."

"Ain't yers to question."

"Nothin' ever is."

"Well then."

As the path widened, sunlight sneaking through, Maureen slowed, put an arm around Tilley's shoulder. "Sometimes I envies him," she said.

"Who?"

"The hermit, I s'pose. I imagines he lives a real quiet life."

"Yeah. Don't have Boyd crankin' up music in his basement. Drive ye nuts."

"I doubts he even got a basement. Couldn't really do it meself, though. Stayin' on me own for years on end. After a while, I'd go right batty with no one to talk to. Guess I'd be talkin' at meself, maybe chat up an earwig or two."

"Why do he?"

"Do he what?"

"Live by hisself in a shack."

"Oh, I don't know. Once I asked Flossie Grimes, figurin' she was old enough to know. But all she told me was that some woman broke his heart when he was a young b'y and he was never the same after. Yer Fadder says beavers is like that. Takes on a hermit's life if they's apart from their loved ones."

"Fadder and his bloody beavers."

"Well, yes."

"Must've been some woman, is all."

"Maybe," Maureen said as they emerged from the overgrown path. "But from me own understandin' when somet'ing like that happens 'tis more often the heart that's special than the actual woman."

Tilley hesitated at the edge of the clearing. "I'll wait here, Mudder."

"I thought ye would. I still remembers that day he shot up yer backside with the salt."

Rubbing his hindquarters, Tilley said, "Like 'twas yesterday."

Maureen stepped out into the warm light, walked to the rickety back stoop. Without knocking, she placed the plastic bag by the wooden door, then turned and left. From his place behind a thinning spruce tree, Tilley noticed a rotted, striped curtain waver, though the window was sealed tight.

Thaw

On Saturday morning well before daybreak, Tilley dragged himself through the woods with a set of near-quadruplets: his father, Earl Payne, Art Knuckle, and Wilf Tippet. Each of the four men wore heavy beige pants, neon orange vests, and striped Chicken Deelicken ball caps atop their balding heads. Tilley was outfitted in pine-green coloured clothes, except for a brilliant red patch of cloth that Maureen had tacked onto the back of his jacket. Even though Earl claimed there hadn't been an accident since Silas Damper blew Clay Potts' ear off, Tilley still sensed that at any moment a bullet might penetrate his small body, end his worries. He tore the cellophane from a second Joe Louis cake and devoured it like it was his last meal.

"I loves a good feed of moose," Wilf Tippet said in a low tone that didn't carry. "'Tis out of heaven, 'cause ain't nothin' like it in this world."

"When 'tis right fresh," Art Knuckle said, wiping a slobbery mouth in the sleeve of his shirt. "Gail makes a wunnerful moose pie. Meat that tender, right like a boil."

"Sunday football," Winse said, "bottle of moose meat in one paw, beer in the udder. Only t'ing make it better is if I got one of them cheerleaders feedin' me. Uh uh. Buddy, I tell ye."

"Now me son." Earl patted Tilley on the back with one hand and flicked left, right, up, down with the other. "Keep yer eyes peeled for any of those signs I told ye 'bout. We'll catch a moose today, buddy. Wait and see. Just wait and see."

"Yes, b'y," Winse said. "There's a million t'ings to watch for. Ye can't have yer head up yer hole, that's for sure."

"I likens huntin' to an art," Art said with a chuckle. "'Tis the sensitive ones that sees the signs."

"Signs?" Tilley mumbled, black Joe Louis crumbs flying.

"Signs," Earl said, annoyed. "Weren't ye listenin'? We's lookin' for fresh droppins."

"Fresh droppins, he says," Winse hollers. "A good-sized

86

dump we's after, now Earl. We's huntin' moose b'y, not rabbits."

"If ye sees either moose footprint, that's often a sign a moose has been 'round," Art said. "They's got a cloven hoof, helps them when they's crossin' the swampy spots." He put his hands out before him, stretched his fingers wide. "Spreads out, they do."

"Traipsin' 'round these parts," Wilf said, "I could use a cloven hoof meself. I wonders if anyone's ever thought to invent it. Moose hunting boots. Buy yerself yer very own pair of handy cloven hoofs."

"Don't sound so bad," Art said, who liked to think he knew a little about everything. "There's grants ye can get for that sort of t'ing. Government grants, me son. Yes sir."

"Now then," Wilf said. "Wilf's Walkers. Every hunter'll be orderin' themselves up a pair of Wilf's Walkers."

"Nah," Art said, frowning. "Sounds too much like somet'ing for the seniors."

"B'ys, b'ys," Winse said, as he moved in a sneaky jaunt over fallen twigs, toe to heel, toe to heel. "Keep it down. Moose got earholes in their heads, ye knows."

Through dense woods they hiked without a path up a steep sweep towards a cliff, then climbed down it one man after the other. For several minutes, they wound their way along a clear trouting stream and Tilley noticed the edges of sky were streaked with dull pink. The sun had begun to rise.

"Here's the spot," Art said, pointing towards the tangle of trees. Though to Tilley the point of re-entry was indistinguishable from any other. Not a qualm from the men. They splashed behind Art, the forest swallowing them, damper now with mossy rocks, spongy footing replacing the twigs and leaves.

"I remembers me first time huntin' with the ol' man," Wilf announced after he threw forth a ball of hawk like a poisoned pellet. "'Twas a time. I had moose so hard on me brain, I minds I shot up half the woods. Comes out with nothin' but a shoulder smartin' like someone took a sledgehammer to me. Me head was poundin' that hard from all the racket, had to traipse backwards in a circle for near three hours before I was rid of it."

"Yes," Art agreed. "Traipsin' backward is the best cure for a headache."

They were moving downhill again, feet shuffling sideways towards an area where the earth flattened into a stretch of black marshland.

"Lookie there," Earl said, pointing towards the barren circle. "Up ahead is a prime, prime area. 'Tis right opened up, a cutover. Trees chopped down, hauled out. Moose likes that. And Tilley, take a gander at the tips of the young trees."

"Buddy, me son," Wilf said. "'Tis chewed right off."

"They's was browsin' here," Art said. "For sure on that."

"Uh-huh," Tilley said, his soggy sneakers now squelching and sucking, his footprints filling with swampy water.

"I'll be damned if this ain't the boghole where Norm Simms got his earlier this year," Winse said, teeth clamped onto his cigarette.

A dried branch snapped.

"Shush b'ys," Wilf said. "Did ye hear that?"

"That we did, sir," Art whispered.

Through the strands of morning light filtering down through the trees, Tilley watched four neon vests freeze, striped caps turning to peruse the landscape inch by inch.

Another snap. Then another. Tilley saw the bull first, so majestic, larger than he'd ever imagined. He held his breath tightly inside his cheeks and lungs, willing those cloven hoofs to dart off in a safer direction. No such luck.

"Over there, b'ys." Earl's voice was thin with contained excitement, as he motioned towards a section of bushes across the marsh.

"Lard, Christ," Wilf said. "He's a real beaut. A real beaut."

Steadily, Earl unzipped his rifle case, slid the 303 from its nest, chamber loaded, ready for action. When he thrust the gun into Tilley's short arms, it seemed to double in size.

"Go, go," Earl whispered. "Give it a go."

Tilley propped the rifle against his shoulder, took aim, hands and heart fumbling.

"For the love of Christ, shoot, me son. Shoot!"

As his fingers, greasy from the Vachon cake, slipped over the trigger, Tilley heard a deafening smack in his left ear. The enormous beast staggered a foot or two, emitted a guttural moo, then toppled over onto the earth, the quake weakening Tilley's legs.

There was a whoop from Earl as he wrapped his proud arm around Tilley's shoulder. "Well, bend me over and call me shitface. Ye got him. Ye bloody well got him."

Art Knuckle stepped forward, dropping his rifle to his knee. "Had to take a go at him, Earl," he said grimly. "He'd be halfway to Labrador 'fore yer b'y there hauled his thumb out of his arse."

Earl's arm went limp with disdain. He lifted his hat, smoothed damp strands of hair across his forehead, then snatched up his gun and buried it in the case with a hasty zip.

"Don't matter," Wilf said, charging headlong toward the clearing. "We got our moose. And by Jaysus, don't doubt if we ain't broke some sort of record. Still got this marnin's breakfast stuck in me teeth."

"Lard love it," Winse said as he leaned in over the hulking frame. "That's some kind of dewlap hangin' off him. Sack like that, must've been real popular with the ladies."

Earl withdrew his hunting knife from the case on his belt, offered it to Tilley, and said, "Missed yer shot, me son. Now's yer chance to finish him off."

"Whatd'ye mean, Fadder?"

"Slit his t'roat that's what, look at him. Put him out of his misery."

The moose's shiny eyes were wide open, staring straight at Tilley through curling black lashes.

"I can't do it," he said, though the knife was in his hand.

"What?"

"I can't. Please Fadder."

Earl looked from man to man, yanked up his pants by his thick belt. "Go on, b'y. Nothin' to it."

Tilley took a step back but Earl lunged forward, clamped Tilley's hand, knife positioned, and forced it towards the throat of the moose. Resistance. Earl increased the pressure on Tilley's fist and hissed, "If ye cuts me, by Christ, ye'll know it."

With a blade like a razor, the knife sliced through the hair, the flesh: it was smoother, butterier than Tilley had expected. He was dizzy now, blood coating his hand, his father's hand, making the ten fingers indistinguishable. Dividing the windpipe, pink bubbles rushed up, one last spruce-scented breath cast over Tilley. Job complete. His hand began to tingle. Gripped too tight, he thought. Then, the other one tingled too. Prickling travelled up through his calves, thighs, over his abdomen, surging eagerly towards his head. Down. One instant appeasing his father and the next, slumped over, as limp as the dead moose that lay beside him.

While the others chuckled at the sight of Tilley, Earl retrieved the knife, swiped the blade across a patch of moss. He said nothing when Art and Winse gripped the broad, flat antlers, rubber band neck, and dragged it upright for a commemorative photo, Tilley's small frame still tangled in the mess.

"Yes sir," Wilf said as he snapped, urged the film forward with his yellowed thumb, snapped again. "This one'll go down in the books without a doubt. 'Moose faints after man kills son.'"

Gulps of dead water. As Tilley surfaced, he felt fingers knotted into the hair on the back of his head, shoving his face down into the bitterly cold marsh over and over again.

"That'll bring ye too," Earl said when Tilley's body stiffened. He released the hair, shoved Tilley backward onto a patch of moss.

Clothes wet and stained with bog and blood, Tilley shivered, drew his knees up towards his chest. A few feet away, Winse was holding up a leg, while Art sliced down through the ribs, along the belly. Rolling the innards out onto the grass, Wilf skulked in, snipped away the liver, wrapped it in plastic, and dropped it into his bag without so much as a sniff.

"Would ye rob me grave as fast?" Winse said, as he dropped the leg. "If ye haves the liver, by Jaysus, I's gettin' the tongue."

After slicing as far as he could go, Art now had an axe in hand, hacking through the empty moose just underneath the floating ribs.

"Don't ruin him, now," Earl said, leaning in. "Don't want no splintered bone through me meat or nothin'."

Art looked up, swiped his brow with his forearm. "Do ye t'ink this is the first time I done this? Ye may know how to cut a fish at the plant, Gover, but I don't need none of yer lip 'bout choppin' through a moose."

Then, Art motioned to Tilley and Tilley rose, unsteady, and swayed closer.

Patting the body, Art said, "Tilley, did ye know his hair is hollow? Helps him to swim."

"Didn't know," Tilley said, feather voice. "Seems too big to be out in the water."

"Ye'd t'ink that," Art said. "But they's wunnerful swimmers. Right graceful. Speedy too."

In no time, while the others smoked, offered a hand from time to time, Art had the head severed, the body chopped into neat quarters.

"Ye leaves the hair on," he said to Tilley. "Else it'll be covered in ol' guck by the time we gets him home." He rinsed his hands in the same standing water where Tilley had been revived. "Winse," he said, as he strolled back to the grassy section, started digging in his bag. "Get a bit of a fire goin'. The b'y looks near froze to death and I's goin' to have meself a wee feed." A nudge to Tilley, wide smile, top teeth missing and a pink tongue poking through. "'Tis easier to cart a lunch out in me gut than over me shoulder. Right?"

While red-needled boughs crackled and smoked in the fire, Wilf sat on the edge of a log admiring the moose and picking things out of the sole of his boot with a thin stick.

Art cracked the lid on a tin of Vienna Sausages, placed them on the edge of the fire, and waited until the label flared up, curled away, juices boiled over. Hand inside the sleeve of his sweater, he plucked the tin out of the fire. "Loves me dogs' dicks," he said. "Ye want one?"

He swiftly tapped the bottom and the middle sausage jumped up steaming hot towards Tilley. "It'll do ye good."

"I got me cakes," Tilley said, as he unwrapped his third, nibbled bits of chocolatey icing to soothe his uneasy stomach.

"Ye want a can of Strawberry Crush?" Wilf said, slurping through discoloured lips. "Hits the spot."

"Alright, then."

"No wonder yer only knee high to a grasshopper," Winse said, licking the paper edge of a newly rolled cigarette. "Eatin' that kind of ol' crap."

"Take this," Earl said, thrusting a sandwich towards Tilley, a can imprint in the centre of the soft bread. "Potted meat."

When lunch was consumed, Art stamped out the fire with his rubber boot, crushed the blackened sausage can. Each hoisting a section of meat onto their backs, they began the trek out of the woods towards their pick-up trucks. Tilley was in charge of the bags, had rifles thrown double over either shoulder. And as he began trudging across the forgiving bog, he turned back for one last look. He did not want to forget. A Bull Moose. King of Kings in the forest. Now just an outline in flattened bloody grass, a vast deserted head with its nose sunk deep into the marshy ground.

eight

At the kitchen table, Boyd sat with a torn scrap of old underwear and a 12-gauge. After removing all traces of dust from the barrel, he snapped it shut, pointed it straight at Tilley's head, and said through bulleting laughter, "Chik chik booof."

Clipper growled, but Tilley ignored Boyd. This wasn't the first time he had served as an imaginary target. He climbed onto a stool and lifted the Styrofoam lid from one of the cold suppers his mother had ordered from the church. Two rolled slices of packaged ham, a scoop of potato salad, cabbage slaw, shiny bun, and stains of beet juice sluicing the works. Tasted just as good as it always did anyway. The back door opened and Earl appeared in the kitchen, hands and forearms streaked reddish brown.

"Got the leg hung up in the shed," he said, as he went to the sink, rinsed flecks of moose meat and bristly hair down the drain. "Let's hope for a cool streak so it don't go maggoty. Though, 'tis an awful dampness in the air."

Clipper continued to growl and Boyd shifted targets. With a second "Chik chik booof" aimed at the narrow dip between the Clipper's black eyes, the dog backed into the shadowed gap made by Maureen's legs.

"What's eatin' at ye?" she said as she crouched to rub Clipper's back.

"Nothin' Mudder," Boyd said, sliding the gun into its sleeve. "Lost me job, is all."

"What happened?" Maureen said.

"'Twas Blackie Tripe done it," he replied, when in fact it was Boyd himself. Billy had caught Boyd sucking on a hefty joint in the backroom, while Boyd's jumble of friends helped themselves to free games of pinball. Immediate dismissal. "Turned me back for a second and the piece of shit rips off the eight ball. Out through the door in a friggin' flash."

"Don't sound that serious to me," Maureen said. "Not like somet'ing to lose yer job over. That's not like the Billy I knows."

"That's just like ye, Mudder," Boyd said, spittle flecking the clean table. "Always pickin' up for anyone but yer son. The prick told me he got to buy a whole new set of balls that's what. They don't sell the one. And he's takin' it out of me bit of pay, Mudder. And I says to him, 'Go fuck yerself, Billy Boyle.'"

Maureen clicked her tongue, stood, and shook the dog hair from her sweaty fingers. "Well, that kinda talk might've done it right there."

Earl pulled up a chair, relaxed. "Don't let that get ye down, me ol' gaffer. That's only a few shackles. Sure, I remembers when I was trappin' beavers. By Christ, one night, I got a real rip on. B'ys to the camp told me I was mad to get back at it, workhorse like I is, wouldn't settle down. Drunk as a bloody skunk. Don't recall much after that but I guess I was rovin' through the woods, scoutin' 'round for a catch. But, I come across me supervisor. And, unfortunate that 'twas, he's there in front of me," Earl smirked ear-to-ear, lowered his voice, "takin' a squirt in the pond. Well, I must've heard that water slappin' or splashin' or somet'ing cause he told me I overtook him, his hand still hold to his dick and I clipped the poor beggar right through the ear."

"No shit."

"Yes, me son. He now, racin' 'round with a striped tag like a peppermint knob hangin' from the side of his head, howlin' like a sonuvabitch. Ye needn't t'ink he kept me on. No sir. I was out on me skinny arse 'fore I could touch me finger to me nose."

"Holy shit, Fadder. That's somet'ing, all right. I don't feel too bad now."

"That's the right attitude, me son. Ye got to buck up, pitch in: there's always another bus. Life's ten percent attitude and ninety percent of what ye do with the shit doled out at ye." Earl pinched a bit of dried blood from his wiry eyebrows and thought for a moment. "Or maybe that's ninety percent attitude, and ten percent shit. Ah, whatever 'tis, fifty-fifty even, any good man'll be back up on that horse."

Lifting a cheek, Earl reached and pulled a worn wallet from his hind pocket. "Never was a wallower, meself. Don't do nobody no good." He dropped a purple bill beside the gun case. "Take it," he said. "Go on. Get yerself a plate of fish n' chips. Everyt'ing seems worse when there's nothin' rattlin' 'round in yer hole."

Boyd snatched it up, said, "How 'bout anudder five spot, Ol' Man, and I'll treat Tilley here to a bite."

Earl shook his head. "That's what ye won't. Fish n' chips for him when he ought to be gettin' a swift kick to the backside. I was that ashamed, I tell ye, the way he got on today. Never knew such a puss in all me years."

"Didn't even want to go, anyways," Tilley muttered through a mouthful of partridgeberry salad, teeth fresh blood red.

"What was that?" Earl was up from his chair. "Keep yer trap

shut, me son. Ye've done enough harm for one day. Laughin' stock I was with all the fellers. Laughin'. Friggin'. Stock." He paced across the linoleum, stole the Styrofoam plate right out from under Tilley's nose. "And who said ye could gorge yerself on me bit of dinner?"

"I told the b'y," Maureen said. "I told him to go on get hisself a mouthful to eat."

"Well, he can get out there and find hisself somet'ing, now can't he? No respect, he got. Nothin' in the world wrong with catchin' a few good meals in yer own backyard. Well, me son," Earl said with a clip to Tilley's ear, "let's see how ye feels with nar bite. I guarantees yer gob'll be waterin' for a taste of fresh moose meat in a couple of days." Earl picked up Tilley's fork, stabbed a roll of ham, and jammed it into his cavernous mouth. "Mmmm. Wunnerful good."

Tilley ran from the table. Out through the porch dodging his mother's lilting voice as it urged him back with promises of a plate of fried bread dough, molasses, sweet milky tea.

But Tilley never ran far. On the back stoop, he stopped short. Tar-coloured clouds cloaked the sky and at once split their seams. Torrents of icy rain pressed down upon Tilley in smothering sheet after smothering sheet. It was almost blinding. He was soaked instantly and water drilled into his gasping mouth, nailed his forehead, pooled deep inside his ears.

Then, as he was about to retreat, he spotted blurred movement, a fleshy mound creeping up the railing. Though squinting, he could identify streaks of a stubby body climbing the slippery wooden steps. It was a woman. She moved towards him with determined footing until there was only a curtain of rain between them. Her belted cotton dress had melted onto her dumpling form and her muddy slippers were like dirty clumps of wet rabbit fur. She was exactly the same height as Tilley.

She stared straight at him through oatmeal eyes and he immediately felt unhinged.

"Where's Harvey?" she said, her voice cutting through the rain. "Little b'y. Tell me now. Where's me Harvey to?"

nine

nnette Boone welcomed them into her parlour, a sunny room overflowing with tightly upholstered furniture, lacquered tables, and bulbous floor lamps. The only exception to this perfection was Hazel Boone's disintegrating chair. Annette placed a crystal tumbler of orange-scented liqueur in front of Maureen and pushed a plate of shredded coconut heaps toward Tilley.

"Go ahead," she said through a reedy smile. "Don't be shy."

Maureen jabbed Tilley with her elbow, then clutching her tumbler, sampled and suppressed a contortion as her tongue went rigid inside her mouth. Finally, she plucked a cookie, handed it to Tilley, and said to Annette, "They looks grand, Missus. Like tiny clumps of frizzy hair. Somet'ing ye'd pluck out of yer drain. Coconut with a home-perm." An arrested giggle.

Annette grimaced. "I made them myself," she said as she seated herself on the very edge of a chair.

"Imagined as much, Missus Boone."

"Annette, please."

"'Tis a right lovely home, ye haves, Missus—Annette. Though, 'tis some climb, I can tell ye that."

"The hill? Yes." Annette emptied her tumbler in one greedy gulp and tapped her diamond wedding band on the glass. "Don't know what David, my husband, was ever thinking. I've learned over the years not to even attempt to understand his rationale for anything."

"Well, I's sorry to say our car's stuck halfway up yer drive. Rain gone and rinsed away a section of yer crushed stone. Wheel is in over the rim."

"Ah," Annette nodded vigorously. "I will mention that to David. It's absolutely treacherous. An utter disaster. The earth seems to be devouring whatever we offer it."

"I pays it no heed, missus. Troublin' over t'ings ye got no hand in. Me husband'll haul that ol' rust box out in the mornin'. Just an eyesore for ye is all."

Dressed in a burgundy gym suit, Hazel Boone wandered in through the open doorway, picked several cookies from the plate, and dropped them into her pockets.

"I dearly hope you plan on actually enjoying those, Mother Boone," Annette said with a sigh.

"Oh, do shut up," Hazel spat back. "I's not yer Mudder, never has been, and God willin' as long as I's on this earth, never will be." Then she wandered out of the room, fresh hard soled slippers click-clacking on the hardwood.

"David is going to be livid," Annette said, as she lurched forward for the bottle and tipped in more tawny liquor. "Entirely livid. I honestly cannot fathom how she got out, not to mention down over that hill. And to end up on your back step? She's slipping away day by day. Day by day. Heartrending to watch."

"Ye never knows what's goin' through the head of someone that age, Missus. Sometimes they's here. Sometimes they's there.

And sometimes they's somewheres else altogether."

"You are quite right, Mrs. Gover. Maureen, if I may."

"She was on and on 'bout some young man named, 'Harvey.' Me Lard, she was right beside herself wonderin' where he was to. What was we doin' there. Offered her a cup of tea to quiet her down a bit but she was awful riled up." Maureen tilted her head towards Annette, whispered, "Actin' like she owned me place, if truth be told, though I didn't pay her no mind."

"Oh my, oh my. Harvey was her late husband. David told me he died some fifty years ago. He doesn't like to talk about it. What a terrible bother for you."

"'Twas no trouble, Missus."

"To your credit, Maureen, you actually got her out of her clothing. That's often quite the struggle around here. More so than I'd like to admit."

"Me love, she was satched right through to the skin. Like a rat. 'Twas beyond pitiful. Had to do somet'ing." Maureen leaned in again and murmured, "Though her undergarments is still wet. I would've offered, mind ye, that sort of t'ing don't bother me in the least."

"Well, you certainly have a way with her. It's quite wonderful, actually."

"Oh. I don't know 'bout that. Comes natural, is all."

Annette bit her bottom lip, then smiled. Her lipstick was smeared across perfectly aligned upper teeth. "Perhaps you might consider coming by a morning or two a week? We had some superb help in St. John's, simply the best, and now, with the move and all, our little routine had to be abandoned. Perhaps we could make some sort of cordial arrangement?"

Maureen went to take a bite of a cookie but it crumbled down over her chest, into her lap, and she covered the debris with her hands. "Well, now. I s'pose I could. Long as she don't mind me company. Don't want to force meself upon the woman."

"Fabulous," Annette said. She stood abruptly, her body unsteady in heels. "Tomorrow morning, then?"

As Maureen rose, shook a shower of crumbs onto the rug, she heard men's heavy shoes on the stairs just outside the door.

"David," Annette called out. "How about a 'good afternoon' for your wife and our company. Maureen Gover and her son."

David came into the parlour and stiffened as though he was flash frozen. The small child he had seen through the window of his old house was seated on the couch. Though now, it was clear he was not a child at all, but instead a boy teetering on the cusp of adulthood. Patchy dark hairs marred the smooth skin on his chin, upper lip, and he appeared awkward with meatless limbs; his body like a stump.

Coming from somewhere in the back of the house, David heard his mother humming. With that sound filling his ears and the boy before him, he felt like he was wading in a swollen river, familiar milky water spooling around him until it foamed, curdled. How easily he could lose his balance, slip underneath, and let the current grip his skeletal ankles. He could do it, all while his wife looked on. Barely able to see past her clumping layers of mascara, she would blame his sudden depressurization on the stroke.

"David?" Annette said, rolling her eyes at Maureen. "A word of greeting, perhaps?"

"I've seen you before," he finally said.

Tilley moved in next to his mother and following Hazel's example slipped the hand-warmed cookie into the pouch on the front of his sweatshirt. "I just lives at the bottom of the hill." His words splintered as he spoke.

"I thought you were just a boy. Just a boy."

"Well he's still a b'y, sir," Maureen said firmly, arm like a sturdy root nurturing Tilley's shoulder. "Barely fourteen now, if ye can believe it."

"What is your name?"

Tilley stared at his sneakers. "'Tis Tilley."

"Tilford," Maureen said, with a nod of confirmation. She nudged Tilley forward. "Tilford Gover."

"Tilford," David said, rolling the name across his tongue. "Tilford. How you remind me of someone."

"Who could that be, David?" Annette asked. "He's not familiar in the least. Not to me."

David's gaze never wavered but his head moved ever so slightly from side to side. "I cannot say." Then his hand shot out and the back of his fingers brushed Tilley's cheek so swiftly, so kindly, Tilley never felt a thing.

And no one noticed. Except Maureen.

"Oh, sir," she said, as she reached to grip David's descending forearm. Even though Maureen knew it would be much easier to say nothing, to keep her son's treasure all to herself, her words spilled forth. "I knows ye knows all 'bout art and that sort of t'ing. And 'tis wunnerful grand that me b'y has the chance to meet ye. He got a real gift, Mr. Boone. Somet'ing honest to goodness, I swears. Beyond what I knows what to do with, that's for sure."

"I," David stammered, his arm freed, and he rubbed the tendons in the back of his neck. "I don't know."

"Ye could learn him, Mr. Boone," Maureen urged, the crows' feet dancing around her close-set eyes. "Learn him real good. Ye'll see what he got. I knows it."

"Well. I guess. I guess I can see you." He shook himself. "Yes. Yes, I will."

"Well that certainly is lovely for Tilford, here," Annette interjected. "A fine young gentleman, that's obvious. Now, back to Mother Boone." She tossed a cashmere throw over the ailing chair. "She really is a dear and lovely woman, Maureen. I assure you, you're going to enjoy your time with her immensely."

After Maureen and Tilley had left and Annette Boone found herself alone, she opened the door of her curio cabinet, switched on the low wattage bulb, and stepped back. She had instructed Marnie to flit delicately in and out with the feather duster, not to disturb a single thing. But on careful inspection it was clear Marnie had shifted things while she cleaned, the fragile heads, the swishing dresses.

Several practised manoeuvres and Annette had returned the entire contents of the cabinet back to its proper location. Now, when she stood on the very corner of her antique tasselled rug every single painted eye on her collection of Coalport figurines was gazing adoringly at her.

David rapidly scanned the treetops through his binoculars, then sat back in the supple leather chair behind his desk. The swirls of smoke were now easy to locate, so comfortably predictable. Second window from the northeast corner, head held perfectly level. And since this afternoon's gale force winds and rain had torn nearly every worn leaf from the trees, viewing was made easier still.

Questions chided with each other inside his mind. *Why haven't I gone yet? Just what am I waiting for?* David was beginning to wonder if he would ever go at all. The sense of urgency coursing through him on that first day had evaporated completely. Perhaps he would simply spy and spy, never moving ahead, never acting. Though, if the truth were told, he'd been like that forever, why change now? Plus, what if he did go? What could he possibly say? "How about 'Hello' for starters?" Not likely, he thought. It wasn't the perfect opener for all occasions.

He slid open the thin drawer just above his knees. Underneath several sheets of blank writing paper and a box of sharpened pencils, he found a razor blade. Something he kept on hand when he was working with oils—he would slice off stray gobs of paint or clean up areas in need of re-touching.

With the razor clutched firmly in his left hand, he dragged it lightly through his stubble, up the right side of his neck, over his chin, and across his hollow cheek. While the white noise from the scraping calmed him, he thought of the boy, of himself, of the stale air that had been trapped in his lungs since he had opened the icebox when he was four years old.

A rapping on the door. Ouch. A nick.

"Dad, are you in there?"

Marnie. Oh, Marnie. The single unintended unintentional thing he had created in his adult life.

"I need help with my Newfoundland history paper for school. Confederation."

David dropped the blade into the drawer and closed it quietly.

"Come in," he said. "I'm here. Yes. Come in."

And she did. Fresh air riding in around her making him feel all the mustier all the more worn.

"Did you scratch yourself?" She leaned in, dabbed his jaw with her finger. "You're bleeding."

"Paper cut," he said, turning the key in the lock on the drawer, dropping it into his shirt pocket.

"Watch it, Dad," she said, hands on her hips like a mock mother. "You of all people should know that that stuff's lethal."

ten

avid Boone kept his painting supplies in a white aluminium shed behind his house. Folded easels leaned against the walls, tubes of oil and brushes were scattered in groups, and stretched canvases were piled in a corner. Along the floor and on shelves old paintings were layered, false starts and incompletes, as well as a handful of gifts from artists grasping for endorsement. Though never once had he been moved enough to grant it.

Compared to the spattered attic where he used to work, the shed was spotless. But really, he had painted very little since arriving in Cupboard Cove, had not even opened a cerulean blue or a magenta. So could he expect anything other than spotless? He felt something like a child's goldfish, out of the bowl and dumped into a clear stream. Surrounded by the same medium, yes, but boundaries no longer as defined.

He took a brush in his hand. Holding it at the very tip like an extension of his fingers, he slid it across some shelving, watched the fine hairs licking whatever crossed their path. Over a copy of Hesse's "The Prodigy," across his solid gold watch with the cracked face, then up the side of a shrivelling Macintosh apple, tickling the stem, and down. How natural everything felt when it came to him through the perceptive bristles of his favourite brush.

Would he paint again? Really paint? He wasn't sure. Something inside him had gone stale since the stroke, his intentions had changed, his wants much more primal. Obscurity took too much effort and he was sluggish. He was forced to view even a slippery tub as a potential death trap. If only he could identify that section inside him that was misaligned, rotten, he would sink a sharp kitchen knife deep into the very spot and cut it away without mercy. But no. That offered nothing but promise, the hope of rapid release. And who could say things would be more satisfying from beyond?

When a gentle rapping came on the shed door, David's breath caught. Somehow he knew the boy's knock would be mild.

"Come in." After he'd heard the boy shuffle through the doorway, he said, "Remove your shoes, please."

Tilley reluctantly bent to untie his shoelaces when he noticed David Boone was sporting his own muddy boots, producing a mess of footprints. David kept his back to Tilley and continued cutting tape away from a parcel wrapped in Styrofoam casing.

"Do you paint, Tilford?" David said without turning around.

"No, never, Mr. Boone." As Tilley considered the luxury of David's space compared to his linen closet shelf, he shifted from one socked foot to the other. The icy sensation on his left heel told him he had a large hole there.

"I didn't either, not at your age anyway." He continued to slice through tape, lifting off segments of Styrofoam, all the while holding the top of the tall, thin parcel in a secure grip. "I would guess I spent much of my time thinking of girls."

Tilley chuckled. Not because he found it funny, he just didn't know how else to respond.

Laying the last piece of Styrofoam aside, David turned to face Tilley. "Do you think of girls, Tilford?"

Against his will, the image of Marnie's ankle flashed behind his eyes, milk flowing down a long smooth trail, gliding over the ripple of her ankle. He felt a flush of excitement, imagined what David Boone would think if he could pluck the cap off Tilley's skull and peer inside. Would the man cry out when he recognised his daughter's ankle? Tilley cleared his throat but the moment he tried to speak he sucked a gob of spit into his lungs, clutched his chest, and hacked. Typical, he thought. Then, finally he managed, "I guess. Sometimes."

David smiled, stern sharp features softening. Tilley reached up to touch his head, skullcap secure.

"Sometimes? Hmm. And just what do you do with the remainder of your time."

More conviction, now. "I draws, sir. Draws whatever I sees. I can hold somet'ing in me head for days, days on end, and then I draws it out right the same. That's what I does."

David did not reply but returned to his task tearing away paper from the oversized parcel. Lifting the object with care, David placed it on a foldout table.

"People shouldn't hover in a doorway unless they are announcing death or going on a first date," David said. "Come forward, Tilford. You may look."

Tilley shuffled toward him in socked feet.

"What is it?" Tilley said, staring at the largest section of bark he had ever seen, nearly two inches thick and big enough to obscure an entire torso.

"Bark. Of course."

"What're ye doin' with a huge hunk of bark?"

"There is no honest reason for me to own it, I simply keep it because it found me over a great distance."

"It found ye?"

"Yes. A man from British Columbia sent it to me. A very sick man, if I understood his letters properly, and that is to say I barely understood them at all. He was moved during an exhibit of a few of my pieces, moved to the point that he felt obliged to express himself."

"So he sent ye bark? That's some queer."

"Not quite, Tilford. I wasn't finished. From what I gathered, he lived alone with his mother and he was troubled by his perception that her head and mouth were expanding day by day."

"Expandin'? She had somet'ing wrong with her?"

"No. Not exactly. According to newspapers she was an instructional sort, apparently. My work spoke to him and after touring the gallery, he returned home and took it upon himself to shrink his mother's head. Used a frozen salmon from her freezer to assist him in the task."

"Holy shit," Tilley said, then covered his mouth.

"Yes," he replied, shaking his shaggy hair—so different from the slicked back style he wore to church. "Desperately sad."

"But why'd he send ye the bark?"

"Pleased with the headway he had made with his mother," David paused for a moment, admiring his pun, "he took a stroll down a nearby trail though an old growth forest. Saw this portion of a tree and it spoke to him. Literally, perhaps, I shall never know. In his correspondence, he indicated that some part of me was trapped inside this section of bark and he took it upon himself to free that part, mail it, and make me whole again."

"Sounds right twisted. Ye'll come across all kinds when yer famous. Real nutcase, that one."

"Hmm. Most likely. Though I believe he fancied himself as a noble sort." David stared straight into Tilley's eyes. "And who are we to argue? Who are you? Who am I?"

David slowly ran his hands over the bark. Tilley remained silent, not sure whether or not he was meant to answer those questions.

After a moment, Tilley asked, "Is it delicate, Mr. Boone?"

"That I wouldn't know," David said. "I've never tried to break it."

"What're ye goin' to do with it?"

"I'm going to have you draw it. I have never seen anything in this piece of bark, other than the obvious. You shall draw it and offer me a fresh perspective."

"If ye wants."

"Yes, Tilford. That's what I want."

David pulled a stool over towards the table, then handed Tilley a thin board with a large scrap of artist's paper taped to it, plus a pouch filled with charcoals of varying diameters.

Tilley sat, concentrated on the very centre of the bark, and decided to work in concentric circles, radiating out from the middle. He figured if he drew the shape, recreated the bark as it was, it would mean nothing to David. Whenever he focused solely on what something was he was more than likely to miss exactly what it might be.

Some time later, Tilley suddenly realised how cold he had become. Finally finished, he stood, and his whole lower body tingled gratefully with re-established circulation. He glanced around. The room was empty. His watch claimed four and a half hours had dissolved, an entire afternoon had slipped away, and inside the shed the light was like thin threads.

He walked out into the backyard, still mostly levelled earth and a few stripped trees. Around the perimeter, a wall of chicken wire had been erected, layers of smooth beach stones piled up behind it. David was in the middle, shoulders against the chicken wire fence, one foot propped up, head facing the woods that rose up beyond. Puffing on a chocolate brown cigarette, he seemed serious, as though he was contemplating the contribution of his strategically placed body: How he alone was keeping an entire mountain from tumbling down.

"Ah, yes," he said when he noticed Tilley. "I see you have finished."

He threw his cigarette to the ground and took Tilley's sketch in both hands. Tilley searched his expression for approval but David gave nothing away as he studied the work.

Tilley was not used to silence. He could not claim to know a single solitary adult who held their tongue. People in Cupboard Cove loved to hear themselves talk and didn't hesitate. At the grocery checkouts, from porch to porch, a road between them, or a stretch of heaving ocean pitching boats left and right. It made no difference where. Mouths flapped and tongues wagged, opinions bounding forth with such speed, it was as though the tongue had a life of its own, the brain retired. Peace was something he was unaccustomed to, something he could not understand, something that made him uncomfortable. And so he said, "I have to wash me hands, Mr. Boone," and took several steps backwards.

"Of course," David said, without looking up. "Straight ahead. In the house."

With slumped shoulders, Tilley left the yard. His head feeling both filled with air and entirely deflated at the same time. Now he understood how foolish he was, allowing his mind to wander, to perceive, to create. He wished he could snatch back the board, tear his childish work to pieces, forget he'd ever been here. He should have simply drawn what was there. A dried cracked fragment of a tree. Finished. But, as Tilley reached the door to go in, David called after him, spoke words filled with such promise that nearly lifted him right out of his sneakers.

"You may come again, Tilford," he said. "You may come when you choose."

Wandering down the main hallway of David Boone's house, Tilley did not know which of the heavy wooden doors led to a bathroom. He passed one, peered inside, and saw piles of unopened cardboard boxes, books scattered on the floor, and an empty mug on a tray.

The next door on the right was open several inches and when Tilley noticed it was a bedroom, he was brazen; he slowed and lingered. The walls were painted in a greying purple, the colour of a confused sky, and all the furniture was pristine white. He positioned himself within the stained doorframe and recognised the figure that was sprawled gracefully on the bed. On top of a satiny violet comforter, Marnie lay on her stomach, elbows bent, palms supporting her thoughtful head. She was reading and biting down hard on an orange pencil. Thankfully, Tilley thought, her feet and ankles were tucked underneath the pile of pillows at the headboard.

"Hi there," she said, pencil released, book lowered.

Tilley's body stiffened. "I...I..." Damn his brain. Betraying him. Stuttering like that. "B-bathroom."

"You can use mine," she said. "Next door down."

Marnie pointed with her pencil and it slipped from her hand, rolled onto the floor. Lunging forward to retrieve it, Tilley struck his forehead on the jewel-like doorknob, said "Shit", as his hands flew up to contain the pain.

She giggled, flattened herself on the bed, and reached down. With the pencil safely back in her hand, she now twirled it through her fingers. "See? I've got it. Thanks though."

Tilley rushed those few steps down the hall into the bathroom, closed the door firmly, and secured the lock. Here he was. In her bathroom. He considered the luxury of it, of having such a space to yourself. And as he glanced around a feeling of loathing and embarrassment rinsed over him. His life spent sharing everything with Maureen, Earl, and Boyd. The soap, the toilet, the damp towels with queer smelling corners, the communal release of billowing body odours. Modest Tilley spritzing the room with aerosol spray, Boyd hollering with intent to share, "Christ, b'y. 'Tis like someone shit under a lilac tree."

He leaned against the cool wood his hand still clutching the doorknob. Mustn't be too long, he thought. Though how he wanted to rummage, permit his fingers to feather over and into everything, explore her medicine cabinet, the cupboards, the double row of drawers, the cartons and jars, bottles and tubes. But, he resisted. He washed the charcoal from his hands with a bar of perfumed soap and took extra care to leave no trace of grime on the lily-white basin. The plush towel he used to dry was not crammed around the rack as it was in his own home but neatly arranged, folded just so. Leaning down, he rubbed his face into that fluffy towel, inhaled a lungful of sweetness that might have come from using a double dose of fabric softener. Her smell. Perhaps something of springtime. An April's day that was certain to be far, far away from here.

The mother had not lied, David thought, as mothers tend to do. Constantly pasting brilliance onto nothing more than mediocrity. Often they would arrive on the stone steps of his St. John's home, young sons like boiled hams held by a cuff, faces scrubbed, belts pinched in around the waistbands of ironed corduroys. These women clutched scraps of paper, "Potential, potential!" they cried, and when David reviewed the offering, they were utterly pitiful. The juvenile lines were smooth and rounded, steady. Certain signs that the mother's hand was firmly and continuously gripping and guiding the boy's.

He would feign mock interest. Mostly, these visits from wealthy woman with over-stuffed offspring had nothing to do with identifying a young budding artist. These women were tired of having everything and were in search of losing themselves, if only for an instant, because some sort of emotion was far better than none at all. They propelled their children towards the kitchen with promises of cookies and milk and replied that a tour of the working space would certainly be most agreeable. "Ooos" over the quaintness of the space, "ahhs" over the canvases that lined the low walls, chirpings of "Superb, Mr. Boone" and "Simply delightful, David, may I call you David?" "Of course, Mrs. Whatever-goes-here." Then, sometimes he would oblige them in his attic. Summoning such a sweaty sheen so that, in contrast, even a warm breeze felt like dead winter. Sensation. It was all about sensation.

More than once, society's best left with daubs of oil paint on the backside of a skirt or smears across the shoulders of a linen jacket just pressed against a wall. On their way down the drive, they always kept a hold of confirmation on their boys who, crammed with simple sugars, couldn't help but zigzag towards the big shiny cars, engines waiting to be turned over. They walked away without wavering—ankles steady in wide wedged-heeled shoes. And mostly, he noticed, they never looked back. Not that he ever wanted them to.

But all that had come to an abrupt end. Since the moment he awoke like a crumpled bag at the bottom of those steep sharp stairs, he had abstained from those pleasures. In fact, he hadn't had a single offer and had barely painted a single stroke. He knew the longing that shadowed Maureen Gover's eyes had nothing to do with what he once could have offered her. She wanted only for her son, almost to the point where he could smell her need oozing out through her pores, off her breath. And from the looks of the boy's work, her calculation was not far off the mark.

There was something special here. Special indeed. David crouched down, not caring that the chicken wire was hitching his woollen sweater. He traced the lines of the drawing, held it at a distance so he could view what was missing, not the charcoal so much as the white. In the negative, smooth ageless faces appeared to melt, meshing downwards, sideways, until they slipped off the paper and continued to repeat through thin air. The faces were eyeless and the mouths were fish-hooked, dissolving, ice thawing, and trickling over lips and endless chins. He recognised something of M.C. Escher in the pattern, but not quite.

He dropped the board to the ground with a soft thud and wrung one dry hand over the other. *How*, he thought, *could a madman who smashed the lacy bones behind his very own mother's face have found him here? A piece of bark. Now the boy, too. And he was even closer still.*

By the time Tilley reached his driveway, the sky was fully beaten and bruised, forlorn, and starting to bawl. Plump droplets of icy November rain began to ping onto his scalp, cut through his thin hair, and roll down behind his ears. For a moment he lowered his eyelids, happy for the rain. It cooled his mind, which felt like a mess of smouldering wires, connections melting, others fusing, a few simply fading away.

A car horn rocketed into his ears. Somewhat disoriented, Tilley had to spring out of the way as Boyd burned up beside him in a beige Chevy Nova. With only inches between a rusty bumper and Tilley's knees, his brother slammed on the brakes with such tremendous force that the backside of his vehicle bounced. Windows steamed, but Tilley was able to see Boyd fumble with a length of rope that allowed the door to slump open at an awkward angle.

"Hey shit for brains," Boyd said as he slid out. "Where're ye comin' from with yer tongue hangin' out? Face on ye like ye just got laid."

Tilley glanced away, up towards the square window in the porch where he met his father's eyes. With lips like a slash, Earl's prominent jowls quavered as he worked something in his teeth.

A sharp kick and Boyd secured the car door. "One day I's goin' to buy me a new set of wheels. When I gets me hands on either dollar, me son. And that might be sooner than ye t'inks."

Boyd brushed past Tilley, tripped up the stairs three at a time, all the while holding his left arm close to his body. Tilley followed close behind into the humid kitchen where Maureen floured and fried cod tongues; Earl salivated next to the stove waiting for his afternoon breakfast.

"Fadder," Boyd announced. "Guess what? Me bus is runnin' and the motor's got a wunnerful hum to it. I got meself anudder job."

Earl clapped Boyd on the back, said, "By Christ, young man. Yer a real go-getter."

"On the door over to Nips-n-Bites. Buddy Johnson says business is takin' off and he needs someone reliable to watch the comin's and goin's. I says to him, 'Buddy, me son, yer man is standin' right in front of ye.'" Boyd's glassy eyes darted around the kitchen from face to face. "That's me I was talkin' 'bout, case yer wonderin'."

"Well, sir." Earl's voice boomed. "Picked yerself up, ye did, dusted yerself off, and got yer arse right back into the saddle. I's that proud. Go on," he said, nodding towards the refrigerator. "Grab yerself a beer, ol' gaffer. 'Bout time ye learned how to handle a drink or two."

Boyd tugged at the refrigerator door and plucked the caps from two bottles with his pocket knife.

"Hey Till-man, guess what I's doin' with me first pay cheque."

"What's that?" Tilley asked, as he smeared a thick coating of smooth peanut butter on a slice of Mammie's Bread.

"Payin' back Martin," Boyd said and he started rolling up his sleeve. "He lent me the money for this." His shirt now pulled up over his left bicep, Boyd picked away at an enormous white bandage and blew a controlled stream of air out through tight lips.

"What've ye gone and done to yerself," Earl said, grabbing Boyd's arm and twisting.

Boyd stepped back, escaped his father's grip, and held out his upper arm. Dressing removed, his face beamed as he displayed a blistering patch of skin, a swollen heart graced with a sash that read "Teena Forever."

"Pretty cool, Boyd," Tilley said with a sticky tongue.

Earl cuffed Tilley, knocking his face forward into his bread. Then he turned to Boyd. "Who do ye t'ink ye is? Degradin' the body God gave ye. And with Wilf's daughter, Boyd? Right next door?"

"Don't go there, Fadder," Boyd said, through clenched teeth.

"What is it, yer too lazy to walk further down the friggin' road? When yer huffin' and puffin' on anudder one, what the hell ye goin' to do with that bloody arm then me son? Tell me that?"

Anger flashed behind Boyd's eyes as they narrowed, darkened. "Ye don't know shit, ol' man," he said, shaking his shirtsleeve down. "Ye don't know fuckin' shit 'bout me, 'bout Teena. 'Bout nothin'."

Tilley pressed his back into the counter knowing that even though Earl weighed more, Boyd had the powerful advantage of rage.

But Boyd did not strike his father. Instead, he tested the hinges on the cupboard door underneath the sink, tossed his bottle of beer into the garbage, and stomped down over the stairs to his basement bedroom.

Maureen flipped the pan upside down onto a plate lined with serviettes, clanked the plate onto the table.

"Well, well," she said.

Earl sat down and tossed a crispy tongue into his mouth. "Too big for his britches that b'y. Mark me words, maid. He's headin' for trouble."

Maureen went to the garbage, plucked the foaming beer out, and took a drink. "And I always thought he'd be after one with 'Mudder' written on it," she said, and smirked. "Well, maybe me Tilley'll do that for his poor ol' woman. Right, me lover?"

eleven

"Now I'll bet that feels better, Missus Boone," Maureen said as she pulled a damp towel away from Hazel's freshly washed hair and hung it over the back of a kitchen chair. "Makes a world of difference, I 'llows."

"Don't like the chill on me head," Hazel mumbled underneath loose dentures.

"Don't ye worry none. We'll be done in a jiffy."

Maureen cut rectangles through Hazel's hair with sharp swipes of a comb, wrapped the wispy strands tightly around black rollers and secured them with a jab of pink plastic pins.

When Maureen paused, Hazel slurped her tea, squirted it back into the cup. "Bitter," she hissed. "That bitter, me dear, can't even get it down."

"I never put no sugar in it, Missus." Maureen reached to take the mug. "I can put in a spoonful. Sweeten it up."

Pulling the cup to her chest, Hazel said, "What? Now yer after me bit of tea?"

"I'll freshen it for ye, Missus. Might've been sittin' too long with the bag in."

Hazel lifted the cup, drank it down without pausing, drops spilling out from the corners of her pasty lips onto her blouse. "And waste a mouthful of good tea? 'Tis easy to know ye didn't want for nothin' growin' up."

Maureen resumed her combing and rolling. "What we don't do to look good," she chirped, changing the topic. "What women don't go through. Cuttin' and paintin' and clippin' and pluckin' and dyein'. Me Lard. By the time we gets a few years on us, we's more processed than a can of flaked tuna."

Rows of curlers complete and Hazel's face with her scalp beyond taut was instantly lifted. She appeared years younger, offering Maureen a somewhat pleasant hint of what she might once have looked like.

"Never went in for all that ol' business," Hazel said. "Never had to. Me Harvey thought I was the cow's cream day he laid eyes on me."

Smoothing Hazel's shoulders, Maureen watched great flakes of dandruff drift off in the sunlight.

"Yer late husband?"

"Oh no," Hazel said, her gullet shaking, eyes suddenly wet. "Me husband still. Always."

"Well, then," Maureen said. "Isn't that right special. Wonders if I'll feel that way when Earl passes on. S'pose I might, I guess. Then again, might be a real weight lifted off me poor ol' back." She sighed. "Yer husband. Harvey. Was he from 'round here?"

"I. I," she stuttered, stared at the residue in the bottom of her cup. "Well, now. I. He."

"Ye remembers how ye met, maybe?"

"I, I. Yes. Well, I don't rightly know," she said, eyebrows struggling to furrow against the tension of her curlers. Then, her face lightened, a nugget recaptured. "Now, then. That Harvey Boone. Dug me mudder's grave. He did. Yes. That's how we met. He was diggin' me mudder's grave."

☙

Born the seventh son of the seventh son, everyone expected young Harvey Boone to have a gift. Members of the small community of Severed Knot waited patiently for some sign, some suggestion that he was going to develop into a healer or have the capacity for second sight. But, much to their disappointment, there never was any such indicator. Instead, he had a queer mix of sensitivities, hated bright light, wept in church when his mother sang, and often complained of discomfort caused by the seams in his knitted socks. With so much unfulfilled promise, people began to slip Harvey Boone into a slot a fair distance away from gifted, a slot they reserved for men who were faint of heart, light-footed, or soft-boiled-runny.

No one turned a head when, at nineteen, Harvey left Severed Knot without looking back. He never left because of others' expectations of him or because he was attempting to cloister his emotionality. Simply put, it had to do with marriage. In such a tiny community and after several generations of ten plus children, Harvey was either a nephew or cousin of every prospective woman in the harbour. At first it was not an issue and he spent an entire year adoring the delicate features of his young cousin, Darcy Button. But when his eldest brother's third child was born with the face of a cherub and webbed fingers and toes, he thought it best to move.

Two years earlier, his sister, Flo, had moved to Cupboard Cove with her husband, Neil Grimes. Harvey figured that was as good a place as any to begin again. Flo prepared the daybed next to the kitchen stove and Neil offered him a space on his skiff during fishing season. After only a short time, Harvey gained the reputation as a generous fellow. He assisted in the reassembling of Neil's stage, hauled out a load of wood for Widow Smith, and burnt his shoulders to a crisp helping Jim Andrews erect the trusses for a roof under the July sunshine. When Lyle and Frank O'Leary came through Flo's back door looking for an extra hand to dig a grave, Harvey was up from his chair, boots on, before they finished their request.

"Missus Keeping passed on," Lyle said, hat clutched in his hands. "Doc Andrews went by this marnin'. Coffin already laid out in the yard. Don't want to be too long gettin' her in the ground, he says."

"Me Lard," Flo said. Her hand went to her chest. "Sickness is draped over that house like a cloth. First the b'y, then the mister, and now the missus. Is the girl alright?"

"Oh yes." Frank sucked air between the generous gaps in his teeth. "Though can't imagine nothin' ever takin' hold to that one. Devil hisself wouldn't touch her s'posing he come up along."

"Not that he wouldn't want to," Lyle said. He chuckled then coughed into his hat as he watched Flo fold her arms across her chest.

Frank rolled his eyes and jabbed his brother in the ribs. "And Harvey," he said, turning back towards the porch, "can ye fashion us some withes. Six in all."

"That'd be no trouble," Harvey said as he crouched to lace up his boots. "No trouble 'tall."

Harvey had a knack for twisting the tough branches to make casket handles. Two stems wound together, ends hidden, then soaked in a pickle. The final product was an indestructible ring. Well, most often anyways. If the withe was too loose, it would unravel; too tight, it would snap. Nothing could be worse than having the handles break when a coffin was being carted out of the church or lowered into its grave.

The three men were sombre as they moved along the dirt road. Just behind the clapboard church, Harvey saw the cemetery. Wild lilacs traced the perimeter, daylilies had overtaken the ditches, and leafy trees flourished among the wooden crosses. When he'd first attended a service in Cupboard Cove, he considered that the location of the church was chosen not for its prominence in the community, but instead with burials in mind. While much of the community was pure rock, behind St. Peter's a stretch of soft soil sloped upwards. Here, graves of a decent depth were dug without so much as a pitchfork or a single word of frustration. As good a place as any, Harvey thought, for a bit of eternal rest.

After Lyle and Frank O'Leary were finished digging, Harvey stayed behind. Only two men could fit into the grave at once and Harvey had spent much of the time shovelling what had already been shovelled, preventing the pile of dirt from tumbling back in on the men. Once they had left he slipped down into the grave, began to smooth the walls with the side of his spade. For him there was something pleasant about being surrounded by damp earth, the stillness that comes from being cut off from the world.

When a shadow cast darkness over him, he glanced up, squinting. First, he saw a pair of paisley shoes, a delicately rounded heel, and tan coloured stockings. Eyes travelling up a navy tubular dress, he noticed pale thin collarbones at the neckline. But it was the hair that made him inhale. Like a mash of red currants, the strands were a wild extension of the glowing horizon just over this vision's shoulder.

Harvey put a hand to his brow to get a better look. As he stared, the vision bent over, scooped up loose dirt, and tossed it down upon him. Particles of soil rushed at his face, over his shoulders, making him shake his head. He heard a ripple of giggling. When his watering eyes opened, he saw this beautiful girl running down the grassy slope, wind fluttering her dress to reveal fleshy curves here, bony knobs there. His eyes followed her until she was no more than a dot. Then he had to lean his forehead on the end of his shovel and wait until his pounding heart calmed to continue.

When he arrived back at the house he told his sister, "I seen a girl today."

"I reckons," she said. Flo was seated in a rocker by the woodstove embroidering violet pansies onto a flour sack apron. "Cupboard Cove's been known to house a girl or two."

"No," he said, frowning. A storm of creases in his forehead. "I means a real girl. A woman."

Her needle stopped crisscrossing and she held the thread still. She looked up. "How do ye mean, real?"

"I s'pose she was real, maid. Though half of me t'inks she was just a dream. Stole the breath right out of me lungs she did. Like nothin' I've ever seen."

"Quite an impression. Who was she?"

"Don't have the slightest," he said. "Though, I can tell ye this: If the Lard sees fit, she's the one I's goin' to marry."

Flo laughed, used to her brother's quirky ways. "Ye is, is ye? What made ye fix on that, now?"

"When I seen her," he said, shaking his head with distrust over his own memory, "she had hair like the hottest kinda bonfire. Couldn't tell where it ended and the settin' sun begun."

"Oh me Lard." Flo's apron dropped to the wooden floor as she stood abruptly. "Don't tell me she was white like the blood were drained out of her?"

"That's she," he said. He leaned forward in his chair, hands clutching his knees. "Yes, that's she, alright. Though that's not how I'd put it."

"Not a word," Flo whispered, her thin lips beside his ear.

"Not one word to no one now Harvey. Ye hear me? That was Hazel Keeping. Her mother was the one just passed. She's s'posed to be in the quarantine, that girl. Scarlet fever inside her house. Anyone hears tell of it and the whole lot of us'll be locked up. Forget 'bout catchin' ar fish. Makin' ar dollar." She stepped back, stared out the window. "Shouldn't be out 'round. Not out through her door. Not one inch. Though I tells ye, no surprise, she don't heed nothin' Doc Andrews says. She don't care. Got a mind on her like no udder." She tapped her temple. "An upstairs room left unpapered. What kinda woman ain't beside herself when half her family passes on? What kind? Fix on that for a spell now then. Fix on that before ye up and marries her."

Flo inhaled deeply to fuel another gust of words but Harvey wasn't listening. Instead he was thinking about this woman named "Hazel" and her expression when she peered down over the edge of the grave. Grief attacked everyone in unique ways: some wept, some swallowed it down, some even laughed uproariously when death spread its dull cloak across their doorway. Hazel was the latter sort; there was no doubt in Harvey's mind. He hurried out the door to break branches from a blooming bush. Flo trailed close behind.

"Me good roses. Harvey, what do ye t'ink yer doin'? Neil had them sent down from Canada for me anniversary."

"Fashionin' a wreath," he said as his fingers twisted vines in and out, blushing red flowers facing upwards. "Pay me respects over to the Keeping's."

"Yer not serious, me son. Surely."

He snapped more branches, jabbing himself, stripping thorns with his bloody thumb.

"Ah, Harvey. Lard have mercy on us. Ye is serious."

"As serious as serious gets, maid."

"If ye marries her Harvey, ye'll rue the day. I can promise ye that. Ye'll rue the very day." She swiped the air with her hands.

"But, go on with ye. Nothin' I says is ever goin' to sway ye when yer fixed. I knows that since ye was a wee lad." Flo turned, started in through the door. Over her shoulder she said, "And leave me a rose or two for God's sake. I likes a bit of class in me garden."

Harvey held the wreath out pleased with his rapid work and went down the lane towards Hazel Keeping's biscuit box. The coffin was still in the yard and the quarantine card still nailed to the wooden storm door. He placed the ring of roses on the coffin lid, stepped around back of the house, and rapped on the window. She was there in an instant as though she were waiting. Just for him. And in the days that followed, he spent hour upon hour there, murmuring through a thick pane of glass, her warm stream of muffled words steaming up the window, his dry face and hands craving every droplet of moisture that settled there.

On a Tuesday afternoon, Harvey noticed something strange but never gave it the attention it deserved. After the downpour had eased to a drizzle, he made his way to his post just outside Hazel Keeping's window. When he arrived, he hesitated. In the worn square where he usually stood, a fresh imprint glared up at him. The soles of someone else's rugged boots had sunk deep into the damp muck. Though the image strained behind his eyes, Harvey closeted it. Pressing in against the window, he shuffled his feet obliterating those prints before he could think too much about them.

As Maureen Gover came into the porch, home from her first day with Hazel Boone, she caught sight of Earl yammering on the telephone. The receiver was nipped in the crook of his shoulder while his two hands fumbled with his belt.

"What kinda bullshit is this?" he yelled. "'Ye don't know?' I'll give ye a week, and ye'll be crawlin'…"

When he noticed Maureen standing just two feet away from him, his voice descended as he wiped away words from the corners of his wet lips.

"No, sir," he grumbled into the phone. "We don't sell no rims and we don't sell no tires. Got that straight?"

"Who was that?" Maureen asked as she slid past him.

"Who was what?"

"That there. On the phone."

"Oh that." A half-hearted yawn, scratching fingers. "Nothin'. Wrong number, is all."

Maureen lifted the kettle from the hotplate, shook it to hear a reassuring slosh, then brought it to the stove. "How come yer up?"

"Up?"

"Yes, up. Thought ye'd be restin'. Long night at the plant."

"Right. 'Twas the phone that stirred me. Ringin' off the hook."

"Sounds like someone with a powerful need for somet'ing."

"Yes, and I told the person-"

"Person?"

"Some ol' man. We don't sell no rims or tires 'round here."

"I heard. Well, then. Cuppa tea?"

"Oh, lovely grand," he said, drawing out a chair. "And a slice of lassie bread for me, maid. I'll take a heel, if ye got it."

Maureen took hold of the soft bread and seesawed the serrated blade down through the tender crust. She could sense Earl's lie perched just behind her eyes as it made the blood throb between her temples. And though she'd been meaning to do it for years, she decided that tonight, once Earl had left for his shift, she would oil every hinge on the two back doors.

twelve

An hour after returning home from bingo, Maureen had fallen asleep in a vinyl recliner, a multicoloured afghan across her knees. The sound on the television was off and Tilley didn't dare turn from the cooking program, as it coated his mother in a reliable, jaundiced light. Darkness would wake her instantly and she would demand to know where he was going.

He wasn't doing anything wrong. Once a month or so, he liked to walk out the back door and head straight for the shore. Sometimes all the artificial noises inside his head, the hum of the refrigerator, the buzz of electric lights, made him nauseous. Although being steps away from hungry waves was not the most peaceful place, at least this sound was natural, rhythmic. Tilley did not want to imagine a space that was wholly silent. The sheer thought of it frightened him.

A car passed and he could hear its wet tires sticking to the road. Water trickled down the gutter, over empty Coke cans, chocolate bar wrappers, and a mess of dead leaves. With each step, a crunch rose up from the gravel shoulder. His ears were more receptive at night. In the white noise of daylight, these simple sounds were easily missed, lost, or ignored.

When he had rounded the bend of Shore Road, he heard a second set of footprints. He stepped onto a grassy stoop, sat facing the sea, crossed his feet at the ankles, and hoped to go unnoticed. Only two minutes had passed and Ida Payne in a strikingly roomy, mint green gym suit and zipped jacket was standing beside him. She was holding an oversized bag of potato chips and her hand fed her mouth in a continuous loop.

Tilley glanced up, thought how unsteady she appeared as moonlit clouds rushed around behind her. "How come yer out?"

"What's it to ye?" she said, plopping down on the patch of withering grass. "'Tis a free country, ye knows."

"Won't anyone be wonderin' where yer to?"

"Oh yeah," she said through a handful of Roast Chicken chips. "Every night, they is. Beside themselves, askin' where's our lovely little Ida? Where's she gone and run off to? They wish."

She finished the bag then let the wind claim the garbage for the sea.

"What's that?" she said, licking each finger.

Out on the water, a spark glowed where black sky met even blacker water.

"Truth be told," he said. "That's nothin' 'tall."

"'Tis got to be somet'ing, ye idiot. I sees it plain as day."

Tilley took a deep breath. "'Round here, we calls it O'Leary's Lantern. Ye sees it on a full moon."

"How come?"

"Fifty years ago, some man took his punt out on the water and destroyed hisself. That there's his lantern, still burnin' in the spot where he drowned."

"That's the biggest kinda bullshit I've heard today," she said, though she continued to squint towards the horizon. "Lantern'd be gone out long ago."

"I knows it ain't the real lantern. I's not that dunce. 'Tis like a phantom ship, sort of, I s'pose. But, 'tis only a phantom lantern."

"Who told ye that? 'Twas Walter, I bet. He's burstin' at the seams with shit."

"Everyone knows it, is all. Some feller years ago went out to sea late one night. They found his boat in the marnin', knocking against the stage."

"Probably just fell overboard. Doubts he offed hisself. No one back then did that kind of t'ing."

"Ye might be right, though there was somet'ing queer got people goin'. On the floor of the boat was his new boots, side by side, and a pair of knitted socks his mudder had made him folded up inside. That's why they says he destroyed hisself. Took care not to ruin a good pair of boots. 'Twas over a woman, I heard."

"Poor suck. If I ever gets that riled up over some buddy, do me a favour and shoot me, will ye?"

"That'd be no trouble," Tilley said. He lit a cigarette and blew a stream of smoke down toward the grass. "Sometimes I comes out just to see it."

Ida plucked a cigarette from Tilley's open case. "Yer soft as shit, me son," she said, and ghost-moaned.

"Real scary, Ida. Ye sounds like an ol' dog t'was struck by a pick-up."

"Ye t'inks? Well, ye sounds like the biggest kinda fag, comin' out here longin' over some dead man."

"Shut yer trap, will ye. 'Tis only a dumb-assed story I was tellin' ye."

She reached over, tugged his ear. "Well, maybe the littlest kinda fag. No bigger than a bloody tadpole."

Tilley snapped his head sideways, away from her pinch, then

drew his knees up to his chest. "No one asked ye here. Ye can get on home out of it."

"Yer some sooky baby," Ida said, showing no signs of leaving.

She leaned back onto her elbows and was sucking on her cigarette as a pale blue Chevette eased around the turn. Thin white hands gripped the steering wheel and a tiny bunched face peered out, scowling.

"Christ," Ida said. "What in the hell was that? She gave me some gawk."

"No doubt," Tilley said. "Lily Pride. She teaches piano."

"Surprised she can reach the pedals. Size of her."

"Oh, she can reach alright."

"Makes no matter to me. I never sat to no piano, and I ain't got no plans to."

"'Tis a good t'ing," Tilley said, leaning over towards Ida. "Parents loves her cause she does good stuff at the church, does the lessons, and then even offers to drive the girls home."

"Nothin' wrong with none of that."

"Best to steer clear. Some of the girls complained ye gets more than a run when she takes ye home."

"Whatd'ye mean by that?"

"Put it this way. Her fingers wants to be playin' more than some piano keys."

"Christ," Ida said. She jolted upright and shot a ball of gum out over the cliff. "She can eye me all she wants. I hates piano. Hates it."

"Yer just her type," Tilley said, smiling. "Young and thin, with a bit of lip."

"I'll show ye lip, me son. Make yers so fat ye'll be able to see it without lookin' down."

Ida punched Tilley in the upper arm and he fell backwards onto the grass. In an instant, she was lying next to him and he could smell her sugary breath, hear her steady breathing. He was frozen for a moment, not sure which part to move, then he sat up, jumped to his feet. Blood rushed from his head, and he wavered, almost plopped down again. "I best be gettin' on home, Ida," he whispered. "Next t'ing Mudder'll be out traipsin' 'round after me."

Ida stood, swiped her hands over her backside. "Yeah, me too. I's sure Aunt Penny is wonderin' where I's to. Or not."

"When is yer Mudder comin' back."

"Soon, real soon," she said. "She called me long distance tonight. Havin' a real time of it, makin' all kinds of dollars with that modellin' stuff. No time she'll be 'round for me, and we'll be buildin' our own place, like that one on the hill." She pointed to David Boone's house that loomed over the entire community.

"Sounds good," he said. "Rollin' in money, ye'll be that stuck up, won't have a word in yer head for me."

For a moment, moonlight poured down on Ida. Slowly, she turned to look at Tilley with an expression of need she couldn't control, and one that fourteen-year old Tilley couldn't possibly understand.

Then she swallowed hard, finally grinning. Punching him in that same tender spot, she yelled, "Last one to Aunt Penny's is a rotten egg," and bolted up the lane.

Stunned for a moment, he swayed in his spot, not having considered walking Ida home. When she was no more than a shadow, he ran to catch up, two steps to her one. By the time he reached the end of Walter's driveway, Ida was already leaning against the front step. She was not winded in the least, while his breath came in short gasps, his lungs squeezed inside his barrel chest.

She shook her head at Tilley, and started to saunter through the unkempt grass. When she reached Winse's handmade lawn art, she stopped, wound her way around them like a curious cat. From plywood, Winse had cut three forms, painted them to resemble little boys, back on, trousers around their ankles, backsides sticking out.

Ida patted the tallest one.

"Can't see the sense in that," she called to Tilley. "Havin' kids constantly pissin' on yer front lawn. Turn it yellow."

Tilley smirked, nodded. "Yer alright, Ida. Ye knows? Yer really alright."

She shrugged, then skipped up the stairs two at a time, and disappeared in through the front door.

thirteen

On the second Thursday in November, winter dropped like an angry fist. School was cancelled. Everything was closed. The first big storm pressed down hard, smothering Cupboard Cove with fat flakes falling thick and fast from a pale pinkish sky. The snowplough had worked through the night, its dull scrape heard from all corners of the Cove, but the roads remained coated and slick.

Along the lane, Penny Payne and her daughter, Missy, trudged inside a pair of wheel tracks. When a truck or car passed, they were forced to step into drifts up on the bank, their feet crunching through snow that came up over the tops of their boots. Even though the Good Hopes was still running, there was no chance Nurse Penny could make the journey over the highroad. But a few dandruffy flakes wouldn't keep her chained to the kitchen like some old-fashioned slave.

Near Vickers' farm, wind whipped off the ocean, swirled snow, collected what had already fallen, and added it to the blanket. A snowplough, appearing as though by magic, barrelled down the lane, coming within inches of striking Missy's face. Penny twisted around to shake her gloved fist, but the snow had already devoured the battered plough. They were walking headlong into the snow again, and as they were rounding the turn, a beige Nova came snaking towards them, fishtailing on top of a thin layer of ice. Rush and fear knocked mother and child flat into the dirty mound amassed on the shoulder of the road.

"Christ Almighty," Penny spat, as she jumped up, lifted Missy right off the ground by her thin arm, and deposited her in the newest tire track. "Teenagers these days. And I believes that was Boyd Gover. I tell ye, if he wasn't a foot taller than me, I'd redden his sorry little arse 'til he thought someone set fire to it."

Of course Missy had nothing to offer, only two ears warmed underneath the knitted flaps on her hat. And the ears were all Penny wanted. So, Missy hopped along silently in a pair of Walter's old boots, too big in the feet, strapped tighter than a rubber band around her calves.

Legs exhausted from pushing a path, Penny and Missy climbed Maureen's driveway sluggishly. Tilley was shovelling, making modest headway as his short arms strained against a constricting one-piece snowsuit, each lift cutting his body in two. He blinked, chips of damp snow clinging to his lashes, and waved to Penny while he hollered "Mudder's in the kitchen, Missus Payne."

In the porch, Penny stripped the jacket and slushy boots off of Missy and plopped them in a pile by the radiator. Taking Missy by the forearm, she plunked her only inches from the television set and flicked it to a nature show, the northern migration of African killer bees. Missy groaned when the screen showed the bees swarming the face and head of an elderly woman who gripped a bright red purse.

"Ah ah ah," Penny said, the noise rising from deep in her throat. "Ye'll watch without a peep, young lady. Don't want to hear one scrap of complaint comin' out of ye. Gets enough of that from yer brudders."

Missy turned her head away as firemen hosed the woman down and zoomed in on her pecked cheeks, swelling eyelids.

"What's wrong with ye, Missy?" Maureen said, twisting her daughter's head. "'Fraid ye might learn somet'ing?"

One last finger wag at Missy, and Penny left the room. With damp pant's bottoms chilling her legs, cheeks slapped from the cold, and a nose like a faucet, Missy tried to focus on the set through lowered lids. When her mother was clear out of the room, she popped her left thumb into her keen mouth, and immediately relaxed while the mad buzz droned in her ears.

At the kitchen table, Penny drew out a chair and slumped into it. "That child makes a constant fuss. Like it since the day she come out of me."

"Now, now, Penny," Maureen said as she hung Missy's snowsuit on a peg, turned dripping boots upside-down on the heater. "Seems like a good enough girl to me."

"Ye don't know the half of it, me dear," Penny said, sniffing. "She's gettin' lippy, takin' careful notes from Miss pain-in-the-rump."

"Ida?"

"Yes, Ida. Who else? Curdles me blood, it do." She rubbed her hands vigorously. "Now, how's 'bout a cuppa tea, maid? I's froze right down to the bone."

Before Maureen put the kettle on the stove, she glanced out the porch window at Tilley and sighed.

"I can't bear it, Penny," Maureen said, as she came back into the kitchen. "He's near growed up. Soon, he'll be havin' thoughts of movin' on."

"Can't be too soon for me own likin'. I'd have Martin and Walter out tomorrow if I had me choice in the matter."

"But Tilley's me last. When he's gone, there's nothin' else. Ye got Missy, at least. And girls never goes that far from home."

Penny got up and found two mugs in the cupboard, plucked the whistling kettle from Maureen's still hand, and began to make the tea.

"Yes, I s'pose. Though I's dreadin' when she starts sproutin' here, puffin' out there, mind gone right to muck over whatever feller crosses her path." Penny lifted a dry teabag to her nose, inhaled deeply, and then jammed it through the tapered neck of her mug. "But, ye know what? As much as girls got goin' on, I figures 'tis the b'ys do more complainin' 'bout all that. I minds when Walter came to me a year back, t'inkin' he had the cancer."

"What? The cancer?" Maureen's mouth hung open an inch, bottom lip pulled in over bottom teeth.

"Oh yes, bulges in his chest. S'posin' he got the idea from Martha Snipe, all the talk 'bout her passin' month or two after findin' lumps in her breast."

"Yes, yes. I recalls. Go on, me dear."

"Anyway, he wants me to feel him, he now, white like someone walloped him with a bucket of flour. I was in the middle of me exercisin', so I was none too pleased I can tell ye. But he whined to the point that I threw down me paperback, the one with the Yoga in it. Lovely book, me dear, I'll have to lend it to ye. When yer done stretchin', ye can put yerself into either position ye wants." Penny winked, threw her steaming teabag into the sink, and went back to her seat. "Anyways, I took a rub at him, up through the mess of layers he got on, the mess of fat, and sure enough, he had a lump, one on either side, right nice and even. Knots, I told him. Some b'ys gets them when they hits, ye knows. I tell ye, his body's growin' in all directions, but his brain ain't keepin' pace. No maid."

"Poor Walter," Maureen said as she sat beside Penny, slurped hot tea, and then split and buttered a biscuit. "Must've gotten a good start."

"I'll 'good start' him," Penny said, shaking her head. "Interruptin' me exercisin' like that. He was mortified, and I tell ye, I snorted so hard with the look on his face, me bladder let go. Couldn't help meself. 'Twas that pitiful. Had to go and change me drawers."

"'Tis a terrible time. Just terrible. Only made worse when ye got the ol' ones tellin' 'tis the best years of yer life. No wonder half the young crowd seems hell bent on destroyin' themselves. If that's the best life got to offer ye, then what's to come?"

"Ye got that right. But, Lard knows, he don't make it no easier on hisself. Course, Martin heard him complainin' 'bout his chest, and for two years has been callin' him 'the royal tithead'. Royal tithead this and royal tithead that. Serves him right, I says."

"Well Penny, he's well on his way to bein' a man, no question." Maureen nibbled and gulped. "Me Tilley now, he's such a wee t'ing, I can't wrap me mind 'round it."

"'Tis all gradual, maid. It don't happen overnight."

"Oh Lard, I remembers the very first step he took away from me. Clear as though 'twas yesterday. Not a real step now, that's not what I means."

"I don't follow ye."

"Just after Fadder died. I minds Tilley was just three, three and a half. We were back from the cemetery, and I pulled the chair over to the stove so Tilley could sit and shove his feet into the oven. Warm air from the fire, and all. Well, Earl went out, Boyd in tow. Don't remember where they went, though I do remember 'twas miserable weather, rain could burn ye almost, 'twas so cold.

"So, 'twas me and him. I was feelin' right drained, lower than low, and he says to me, Mudder, we can play a little game, cheer ye up. So, I says, 'alright.' And he tells me he'll be Mr. Gristle and I'll be Missus Fat, and can I cook him up a nice cup of hot chocolate. So, I says yes, honey, I surely can. And he reminds me, I ain't yer honey, he says, I's Mr. Gristle. Tough as a gad."

"Some mind on him."

"I knows that," Maureen said, cocking her head. "We goes on for some time, havin' this sweet talk 'bout—oh, I don't even know now. But, I looked down at him, a tiny man in a black suit sittin' by the woodstove, wearin' one of his Fadder's ties. That big now, seemed to cover up half his front. So adorable, me Mr. Gristle was, that I leaned down and kissed him right on his chocolatey lips."

"Well, that's a lovely story, maid."

"No, that's not the end of it. Tilley got a real fright, spillin' his drink right down over the cotton shirt I'd pressed only hours earlier. And he stares at me with this queer look in his eyes, right queer, maid, and I knowed I done somet'ing wrong. Crossed some sort of line. I reckons he wondered what Missus Fat was doin' kissin' Mr. Gristle. Guessin' I broke the rules."

Penny giggled. "Only a childish game, Maureen. Not worth that much thought."

"I ask him what he was he t'inkin', and for the first time since he learnt to talk, he says nothin'. 'I wasn't t'inkin' nothin'.' And then I knew. He'd started movin' away from me. Buildin' up some sort of inside world I weren't privy to. Keepin' a secret up there in his head. As wee as it might've been. The secret, I means, not his head."

"Me Lard," Penny said, shooting out a loud wind through pursed lips. "Ye needs to get out and do somet'ing with yerself. Go buy yerself some new shoes or go get yer hair styled over to Sally's. Too much time if the likes of that silliness is weighin' heavy on yer mind."

Maureen got up from the table, opened the refrigerator, and

took out a worn ice cream container filled with thawed cod. "Ye might be right," she said. She took the lid off, poured out the water, patted the fillets dry with a fresh dishtowel. Turning to face Penny, she leaned against the counter, unconsciously ran the back of her hand over her lower abdomen. "Would've had a dozen, ye knows, Penny girl. Honest to me soul, if God had seen fit, I would've had a whole dozen."

Beyond the fence that marked the western side of Vickers farm, a steep but steady slope rose up to meet the clouds. After a storm, the best sledding in Cupboard Cove could be found there. Though it was the destination of dozens of children, it was not without its perils. Sledding on this hill had to be a controlled affair, veering to the left meant out into traffic, veering to the right meant plummeting over disguised and deadly cliffs. And straight ahead without braking meant trespassing onto Vickers' farm, which was considered a fate worse than the former two.

But this did not stop the hordes. As soon as the storm eased, the hill was specked with dozens of brightly clad balls of snowsuit, bits of cardboard, long toboggans, or neon crazy carpets. Considering himself clever, Walter had cut two leg-holes out of a green garbage bag, climbed in, and electric taped the top around his chest. "Now all I needs worry 'bout is gettin' me own arse up over the hill."

Tilley used a sawed down crate that he stole from the garbage bin outside Samson's Grocery. Being so light, but having manoeuvrability, he was able to whip down over the hill faster than anyone else could. With each pass, he gained confidence, feeding off the whoops that erupted from the younger children when he took to the air after conquering an enormous ramp made of packed snow. Next go, he steered using only his foot, and after that, he blasted down the hill backwards, arms above his head like an athlete.

With each ride, he got cockier. When he lay back, arms straight down by his sides, he reached his fastest speed yet. Closing his eyes, he gave himself over to pure gravity and let it pull him downward. And before he'd realised, he was bounding towards Vickers' fence at an uncontrollable speed. Two years earlier, Mr. Vicker's had replaced that section of his frequently busted picket fence with a double layer of barbed wire.

Tilley held his breath as he slid underneath it. Barbs tore neat lines through his grey snowsuit, the stuffing hitched and poking out. Pinned by his chest, homemade sled locked underneath him, he wriggled but the wire secured him firmly in place. His neck was limited in movement, but he managed to twist it enough to spot an orb of blistering magenta tripping over the drifting snow.

"Looks like I got ye where I wants ye," Ida said with a snicker as she stepped over him, one foot on either side of his head. "Could have me way with ye."

"Come on, Ida," Tilley said. "Haul up the wire. Let me out. Me suit is right ruint."

"Not so fast," Ida said. "Set ye free before we haves a bit of fun?"

Tilley strained against the fence, Ida's legs feeling like additional binding. "Let me out, will ye."

Ida ignored his pleas, swayed her hips. "Whatd'ye t'ink of me new suit?"

With her feet and ankles clamping his head, Tilley couldn't help but stare right up between Ida's legs, at the point where her silver zipper started. That point seemed to be in constant motion, waving, shifting, disappearing in a fold of fabric only to re-emerge a second later.

"Mudder sent it to me from Californier."

"I 'llows," Tilley said as he tried to focus on the very tip of his nose. "Snow gear in every shop down there, I bets."

She stepped aside, her boots scraping roughly over Tilley's ears, and crossed her chest with her arms. "Maybe 'twas Halifax. Maybe 'twas Tronto. Who gives a shit? She sent it to me, that's all I knows."

"'Tis gargeous, alright? Nicest suit I ever seen. Now let me out."

"Saucy little fucker, aren't ye? Half a mind to leave ye. No one else seems to be missin' ye. Walter there, the biggest kinda dickhead in fuckin' plastic bag underwear." Ida turned back towards Vickers house. "And ooh la la, look who we got comin' now."

Lifting his head, Tilley became aware of its full weight. Mr. Vickers was trudging slowly across the snow, wearing a pair of high black rubber boots that made Tilley nervous. He was stout, old, but his hands were massive. Good for gripping.

"Yer goin' to get it now, b'y. Colour of yer outfit, oh Lard, he'll have a real time with ye. Heard he got a t'ing for dirty sheep. With yer insides sticking out, ye could pass, no trouble."

Tilley started to whine, writhe underneath the fence, as the barbs dug deeper into the fabric of his suit. Ida stood by, watching him, smiling, and waving at the approaching farmer. Now, behind him, Tilley heard a "shick shick." Friction from Walter's thighs. When Walter was a few steps away, Ida hauled rapidly up on the wire, and Tilley flopped onto his belly, slid himself out to safety, sled abandoned.

Halfway across his yard, Mr. Vickers raised and threw down those colossal hands, turned, and started back towards his house.

Tilley breathed a sigh of relief, then stared down at the gashes in his suit, and frowned. Wind snuck in, chilling his legs, his lower body. He unrolled the rim of his woollen hat, tugged it down over his ears.

"What the Christ happened to ye?" Walter said. "Ye was doin' great."

"Mudder's goin' to skin me," Tilley said, and then he laughed. "Though 'twas some rush."

"Yes now," Walter said. "Ye'd get some rush if Vickers reached ye. Shit, ye looks right like a half sheared, grimy sheep."

"That just what I told him," Ida said, stepping in next to Tilley. "Told him not to budge, I'd give him a hand."

"Like shit, Ida. I saw what ye was doin'. Apple don't fall far from the tree."

Ida lunged at Walter, and even though she was half his weight, she managed to topple him. Within a second, he scrambled back to his feet, blushed, a meteor hole in the snow behind him where his backside had landed.

"Take a look at yer own tree, ye fat faggot," Ida yelled. "No roses growin' on there, that's for sure."

"Last time I checked, Ida," Tilley said calmly, poking stuffing back into the wounded suit. "Roses growed on bushes. Not on trees."

"Fuck the load of ye," Ida said. She tried to stomp, but the snow sensed her wrath and gave way beneath her feet. Squealing in frustration, she said again, "Fuck the fuckin' load of ye."

Half walking, half crawling away from the giggling of a scored Tilley and a diapered Walter, Ida called to Jimmy Horwood who had just safely descended the hill and was making his way back up, "Wait up, Jimmy. I'll ride on back with ye. Give ye the ride of yer life, me son. I will. The ride of yer friggin' life."

fourteen

athing Hazel Boone would be no simple task. In all the weeks Maureen had climbed the hill to attend to the old woman, wrapping her hair in rollers, scraping and clipping her brittle, yellowing toenails, she had not once helped to wash her. But that morning, when Maureen arrived in the front porch, hands still hidden inside rabbit-fur mittens, Annette made her wishes crystal clear. Maureen would not be paid a red cent unless, by the end of the visit, the old woman had adopted a distinctly different odour than the one she now possessed. "I don't care how you manage it," Annette told her. "If you've got to drown her in the process, so be it. I won't abide that stench in my home for another single, solitary day."

When Maureen entered the kitchen, Hazel Boone was sitting at the round table, staring into space. Maureen rolled up her sleeves, clapped her hands together sharply, and started in. "Ye'll feel right wunnerful, Missus Boone, right fresh and relaxed after ye has a rinse in the tub. Drop in a cap of lovely bath suds, a spoon of salts, or what have ye." The old woman never blinked, never flinched. So, in the next hour, after serving Hazel a cup of tea, Maureen moved on to gentle prodding, "'Tis not healthy to go so long without washin', Missus. Yer skin needs to breathe." This caused Hazel to scowl, "A bath'll be the death of me. And I knows that just what ye wants." Maureen tried bribery. "I'll make ye up a grand lunch after yer wash, Missus, scrambled eggs and some fine soft toast." Hazel glared at Maureen. "Ye must t'ink I's nuts. Ye got nar idea how long that carton of eggs has been sittin' in the fridge? Pure rot." Finally, Maureen resorted to an authoritarian approach, "Ye'll be havin' yer bath, Missus Boone, before I leaves here this day. Just mark me words." But Hazel held firm, said, "That's what I won't then, ye saucy little minx."

That set the devil in Maureen. With feet well spaced on the linoleum floor, she gripped Hazel's frail arms and began to hoist her out of her chair. Expecting a struggle, Maureen was surprised when Hazel did not resist, but began to lift herself up. Though halfway, still bent at knees, hips locked, Hazel stopped. Her body went rigid. Wet lips pursed, eyes squeezed shut, a grunt snagged in the old woman's throat.

"Oh me dear Lard in heaven," Maureen said, turning her head away as ripe warm air wafted up.

Undersides soiled, Hazel was now smug, agreeable, waddled willingly to the bathroom. "Yes, Missus Gover. Ye might be right. A bath would be lovely."

Maureen resisted the temptation to scissor the soiled clothes from Hazel's body, even though Hazel offered no assistance with her own disrobing. As Hazel settled onto the no-slip sandpapery flowers that lined the tub, Maureen could easily spy a greasy film spread out over the surface of the water. Like turpentine daubed on the end of a stick and stuck into a clear puddle. Selecting the first of three washcloths, Maureen lathered with floral soap, rubbed at the tissue paper skin, and lifted greying folds to reveal shiny crevices. Well-soaked, dead skin seemed to rumble away beneath Maureen's fingers, as though she were running her hand over a great piece of damp cheese. But, no matter. With some work, a clean Hazel emerged, her faux jaundice now but an inch-wide ring around the tub.

After drying, dressing, and walking the old woman to the kitchen, Maureen returned to the bathroom to sop up copious amounts of water on the floor. She gathered the filthy clothes, stiff from grime and caked on bits of food, and carried them to the washing machine. Sprinkling extra detergent onto the mound, she allowed some to spill over her damp hands, and rinsed them quickly in the stream of scalding water that poured around the agitator. Against the white of the washer, Hazel's pants were the colour of a stained robin's egg. Initially, Maureen had thought to burn them, but as clean water buried them, and fragrant bubbles cut through the sour smell, she was pleased that she didn't. "Waste not want not," she always said.

As she dropped the lid on the washing machine, swiped her wet hands across her backside, a shriek came from the kitchen. Maureen rushed in to find Annette standing red-faced amidst a mess of crumbs. Spanning the kitchen, someone had stomped and kicked, crushed and scattered an entire box of biscuits.

"Who is responsible for this?" Annette punctuated each word while her eyes roved between Maureen and Hazel.

Maureen's mouth hung open, over-bite protruding.

Flecks of cracker clung to Hazel's slippers.

"Maureen?" Annette said sternly. "Weren't you attending to Mother Boone?"

"I- I-," Maureen stammered.

"Ye knows I likes lemon creams." Hazel's rasping voice interrupted Maureen. "Not those dry t'ings yer fillin' the cupboards with. I won't eat them."

Annette huffed, shook her head, and spoke slowly. "You are truly impossible, Mother Boone. If you think your preferences take priority in this family, then you are sorely mistaken. Far too used to getting your own way, if you ask me." She surveyed the floor again, said under her breath, "Honest to God. If I had a choice."

At once, confusion clouded Hazel's eyes, and she hobbled out of the kitchen, her sliding slippers leaving two trails through the crumbs.

Once Hazel was well down the hallway, Maureen said, "I can't do it no more, Missus Boone. I just can't."

Annette's face softened. She tilted her head, lowered her eyes, expression demure like a nun's. "It's Annette. Pleeease." Then she walked over to the section of countertop that had been transformed into a desk, tugged open a drawer and retrieved an envelope.

"Ye needs someone who knows how to deal with that type of person, and that ain't me. Someone who got the patience."

"I admit," Annette whispered, as though confiding to a friend, "mother Boone can be somewhat cantankerous. And she is most definitely used to getting her own way. To be truthful, Maureen, she finds it terribly difficult to control herself." Crossing the kitchen again, Annette slipped the padded envelope into Maureen's hand. "But she says such lovely things about you to both David and myself. What a pleasant time she's spent with you."

Maureen pinched the envelope, felt the wad of dollars inside, and thought of the white winter wool coat in Pustin's store window. She thought of Tilley and all the things she could afford for him with this extra income. "To David? Really?"

Placing a hand gently over her heart, Annette nodded. "Honest to my God, Maureen."

Maureen kicked a few cracker pieces with her toe. "Well, I'll keep on, then. For a while anyway. Seein' as that's the case."

"Superb." Annette said with some gusto, then she sighed. "Ah. I've so much to do. Dinner is such a bother. And David needs to eat food to make him vigorous. I've got some lovely bones to make a hearty stew."

"A soup, ye means. With bones."

"No dear, I prepare a wonderful stew. Frozen peas, instant rice. It's a snap really. I have a secret ingredient."

Annette's mention of a secret was an invitation to Maureen, and Maureen accepted. "And what's that? Yer special stuff."

"Ask most women," Annette said with precision, "and they'll quickly tell you that a diamond is a girl's best friend. Well, after being married for nearly two decades, I can tell you without an ounce of uncertainty, that it is a good quality can of gravy that will take you the distance."

"Oh goodness." With the mention of rich gravy, Maureen's mouth watered involuntarily, and she slurped slightly.

"I kid you not, Maureen. We women have lives to lead—that cannot be denied. It's simply no longer necessary to reside exclusively in the kitchen."

"Well. I guess."

"And you do guess correctly," Annette said with a maple syrup smile. Then she turned on her heel, and with her back to Maureen, words trailed behind her as she sauntered away. "And do be a dear, will you Maureen, and straighten Mother Boone's little mess? I so despise a dirty floor. The upright is in the hall closet. Second door on your left."

Maureen recognised a question when she heard one and knew this wasn't a question. She went to the closet, returned to the kitchen with the vacuum. A new model, it purred like a content-ed kitten. Unlike hers at home, these attachments were without cracks, void of drips of old glue, scads of tape. She tucked

Annette's tone away and stole a moment's pleasure in cleaning with such a fine machine.

Hazel had retreated to the parlour, threw Annette's throw blanket onto the floor, and eased down into her chair. The vacuum whined in her ears, filling her head with a drone that made her reel. She gripped the arms of her chair and ground her toughened gums against her dentures.

Inside that sound, Hazel could not help but hear a tired child howling. And to quiet it, she began to sing a jumble of words. Her irritated voice was a needle skipping over a scratched record. "Peas porridge hot, peas porridge cold, peas porridge cold, porridge cold, porridge cold, porridge cold, cold, cold."

The second time Harvey Boone saw Hazel Keeping outside of her home, he was forking fish from the floor of Neil's skiff up onto the stage head. The skiff was rising, dropping on a gentle wave, and Harvey gripped the long smooth handle of his two-pronged pitchfork, jabbed the heads with precision, and hoisted them in fluid movement. Then, as a forkful of fish slapped onto the floor of the stage, he looked up and noticed Hazel standing at the shoreline, her fiery hair burning off the milky fog.

For a moment he didn't blink, though his arms and shoulders continued their work at a relentless pace.

"Christ, b'y," Neil yelled down from the stage as Harvey stabbed a fish right through the body. "Yer ruinin' a day's work, me son. Watch yerself."

After scrubbing hands and forearms to freshness and donning clean pants, he set out to find Hazel. Just off Shore Road, he discovered a thin trail of bent hay, rushed down it and found her at the end, eyes closed lying in the shade of a damson tree. She started smiling as his feet approached. Harvey knew she wasn't sleeping.

Out of breath, he wheezed, "I was lookin' for ye."

Hazel didn't open her eyes. "I thought ye would be," she said. She raised an arm and pointed to the highest branch jutting out from the tree. "Pick me a few of those damsons, will ye? They've been stuck in me mind all week."

"Got a fine bunch right here in front of me," he said, reaching out to pluck them.

"No, they's not as good. I wants them ones up there. They's the sweetest."

"Well, what ye wants, ye'll get."

He ploughed up the tree, thighs pressed around the trunk, hands clutching, grabbing, and feet sliding over the smooth bark. After he spidered up through the centre branches, he eased his body down and inch-by-inch, he slid out onto a weak section. Eyes blinded by leaves, he tried to determine his distance by the bobbing of the branch. Even with his fingers extended, he still was unable to reach the cluster of plums Hazel desired.

"There's no way. Me arm ain't goin' to stretch that far."

One eye fluttered open. "Fly, then," she said through a smirk. "Yer goin' to have to fly."

All that he needed was her suggestion. And in that moment he pushed off with his feet, he actually felt as though he were flying, soaring through the air. When his fingers encircled the branch, he held tightly, but it cracked instantly with his weight. Back to earth he dropped with a dull thud, the branch splayed, fruit tumbled down the incline towards Hazel. He sat up, tried to pick them up, but his limp arm hung from a dislocated shoulder.

When he watched Hazel select one of the succulent damsons, and drop the whole fruit into her mouth, a sensation of pleasure crept over Harvey's body. Like a gift, the very sight of her with juice shining on her chin numbed every ounce of his pain.

Three weeks later, they fumbled onto the stage, through the door. Darkness tucked itself around them, waves crashed underneath, and the whole structure swayed with the power of the ocean. Salt hung heavily in the air, and Harvey tasted it when he licked his lips—which he couldn't help doing often. He cracked a match, reached up to light the stage lamp, but Hazel took his hand: no.

"Do ye want me to strip?" she said, reaching behind her neck.

Harvey's whole body felt hot; his hands were suddenly slippery when he rubbed them together. "No, no, maid. Not in this kind of place."

She lay down on the rough floor of the stage. Her knotted hair glistened about her head like a mound of netting, catching every shard of moonlight that snuck through the many holes in the roof. Water splashed up from the opening where fish innards and heads were discarded. Her hands worked to lift her dress, and when it was almost to her hips, she looked him straight in the eye and said, "Help yerself."

Dropping to the floor beside her, he threatened the boards with his sudden shift in weight. She gripped the legs of the splitting table where the fish were beheaded with a stubby knife, gutted, and then rinsed clean. In those moments, she was thankful the legs were secure, nailed down to the floor of the stage.

As he moved over her, those words echoed inside his head, 'help yerself'. He knew that he was doing just that. Fully helping himself to everything she offered. And at the same time, he was also certain he couldn't help himself, couldn't stop himself even if he tried. Somehow from the moment he stood in the grave and his eyes watered from that fistful of thrown dirt, he knew it would be this way. So easily, his will had disintegrated, a rotten piece of fabric, eager fingers pushing through.

After they had finished, Hazel and Harvey slid out into the damp night. She was wearing a blood red dress, and under the starless sky, it appeared black. Darkness swallowed her, while Harvey's wrinkled white shirt radiated. He was easy to spot. Like a single spark moving along the dirt road, he appeared to be alone. And for those who stared out their windows at that late hour (and there were always a few), they never thought much of it.

The following morning, when Neil Grimes opened the rickety door to the stage, he saw a faint imprint on the floor near the gutting table. He bent to one knee, ran his thick-skinned fingers over the weathered wood. How very strange, he thought. The wood was burned slightly. Much like a splash of fire, or long wispy hair spread out in a haphazard halo.

fifteen

O n his way home after the sliding mishap, Tilley passed a mountain of snow, so high it obscured all but the puffing chimneys of the homes just beyond. Near the base of the mound, three rounded tunnels had been hollowed out. Like moles, children had created a series of passageways and miniature rooms inside the bank. As he walked by, Tilley felt drawn towards the middle one for no other reason than to discover where it led. Somehow, a hole offered a promise. *Was there something beyond it or did it only lead to a dead end?* Most likely deceptive, but tempting nonetheless. On all fours, he climbed in to find out.

He had to squeeze through the mouth, but once inside, the tunnel opened and the air turned into a surreal bluish grey. His torn snowsuit grazed the soft walls, and the sound of cars rushing through slush just outside the entrance was muffled. When he was several yards in, he considered backing out. But there was no way to turn around. The tunnel wasn't wide enough, and when he realised he couldn't shift left or right, he became aware of a pulse point at the base of his throat.

Legs constricted underneath him, he whispered to himself, "Shit. What's wrong with me today? Stuck once, stuck twice."

Though this time, he wasn't really stuck. No larger than an elementary school child, he could have easily flattened his body and slid back out onto the road. But the feeling still lingered. He found nothing particularly appealing or inviting about being enveloped in snow. For years, Boyd had practised his one and only sport (winter football—no ball was actually involved) with Tilley as his only opponent. "Hutt hutt," Boyd would holler as Tilley tried to scuttle away through the drifts, feet moving at a nightmarish pace. Overtaking him, Boyd would knock him forward, and when propelled, Tilley would invariably start what could have been the perfect snow angel. Then, sitting squarely on Tilley's shoulders, Boyd would press Tilley's howling face deep into the icy blanket, and count, "One Mississippi, two Mississippi, three...." At first, Tilley thrashed about, but quickly realised he needed to remain calm to find his breath through the snow. Once Tilley went limp, Boyd would finally rise and Tilley would lie lifeless, cheeks prickling, begging for release. But he would deny himself, until Boyd bored and wandered off.

No, Tilley didn't like being surrounded by snow at all. But who could resist the offer of a tunnel, the potential of a cave? The possibility, however slim, that it did lead somewhere, into another world. *Hell*, Tilley thought, *Lucy found a whole new reality through a false back in a wardrobe, why couldn't he disappear through a tunnel of dirty snow?*

When he rounded a turn in the tunnel, and smacked his lowered head into a wall, he wasn't surprised. Most of his mind knew that things in Cupboard Cove never really went anywhere. This wasn't England, and he wasn't visiting a professor with his charming siblings. He lived in a saltbox house, and had just ventured down a hole made of snow scraped up from a potholed road, shards of rock sticking out, and streaks of grime abounding.

Tilley rolled over onto his back and leaned his head against the icy wall. Staring out towards the road, fully aware of the outport community lying beyond the entrance, Tilley felt a childish sense of disappointment wrap around his chest. His head lolled forward, jaw dropping slightly. He breathed deeply and air that tasted of car exhaust filled his mouth. Everything deadened, cozy inside his hole, he had the urge to doze off. Lashes fluttering.

A light crunching beside his left shoulder made his eyes pop open. Turning his head, he saw a bright red mitten moving behind a thin wall, then breaking through. That mitten, formed into a fist, punched away at the snow, spraying it up onto Tilley's face. Once the hole was the size of his father's head, a brand new shiny leather boot started kicking the barrier between the two tunnels. To avoid the oncoming boot, Tilley slid as far to the right as he could. And when the boot withdrew for the last time, a flushed face appeared, smiling.

"God. You'd never find anything like this in St. John's." Marnie Boone was peering up with shiny cheeks, strands of hair poking out from underneath a matching hat. "Hi, Tilley," she said, as though finding him there came as no surprise at all.

Tilley twisted his body to hide the rips in his suit, but her hand darted out, a red mitt batting at a trapped rabbit, and she yanked away a tuft of stuffing.

"You were lucky," she said. "You could've really hurt yourself."

"Nah," he said with a dismissive tone. "I knew what I was at."

"Certainly looked like it," she said playfully. "I could tell." She bit her chapped bottom lip. "I was going to help, but that girl beat me to it."

"Who, Ida? Nothin' but trouble, that one. Mudder says—," he began, but stopped himself.

Marnie stared intently at Tilley and removed her red mittens. Tilley thought he should do something too, but wasn't quite sure what. Inside his own mittens, his palms were sweating, clinging to strands of moistened wool. He noticed a grilled pattern melted into the cuff of his snowsuit, no doubt from drying it on the radiator. Trying to hide his hand, his ill-fitting suit was all the more obvious, and he squirmed.

"Did ants crawl in through those holes in your snowsuit or something?" Marnie said.

Tilley blushed, tried to relax one knee, and slowed his breathing to a nonchalant tempo. "Ha, ha. Very funny." He unzipped a few inches near his neck, and his hand dove down, retrieved a package of cigarettes and lighter.

"Those are my father's."

"Yeah. Want one?"

She shook her head quickly.

Holding the thin box in his mitten, he realised the smoke would choke them both, drive Marnie out to fresher air when everything in him wanted her to burst down the remainder of the wall, join him in his own tunnel.

"So," he said. "What's it like, livin' with someone…?"

"Someone what? Famous?" Amused, she spoke loudly. And her voice echoed gently, filling Tilley with pleasure over hearing her words repeat themselves.

"Yeah, I guess."

"Well, you'd know better than I would," she said. "You've spent more time with him these past weeks than I've spent in my lifetime."

Tilley detected the slightest smidgen of disdain, though perhaps it was his imagination. He let the package of cigarettes rest on his chest, drove a mittened finger into the snow, and carved away a little hole. For weeks now, he had been spending his afternoons with David Boone. At first the visits were strained, but gradually, Tilley grew comfortable drawing outside the confines of a linen closet, having ample room for his elbows, his knees. While Tilley sketched, David's hands were most often still, but occasionally they came to rest on Tilley's shoulders, and once or twice on the small of his back. Touches that were only meant to keep Tilley grounded, focused, riding in the space where he should be riding. *Somehow from the house, had she been able to see?*

Inside the small quarters they shared, Tilley could smell Marnie's breath, yesterday's garlic, maybe curry or some other sweaty spice. The same scent as her father's. He wondered if he was exhaling canned chicken noodle, salted crackers, Tang. "I just thought," he said.

"Did he say something?"

"No, nothin' like that. He doesn't really talk much."

"Oh."

"I just had the feelin' ye was, ye were, ye got on good with him."

"Oh, we get along fine," she said. "Don't get me wrong. He's a man, I guess. Doesn't know what to do with a girl. Wouldn't know where to begin." On top of her mittens, she folded her hands together, placed her chin on her knuckles. "My mom says I should consider myself blessed."

"Why's that?"

"She says I was very much an accident. My father never wanted a child."

"Ah," Tilley said. "All parents says that when they's pissed with ye. 'Ye was nothin' but an accident. Never wanted ye in the first place.'"

"Your mother?"

"Mine?"

"Of course, yours. Is there anyone else in here that I don't see?"

"Um."

"Well, did she ever say that to you?"

At once, Tilley thought of his toad-in-the-hole breakfasts that his mother prepared on Sunday mornings. The hole in the bread was never a straightforward circle, but formed ever so carefully with a heart-shaped cookie cutter.

"Well. Hmmm. Well, I's sure she must've thought it." That was the best he could offer. But he knew it was an outright lie. And as he smoothed the snowy wall of the tunnel with his wet mitten, he wished he hadn't said it at all. Even the very notion of it felt like a betrayal.

From her perch atop the snow-covered stone pillar that marked the corner of Vickers' farm, Ida squinted with the brightness. She was surveying the three dark tunnels near the bottom of the snow bank. Marnie Boone had been in there for some time, and even though the sky was fading to grey, Ida would not budge until that girl came out.

Scooping snow, she squeezed it into a hard ball, and started sucking. *Where was Tilley, anyway?* Shouldn't he have gone home, the state he was in with that suit? Ida bit deep into the snowball, and the chill on her teeth sent a stabbing pain between her eyes. She cursed, threw it as hard as she could, but the ball just made a mundane plop, and was lost in the mirror of whiteness.

Finally, after what seemed an eternity, Marnie's head emerged, shoulders next, and Ida watched her daintily slide out onto the road. Tilley did not follow. *Still recovering from whatever that girl had done to him. No doubt.* Then she noticed Marnie wasn't wearing any mittens. Why had she taken them off?

To handle him, Ida thought. That was the only reason that made sense. Exposed skin in this insane cold.

Ida shivered. And way down inside her shapeless torso, a well-established knot started to tighten.

sixteen

"**W**ham! Right in the noggin."

"Wham?"

"Yes wham, missus. Yer that daft." Earl stumbled into the kitchen, sobered mind, limbs drunk. Cotton batting for a tongue.

Maureen drew out a chair from the table. Earl swaggered to the seat with fists clenched, blood oozing down his cheeks, a boxer in centre ring.

Standing at the stove, Tilley had been scooping overly swollen spaghetti noodles and rust-coloured sauce onto a plate. When he heard his father's rasp, he turned swiftly. The slippery mass slid sideways, abandoned the plate, and landed with a soggy splash on the linoleum.

"Christ, Christ, Christ," Earl moaned, as Tilley bent, trying to scrape the fat strings onto the plate with his bare hands.

"Never mind," Maureen said, flustered, hands like chicken

wings. "Never mind that. Tilley b'y, run and check the corners for a cobweb. I'll put it on his head, help slow the bleedin'."

Earl grasped his oozing head with both hands. "No wonder half the world t'inks we Newfies is stunned as a boot. Sendin' the b'y after a friggin' web when me goddamned face is hangin' off."

With her first finger pointing, she said, "It works, Earl. Ye can't say it don't."

"Well, I don't want him gettin' nothin'. He's the root of me troubles."

Maureen rinsed a dishcloth in soapy water from the sink, pressed it against Earl's forehead. She watched the coagulating blood creep out and along the fabric.

"I tell ye one t'ing," Earl said, as he swayed dizzily. "I's damned delighted that I's soused. Lest I be feelin' this full on."

Maureen lifted Earl's limp hand, placed it over the cloth. "Yes, Earl. Ye looks right like lady luck is on yer side this evenin'. Tell me exactly what happened. Every bit. Right from the start."

"Alright," he said with a heavy breath. "I goes to Nips-n-Bites, see?"

"We knows that. Come on, now. Skip ahead. Skip ahead. Cut to the chase."

"Right. Don Morris, then. Cut me up with a bloody beer bottle. I shook me fist in his face, told him I'd rip out his t'roat if he said anudder word, and he cracked me one. The dirty bastard."

"Me Lard." Hands sprung to her throat.

"I'll have his head on a platter, I can promise ye that. I'd have half a mind to call Constable Johnson, but he was at Nips-n-Bites hisself passed out beside the bar. Dozen ol' wet coats piled up on him. Lot of good, there."

With short gasps, Maureen punctuated Earl's account at suitable intervals.

Earl eyed her from underneath the cloth. "Stop yer gawkin', woman, and take a few snapshots. I could have real damage here.

Serious damage. Sue Don's ass right off him. Won't have a goddamned pot to piss in."

"What was he sayin' to ye, Fadder?" Tilley asked meekly from his position near the spaghetti spill. His hands were stained with sauce as he gripped the white plate, smeared top and bottom.

Earl spoke directly to Maureen, as though Tilley had somehow evaporated. "We started out all cordial like, rantin' 'bout Harold Gullage over to the bank. How he's makin' a bloody mint off us, slappin' us left and right with costs for this shit and that shit, processin' and handlin'. Christ, ye don't see nar cent in interest. Nar cent, 'tall."

"Well, that's no reason to clout ye."

"Will ye listen, missus? 'Fore ye starts up with yer tongue?" Earl peeled away the cloth, stared at the dark bloodstain, then pressed it back onto his forehead. "Don starts goin' on 'bout Gullage keepin' a fresh piece of arse in a basement apartment in the Gut. Barely nineteen. Sweet as molasses taffy, he says, and he had a gander at her once." He paused to lick his lips. "Anyways, that's not his first girl from the Gut. Seems he likes them cheap and poor. And how queer 'tis, Don says, all kinds of money he got, most of it bein' ours, and he can't manage to get hisself a decent piece of tail from some udder place."

"I beg to differ with ye there," Maureen said stoutly as she rummaged through a junk drawer, shovelled out loose cards, a screwdriver with a cracked handle, a coiled white leather belt, finally finding the Kodak camera. "He must've managed a t'ing or two with his dear wife, Missus Gullage, at some point. Them havin' a handful of children and all. And, for yer information, she was born and raised right here in Cupboard Cove."

"I guess Don stands corrected."

"Still. 'Tis no reason to clobber ye."

"Oh yes," Earl said, remembering his head, the point of his story. "So I tells him I can barely stand to go to the teller now with all those disgraceful pictures hangin' on the wall. Sight of them makes me feel right sick to me stomach. Queasy, like. Scantily clad youngsters. 'Tis disgraceful. Don't know why Gullage took down those shots of skiffs and whitecaps, the one showing a hot bowl of hurt puddin'. Now they was lovely grand. If ye asks me, 'twas a downright piss poor attempt to get Boone's business, when anyone with a grain knows that feller likely got all his money tied up with investments in St. John's. I tells Don I t'inks that David Boone is a fruitcake, honest to Jaysus. The way he strolls 'round the cove on his tippy toes, gawkin' out through those ferrety eyes.

"Then he winks at me, and says, ye'd know alright. And I scrapes me stool back from the bar and says to him, what the hell is ye tryin' to say, arsehole. And he goes on that he knows all 'bout me son. Sayin' me b'y is light as a feather. Queer as a three-dollar bill."

"What son?" Maureen said as she fumbled, cranked the film. "Why ye can't be more manly than Boyd. By jumpins, he got anudder tattoo on his shoulder. A scaly mermaid with nar bit of shame. Saw her on him tonight when he was comin' out of the bathroom. Towel wrapped 'round his waist."

"Not Boyd, maid."

"What? Tilley?" Maureen clicked, the flash making both father and son wince simultaneously. "That's utter silliness."

"Told me he sees that little bugger climbin' the hill every afternoon like clockwork. Goin' to that Boone feller's house. Where no doubt the old man sticks it to him. Or else gets him to unstrip, then paints him or somet'ing. I couldn't hear no more of it. I hoved me drink at him and he grabbed me by the back of me head, walloped me with his bottle."

Tilley's hands opened, plate released, a loud crash, shards spreading across the floor.

Maureen's voice wavered, dropped a notch. "He must be mistaken, Earl."

"By Christ, he better be. Me sons are men. Ye hear me? Men. Men. MEN." Blood started dripping from underneath the cloth, skidding down over his shirt. "Good strong sturdy men. Through and through. Hard workers. The toughest. Not ones to get roused up, pummelled 'round by no faggoty artsy types."

When he finally spoke, Tilley's face was a bleached sheet. "He's no faggot."

"What?" Earl said, dropping the cloth onto his blubbery belly, twisting rough fingers inside his ears. "What?"

"I said he ain't no faggot, Fadder." Stronger now.

Earl lurched towards Tilley. Wanting to clutch the boy's cheeks, skinny neck, his baby hair. Blood oozed into his eyes, clouding his vision but leaving his anger intact. A deep step and Earl's legs splayed, winter boots sliding on spilled spaghetti. Crashing onto the kitchen floor, Earl seized his hip, the base of his skull, his left shoulder, his hands roaming furiously over his aching body, not knowing where to settle, what to soothe.

Even though his heart was tumbling over, revving inside his chest, Tilley stepped cautiously around Earl, avoiding the buttered noodles, and splinters from the plate. Earl's hands flailed, reaching for Tilley's ankles, but Tilley was beyond their grasp. Tilley felt coldness inside his body, but little else. His senses were numbed. And somehow it seemed as though he were moving through a soiled dream, taking great moon leaps, floating out into the porch, and with exaggerated motion, tugging a downy jacket from off a hook. On his way through the back door, he turned down the volume on his father's voice, as it slurred with protracted agony.

"Yer lying to yer Fadder. Yer a liar. A liar. If ye ever gets a name for bein' that in the Cove. If ye ever. Tilley, me son, come back here. Right now. Come back. If ye does. If ye does. Tilley, me son." A moan. "Ye'll never be nothin' else."

When the door thumped shut, Maureen stooped, shoved her hands up into Earl's armpits, damp even through his wool sweater. Open wounds on his forehead and to the left of his eye, which shone for her under the fluorescent light. Black blood had dried in every wrinkle; a rapid etching of unattractive broken lines now outlined his face.

To steady himself, Earl wrapped his arms around her neck. He let his slashed face tilt onto her shoulder, and inhaled the smells of deep-fried halibut and flowery perfume that circulated through the fine fuzz growing at the nape of her neck. Maybe he was still drunk, but in a single breath, everything started rising to the surface, breaking through.

Ah yes. Time, that slippery eel, might deny him a solid grasp on any given moment. And his children, two familiar strangers, might stray far from him. But his wife, his original darling, she would remain close by. He could feel the strength in her hold. Maureen. How he had loved her all those years ago. And she was here for him, just like she'd always been. So very solid.

As Maureen hoisted her husband onto the chair, she gazed into his eyes, saw a peculiar oil-water emulsion of rage and regret. In a flicker, his greasy temper separated out, obscuring the certain sorrow hidden underneath. But Maureen savoured it. Could almost taste those bubbles of weakness gliding across her tongue. She stored away that image, and for a stolen moment, permitted unseen beads of satisfaction to sweat out through awakened pores.

Then she forced herself to focus on something else: her two feet, firmly planted on the floor of her kitchen. She leaned in close to inspect the gashes. "I'll call Penny," she said. "She can bring her kit. Be here in ten minutes. Less, maybe."

"That's what ye won't."

"Why for ever not, Earl?"

"Don't want her goin' all to pieces over a few scrapes. Listenin' to her chirpin' in me ear." He squirted blood-streaked saliva into a fresh towel, inspected it.

"She's a nurse for heaven's sake. And they's hardly scrapes. Any deeper and yer polluted mind'd be fallin' out onto the floor."

"No to Penny, Maureen. Ye can let the goodness drain right out of me, for all I cares, or cart me over to the Good Hopes, if ye wants. But no Penny. And that's friggin' final."

꧁

As windshield wipers swished sleet off into the night, Maureen drove cautiously over icy roads. Arms snug against her sides, she was wearing only a thin rain slicker, her winter's coat gone missing from the hook by the back door. In the passenger seat, Earl drooped, partially mummified with a clean dishcloth wrapped and secured in place with the severed leg from an old pair of nude pantyhose. Though he droned on, his voice drifted in and out of Maureen's consciousness. Instead, she was thinking about where Tilley had gone, how long the wait at emergency would be, and the tedious task of cleaning dried on spaghetti off her good linoleum floor that awaited her.

But when Earl mentioned their saltbox home, the whistling wind diminished, scratching snow faded away. Maureen's full attention was suddenly inside their car, now stifling hot from the blasting heaters, choking with the sweetness of recycled yeast from Earl's breath.

"What was that?" Maureen asked. She leaned forward, gripped the steering wheel. "What was ye sayin' 'bout the house?"

"Oh, 'twas Duncan Murphy shootin' his mouth off, 'fore Don struck me. Murphy now, drunk as a bloody skunk. Hobblin' 'round with his goddamned walker, smackin' into chairs, knockin' over drinks, goin' ass up, and stayin' there 'til someone sets him right. Sherri shouldn't let him out, let alone into Nips-n-Bites."

"She ain't no kind of daughter, that one. Lettin' him make a show of hisself like that."

"So, he sidles up 'longside me, got somet'ing stuck in his craw, he says, these years. Then he goes on 'bout somet'ing awful terrible happenin' in our house. So unnatural—"

"Unnatural?"

"That's the word he used. Yes, maid, that was it. He said ye won't find none of the old folks to even talk 'bout it. Why do ye t'ink 'twas boarded up all those years, he says. Why do we t'ink we spent near nothin' for it?"

"Me Lard. Brazen beyond belief. 'Tis none of his business what we paid for it."

"I tells him I don't give a rat's sweet furry arse what went on. Livin' here near twenty years, then havin' to listen to him gettin' on with that shit. Pure and utter shit, is all. Pure and utter."

"Proper t'ing, Earl," Maureen said calmly, though her knuckles were white on the steering wheel. She had long ago given up wondering why the house was so cheap when they bought it, but here it was again, a niggling reminder, an inkling creeping up the back of her neck. As a child, she had walked by the sad little saltbox, its symmetrical eyes blinded, mouth sealed with lengths of weathered clapboard. But when she married Earl, there wasn't enough time to build a new home, or enough money to even buy a plot of land. Her father had railed against the old house, but when he found out she was in the family way, he relented. "'Tis only four walls," he had said. "They's four walls as good as any." And he was right. What difference did it make? History wraps itself around people, but wood, and nails, and plaster, and linoleum should be free and clear. Surely. Maureen tried to settle her mind, held the wheel with her thumbs, and wiggled her cramping fingers.

"Proper t'ing," she repeated, pulling into the near-vacant parking lot of the Good Hopes Hospital. She could see the brightly lit emergency entrance through the December storm. "No, siree. It don't matter nothin'."

When Tilley crept around the back of David Boone's darkened house, he was relieved to see windows glowing in the white shed. Approaching the door, he realised his boots were unlaced and that it was his mother's unzipped jacket he clutched to his body. After three steady knocks, David cracked open the door, peered out, then stepped aside and let the door swing on its hinge. Tilley wasn't wearing a hat, and the moment he stepped into the warmth, his ears began to throb as though they were growing uncontrollably.

"Let me take your coat," David said. No question as to why Tilley had arrived near midnight, drowning inside woman's clothing.

David tussled flakes of snow from Tilley's head. "Come, come, Tilford. Warm yourself by the woodstove."

Tilley swiped away a lock of hair that had fallen into his eyes and followed close behind David. For minutes, he continued to feel the sensation of David's fingers on his chilled scalp and he was certain that only fondness lingered in that touch. No matter what his father had the gall to say. Fondness. Nothing more.

And Tilley was familiar with the 'more' part. Likely, most of the boys who played volleyball at Cupboard Collegiate had some experience with the 'more' part. Mr. Bightford was their gym teacher, a sinewy bicycle-riding sort who blatantly wore size XS T-shirts and skimpy white tennis short-shorts that had two navy stripes up either side. His aged skin was an ill-coloured yellowish green, like an inside leaf on a tight head of cabbage. And that tone, plus a mat of salt and pepper fur, covered him entirely. Anyone who instinctively dove for the ball, sliding onto the wooden gym floor, could attest to it. Mr. Bightford was there in an instant, legs over-sprawled near the boy's head, whistle blowing with a hearty wink.

When he taught each boy to serve the ball over the net, he was oh so touchy, touchy.

"I don't want to hear no balkin'," he said, tapping a spotless sneaker and wagging a thin finger at lightening speed. "Ye can make yer whole game with a decent serve."

When the time came, Mr. Bightford shaped himself around Tilley's body, his over-burdened ring of keys jabbing into the small of Tilley's back. "Oops, pardon me, pardon me," Mr. Bightford said, which made the other boys snicker, punch each other, and howl. And then, he snuggled in close, warm knee behind warm bended knee, his arm stretched underneath Tilley's own, guiding it gently, following through forcefully, ending when Tilley smacked that imaginary leather ball to hell and beyond. Then, all at once, Mr. Bightford pulled back, rushed off to answer a phone in his office that rarely rung, and Tilley lifted his hand to his neck. He felt a definite wetness there. The sick chill of evaporation.

"We seen it," Louie Rund cried, whooping with laughter, rolling on the bleachers in near spasm. "He tongued ye. He tongued ye. Buddy, luh. Ye've been tongued."

Tilley wiped his palm in his shirt. He couldn't understand why it was all so amusing. Apparently, Mr. Bightford had tongued them all, even Boyd several years earlier. Now that Tilley thought about it, he recalled a rumour that Boyd had been a favourite, at first a willing volunteer to demonstrate his serving prowess, then a reluctant participant. Someone even scratched Boyd's initials on the wooden wall of a bathroom stall, equating them with

Mr. Bightford's. BG=GB. Gerry Bightford. Perhaps it was a different BG and GB, but for weeks after, Boyd ground his teeth so loudly in his sleep, it could be heard throughout the house. And shortly afterwards, he dropped gym class, Boyd bought (stole) his first leather jacket, started smoking whatever he could swipe, and refused to ever let his mother buzz his hair again with those vibrating clippers.

Tilley had the urge to march up onto those bleachers and smack Louie Rund right across his greasy chops. But, he resisted. While Louie laughed, the truth was he had been tongued too. Likely he understood it to be their collective shame, and could find no other way to package it.

A communal sigh of relief arose when Mr. Bightford didn't show for work one Monday morning in November. Someone mentioned they saw him riding out of town on his bicycle, wearing knee-high, glossy black rubber boots with a sport fisherman's cap on his head. The only person who missed him was Walter, who complained bitterly that the one teacher who ever appreciated him had just up and just disappeared.

"And in his defence," Walter had told Tilley as his fingers stroked the cabbage moth in his hair. "P'raps he had some sort of queer disorder. Desperate need of salt or somet'ing. Ye never knows."

"There's coffee in the thermos there. On the shelf," David said.

Tilley shook his head no. David shrugged slightly, and returned to his painting, holding a razor blade at an oblique angle, scraping away excess paint. There was little light in the shed, mostly a warm reddish glow from the sooty window of the wood-stove. Rosy hues disguised David's drab pallor, washed him in a youthfulness that Tilley had never before seen. On a swivel stool before his canvas, David worked eagerly defacing the painting, and Tilley fidgeted as soaked sections of his jeans scorched his skin. *Should he leave?*

As though Tilley's thoughts had floated out, snagged in a gaping net, David said calmly, "You're not disturbing me. But if you keep shuffling like that, you might wear a hole in my floor."

Tilley relaxed his feet, and felt a flush of admiration colour his cheeks. *How could this man, so entirely unlike his father, seem to care so much for him? Why did he bother to encourage him, embrace even his mediocre efforts?* Those subtle nods, tempered blinks, a checkmark in the air with a dry finger, offered a recognition that lifted Tilley's spirit far beyond the claustrophobia that was Cupboard Cove.

And Tilley had done nothing to deserve it. Nothing but draw, sketch, and smudge pencil lines with his thumb: things he loved to do anyway. Now here was David Boone, a solid practised man who quietly believed in him. His near silence making the conviction all the more profound.

A tremendous longing teased Tilley's skin, and weakened his heart, his knees. He wanted to dart across the shed, bury his miniature head in David's wool sweater, expensive but still flecked with splinters of logs, flakes of brown bark the size of fingernails. He could suffocate himself in that sweater, fade away in this fourteenth year of life, and be content.

And it was all so innocent, right? No question. Tilley made a conscious note to correct himself.

Stepping away from the woodstove, an immediate chill replaced the blaze that had likely splotched the skin on Tilley's back. Instead of rushing, he calculated the steps between David and himself carefully. Then, he unlocked his nervous jaw to let his innermost feelings slide out into the room. Be loose, he told himself, don't consider too long. But after he had spoken, he was shocked to hear what another part of his mind, a veiled and devious part, was really thinking.

"Me fadder told me yer sick in the head."

Somehow it had managed to escape before a hand clamped over his mouth.

While Tilley feared the sting of those words, David seemed unfazed. He leaned closer to the canvas that was just beyond Tilley's view. In his hand, David held a wide paintbrush laden with a thick glob of sparkling black paint. He closed his eyes and swiped randomly, slashing his work with exaggerated swooping motions, dancing about infinity. Opening his eyes, he looked satisfied with the destruction, and considered that after the fresh strokes dried, he might once again start to re-paint, re-create, layer upon layer until his original intention was entirely masked, hidden from the prying glances of any observers. That was his great secret. He had to smile inside. No one had ever really seen his one true painting. Repeated on every canvas. His precise vision laden with frozen intention.

He swivelled on his stool, finally faced Tilley in order to respond to him. The same idea he had so frequently asked of himself. And even though he was light-headed, he did not waver, and said simply, "Did you ever consider that your father is right?"

꩜

The following afternoon, Maureen tromped over to Flossie Grimes'. She didn't rap on the back door, but let herself in. People seldom ever knocked in Cupboard Cove. Why would they? It would only bother the owner, force them to abandon their task, trudge out through the porch, and open an unlocked door. Surely callers in good health were able to lift the latch and let themselves in on their own. The only exception arose with a set of frozen fingers. This happened on occasion during the winter months when children roamed too far away with soggy mittens or when temperatures dropped while husbands hauled logs from the woods. Though, when Maureen considered it, this was never a knock, but the side of a boot striking the door, often accompanied by either whimpering or cussing.

Maureen blew into the porch. She could see the outline of Flossie standing before the woodstove stirring a polished silver pot. Maureen's glasses fogged with the steam of baking bread and cooked fish, but she did not remove them. Instead, she slid her feet from her boots, trod into the kitchen by tilting her head, peering straight out underneath her thick rims.

"Come in, me dear," Flossie said with her crinkled voice. "Won't be anudder minute with me chowder here. Warmin' the cream through." She leaned her fat body over the pot, took several sniffs. "'Tis goin' to be some lovely. Got to watch it like a hawk though. Don't want it boilin', now. Cuppa tea?"

Maureen sat on a spongy chair at the kitchen table, the wood laminate surface gleaming. "Ye knows I would Missus Grimes. Just got somet'ing on me tongue to ask ye, is all, and if I drinks it down on a drop of tea, I 'llows I'll never get 'round to it."

Flossie continued her methodical stirring, knuckles on her hand the size of quarters. "Go on then, maid. Have yer say."

"The house." Maureen stammered slightly, cleared her throat. "Me house. Earl's house. Can ye tell me who was livin' there 'fore we bought it up?"

"Me lard." Flossie stiffened. Carefully, she balanced her wooden spoon on its rest and placed a cover over the pot. Clasping the delicate gold cross that dangled on the chain around her neck, she turned away from the stove and said, "No, me dear. No one for years. Not a single soul. Sure, ye knows that."

"But before that. When 'twas built."

Flossie slid the cross back and forth, grating at the gold. She was about to speak, but an angry shishing sound cut her words short. Boiling cream sputtered and tumbled out from underneath the lid, coursed down over the sides of the pot, and blackened immediately on the stovetop. Smoke began to rise, and Flossie grasped cup-towels with rickety fingers. Jolting up from her chair, Maureen tugged the towels from Flossie, unstuck the pot, and slid it over to a cooler area of the stove.

Flossie's face fell flat, defeat weighting her jowls. "Ah. Me chowder is spoilt."

"'Twill be fine, Missus Grimes." Maureen managed a smile. "Smelled grand when I walked in."

"No, 'tis spoilt." Her hands were folded over her heart. "Cream curdles when it boils."

And now it was Maureen's turn to sink down inside. She chastised herself. Foolishness was all. Being a nuisance to an old woman, and Christmas just a stone's throw away. She should be ashamed of herself, and thankful that whoever did build the house took such care in the construction. Their home had withstood decades of battering from salty winds on the outside, and almost as long with quarrelling and sickening appeasement on the inside. Instead of questioning, Maureen should be grateful the whole structure hasn't simply disintegrated, crumbled around them.

"I's right sorry, Missus Grimes," Maureen said on her way to the porch. "'Twasn't me intention to ruin yer dinner."

Flossie shook her head, turkey neck quivering. "No maid. 'Twas me own fault. When somet'ings on the verge or trouble's afoot, ye should never cast a blind eye. Then ye takes a hand in it, whatever comes 'bout. Ye sees?"

"Yes, Missus Grimes." Maureen nodded, but as she slipped back into still-slushy boot, she couldn't help but wonder if Flossie was talking about something else besides curdled chowder.

Then, when her hand was reaching for the door, she heard, "Maureen?"

"Yes, Missus Grimes?"

"Ah. 'Twas a young couple," Flossie said. "Yes, a young couple. Never knowed them much. I minds they saw good fortune. Seemed to settle down, then carried on to St. John's when they came into a bit of money. No one with either dollar was apt to stay. Too much struggle here. 'Twas the way it went."

"Thank you, Missus Grimes."

Out into the snow, Maureen trudged across the property line and stopped for a moment to admire the spruce trees. Their boughs drooped, as though they were laden down with sweet mounds of double-boiler frosting. Her stomach growled. Shortly, she would have to make a breakfast for Earl, and she'd take a light lunch herself. A cheese slice and a few crackers.

Maureen swallowed the saliva welling up around her tongue, then considered Flossie's chowder and her parting words. *Never knowed them much?* The phrase skipped around inside Maureen's mind. Had Flossie forgotten? Earl had paid her for the home. Flossie did the selling, banked the money, even though she claimed it was in trust for the owners. *How could she hardly have known the young couple, if they permitted that transaction?* More questions.

Maureen pursed her lips, tightened her grip on the neck of her coat. She would not ask about the house again. Some things people are just not meant to know, it's not their business. *Best to let sleeping dogs lie*, she thought. *Lest you get a nip*. No, she would leave it be. Not utter another word. Even though, and perhaps mostly because, Flossie Grimes was lying.

seventeen

On the way to their brand new home, built strong and snug by Harvey Boone's own hands, they passed the old cemetery. Lush shrubbery lined the roads. The heavenly fragrance of lilacs and honeysuckle draped the air like a damp cloak. Though clouds had consumed the sky the headstones seemed to come alive and radiate in the darkness. Hazel encircled Harvey's waist with her slender arm and guided him through a gap in the layered shale fence.

He held back, said, "'Tis not right, Hazel. Traipsin' 'round here this time of night. On this special day."

She turned to face him, her skin and wedding dress appearing grey and speckled, and beckoned him with a saucy smirk and curling gloved fingertips. Slowly, she stepped backwards, the heels of her good shoes sinking into the soft grass. And as quickly as that, she vanished into overlapping shadows.

Only a penetrating laugh and her whispering voice remained. "Don't tell me I's gone and married an old fuddy-duddy."

Blindly, he rushed into obscurity, only to feel a reaching set of fervent hands clutch his best shirt. She tugged him into the bushes, he tripped on knotty roots, and his face pressed so hard into her hair, he detected the smell of rust in her hairpins. But still, he was relieved to be beside her.

Then at once, his body was missing her again. She had released her hold and was darting out among a stretch of older graves, longish grass and soft earth soiling the bottom of her dress. Now, cat and mouse through disintegrating tombstones, an angel with a missing hand, cherubs rained away. Wild pursuit, he shifted this way, that, only to reach the very stone where she was hiding, and hear her giggle just beyond.

Above, two bulky clouds parted, allowing the moon to beam down and cast an eerie clarity over the grounds. Hazel's gown reflected the light, making it difficult to conceal herself, and she hastened towards a growth of variegated dogwoods. Harvey watched her gather her skirt into a pile. She was strong on her feet, like a wilful ghost. And, of course, he followed her, his excited heart beating up in his ears, smooth soles of his church shoes skidding on patches of wet grass.

Through the spindly branches, he saw the dress first. Emerging on the other side of the dogwoods into a newer section of the cemetery, he discovered her standing by the side of the open grave he had helped to dig a day earlier. Like a cavernous black mouth, it appeared ready to consume Hazel without a second thought. Tips of her toes were taunting the very lip, and he flung his arms around her waist, tried to yank her away.

"Me Lard, missus," he said, gasping. "Ye could tip right over. Lose yerself."

She twittered, defiant, and swirled inside his band of arms to face him. Her cheeks were on fire. Skin, nearly translucent. Harvey imagined he could see her very blood coursing through her veins. He plucked away a few strands of hair that had escaped from their constraints, blown across her eyes, and clung to her panting mouth. Dropping his hand to his sides, he stopped his touching. For a moment, he just wanted to stare. The mere sight of her, alive and lovely under the melancholy moon, made him tingle with anticipation. Like bee stings across his torso. Consuming love, to the point of pain.

"C'mon," she said, turning again, dropping onto her backside and letting her feet dangle into the pit. "Let's get in."

Harvey only stepped back inside his mind this time. "Don't be actin' crazy, now Hazel. Isn't ye lookin' forward to seein' yer new home?"

"That can wait," she said firmly. "Now, help me in, or else I's goin' to break me ankle goin' down. And what a story that'll make for yer dear sister."

Harvey sputtered with displeasure, but crawled down over the side, and sprung backwards onto the floor. He half expected to feel a wooden box under his feet, and sighed with the thump of solid clay, the shock to his shins. As he helped Hazel ease into the blackness, his rough face skimmed over her smooth dress, passing her calves, her thighs, the roundness of her bottom. Each button up her spine delightfully stubbed his cheekbone. Cradling her against the wall, every inch of her was soft, yielding, and now she fully belonged to him.

"'Tis cool," she murmured in his ear as she ran her hands over the inside of the grave. "'Tis no cooler place on a hot summery night, ye knows."

The comment was lost. Harvey never wondered if Hazel had been deep in the earth on previous occasions as he was too busy admiring her neck, the perfect V of her jawbone when she tilted her head, exposed her throat. He put his mouth there, sucked gently, right on the tip of her chin.

"Yer dress?" he mumbled. "The muck."

"Never mind me dress, Harvey Boone. 'Tis not like I's ever

goin' to wear the t'ing again." She had made her choice today. In front of everyone.

He laughed abruptly, though the sound of it was distant, foreign to his own ears, like a man lost out on the ice, hungry for home cooking. Lying down on the chilly mud floor, Hazel straddled him. He slid his sweating hands over her hips, but she reached to remove them, and folded them neatly across his chest.

"Don't squirm," she hissed as she fiddled with her dress, his trousers.

Moonlight hit the grave at a sharp angle, creating a line down the centre of Hazel's face. It was so much like a dream, the muffled hums, the pleasant scent of ancient earth, and the sensation that those from beyond were peering down. In her simple off-white gown, Hazel glowed, and swathed half of his body in a luminous heaven, half in untouchable night.

Afterwards, Harvey laid still. His eyes refused to blink as they watched cloud after cloud scuttle across the dimpled face of the moon. There was not a breath of wind that evening and he could not help but wonder what force of nature was behind it all.

"'Tis a blue moon," Harvey said joyously as they strolled out onto the gravel road.

"Blue moon?" Hazel did not look up.

"Yes, 'tis a rare t'ing. Two fat, full moons in a single month. Second one they calls a blue moon."

"Now who's they?"

"Oh, science people, I figures. People with smarts."

"I never knowed," Hazel said.

"Don't ye worry none, me dearie. I's goin' to learn ye lots of that stuff." He nodded, caught Hazel's swinging hand. "Let's go on home now, maid. 'Tis an awful hour."

Harvey was excited for her to see the results of his efforts. For months, he had sweated and toiled with the help of his brother-in-law, Neil Grimes. Tonight, he was bursting with pride over the solid respectable saltbox home he had created with his own two hands. She would be satisfied there, he was certain. Even though his sister, Flo, claimed Hazel was the sort who would never be satisfied.

"Mark me words," Flo had said to him only hours earlier at the wedding dinner. "Ye could build a house to the high heavens and t'wouldn't suit her."

"Home," Hazel replied. "Yes. Home. 'Tis just as well."

Picking up the pace, they moved through the still night, arm in arm, together. Everything would be fine, Harvey told himself. He just had to care for her enough. Give her only good love. Wrap her up in all the compassion he had to offer, and gradually she would become the wife he always wanted, the mother of a swarm of adorable children. As the swirling notion of it gained momentum inside his mind, he trembled with delight.

But how that trembling confused his senses, coated his nerves in a thick numbing plastic. For, if his floating feet had any contact whatsoever with the gravel road beneath him, he just might have caught the absolute flatness in the voice of his new bride.

eighteen

Maureen was running late. At the very last minute, she decided to mix a batch of oatmeal raisin bread, and before leaving, she wanted to have the dough kneaded thoroughly, plastic container sealed, everything wrapped and ready in a thick blanket beside the stove. Then, by the time she arrived home after her visit with Hazel Boone, the dough would be pressing against the lid, threatening a yeasty explosion.

With her arms deep into the Tupperware container, she bore down on the bread, shifted with a twist of her elbows, and bore down again. The sweetness of oats, melted butter, cinnamon, a pinch of cloves rose up around her, and filled her with a sense of wistfulness. Spices, when mixed with other Christmas fragrances, always pinched her slightly, revived dozing memories. She inhaled deeply. Funny how her mother came back to her through her nose. Never a concrete image to accompany this vague awareness, just a consciousness, an impression of belonging, of love.

A shrill ring from the phone interrupted her reflection, and she stared at it as though the olive green box were somehow animate and living out its years on her wall. If Earl hadn't been sleeping in the next room after his night at the fish plant, she would have let it ring. "Isn't it always the way," she murmured as she withdrew her hands from the dough, and went to answer it.

But when she plucked the receiver with her great floury mitt, she met with near silence. Only a muffled sound, as though someone on the opposite end were sliding a sweaty palm over the mouthpiece. Maureen replaced the receiver, gave it an angry glare, wishing now that it would speak, offer some insight.

As soon as she turned to continue with her kneading, it rang again. Swiftly this time, she scooped the receiver from its cradle, squashed it against her ear.

"Hello?" she said, imploring an answer. Nothing. "Who's this? Who callin' here?"

Maureen listened hard. Still nothing. But just before the person on the other end slammed down their phone, Maureen thought she heard the thin squeal of a young child, followed by an incensed foot stomping once, twice. She gently returned the receiver to its bed again, determined to ignore future ringing, whether it woke Earl or not. Only now, it sat there, prim and soundless.

Using the blade of a sharp knife, Maureen scraped excess dough from her palms, from between her fingers. She liked that sensation, the practised glide of the knife. Rapidly, she worked it into the leftovers, swaddled the covered container in an old wedding-band quilt, and plopped it down into her rocker. She drew the rocker close to the woodstove, making sure it did not sway on its own. An empty rocker rocking could only bring the worst kind of luck.

On her way out, she glanced back at the telephone. Bits of dough, floury fingerprints, still clung to the thin body of the receiver. She never stopped to clean it.

Hours later, when she arrived home, the phone was clean. She found Earl still tucked into their bed, snoring like a baby with a belly full of milk. His face leaned towards the door, and across his forehead, fuzzy caterpillars' stitches crawled left and right. She tiptoed in closer and sighed quietly. *Why was she not surprised to see a suspicious dusting of flour coating his right ear, specks of dough snagged in his stubble?*

❧

Young Hazel was in her mother's kitchen. Rows and rows of sea green glass jars with painted metal lids were lined on the wooden table. She scanned them all, contemplating which one to twist off first. Up on the tips of her toes, she started tapping each lid, reciting 'farmer, farmer, shave a pig.' Oh, what a treat, to have discovered so many hiding places.

In the first four jars, she found flour and sugar, loose tea and cherry jujubes. She delved deep into the candy jar, and jammed a handful into her mouth; she chomped heartily. The next jar contained sealed envelopes, her maiden name inked in manly script across the fronts. She tore open one, then another, and another. All were filled with crisp white paper, sharply creased in neat squares, but bearing not a single word. Frustration bubbled just beneath her skin, as she was certain text lined those papers, though she didn't know how to unveil the disguise. She dropped the letters to the pine flooring and grasped another lid. Peering into the jar, she found a seething mess of carpenters, that sort of wood lice with steely armoured bodies. As she stared, they balled like porcupines in danger, and dropped to the bottom of the jar. She did not recoil, but quickly lifted the next lid, and then the next, tossing each one aside with a tinny clatter. The remaining were empty, and she pouted and flounced onto the floor, her cotton skirt poofing with air then settling around her. Even distressed carpenters were better than nothing at all.

Then, just off in the distance, she heard a thin scraping sound, as though somewhere a man was scouring loose flakes of paint off the underside of an upturned skiff. Her heart leapt inside her blouse. She knew who it was, and rose to her feet. Her whole body missed him, as one piece of a two-piece puzzle might miss its match. *It would, wouldn't it?* And now he was labouring, perspiring in her very backyard.

She rushed out onto the splintery stoop, but fog blinded her. So thick and cottony, it was as though dozens of damp feather dusters were slapping her face. She grew unstable inside the clammy mist and crouched down to feel the heels of her shoes. To her surprise, they were worn heavily on the outsides, twisted, or as her mother would have said, "*squoiled.*" Hands groping, and she unexpectedly felt the slippery thin bodies of caplin surrounding her feet, washing in over the stoop in living waves. The caplin were seething in their own warm spawn, and she sensed them moving up over her shoes, to her ankles. She could barely see it, but the spawn felt like thinned overcooked cornmeal. It would not stop, and she stood, tried to balance on her rickety shoes. Rising reliably, it climbed past her calf to her knees, tickling her while spoiling her stockings. She would drown unless she could move. Surely, she would. Why did the scraping continue? Like a steady hacking. Behind her now. Or to the side. Oh. She was lost. Completely lost. And so undeniably stuck.

Hazel bolted upright in the bed. There she was, safe inside the plain box of a room Harvey had built. Sweat coated her forehead and she struggled to unpin the covers that were binding her legs. Harvey had let her sleep in again, and had tucked the sheets beneath the mattress as though she were two, maybe three years old, and in danger of rolling out.

When she went to the window, she met a fine bright day, and noticed Flo Grimes, her reliable sister-in-law, already hard at work in the garden they shared. Hoe in hand, scrap of polka-dotted material tied over her hair, Flo chopped at the dirt and trenched up the flowering potato plants. Ah. The scraping sounds in her lucid dreaming. Hazel quickly hauled her dress down over her shoulders, twisted and pinned her hair, ignored tea pot and cozy on the kitchen table, and darted out the door. Flo Grimes would not get the best of her.

Not knowing how to use a hoe, Hazel began working with a handheld shovel. Easing along each row, she scooped dirt up and underneath the plants and patted it down. The soil in their garden being more stones than earth, her shovel often struck rocks and Hazel worked to release them. When she glanced up, which was infrequently, she found Flo staring at her, clucking her tongue ever so quietly. Hazel felt exposed, and the more times she caught Flo's glassy stare, the more she wondered if somehow her wicked dream was hovering in the humid air just above her head.

"'Twas some grand this mornin'," Flo finally said as she and Hazel shared the work along a row. "Expects Neil and Harvey back any time now."

"Harvey never woke me," Hazel said in her own defence.

"Neil don't have to wake me. I knows me place. And though 'tis lovely here, can be bitter out on the water. The sea castin' itself over top of ye. Wouldn't t'ink of sendin' someone I loves out with nar bite in their bellies. No, maid." Flo snapped her mouth shut, hoed double-time.

Though she didn't care for Flo's pointed method of delivery, Hazel thought she should support the message, and replied, "Yes, Flo. I reckons yer right. 'Tis not good enough on me part. Just I can't seem to get enough rest these past weeks. Tired to the bone."

Flo's hands stopped and her eyes settled on Hazel with a strange intensity. She let the hoe drop into the trench. And stepping over the potatoes, she took Hazel's hands in her own, examined the mud-caked puffy fingers, and said, "Well, now. I'll be. Not married two months, and ye got yerself underway. Ye don't get swoll out like that from eatin' too much salt fish."

As Hazel held her hands out to examine them, Flo turned swiftly and marched past the potatoes, leafy carrot tops, and the row of cabbage heads. Coursing straight through the pea plants, she scolded them softly as they tried to snare her dress, her wrists with their tendrils. It just didn't seem fair. Where was the balance in this? Friday night after Friday night, faithfully for six years, Flo and Neil had tried. And still the good Lord had brought them nothing.

Considering what was now 'underway', as Flo Grimes had so aptly put it, Hazel wondered how she should present herself to the world. *Should she adopt a position of constant elation over her state, or maintain demure poise?* Surely, she couldn't brood. Expectant mothers never brooded.

Hazel sighed and twisted the snug wedding band around her swollen finger. At that moment, it was all too much for her to bear, but she would have to decide on some reaction soon. Harvey would be arriving home and Flo would waste little time in announcing her tidbit of news. That would be just like Flo. That woman wasted little time, regardless of what she was doing. *What a shame that was*, Hazel thought. *How could someone be so oblivious to the benefits of the occasional diversion? The sporadic delusion?*

As Hazel pondered appropriate facial expressions, a fat brown spider crawled among the potato stalks and crept over the dirt towards her. Underneath its bulbous abdomen, it carted a perfectly round, dimpled, white egg sac. Using her shovel, she knocked the egg sac aside, and watched as the spider frantically retrieved it. She repeated this again and again. Instincts had always fascinated her. But when the reaction was no longer of interest, Hazel lifted the shovel a few inches above the pebbly soil, and with tremendous precision, slashed a permanent metal wall between the spider and its multitude of babies. Motionless, the spider seemed to be waiting for some clue, some direction. Hazel decided not to offer it. Instead she stood, paused for a moment to feel blood rush down through her cramped legs and then walked away, leaving the dusty shovel stuck firmly in the earth.

nineteen

*T*illey could not remember the exact winter that Christmas Eve skating became a tradition in Cupboard Cove. Maybe eight years ago? Maybe ten? Before that, mummering was the standard event for the evening. After darkness sucked in around the homes, men would don homely dresses and wigs, masks and mittens, rubber boots and Sunday hats. Banging on doors, bowling into kitchens, they would sing and cajole, dance a jig, and drink a pint. Oh, it was all in good fun until a swarthy pair swarmed into Widow Johnson's house, and while one twirled her around her kitchen, the other stole the sizeable turkey and fixings right out of her fridge, and can of cranberry jelly from a shelf in her cupboard. Everyone claimed the two came over from the Gut, but there wasn't a shred of any proof. Some even said Widow Johnson made the whole business up to save a few dollars on a holiday dinner. Nevertheless, Constable Johnson missed his mother's cooking that year so fiercely, he made it known that anyone seen dressed like a fool during any future Christmas season would be promptly arrested and handcuffed to his police car.

So now, every Christmas Eve, several men broke a path along Wrinkle's Rub Trail and carting shovels up to Long John Pond, they spent the morning scraping away the foot or so of snow that covered the frozen water. Early afternoon, children would arrive to putter around the lake, squealing as they passed over sections where gusts had rippled the surface of the ice. Then, after dinner, a young crowd would gather, light a fire on the bank, skate, smoke, and drink until midnight.

Tilley had been in the afternoon group until he was twelve, so this was only his second winter skating during the evening. Already the ice was slashed and pricked from the mess of hockey and figure skates, and Tilley tied his zebra-striped laces with flying fingers. As he looped the bow, Boyd stomped up behind him, dressed in a thin leather jacket, slick jeans, his long arm dangling over Teena's well-padded shoulder.

"Hey, dickwad," he hollered, though Tilley was only a breath away. "Where's yer girlfriend?"

"What girlfriend," Tilley said without twisting around.

"The one with the fat tits. Walter, of course. Who else did ye t'ink?"

"Yer some funny, Boyd."

Tilley felt the slap of a wineskin against the back of his head, heard it plop down.

"Have yerself a drink," Boyd said. "'Tis a night for celebratin'."

"What's to celebrate?" Tilley asked as he turned and plucked the pouch of sloshing liquid from the snow. The suede was warm. Boyd must have had it tucked inside his jacket.

"Never ye mind, ye nosy little bugger." Boyd kicked a damp clump of snow onto Tilley's knitted hat. "Yer worse than

Mudder, wantin' to know everyt'ing. Go on now, have a swally for a bit of good cheer."

"Nah. I don't touch that stuff."

"Go on, I said." Jaw clenched.

Tilley unscrewed the cap, squeezed the pouch gently and fumes of alcohol flowed out into his eyes. He held the spout to his mouth, just about to wet his lips when he heard Boyd howl, "Let's get him, b'ys." Tilley was pinned beneath a blur reeking of wet leather and cigarettes. Boyd then sat astride his chest, clutched Tilley's head with his knees. Straining inside his snowsuit, Tilley couldn't help but wonder how he looked. His mother had sewn up those previous rips with an unfortunate choice of violet thread.

He squirmed, but could not budge an inch, and wondered if this was to be a winter of constriction. Prying his mouth wide, Boyd shoved the neck of the wineskin down Tilley's throat and squashed it. Either swallow or inhale, those were the choices, and Tilley's throat gasped only once, then opened up, allowed the burning liquid to surge onward.

"'Tis jungle juice," Boyd said with a proud snicker as he stood, stepped away from Tilley.

Tilley sprung to a sitting position and shook himself with a shock that radiated out from his searing guts. "Not Fadder's," he said as he choked, coughed hot droplets of the potent mixture from his lungs.

"Yes, 'tis. Ah, the ol' geezer won't miss an ounce."

"I 'llows he'll skin ye if he finds out."

"Skin us, ye means." Boyd laughed, slapped his thigh with a bare hand. "Don't go bein' sick, now, me son. That was quality stuff." Then, nudging Tilley with his boot, nodding towards the ice, he said, "Get on out there. Ye got a gutful of liquid courage and ye can find yerself a little kitten. No bigger than a doll ye is, me son, and girls loves dolls. Don't they Teena? B'y, ye got that angle right cornered." Boyd scratched his groin, then harvested a flaccid cigarette from behind his reddened ear. "Christ, by the time I was yer age, I'd be walkin' down the street and the noise'd be right deafenin'. Pussies snap snappin' for me. Snappin' hither and yon. East and west. Callin' out to me. Boyd. Boyd over here. Boyd!" His cigarette clamped in his teeth, he ran one hand over Teena's blubbery rump as he flicked his lighter with the other. "But, I's blind to it all, now. Right blind. Deaf, I means. Gone right deaf. Ain't that the truth, baby duckling?"

Before words could emerge from her scowling lips, Boyd yanked Teena's free hand, and her face lurched forward, rammed into the can of Pepsi she was slurping. Icy cola shot up her nose and she cursed, hurled her can into the snow. When she slapped the back of Boyd's head, Boyd's gallery of friends snorted and guffawed, then throttled the tapered necks on their own wineskins.

As Tilley watched Boyd tug at Teena, grope her backside, and then reach up to tug a strand of her brittle hair, something very simple occurred to him. His older brother had never learned how to touch. Boyd's hands were incapable of being gentle; it was always a jab or a punch, a kick or a smack. Often pure aggressiveness was the root cause. Though to be fair, sometimes Boyd would strike out, clout Tilley over the head or between the shoulders with the utmost of brotherly affection. Just now, Tilley understood that Boyd had knocked him down and pumped him full of whiskey-screech-vodka-rum mix not because he was angry, but because he was excited, and wanted Tilley to share that excitement. Either way, Boyd Gover had a difficult time controlling himself.

The more Tilley thought about Boyd, the more impressive his appraisal seemed. After about twenty stunned minutes of being parked in the snow, Tilley suddenly considered himself downright brilliant, and a sense of pride welled up inside his small body. *How could he not have noticed Boyd's significant flaw earlier?*

Could it be repaired? Were touching lessons available some-where? A therapist? St. John's? Fly Boyd straight into Halifax? Toronto, even? Maybe if Tilley reached out on his own, tried to hug Boyd more often, shook his hand firmly every morning before breakfast, he could start Boyd on a whole new path. Anything was possible. People could change. They really could.

Tilley swayed slightly, and found it hard to suppress a con-tinual giggle weaving in and out of his ribs. *I want to feel like this forever!* he decided as he forgot loops and bows, instead wrestled his black and white laces into a length of overlapping knots. As his thumbs and forefingers tangoed above his skates, Tilley had another revelation. This time about himself. Like a wisp, it was almost too thin to grasp, but in that moment, it made perfect sense. He was exactly like those laces. Two complimentary strands of thread woven into a pattern, distinct, yet all contained within a single functional package. Before this, he had not realised that he was a striped shoelace. But now that his two halves had melted together, everything he saw was crisper, and sounds pinged onto his eardrums with razor blade sharpness. Never had he been more alert, confident. The journey hadn't been pleasant, of course, but the destination was so sweet. And if this was the meaning of tipsy, Tilley thought, he could comfortably reside inside a tipsy body evermore without a single complaint.

Rushing air made Tilley's eyelashes flutter, and when he glanced up, he saw Marnie Boone glide by on pristine skates, her body positioned in a stout 'T'. He was almost pulled onto the ice and wondered when had Marnie become magnetic, in what moment had he been transformed into metal. He swallowed down mouthfuls of cool air, stood up, marvelled how he felt so lofty, limber, like that shoelace. He was an Irish wolfhound trapped in the carcass of a lap dog.

"Jeesh. What a show-off."

Walter's voice behind him, gum cracking like miniature fireworks.

"Knows what she's at, is all," Tilley replied. What sort of things did Walter appreciate? Not much, that's for certain. He was the kid in first grade that adored the taste of Elmer's glue; the one who made and wore metallic necklaces from carefully folded Juicy Fruit wrappers.

"Don't get defensive, b'y. I was just sayin'."

"I's not defensive."

"Ye was too. Ye likes her, I can tell."

"Ye don't know nothin'."

"Shit, Tilley. I's s'posed to be yer best friend."

"Look. I don't like her, alright? In fact, I t'inks she's a stuck-up priss."

"Well, just don't let Ida know. She got her exercise books all marked up with yer name. She's liable to rip that one's face right off."

"Like I said to ye," Tilley said as he reeled out onto the ice, scrambled after Marnie. "I-Don't-Like-Her."

Striding side to side, cutting in and out of other skaters, Tilley fancied himself a professional hockey player performing for the crowd. Bent low against the wind, he traced his exact path with his eyes, and his skilled feet followed through. When he passed on the inside of Ida, she lunged towards him, tried to clasp his hand.

"Take me 'round," she cried, her feet managing unsteady baby steps. "Stop, b'y. Stay where yer at. Take me 'round." Her direction was in constant flux as other skaters knocked her this way and that.

"Can't," Tilley yelled over his shoulder. "Too busy."

Ida flumped down in the middle of the ice, pouted.

When Tilley whirled past her again, he felt brazen, and

slowed to say, "If ye don't move yer stodgy arse, Fried-Egg Ida, someone'll slice yer fingers right clear."

"Shut-up, ye smart-ass," she wailed, stuck out her chest. "More than bloody yolks here, me son. Wouldn't ye love to know?"

As Ida started bear walking off the ice, Butchie Appleby jammed her thick fingers into her mouth, emitted a piercing whistle. It was time. With the power of a bulldozer locked in her meaty thighs, no one could match Butchie's strength for cracking the whip. Not breaking a sweat, she could haul dozens of people around the ice, thousands of pounds coasting with her momentum.

Everyone loved Butchie in the wintertime. People liked her well enough in the summertime too as she was always cheerful, but no one would chance getting close to her. Penny Payne once said, "That girl reeks so bad, couldn't be worse 'less her bowels were strung on her hip." While Boyd thought she should get friendly with a bar of soap, Maureen suggested there was some sort of illness inside her, rotting from the inside out. Whatever the explanation, it changed nothing, she still smelled like a compost heap. But in wintertime, with sub-zero temperatures and layers of clothes, the hot gusty days of July were forgotten. Besides, she cracked a mean whip.

"Hop to," Butchie hollered. In the air, she waved a pair of navy mittens with bright white anchors on the back. "Hop to, fellers. Train's a' leavin'."

One by one the links in the chain were formed, Arnold Harrison clutching Butchie's hips, Randy Bund grabbing Arnold, Anita Stevenson holding Randy. Marnie was midway down the chain, and near the end, Tilley managed to catch hold of Walter. For several moments, Ida looped wildly at the lethal tip of the whip, but when Butchie veered mercilessly to the left, Ida spun off, landed headfirst in a snow bank.

With sheer exhilaration from the speed, there was a flourish of wild squealing. Bitter winds lashed Tilley's face, tears coursed down over his rosy cheeks, and his nose maintained a perpetual drip. Even though the tips of his fingers dug deep into Walter's hips, holding on for dear life, with a second sudden crack of Butchie's whip, Tilley broke loose. He sliced across the ice at lightening speed, hurtled into a clump of spruce trees. Rolling over onto his back, he was dizzy and elated, and as he continued spinning inside the stillness of his snowy crib, waves of nausea pressed him flat.

Keep your eyes open. Better that way.

Beside his head, two-by-fours had been nailed onto a spruce tree in the fashion of a rudimentary ladder. Tilley glanced up the length of the trunk, but the ladder led nowhere, not to a lookout, not to a tree fort. Perhaps it was a project, started zealously, but abandoned begrudgingly.

Between two of the rungs, someone had carved shapes—a pencil thin penis with a bulbous tip aimed at an appendage-less torso, absent of gender minus two half-moons scratched out near the top. Tilley raised a hand to his mouth, bit down on his mitten and pulled. With a bare index finger, he mindlessly traced the lines sculpted into the wood.

"Working on some new artwork?"

Tilley heard a promising crunch of snow beside him, and there was Marnie, breath rising over her like steam off hot bread.

"No. Not me," he said as he thrust his hand back into his damp mitten. He was woozy, but sat up, leaned his back against the spruce. "'Twas there all along. That's the truth. I could tell, see. Wood's all dried up 'round it." He was talking too much. Slurring slightly.

"I was only joking." She nudged him.

He nudged back. "Yeah, me too."

"No you weren't."

"That I was, then."

"You were not."

"Yes I was too."

"Yes you were."

"No I wasn't."

"Ha," she said. "Gotcha."

Got me indeed, he thought, his eyelids drooped. His mind raced through a dozen possibilities for banter, trying to capture one that was witty, insightful, intelligent. Nothing came, just fleeting memories of a lobster boil, his father scraping steam from the kitchen window with the side of his fist, an unholy yowl, Clipper scampering, a blur of bright mottled green attached to his tail, snickers from Boyd as he tossed two wooden claw pegs into the stainless steel sink. *Would she want to hear about that?*

"You're cute," Marnie said.

Tilley pretended to be disgusted. "'Cute', she says. 'Cute!'" Then he pounded his chest with his mittens, specks of melted snow flying up onto his chin. After a fit of coughing, he said, "Just ye wait and see, maid. Watch now, I's goin' to grow to be the biggest, handsomest feller 'round here."

Scooping a liberal handful of snow, Marnie rubbed it over Tilley's face. His hands never lifted as she polished him, and he was smiling so wide that the snow stunned his sensitive teeth.

When her hand dropped away, he said, "I'm goin' to get ye, ye knows."

"Are you?"

"Yes, me dear." Even though Boyd's drink still coursed through his tiny body, he hesitated, could not trust his tongue or his fourteen-year old hands. "But not right now. Later, though."

"I can wait," she said, and she popped up, glided out onto the crowded ice, linked onto the chain that still snapped with Butchie at the helm.

For what seemed like hours, he followed her lithe body as it coursed confidently around the ice. He watched Arnold Harrison trying to encircle her hips with his arms, paw at her, but she joggled away, increased her speed until her legs were humming-bird wings. *Oh God, she was amazing.*

Visually satiated, Tilley slid down against the spruce, revisit-ed their conversation, and tried to capture her tone. *Was she being saucy with him?* If yes, and how he hoped it was yes, he didn't mind in the least.

❦

"Come see what I made for ye for Christmas," Harvey Boone said to a rapidly ripening Hazel. "And yer birthday too."

She laid aside her knitting, folded her hands over the hard lump that was beginning to form underneath her dress, twice the size of what it should be. "What's that, now?"

"Come on, maid. Yer life won't never be the same."

"Well, if that's the case, then I best come have a gander."

In the dimly lit porch stood a thin wooden box that reached the height of Hazel's ribs. The wood was sanded smooth and finishing nails were hammered so precisely, they were hardly visible. The box was divided into three neat compartments, two on one side, one long one on the other.

"I knows ye can buy them, but I thought I'd try me hand at makin' one on me own."

Hazel seized Harvey's shirt collar and shrieked.

"I loves it. I just loves it."

Harvey gripped the icebox, shook it, banged the top section.

"Couldn't be no sturdier. Whatever goes in ain't comin' out 'til ye lets it out. That's for darn sure." He flipped a wooden clasp to open the upper left section. "We's goin' to buy hunks of ice to go in here. I got a handy dandy sign for the window, tellin' what size pieces we needs. Mort Cooper over to the shop says he'll deliver. Whatever we needs."

"Buy ice?"

"Yes, maid. Ye got to buy yer ice."

Hazel ran her hands over the wood. "Well, that's foolishness if I ever heard it."

"Foolishness? But Mort's got to saw them out in winter, lug them back to his barn, pack the chunks in sawdust to keep 'til summer. 'Tis an effort, ye knows."

"Still. Spendin' money on ice that just melts away and don't cost neither cent to make. Seems to me yer spendin' money on nothin'. Pure and simple."

"Well, show me a new way for the icebox to work, and I'll be all ears."

Hazel pouted, while Harvey smirked, shook his head. "Never knowed ye was frugal, maid."

"I ain't," she said.

He smoothed the back of her head, his rough skin snagging her hair. "There's a cost to everyt'ing, me darlin'. No matter what, there's no way 'round it. What ye wants always comes with a cost to it. Some way or anudder, ye got to pay."

"For everyt'ing. Yes. I s'pose." Hazel spoke slowly, deliberately, as though her tongue was shaping the words independently while her mind travelled somewhere else, a secret place where every single one of her wants were organised, labelled. Then, snapping back to the porch, to the icebox, to Harvey, she said, "Come on, now. Show me how it works."

"Alrighty, then." He pointed to the lower left cupboard. "Now ice drips down through there into that tray. Just ye got to mind the run-off. Don't want a watery mess all over yer good floors, right?" He opened the long part, knocked his knuckles on the inside. "Ye store yer few t'ings in there. Metal liner'll help to keep it cool." He looked at Hazel. "I can build ye some shelves or leave it as 'tis. Whatever ye wants, me lovey."

Hazel caressed the ornate silver hinges. She could do this, she told herself, she could be a housewife. Then, she turned to kiss Harvey, running her hands inside his suspenders, up and down his wrinkled shirt. Underneath the cloth, Harvey's ribcage was prickling, blushing with the heat from her palms.

"Oh, 'tis grand," she murmured. "Lovely grand."

As she spoke, gusts of wind drove hard flecks of snow against the porch window, sounding like brittle fingernails rapping against the glass.

"Not much use now," Harvey said, nodding towards the window. "No doubt we got the world's largest ice box right outside that door there. But, when summertime hits, it'll be real handy. Cool drinks and fresh meat. Ye'll see, maid. Real handy.

twenty

Everything was set, the buttercup linen tablecloth, the red and green candles, and her dead mother's white china plates. Christmas Eve dinner would be a late evening affair, but it would be perfect. Annette washed her hands, dried them in the ironed tea towel. She smoothed her ruffled apron, its colour not a perfect match to the tablecloth, but annoyingly close.

Fish on Christmas Eve, David had requested. What sort, she had no idea. So she had gone to Seymour's Salty Shack off Main Road, frowned at the idiotic logo painted on his sign that read: "Sea-more Fish Here!" Inside the shop, she fought back the urge to pinch her nose, instead deliberately pacing her breathing and quickly pointing to the contents of the cleanest looking pail. Lengths of something white and fleshy. "That's some fine fish, Missus," Seymour himself had spoken, an exaggerated and unnecessary wink accompanying his drawl. He probed among the pail with mint green rubber gloves while staring at Annette in a way she could only describe as familiar. She considered turning her face away, but didn't. Then he said, "Ye can't go wrong with these dandies. Right gargeous."

Heavens above! Would she ever get used to outport living?

Inside her sparkling kitchen, she untied the knot in the plastic bag, let the fish ooze into a glass-baking dish, slopped in juices and all. Spreading the Cheese Whiz with a butter knife proved something of a challenge, but in the end, she warmed the bottle, and managed a thick layer over each fillet. A sprinkle of coarse breadcrumbs, dollop of heavy cream, salt and pepper, and Annette stood back, pleased. Cod au gratin, her first attempt. And to think, an original recipe.

She daubed her brow with a clean tissue. Now, something to complement. Biscuits, perhaps.

Rifling through her sparsely filled cupboards, she found no yeast, no baking powder or soda. She withdrew a box of instant pancake mix from the bottom shelf, read the instructions. Yes, plenty of water available, and she decided to improvise. She would pour the mixture into an eight by eight-inch, bake it alongside the fish, and slice it into nine equal pieces. Who would ever know the difference? That, plus two cans of green beans. "Haricots vert," she said aloud. Dim lighting would mask their dreary green, and Mother Boone would appreciate the texture. Annette would let them stew so that chewing was optional, a firm tongue would do the trick.

They would eat together as an ordinary family. It would be pleasant, Annette decided, if it took every ounce of her strength to make it so. But there were so many variables to consider. Her Marnie, who refused to erase or even acknowledge the silly teenage angst clouding her pretty face. "You will never fit in," Annette had informed her, hoping to ease her struggle. "Why bother?" Marnie had responded with a slammed door. All so perfectly trite, Annette could not resist grinning.

Then there was David, the husband she had longed to acquire. He could present his ageing body at the dining room table, but was adept at keeping his softening mind firmly planted on whatever image lay beyond those conservatory windows. Hour upon irksome hour, he lingered in that room. And if he ventured out, it was invariably to fawn over that minuscule mouse of a boy.

Of course, Mother Boone was not to be forgotten. Annette shuddered. Oh, too many loose wires to consider. *What horror would she execute tonight?* During meals, Hazel ground her food, and then let her jaw hang open, much to the dismay of onlookers. More than once had she carried them through a main course singing hymns with her reedy voice, all the while slipping food to an invisible dog that begged incessantly beside her (Annette suggested putting it outside during dinner, but Hazel refused). And once, Hazel had even mistaken the silk-covered dining room chair for a deluxe cushioned toilet seat. Yes, Mother Boone was chock full of nasty surprises.

While the odour of baking fish and flapjacks radiated from the oven, crept into every corner in her home, Annette dashed to her bathroom mirror, added additional pins to her hair, and touched up the powder on her forehead. With a professional smile, she chimed, "Merry Christmas," to herself in her most joyous voice. No matter the angle, the perspective, this was still her life. She may as well look beautiful in it.

Even as a child, he could never wait to open a gift.

So when he heard the buzz of a skidoo, the thump on his stoop, he forced himself to count backwards from fifty, and then ambled to the door. Outside, the night was clear, sky aglitter with stars, but the wind felt vicious, like it would slash if it had the chance.

The hermit picked up the discarded cardboard box, noted the one pair of boot prints in the snow leading up to the stoop and back. He remembered some years ago when there had been two.

Inside, he sat on his daybed next to the woodstove. Embers glowed, casting a festive red light over everything. His miniature home was pristine. People most likely wouldn't expect that. From the outside, his world appeared dishevelled, the wood on his shelter was compromised, much of the ground unattended and overgrown, and the pile of useful things in his yard was on the verge of being labelled junk. But inside, his house was spic and span. No scattering of fish bones or peelings, no mound of soiled clothing, no infestation of diseased mice. His only concession were the spiders, he refused to squish a single one. And so, he had more than his share of gauzy strands, corner webbing.

He also kept himself clean. Every Sunday he trimmed his beard and the band of hair at the base of his skull. Each morning he washed his hands and neck, washed each part once a week in summer, once every two in winter. He knew the importance of taking care of his nails, so many a night he smoothed them down with foot-long metal file he had found in the rubbish outside. Unconventional, yes, but it worked like a charm. The hermit knew he would be that way until he died. In his youth he had never been slovenly. And people don't change.

With a dull knife blade, he broke through the tape, peered into the Christmas box his brother-in-law had brought.

He smelled the fruitcake before he saw it, wrapped in strips of rum-soaked cheesecloth. Alongside, there was a small flask of whiskey. And a new plaid shirt, no two, rolled up next to the flask. He ran his hand along the inside collar, felt that the labels had been neatly cut away, all loose thread snipped and discarded. His sister had included three matching sheer curtains to replace the yellowed ones on his windows that were nearing disintegration. A bag of peppermint knobs. Package of Purity Jam-Jams. Ginger snaps. Beef jerky. And finally, a crinkled parcel, wrapped in blue paper patterned with childlike angels. It contained three pairs of hand knit socks, made from the softest wool he had ever felt. He slipped one on over his hand. They came to a point at the toe. She had knitted them on circular needles. And the socks had not a single seam.

The hermit's eyes moistened. Year after year, she had remembered his childhood peculiarities.

Almost midnight, and Tilley started to climb the driveway to Marnie's house. In his hands, he clasped a weighty glass jar. When he reached her backyard, he would pelt snow against her window—he knew which bedroom was hers—to wake her, then offer up the jar. Not wanting it to seem too much like a gift, he didn't take the time to wrap it.

Even though it was salted, the driveway was still riddled with patches of slick ice. And the mittens he had hauled on as he tiptoed through the porch remained soaked from the evening of skating. So when he skidded slightly halfway up the hill towards her darkened house, the jar easily slipped from his grasp and fell straight down. Through the 'O' formed by two empty hands, he saw shimmering glass, smashed in a thousand shards around his boots. He circled just in time to see what remained of his gift, as it cruised away. A bad joke. The lid from his jar rolled down the hill like a rickety wagon wheel, and two-dozen spongy pickled eggs, shiny white in the moonlight, bounded after it.

Tears sprung to Tilley's eyes and he wiped them away with the back of his mitten. It had seemed like such a good idea when he clawed himself out of dead sleep, left his warm bed, and snuck out of the house. Only the unplugged Christmas tree noted his absence. *Could he have chosen a better gift? Something she loved more than pickled eggs?*

As he loped home, salty crystals forming on his eyelashes, he felt miserable, brain expanding inside his skull. But even though all seemed lost, he had a sneaking suspicion he might be grateful in the morning.

twenty-one

*E*arl considered himself to be quite the trapper. Of six snares, one remained untouched, two were buggered, and three had snagged a respectable catch. He discovered a live rabbit fruitlessly trying to scamper away, foot quivering in the snare, but he made short work of it—with a swift crack of the blunt side of his tomahawk.

As he passed along, Earl stopped to drop a glassy-eyed hare on the greying stoop of the hermit's house. Clipped on either side of his belt, the others dangled like furry cowboy chaps. Certain he was unseen as he continued trudging out of the woods, Earl swayed his hips, relished the feel of the stiff lean bodies when they knocked against his thighs. To the onlooker, it would appear as though their front paws were stretched out before them, and they would leap away if only their captor would untwist the wire binding their furry ankles. But the notion of releasing them never entered Earl's mind.

It was Sunday, and he had skipped church. Sunshine gleamed down through naked trees. Unseasonably balmy temperatures had melted much of the snow. Warm air crept through the underbrush leaving spongy trails, soggy patches of yellow grass in the clearings, and a thick coating of water over the ice that clung stubbornly to the rocky bottom of Push-Along Pond. For a February day, everything was perfect. Surely it would be a sin for a man to waste his only day of relaxation cooped up in an overheated box listening to Reverend Grimes drone on about leading a decent life. Earl figured God would consider it far superior to conduct your business accordingly. Live life rather than merely listen to someone talk about it.

As he reached his backyard, his boots squelching through Maureen's thawing flowerbeds, Earl delved into his front jeans pocket for a much-needed scratch. When his fingers roamed freely, easily relieving the itchiness in his crevices, he realised his hand had a good deal more room than it should. His pocket was empty. Somewhere along his route, traipsing through the brush of spruce trees, he had done the unthinkable. Earl had lost the only thing his father had ever given him. A shiny silver pocket knife.

Bowling past Maureen into the kitchen, Earl untwisted his rabbits, thumped them onto the table, and nearly upset Tilley's bowl of tuna fish casserole.

"C'mon me son," Earl said, snorting. His nostrils had started leaking with the sudden heat of the kitchen. "We's headin' back in."

"To where?" Tilley pulled his casserole lunch closer and made a protective cove with his elbow.

"Can't ye see the b'y is eatin', Earl? He needs his nourishment. He's a——." She was going to say growing boy, but decided against it.

"Give him a pocketful of hard-tack, he can gobble that on the way. I lost me good knife. Me good knife! Can ye believe I'd go and be so stupid?"

Maureen snorted.

"Well, I needs the b'y. He got eyes on him like a hawk."

Maureen had to agree. She said to Tilley, "Fresh air'll do ye good," while filling a paper bag with several perfectly smooth oval-shaped biscuits. "Watch yer teeth on these, me son."

Stepping out through the back door, Earl hollered back to Maureen, "Nar bit of thanks for the fresh meat? What's the world comin' to?"

"'Tis lovely, Earl. I's goin' to skin them while yer out."

"Don't heave out all the feet. Promised Missy I'd save her a lucky one."

"Missy?" Maureen moved out into the porch, spoke through the cool breeze drifting in the screen door.

"Yes, Missy. Penny's girl."

"Where did ye see Missy to?"

"What's with the grand exam here? Yer some kinda legal eagle now? If ye wants to know, 'twas at the gas station. Winse was there fillin' up."

"Oh. Alright, then."

"Yes, 'tis alright is right. Best kind of little girl, she is. Penny's doin' a top rate job." With a jab of his baby finger, Earl checked the status of his zipper. "Now, don't forget that foot."

"Well, I guess I can manage that." Maureen pushed open the screen door and held it while Tilley scuttled underneath her arm. She felt his hair brush along her skin, tickling her.

Squinting with the brilliance of sunlight on glistening snow, Maureen watched Earl skip his heavy frame down over the steps, his bowed legs like broken sticks. Feather-light Tilley followed close behind; the polyester scarf she had knit for him sprawled uselessly over one shoulder. No hat either. She bit her tongue, and didn't say a word.

⚘

"Up the pace a bit, me son," Earl hissed as they rounded the corner of the house.

"Shouldn't we be walkin' that way?" Tilley asked, pointing towards the mouth of the trail leading out from their backyard.

"Nah, thought we'd try a different route. Down along the water."

"But what about yer knife?"

Earl stopped, stared, and burnt holes through Tilley's head. "Don't ever question yer Fadder, me son. I knows right where I lost that knife and I don't need the likes of a little shit like yerself tellin' me how to find it. I thought ye'd be grateful to hike on a different path."

"But I never went with ye this marn-."

"Christ," Earl muttered, cutting Tilley short. "What did I just say? Don't they teach ye nar bit of English at that bloody school?"

Tilley maintained a distance of several yards behind his father, inhibiting conversation or comments about his clumsiness. They walked out the driveway, down the lane, past Vickers farm, and cut over onto the jagged cliffs that lined the harbour. Daringly, Earl slogged along at the edge of the wet navy rocks. Snow never lasted along the sea; salty gales wasted no time in dissolving any settlement, revealing its sharp precipice proudly once again. Tilley cringed with each brash step Earl took, but he knew his father would not slip. He never slipped.

From his position behind his father, Tilley was surprised to notice that he had the gait of an old man. He had always thought of his father as unchanging, sturdy, ageless. Now, his head hung forward on a slightly wrinkly neck like a lazy turtle's would and his sloping shoulders formed the shape of a downward-pointed sickle. Gusts of wind ridiculed his comb-over, snapping it upwards into a rooster's comb, though Tilley did not laugh, did not even smirk.

When Earl stopped to catch his breath at Gone Down Point, Tilley was relieved.

"'Tis grand, don't ye t'ink?" Earl said, indicating two dagger-like rocks rising out of the ocean, waves churning and frothing around them. "Oh yes, sure they's got their Hare's Ears up 'long, and down a ways, but they ain't nothin' compared to these here. Right up, even, and perfect. Ye'd gut yerself if ye run up alongside. More than one skipper crashed his dory, drowned right out there. Oh, yes." Earl puffed out his chest, adjusted his belt. "Used to come out here as a b'y, warm raisin biscuits wrapped in a cloth. Mudder missed them biscuits, I's sure of that, but she never said a single word to me. Used to eat me fill, then gorge meself on blueberries 'til me belly was so fat, ye'd t'ink I was spawny. Lard, I was seeing blue. I minds havin' a rest here, dozin', and those Hare's Ears would wag up and down. Put on a bit of a show, just for me. They's solid stone, I knows that, ye don't need to tell me, but 'twas some grand imaginin'." He smiled, dewy eyes distant.

"I bet 'twas."

"Yer bettin' right, me son. She was some woman, me mudder. And so is yer mudder, ye knows."

"I knows that."

"Used to bring her here too. Talk a bit of poetry to her."

"Poetry? Yer jokin', right?" Tilley laughed.

Earl's face remained stony. "Wipe that dumb face off ye, 'fore ye gets a smack in the gob."

Tilley's smile evaporated.

"Whatd'ye t'ink, yer fadder's a buffoon? He don't know nar t'ing 'tall? We had to learn ourselves poetry in those days, me son. Learn by heart. I even used to add in me own words. Have yer mudder in stitches, cracked right up. I minds when this whole field was covered in dandelions, I says to her:

> I wandered lonely as a cloud
> That floats right high over valleys and hills,
> When all at once I seen a crowd
> A host of yellow piss-the-beds.

Earl had one hand over his heart, as though reciting an anthem. "Or, somet'ing like that, anyways. Women loves that stuff."

"Ye made it up?"

"No, me son. That's right famous."

"'Tis? Well sounds like ye made it up, then."

Earl hawked, spit, then turned, and marched on, following a trail of decayed footprints that led across a field and into the thick woods.

He grumbled, "What do kids know nowadays? A big goddamned nothin'. That's what. A brazen bloody bunch, they is. All day, gawkin' and droolin' at the television, t'inkin' 'bout friggin' girls and how to get a rub through the jeans. No concern for their families. Nar thought on how to better themselves. And all this loveliness right outside the walls of their own houses is forgotten. Flouted. Why, when I was a b'y, ye couldn't drag me in. If 'twas fit, that is. No sir. Wouldn't hear of it. Summertime, I was black as tar, sun and dirt caked onto me in layers. No such t'ing as a shower in them days. Bucket and cloth. Ye don't know what ye got. Ye don't."

A short distance into the woods and two paths joined, so Earl was once again travelling along his original route. He wiped his forehead with his sleeve, threw his cigarette down, and said in wheezing breaths, "Lard Jaysus, I's sweatin' bug juice."

When they reached Push-Along Pond, Earl slowed his pace, bent towards to the ground, scanning this way and that. "Keep yer eyes peeled here," he said. "I's bettin' ye'll find me knife, sure as there's shit in a cat." A moment later, he half-sung, " Well, well, well. Will ye lookie there."

"What? Ye find yer knife?"

"Nope. But luh." Earl waggled his finger towards the lip of the frozen pond. "I passed by here not two hours ago and missed them. Decent set of rubbers. Who'd go and throw away good rubbers?"

Jutting from the cloudy ice were two shiny black boots with rosy tips on the toes and heels.

"Maybe they's ruint."

"Too much money floatin' 'round these days, if ye asks me. Waste has never been more plentiful." Earl clucked his tongue. "Christ, that's some balancin' act," he remarked when he closed in on his find. "Froze in the ice like that. But they ain't new. Soles half worn off."

He grunted and strained. With a sudden release, the boots slipped out of their hold, and Earl held his prize high. Then he frowned, said, "Well, I'll be pissin' in the wind. Ye was right, they's spoilt. Buddy here had his feet wrapped in plastic bags." Then, as his mind caught up with his words, his voice splintered. "Buddy?"

Dropping the boots, Earl plunged backwards and crab-crawled away over twigs and wet clumps of snow. Descending onto his rump, he joggled his hands now, chest heaving, mouth taking audible sucks of air. His face, normally flushed from the drink, was so pale that from a distance, Tilley could identify the craters from Earl's teenage acne.

"See." Earl voice sizzled and popped. "Feet. Goddamned feet. Christ. Christ. Go take a look. Go, will ye. Go."

Tilley sidled in. Sure enough, Earl was right. Sticking out were two bootless feet, wrapped in plastic bags, secured at the ankles with rubber bands. He had seen a dead person before, but only within the confines of a church, a coffin. Never just a pair of dead feet. When he peered down through the watery ice, he could trace the two legs, bent at the knee, dull beige trousers fallen down to reveal a strip of pasty blue skin, long sprigs of anaemic hair. A man. Or else a manly woman. His or her dead feet, and dead legs.

Tilley was cool, composed. Whoever it was had been frozen for a while. Was frozen still, if truth be told, and obviously not in a hurry to go anywhere. "I sees now, Fadder. They's spoilt. Feller won't use bags unless they's leakin'."

"What is we s'posed to do?" Earl whispered.

"I can't hear ye, Fadder."

"I says, what is we s'posed to do. Goddamnit." Snarling.

"How should I know? 'Tis too late to give him mouth to mouth. If ye can find his mouth."

"Ye lousy bastard." Earl got to his feet, his backside a damp dark circle of wetness. "Mockin' me, is that what yer doin'? Gettin' lippier by the day, ye is."

"Sorry Fadder," Tilley said. "'Tis all a bit queer." He took a few steps towards his father, who shook on unsteady limbs. "C'mon. We goes home, calls Constable Johnson. Some of his kind'll come out and crack the poor bugger free."

❧

"Smells wunnerful good, Missus Gover." Constable Johnson hovered in the doorway of the porch. "'Tis rabbit?"

"Just stew." Maureen blushed. "Nothin' to get excited over, really."

"All the same, smells grand." He removed his cap, jammed it into his armpit. "For dinner tonight?"

Each time Constable Johnson opened his mouth to speak, Maureen could hear his dry tongue unlatch from the roof of his mouth. "No, I's goin' to freeze that up in a few batches." She held up the bloody knife that she was using to slice through a slab of partially frozen meat. "Tonight I's tryin' somet'ing new from me cookbook. Got recipes from all over. Havin' a go at somet'ing Japanese, though I reckons they never counted on moose meat being the main ingredient."

"Well, me lard," Constable Johnson said, rubbing the rumbling ball underneath his shirt. "Japanese, hey? Well, I be darned. Yer somet'ing else Missus Gover."

Maureen smiled at the compliment. "There'll be plenty. Stay for a plate?"

"No thanks. Mudder's got a roast chicken on. She'll be right up in arms if either bit of it goes to waste. Ye knows Mudder."

Whistling, Boyd strolled into the kitchen, abruptly switched directions when he saw Constable Johnson.

"Afternoon, Boyd." Official sounding.

"Yeah."

"Keepin' yerself out of trouble, young man?"

"Like always," Boyd said. He knocked Maureen on her arm. "Give me that knife, Mudder."

With eyebrows startled into outer space, Maureen said, "Whatd'ye want me good knife for?"

"Cut up yer moose, me dear. Can't a b'y offer his mudder a hand?"

"Get on with ye, me son." Maureen nudged him away with her elbow. "What on earth has come over ye? Doubt ye ever sliced meat in yer life."

Boyd slinked over to a kitchen chair and plunked himself down on his hands. Constable Johnson positioned himself in the opposite chair, back ramrod straight.

"Well, I knows yer all wonderin' who 'twas, and seein' as ye folks all reported him, I thought I'd do ye all a good turn and come let ye know before ye read 'bout it in the *Full Bucket*."

Maureen stopped her slicing, turned her back on the meat.

"'Tis a he, then?"

"Yes, ma'am."

"And?" she asked.

"'Twas Gerry Bightford. Gone missin' late last fall, if ye minds."

Boyd's leg twitched, plastic salt and pepper shakers vibrating on the tabletop.

"Mighty gash 'cross his forehead, head split right open. Lard, ye can gaze right into it. 'Tis lookin' like he was climbin' up some tree for God only knows what reason, lost his balance, come straight down, powerful hard on his noggin. Seems he bit the top inch of his tongue clear off. Fellers over to the hospital reckons he stumbled right into the pond, arse up, and there he stayed when the big freeze come on."

"Well that sounds mighty suspicious if I says so meself."

"No ma'am. No foul play is alleged here. None 'tall. Cupboard Cove's got a perfect record for that sort of t'ing. We's seven months shy of ten years without a murder. Last one was a doozy though, Mary McNulty feedin' her husband a nice raisin pie sweetened with rat poison. He might've survived the one slice, but the mister went back for a third and fourth servin'. Ate enough of the poison to fell a cow. 'Tis greed that got him in the end, the missus claimed, but me off-the-record opinion is that he made a poor choice in wife. Though, I recalls eyein' the pie meself when I was up to the scene. Flaky pastry, plump raisins, oh me Lard. Lucky I never ended up in the same predicament." He peeled the wrappers from two lengths of chewing gum, shoved them into his mouth. "But nothin' like it since," he said between juicy chomps. "And if we manages to make ten years, we gets an engraved medal from our local Member."

"Gerry Bightford, eh?" Earl said behind the lip of his teacup.

"That's what they t'inks. Wallet in his back pocket, not a cent missin', so no thought of theft. Found all his identification. There ye haves it. Open and shut."

"Good riddance, if ye asks me."

"Earl!"

"'Tis, Maureen. Don't give me that look, maid."

Maureen shook her head. "Still, a life is a life. Right? Terrible way to go."

"I can t'ink of worse," Constable Johnson said. He picked up his hat and stood. "I heard drownin' offers a wunnerful peace."

Boyd snickered. "Next time I has a word with someone drowned, I'll be sure to ask him."

"Watch yerself, me son," Constable Johnson said. "Else ye'll be findin' yerself in a heap of muck."

"Will do," Boyd said. He jumped up, saluted.

"Have yerselves a good one, folks," Constable Johnson said as he strolled out through the door. "And enjoy yer dinners."

No one said a word. The only sound was ice crackling as Maureen continued to press the thin blade down through the frozen meat.

Standing with feet wide apart, Boyd rubbed his remarkably clear eyes, and yawned so that his pale pink tongue dangled from his stretching mouth. His T-shirt slid up over his stomach to expose a dark carpet of fur radiating out from his belly button. Then he shuddered visibly, as though tossing something off his back, and cleared his throat. An announcement.

"Now's as good a time as any to tell ye's."

"We's listenin'," Maureen said. "Whatever 'tis. Go ahead."

"Me girlfriend. Teena. Well. Ye sees. Well." Fists clenched. "'Tis like this. She's growin' a baby." Words tumbling now. "And I knows bloody well Fadder don't want me 'round here with that scrap of news, so I took the apartment up to Roland Roberts. Ye needn't worry, Fadder, and ye can keep yer trap shut. It ain't yer problem. I'll be out of yer hair by tonight. I don't care if she lives next door or on the udder side of the fuckin' moon. I loves her. And I's happy as a pig in shit. So there. Whatd'ye got to say 'bout that?"

"Christ Jaysus," Earl managed, as he wiped the back of his hand over his mouth.

"How far along?" Maureen whispered. Once again, her knife stopped, hovering.

"Five months, she tells me."

"I thought she was gettin' a bit thick around the middle," Maureen said, facing Boyd. "Seen her smokin', I did. Just last weekend outside the Chicken Deelicken."

"She's tryin' to quit."

"I should hope so. Ain't good for the baby."

"Luh. Callin' the kettle. Ye was like the tilt, and we turned out decent enough. Well, one of us, anyways." Boyd licked his fingers, smoothed his twiggy sideburns.

Maureen's lips thinned. "They knows more now than they did when I was yer age. Is ye still smokin' yer pot?"

"Me pot? What pot?"

"Ye t'inks we's blind, deaf, and dumb to yer ways, me son. But we ain't none of it."

"I's goin' to quit soon as the baby's here. Maybe sooner. No, fuck it. I's goin' to quit today. Ye knocked the nail, Mudder." Boyd flexed, action hero style. "I'll start workin' out everyday, I figures. An hour. Maybe two. Feel real good 'bout meself."

"While yer at it, ye could get rid of yer dirty mouth along with yer dirty habit."

"Get off it, ol' woman," Boyd said as his brazen hand whipped over, stole Earl's cigarette right out from between his lips. "He's goin' to be strong as an ox, the little nipper. She felt him kick on Christmas Eve, she did. 'Twas somet'ing else. Best news of me life. He knocked her so hard, she fell onto her arse." Boyd beamed.

"Well, now. What'll ye do for money?" Maureen, all business again. "Babies costs money, Boyd. There's no way 'round it. They needs clothes and diapers and bottles of special milk and bibs and jars of food and the scatter toy and…" She stopped herself, pinched that desire that was taking hold of her stomach, her intestines. If she breathed deeply enough, she could almost smell that sweaty baby scalp, like sweet curry underneath fragranced shampoo.

"Don't she make her own milk?" Boyd asked, patting his chest.

Tilley had to concentrate on keeping his mouth closed. It longed to drop open with astonishment over the genuine xpression on Boyd's face. Who was this person talking about infants like it was old hat? Still Boyd, yes, but a newer Boyd. Edges filed down, brimming with adoration.

"Yes, Boyd," Maureen said, rolling her eyes. "But the stuff they's sellin' now in the shops is far better for the babies. Got more good in it. Not like the thin watery drink that comes out of a woman. Lard only knows how youngsters ever survived 'tall on it. Besides, like I says, ye got more than just a few bottles to worry 'bout."

"Well, Teena knits these tissue box covers she's tryin' to sell. Ye knows the ones with the plastic doll sticking up in the middle? Goes on the back of yer toilet?"

"I knows the ones."

"So she can keep on with that."

"She could try shippin' a load out to St. John's. To the shops there on Water Street. Tourists eats that handmade stuff right up. Pay a right wicked fortune for it."

"I'll tell her. Thanks, Mudder."

Seated quietly at the kitchen counter, Tilley waited patiently to wake up from the entire day. It was all too surreal, too great for his young mind to grasp. Not so much his father's limp poetry, the plastic bagged feet, or the frozen body of the late Mr. Bightford. No, that he could handle. But this honest-to-goodness brainstorming between his mother and Boyd, now that was entirely dreamlike.

"And yerself?" Maureen continued.

"I's been at Tubby Gould's now for three nights, makin' a decent go of it, if I says so meself. Nar sign of Blackie Tripe too, messin' me up like he did over to Boyle's Billiards and Nips-n-Bites. Though, thanks to Fadder's grand show there, they was waitin' for any ol' excuse to oust me. But Tubby took me on."

"What's to prevent that Tripe b'y from loiterin' at Tubby's, rilin' ye up. Ye knows it don't take much to trigger ye. Next t'ing ye'll be fightin' again, whip yerself smack back to square one."

"Martin told me Blackie was shipped off to the penitentiary over to Bitter Butter Bay. Happened on his way home 'round Christmastime, loaded up to the gills and rams his pick-up right through someone's fence, down over the lawn. Landed the whole truck, the works of it, into the basement. Some ol' couple was sound asleep in their beds, almost gave the beggar a heart attack. I can well imagine, rousin' to see a set of big wheels spinning at ye. Martin told me the feller never minded the truck, or the giant hole in the side of his house. Not 'tall. 'Twas was the sight of Blackie Tripe's ugly mug that almost put him under."

"That's a stroke of luck, I guess. Times is tough. Got to count every blessin' ye gets."

"Ye can say that again, Mudder."

Tilley cleared his throat, searching for his voice. "Congratulations, Boyd."

"Thanks, buddy," Boyd said. Knees bent, hands in boxer defence position, he bounced around the counter, and took two speedy stabs at Tilley's upper arm. "I's goin' to be the World's Best Fadder. Get meself a mug with it marked right on it."

Tilley's eyes watered with the pain as tiny blood vessels

ruptured near his shoulder, but he didn't mind it. Maureen sighed her boys-will-be-boys sigh, started slicing again.

For several moments, Boyd leaned against the counter grinding his teeth, and then stalked over to the sink, squashed his cigarette in the wetness near the drain. "And just in case ye's wonderin'," he said, "I can do the math for ye. Teena told me the news right near the time when that fairy queer Bightford lost his way, had his awful accident up there in the woods. Some coincidence, if ye asks me. Don't ye say?"

Maureen jolted, pressed the knife down over the pad of her thumb. She did not feel the pain. After gripping the slab of meat for so long, the ice had numbed her. Holding it up to the light, she saw her thick bright blood seeping out, blending with the muddy-coloured moose's blood. And she remembered. Those few months ago. Scrubbing stubborn stains from Boyd's jeans. At the time, she thought he had spilled red wine. Maureen twisted a tissue around the wound and in spite of the situation, in spite of all the potentially horrendous outcomes, she felt light-headed, and giggled. She refused to let her mind travel across that slender bridge, make that deadly connection about her son. Instead, she crazy-glued herself to the asinine theory of Boyd sipping wine. Now, that was truly hilarious.

❧

Standing at the tip of the basement stairs, Maureen could see only a portion of Boyd. He was hunched over in his room stuffing clothes, clean-dirty-folded-not, into a roomy duffel bag. Tilley sat on the edge of Boyd's bed, his feet swaying.

In a couple of hours, her first son would be backing out of the driveway, belongings, stereo system, and tufted vinyl ottoman jammed into the Chevy, soiled mattress lashed to the roof. He would drive seven homes up and unload his gear in his new rented space—a mildewed room the size of a generous closet in

Roland's basement.

She glanced down again, saw him toss a stiff grimy sock into Tilley's face. Then Boyd yanked out the 8-track, inserted a new one, and played his air guitar with awakened vigour. He seemed in no great hurry to start his new life. *Would he stay to dinner? Would he make a habit of coming home?*

Earl had not budged from his perch at the kitchen table. He sighed, gazed at the space between his feet, bemoaned, "Guess me good knife is gone."

"Guess so," Maureen said. She drew a deep breath, consulted her recipe. Were would she ever find 'Bamboo Shoots' in Cupboard Cove? As far as her world went, that sort of thing did not exist.

"Nar bit of sympathy? 'Twas the only t'ing me fadder ever gave me."

"Go on with ye, Earl." Maureen did not look up from her book. "Only t'ing yer fadder ever gave ye was a sharp crack over the head. Ye stole that knife. Ye told me so yerself."

A tinny laugh. "Yes, yer right. I did."

After a moment, she paused, tapped her finger against the clean page. "Earl, do you s'pose-"

"S'pose what?" Earl said with a grimace, chin transformed into peach pit.

Maureen shook her head slightly as she went to the fridge, collected several carrots. She would slice them like slender pieces of tape, creating something bamboo shootish. At the cutting board, she was careful now, removing the sprouted tops with the knife, using her bandaged fingernail as a guide. It was too easy to proceed swiftly, without thinking.

"Well?" Earl said.

"No, never mind." Maureen reconsidered her words as the peeler shaved off grubby strips of skin. "S'posin' never got no one nowhere. No sense to it. No sense 'tall."

twenty-two

Hazel reached up behind her back, and unbuttoned her floral cotton dress down to her hips. She withdrew her arms from the sleeves, tugged down over her silky slip, and let the whole works dangle around her waist. A large basin of warm sudsy water sat on the dresser, a block of slimy brown soap on a plate. She dropped in a fresh washcloth, soaked it, and squeezed out the excess liquid, letting it run down her forearms.

In a dozen lifetimes, she could never have guessed how much her body would change. Her skin had once been the object of envy, like a pearl, smooth, creamy. Almost overnight, it had transformed. Her abdomen was now discarded pudding skin, her armpits laden with walnut lumps of untapped milk, her breasts, like true glands, resembled two prize-winning potatoes. Everything had puffed, then deflated miserably in a matter of months.

She washed to rid herself of a smell she despised. Sour milk lurked in the hidden crannies of her chest, and in the folds under her arms. As she slid the cloth over her chest, she took extra care not to knock one of her nipples. This would send a persistent shower of milk, spraying out onto whatever lay in front of her. Somehow her body was unconcerned about the surface, wood, mirrors, bed sheets; her milk once dripped out through her woollen dress and onto the Sunday dinner. Leaching, that constant animal leaching. Her mind blurred as she thought about it, and as they watched her. The identical set of them, with soft mouths formed into 'o's, insect-sized eyes fixed upon her drooping teats.

She had plunked David and Levi, her twin babies, nearby on a crocheted blanket. David (born first) leaned on his chubby arms, while Levi (screeched out ten minutes after David) flopped forward and sucked the knitted navy toes of his sleeper. Though they were stout, Harvey's sister complained frequently that Hazel wasn't feeding them enough. But she could do no more. Already, she felt eaten alive, nearly pecked to death.

Hazel washed up around her neck, following the path of her hand in the mirror. Such a pretty mirror with its arched wooden frame. It had been her mother's, though her mother never used it. She would skirt past, ignoring her reflection, considering vanity to be a deadly sin. What absolute silliness. Hazel often wondered how she could be so different from her mother, as she found there had been no greater pleasure than in seeing herself, admiring her own beauty. Why would God have made her so striking unless she was meant to be adored? It simply wasn't logical.

She allowed her eyes to flutter up from the reflected image of her chest onto her face. When she noticed how sallow she was, she dropped the cloth onto the floor, and gripped the sides of the dresser. Leaning forward so that her nose was only inches from the glass, she could feel the buoys on her chest hanging down, straining her thin back. Who was that woman staring back at her? Surely that couldn't be her. Hazel rubbed her cheeks until they were blotchy. In the bright sunlight, her mask of pregnancy was glaring; unsightly discolourations that her sister-in-law had promised would fade back to nothingness after childbirth. But no, here they were, as prominent as ever, darker even, covering her cheeks, and the undersides of her jaw. Then beneath this dirty veil, her skin was pallid, almost jaundiced. She felt a rush of fear, clapped her chest, and her breasts began to percolate. She collapsed onto the rug beside the bed, though she had not fainted. Instead, she was deep in thought. *How could she, with a face so foreign, so uninviting, ever step outside again?*

✺

With his mother lying flat on the floor, eyes wide open, but body sedate, David recognised an opportunity. He crawled over to her side, nestled into her armpit, and attached his hungry little mouth for an unhindered drink. Levi was reluctant, but after several moments, he followed his older brother's lead, latched onto her other side, and gulped greedily. Hazel did not budge, but her eyes slowly travelled up into her head.

When Harvey entered the room, dragging his heels in heavy work boots, he roared with laughter over the perceived quaintness of the scene. Then, he opened the top button of his lumberman's jacket, leaned over. On the rug beside Hazel, a tiny ball of plush yellow fur tumbled out.

"Room for one more?" Harvey said with a jubilant laugh. "Thought with all the men here, ye'd like a little lady around. 'Popcorn's' her name."

Hazel snapped back to life.

"I don't want no dog," she screamed. Scrambling to her knees, the two miniature vice-grips suctioning her chest were lifted several inches, then dropped. Popcorn yipped near her calves, grabbed a mouthful of her hem, tugged and growled. On her feet now, and with a swift kick, she spun the yelping puppy across the wood floor. She tore at her loose hair, cried, "Don't ye see, ye stupid, stupid man? Don't ye see I got more than I wants? More than I needs." She began to weep, though her face was still twisted with anger. "There's nothin' left of me. Don't ye see? Where is I gone? Where is I gone to?"

Seeing her standing there was nearly too much for Harvey. Her upper half glistened, her wild mane was pure brightness, and her rage gave off an exhilarating heat. He clenched his fists and averted his eyes; he was embarrassed by the senses of arousal netting him at every step. He turned and walked out of the house, stepping out into the yard where the air was crisp, traced with pungent smoke. There he found the pile of wet spruce logs he had hauled out of the woods over a snowy trail. He would pluck off the Old Man's Beard and start sawing. Saw, and think of nothing. Nothing only the blade's curving pattern and how it managed such a fine, fine job on the dripping wood.

"Had three die this week. Three. No less."

Penny Payne sat at Maureen's kitchen table, a brimming cup of tea, plate of gingersnaps before her.

"Not true."

"Yes 'tis, maid. By the looks of t'ings at Good Hopes, our geriatric community is diminishin' by the day."

Maureen, seated opposite Penny, shook her head. "That's too bad. Sometimes when I t'inks of that, I wonders 'bout all they knows, all that's lost when they passes on."

"Well, I can tell ye this with utter confidence, me dear. By the time some of them crosses over, they don't even know how to wipe their own arses. And that's the truth. So, ye can judge yer loss accordingly."

"Still."

"No still to it, maid. That's the way 'tis. God, one ol' woman this week, mustn't of had more than a dozen strands of hair stuck to her head and all her faculties, long since sucked down the drain. Starts on 'bout angels, she do. Sayin' she can see them on the ceilin', and they's a grand sight for sore eyes, and how much she wants to be on the ceilin' herself. And, by jumpin's, if she ain't tryin' to hoist herself out of the hospital bed. Don't know what she was t'inkin'. I had to hold her down, tucked her in good and bloody tight, I'd say. And I tells her, listen, me dear, there's no way yer gettin' up to that ceilin' when I's on duty. Ye can hang tight 'til the next nurse, maybe if ye minds yer 'p's and 'q's, she'll round ye up a good sturdy ladder. Wouldn't ye know it, me breath wasn't stale, and she was gone."

"Gone? Don't tell me she managed to squeak out of the bed?"

"Matter of speakin', I s'pose. Eyes rolled up, smile on her a mile wide. Dead as a doornail. For a minute, I was awful tempted to look up, have a gander at the ceilin' meself, but did I? Ye can bet yer bottom dollar I didn't. I don't feed off that sort of ridiculousness. No room for it in the land of the livin'."

"That's so sad. Must've took the good right out of ye."

"Sad? Makes me wonder why I ever choosed to become a nurse. Got rocks in me head, I does. I'd be better off scrubbin' toilets." Penny dumped three heaping spoonfuls of sugar into her tea, stirred and slurped. "So, ye never said a word 'bout me hair."

"No." Maureen scratched behind her left ear. "'Tis nice, Penny. No, maid, 'tis lovely. Right smart on ye."

"After the hell week I had, I went right over to see Sally. I told her, take me, maid, I's all yours. Do what ye wants with me, me dear. She called it copper wire."

And it was, Maureen noted, in both colour and texture.

"Well, she knows what she's at. That Sally."

"So, do ye agree with me, then? Ye needs an outlet? Somet'ing to take ye mind off the daily grind as we knows it?"

"Oh yes. Of course, I does. Every woman needs that. Surely, to God. With all we does. Whether 'tis havin' yer nails painted or yer hair styled. We all needs that."

"I can take everyt'ing thrown at me, but I can't stand old folks. Pieces of them dryin' up and fallin' off. Makes me right disgusted. I swears I'll chop me own head off, copper wire colour and all, if I ever gets within ten feet of bein' senile."

Maureen shot a look at the clock, then scraped back her chair. "God help me, I don't believe meself. I's late again."

"For?"

From the porch, Maureen continued talking. "Annette Boone is havin' a dinner. Her sister, out from St. John's. Right hoity toity. Seymour at the Shack told me she came in lookin' for the priciest thing he had to offer. Of course, he tried to offer up hisself, the dirty beggar, but she ended up with a bag of scallops, shrimp. I reckons no matter what, she'll crucify it." Maureen drew her brand new white wool coat down from the hook in the porch, then peeked around the corner, cocked her head. "Didn't I tell ye all that?"

Penny jabbed her damp teabag, licked her fingers. "Ye might've. I don't remember."

"Well, anyways, I told her I'd handle Missus Boone while she cooked. And I tell ye, by the queer smells comin' out of her kitchen most days I's there, she needs all the help she can get. Is ye almost done?"

Running her chubby finger around the sharp edge of her cup, Penny said, "No, not by half. I can drink up and let meself out though." She sighed. "Have a moment's peace, here. If ye don't mind."

Waving her hand, Maureen said, "Not 'tall, maid. Take yer

time. Long as Earl's snorin' don't bother ye. I swears I's tempted to tape his mouth right shut. See how he fares. Don't know when I last had a decent sleep. I feels crazed half the time."

"Me too, maid. Like I's livin' in a dream." Penny craned her neck to sip her tea. "Go on, then. We quits chewin' the rag. Don't want to make yerself even later."

"Yes, yer right. I hope ye feels better. Yer a good friend, Penny Payne."

"I is?"

Maureen buttoned her coat, smoothed her hands over the luxurious fabric, and then waved her hand again. "Yes. Best kind," she said and hurried out through the door.

twenty-three

"Did ye hear a polar bear come 'cross on the ice?" Earl asked as he waited for his late afternoon plate of breakfast. "I seen it last night, I did, on me way to Nips-n-Bites."

Maureen cracked three eggs into a pool of bacon fat and stepped back from the stove as they bubbled angrily. "Is ye sure 'twasn't on yer way out of Nips-n-Bites?"

"Don't be stupid, maid. I knows if I's comin' or goin', and I only had the one drink before me shift. I told the b'ys all 'bout it. Enormous, 'twas. Clamberin' up off the beach, yellow fur on him like he smoked three pack a day. Up over the rocks and he scuttled down the road just ahead of me. Ye needn't say I didn't clip it in the opposite direction."

"He scuttled, did he? On his hind legs, I s'pose." Maureen twittered, spooned fat up and over the crisping eggs. "Joggin', maybe. Or, 'twas he sprintin'. On a marathon through the Cove."

"'Tis too much effort to talk civil to yer husband, is that it?"

Maureen dropped the plate in front of Earl and he dove into burnt toast, lengths of shiny bacon, and slippery eggs. With a tea towel, she gripped the metal handle of the cast iron frying pan, dumped the smoking contents into an empty corn-on-the-cob can, and then slid it into the sink. Greasy steam hissed up her nostrils, around her head, coating her hair, when Earl, mouth full, hollered, "Turn that up. By Jaysus. Turn that up."

She reached across and twisted the volume dial on the miniature radio. After a grating introductory chime, and a brief ditty, Ray Foote read the local news with his trademark tone of deathbed incantations. And sure enough, he announced the arrival of Cupboard Cove's newest member, an adult polar bear who had travelled down from Labrador on the ice floes. Locals were advised not to travel far, avoid wooded areas, and by no means attempt to approach the animal. An attack could be deadly. Experienced government employees would be working around the clock to sedate it and transport it back up north to its natural habitat.

Maureen covered her mouth with her hand. "Oh me Lard. I hope Tilley's alright. I should pick him up. Should we keep Tilley home from school tomorrow?"

"Nah. He'll be fine. They'll have it caught by then, I 'llows. But I'd watch meself, if I was ye. Don't be gettin' dolled up in that new white coat of yers. Traipsin' 'bout. With the size of ye like a barn, yer apt to feel a tranquilliser pinch ye right in the arse."

Maureen smiled, put her hand on Earl's round shoulder. "Sorry I laughed at ye, darlin'. I thought ye was pullin' me leg."

Earl did not look up at Maureen, but continued to pack food into his chipmunk cheeks, yolk dribbling down over his dimpled chin. "Don't make no difference, maid," he managed between hard swallows. "Laugh all ye wants. I don't even listen. I stopped hearin' ye long, long ago."

❧

"How is she anyway?" Tilley said as he laboured over his drawing in a sunny corner of David's work shed. "Me Mudder says she's gettin' on good."

"My mother is well, Tilford," David replied, pacing back and forth behind Tilley. "Thank you for asking. Your mother has likely told you her senility is palpable. Often she is bewildered, lost among her urges. Like a child. Living each moment without a past." He stopped for a moment and smoothed away a streak of dust coating a canvas that was stretched over a wooden frame. "Sometimes I cannot help but wonder if that isn't a delightful place to be. Would you think?"

Tilley shrugged, recalled Marnie's pale hand wiping strands of her bangs out of her eyes, that one-penny space between her front teeth. "That ain't for me. No sir. I'll hold tight to me mem'ries."

"Yes, yes, of course." David laughed lightly, shoulders hunched inside his cardigan. "I am very nearly an old man and have forgotten what it is like to be fourteen. Falling helplessly in love at every junction." He stopped his shuffling. "Are you in love, Tilford?"

Mid-cough, Tilley stuttered, "No, no, Mr. Boone. Nothin' like that." He never knew how to respond to David's direct probing. It forced him to dodge about, perjure himself, even though he felt David already knew the answers to many of his questions.

"Just as well, I guess." Moving again. "Love is something very difficult to get right. It often does more harm than good."

Jumping down from the stool, Tilley stood back from his work. "There. I's done."

"Well, Tilford," David said, turning and putting a hand on Tilley's shoulder. "You've almost created an exact replica."

"Thanks," Tilley replied. His hand throbbed from gripping charcoal, and his face was smudged with sooty streaks.

"I'm sorry." David paused, words tugging like thread from a snarled bobbin. "I didn't intend it as praise."

"Oh," Tilley said, frowning now. David's comments were often so irritatingly difficult to decipher.

"I said almost. Of course the lines are perfect, you are truly a gifted artist."

Yo-yoing, Tilley felt proud again, puffed out his chest.

"But," David continued, causing Tilley to exhale. "It simply lacks depth."

Hackles rising, Tilley said brusquely, "Whatd'ye mean, depth? I done what ye asked. Drew the picture of yer mudder. Plus ye made me sit in the sunlight and I was sweatin' like a roasted pig."

"Yes, I wanted you to be distressed as you worked." David's tone was level, calm. "I wanted to determine if that emotion, or actually any emotion, would weave its way into your portrayal. And I see that it hasn't. Your lines are precise, yes, but the composition is empty. Void of passion. The sole message it conveys is that you, the artist, are spiritually immature."

Tilley yanked down his shirtsleeves and tried to absorb David's words. "What do that mean? I's small, that's right, but I ain't no baby."

"No."

"And I ain't had no easy ride of it, neither. No sir. Not with a fadder like I got. No easy ride, is right."

"No."

"So, I respects ye, Mr. Boone. But, I can't abide ye callin' me immature."

David continued his pacing, his skeletal hands clasping and releasing, clasping and releasing. "Perhaps I misspoke. What I meant was that your soul is youthful. Somewhat unsullied, if you wish. Though I would have expected nothing else. If you will indulge me for a moment?"

"Go on," Tilley said, staring down at his cold feet. He wished now he was wearing his sneakers instead of only thinning sport socks, a gaping hole exposing much of his left heel. Lately, it seemed every pair was faulty.

"Let us scrutinise the image again."

"The photo of yer mudder?" Tilley glanced over at the black and white, fractured finish, ribbed edges that David had attached to the easel.

"Yes. What do you see?"

"I sees a woman in a flowery dress."

"Anything more?"

Tilley leaned in close to the photo, searching for a clue to quell David. "She's sat in a chair."

"And?"

"She got neither ring on her finger."

"That's it?"

"Yup."

"All fine observations, I will admit."

"Well, I don't know what ye expects me to see. 'Tis a photo. Ye told me to draw it and like I said, I done what ye asked. And a good job too, if I says so meself."

"But you've missed her whole inner world, Tilford." David ran his index finger over the face in the photo. "The eyes you've drawn are strictly eyes, the lips, clearly only lips. What do the position of her hands reveal about her? The slight turn of her shoulder? Am I making sense? Can you grasp what I'm attempting to explain?"

"No sir, I can't. Not one iota of it."

David sat down on the stool, folded his hands together. "When you generate a piece of artwork, Tilford, whether it be a painting, a sculpture, or a piece of jewellery, one of your goals is to convey an emotion. With regards to this snapshot, you have to reach inside the subject, feel around, ascertain the very crux of her motivation, then capture it."

Tilley could listen no longer. "Ye t'inks I's stupid, Mr. Boone, but I ain't." He jammed his feet into his sneakers, crumbling the heels. "What if I don't want to reach inside, feel around? What if I got no yearnin' whatsoever to get anywhere near to what makes her tick? I knows she's yer mudder and all, and I don't want to offend ye but I don't want to get near her crux, as ye says." Pulling on his hooded sweatshirt, he strode to the door of the work shed. "Having her gawkin' out at me for all those hours gave me the creeps. She looks cracked, like she's gone right 'round the bend, and I couldn't draw that for ye, now could I? So I took what I could from the photo and left the rest."

He twisted the handle and a gust of fresh spring wind forced the door to swing wide, almost knocking Tilley to the floor. "Sorry if yer mad," he said as wind flattened his hair, filled his ears.

"No, not at all," David replied, moving to grip the door as Tilley walked through. "Go on home, Tilford. I'm the one who has made a mistake here. It's me. As for you, you've done well."

David watched through a rattling window as Tilley disappeared around the corner of the house. Then he returned to the stool, perched himself before the latest drawing. It was a curious experiment, having the child draw his mother, something he likely should not have done. But, he wanted to establish if Tilley knew her, could feel her. And yes, according to what he said, he could, but wisely choose not to replicate it.

In hindsight, David had miscalculated, giving Tilley such little credit. After their latest exchange, David decided the boy was a lot cleverer, a lot more knowledgeable about human nature, than he had originally thought. Perhaps he should not be so surprised. After all, David had grown absolutely certain that Tilley Gover represented a ghostly second hand shadow of himself.

twenty-four

In early spring, Tilley began escorting Marnie home from school. Scuttling on stumpy legs a pace or two behind her, he almost skipped trying to keep up. In his aching arms, he carried her bundle of books, scaling the steep hill to her house, avoiding potholes so large they could swallow him. Occasionally a fragrant waft of shampoo or lotion would drift back and Tilley was quick to suck in what he could, hoping to lock it into his memory. On weekends, he would sneak down the ladies necessities aisle in Snook's Drugs sniffing all the tubes of creams, bottles of conditioner, deodorants even, but was unable to identify which scent belonged to her. If he had, he surely would have purchased it, hidden it inside the faded belly of his zip-up lion where, as a child, he had tucked away his diamond-patterned pyjamas.

Walking with Marnie meant Tilley had to abandon Walter. And after the first week, Walter no longer waited for him at their usual meeting place—the corner of the school where smokers gathered and delinquents had carved "Fuck Off if your reading this" into the soft wood. Walter griped at first; *"best friends don't do that."* But late March, a curious fever came over him as Christina Wong took the empty desk beside him in Honours Math. Christina had transferred to Cupboard Collegiate from a place Walter couldn't pronounce and her family opened a Chinese take-out, four doors up from a disgruntled Tubby Gould. Boys called her 'Slit-Eyed Frog,' girls, 'Chinky Bitch,' but she seemed unfazed, told amicable Walter the world was a shrinking community and they would come around. Come around to where, he wasn't sure. How long before she realised that Cupboard Cove was already shrivelled beyond repair? Though when she offered him free crispy egg rolls stuffed with spicy chicken, shrimp, and stringy vegetables, he was hooked on both her and the distinctive snacks she provided.

It was during this season of first love that a pliable wedge began to softly manoeuvre its way between Walter and Tilley. Neither acknowledged the waxed paper obstruction, it was not a subject growing boys would ever discuss. Individually, though, they held similar theories. Each maintained that now, as teenagers, they no longer needed each other the way they did when they were children. But there was an additional, unspoken level that surpassed childhood and mushrooming emotions. And that involved ability. While Walter attempted to embrace an irrefutable future of slouching around Cupboard Cove, Tilley harboured a suspicion he was bound for something more. And though Tilley never once uttered this hunch to a single soul, somehow Walter seemed to know it too.

Ida Payne didn't appreciate the newness of wandering home on her own. It seemed to have happened all at once. Over the winter term, she had grown accustomed to striding up her side of the chain-link fence only to meet Walter and Tilley at the icy parking lot. They would amble up the frozen streets together, Ida often sprinting ahead, hammering snowballs, handfuls of drippy slush back at her followers. On bitter days, they would stop at Tubby Gould's for a cardboard tray of fries, peas, and chicken gravy. But when warm winds braved the cold, platters of soft snow slid off roofs, and snapping ice interrupted class discussion, Ida discovered Walter standing alone beside the rusting hulks of salt-stained cars, mud-caked along the side of the road.

A fissure opened up inside Ida. She was certain Tilley liked her. Who had skipped rocks with her beside the beach? Who dragged her out of the water while they were panning and she had slipped down between two colossal shards of ice? Who had insisted on hauling her out to the cliffs to show her O'Leary's Lantern? Well, okay, she had happened upon him that night and asked, but still, the sharing of local tradition was significant. Wasn't it? And, she had caught him staring. More than once. So, why wasn't Tilley waiting for her after class? Most days she didn't even bring books home, so his load certainly would have been a great deal lighter. *What was so exceptional about Little Miss Priss anyways?* Nothing but an instigator, she was. Chasing him, teasing him, flaunting her money. Some girls were just blatant about it all, would do anything to snatch a guy. Turning a level playing field into heaving waters. That was almost criminal.

Ida stomped up the street, coursing through every mound of slush like a bulldozer. A vinegar jealousy welled up inside her as though someone had twisted the spout. Sourness pouring out.

No. Fried-Egg-Ida would not go over-easy.

Every afternoon as Marnie and Tilley passed by the cemetery she would slow, glance in wistfully. This occurred for two weeks, until one day, she stopped completely, announced, "I had a grandfather that lived here, you know."

Tilley stopped beside her. "Yeah, me too. Couple of them. They's in there somewhere." Pointing towards the graveyard, he said flatly, "We don't never visit." He gazed in, wondering for just a moment if he would ever have a need to pop in or if he would ever be popped in on himself. And then, would someone visit him? It was easy to tell which burial sites were popular draws as stomped down, hardened snow refused to melt, leaving a white ring around the grave.

Marnie hesitated, stared through the peeling fence. "Are we allowed in?" she asked.

"'Tis public property. Ye can go in long as ye don't take a hammer to nothin'."

She smirked. "I wouldn't do anything like that. I just thought we could go in, poke around a bit. See if I can find my grandfather's grave."

"If that's what turns yer crank."

"Not really I guess. It's just I have no idea how he died. My father won't talk about it, just says he was very young when it happened. And my grandmother, all she says is that he left her alone. Maybe we'll come across something. Sometimes gravestones give hints. Look, like this one here." Marnie stepped through the fence, pointed at a slick wet headstone. "Irving Baker, beloved Son and Captain, loved the sea and lost." My guess is that he drowned."

"I'd imagine," Tilley said, moving along the slushy trails between graves. He pulled down a handful of dried dead grass obscuring an epitaph. "Whatd'ye t'ink this means? 'William Williams, died due to his own gullibility'."

"That's strange. You've got me. Maybe he ate a poisonous apple after a beautiful girl told him it was delicious."

"Good guess," Tilley said with a smile as he stepped over William Williams' grave and read the tombstone next door.

"Listen here to Kenneth Kennedy. 'Where you are, I once was. As I am, soon you will be'."

"Geez, talk about comforting. And what's up with the names? Lacking originality, at best." She sniffed the air. "God, the air stinks in here."

"Yeah, not what ye'd expect for a cemetery, hey?"

"Like fried chips mixed with rotting cabbage."

"Tubby Gould's and the new Chinese take-out. Not the best combination."

"If I was buried here, that stench would make me roll over in my grave."

Tilley put his hand on a tombstone and gaped at her. "Don't go sayin' stuff like that. Not when yer standin' here. It's like talkin' 'bout someone's illness and pointin' it out on yer own body. Mudder says 'tis a bad omen."

"Well, your mother is a silly woman, Tilley," she said flippantly as she meandered into another section of the graveyard. "Hey, listen up. Says here this youngish woman died of a broken heart. Poor thing." Marnie bent, fingered a clump of weathered plastic tulips wedged in beside the marker, and said, "Someone must love you, Mary-Anne Anderson. You're the only one with flowers here, fake or not."

Several yards away, Tilley called out, "Wow. This woman here might've had a broken heart too. Says she plummeted into Devil's Ravine."

"You mean threw herself in?"

"I don't know. Wouldn't be 'llowed to bury her in here if she done away with herself, right?"

"Not sure. What's Devil's Ravine?"

"'Tis a crack in the cliff about a forty-five minute walk that way." Tilley pointed towards the inky sea, a ledge of rock.

"Why is it called that?"

"If ye looks down into the crevice, ye can see sections where the rock has fallen away. Right smooth, looks like links in a chain. People says years ago the Devil got stuck in there and got so angry, he turned red-hot. And the chains that wraps 'round him melted right into the rock. When he managed to free hisself, he left his impression. Everyone says Cupboard Cove is special cause we managed to get the Devil in a pinch. But he got away."

"I never knew the Devil had chains. I thought he wore a red suit. With the forked tail and stuff."

"Everywhere's got their own Devil. Maybe in St. John's he wears red, but here he likes to rattle his chains."

"I'd love to see-."

"I'll take ye there," Tilley spouted, stepping forward. Then he eased back, embarrassed. Here he was again, jumping in so swiftly, always too eager, too obvious for his own good. "I means if ye wants. Sometime. If I's goin', ye can come along or somet'ing."

"Sure. Alright. I'd like that."

"If I goes," Tilley repeated, rubbing his reddened nose stiffly along his index finger.

They spent another forty-five minutes sifting through the graveyard, giggling at unusual epitaphs, pondering peculiar ones. Though he did search, frequently he peered across the stones, the unkempt grass, to sneak a peek at Marnie. Cruising so effortlessly among the dead with sunlight streaking through her hair, she appeared even more alive, more beautiful. As his boots mashed into mud on the side of an old grave, he decided someday he would draw her. Exactly how she was.

"Well, I don't think my grandfather is buried here," Marnie finally said. "We've looked at everything in the old section. Nothing with Boone."

"What about those?" Tilley motioned towards a series of miniature beds, stones with eroded cherubs and lambs.

"That's for children, I think. Boy, what a sin. Look at all the kids that died back then. All kinds of sickness, I suppose. Not like today."

Tilley and Marnie picked their way through them. "Look at this," Marnie whispered, bending near a tiny picket fence. "'Thomas Earle, I will not forget you, I have you carved on the palm of my hand.' So sad." Marnie took a quick sip of air. "And here, look. 'Gavin Foote, our tender little lamb, died aged 11 days'."

"Ugh," Tilley said. "Sounds like he was some sort of roast. Not a baby."

Marnie scowled. "Don't be mean, Tilley. It doesn't suit you."

Believing every word that emerged from Marnie's mouth, Tilley said a rapid "Okay" inside his head. If being mean didn't fit with her perception, then he would be the opposite of mean. From then on, he would pet stray dogs, hold doors for sluggish old women, and never filch another box of Girl Guide cookies from an unattended cardboard carrier. He thought to tell her but then grounded himself, bit his willing tongue in case the words slipped through.

"What's this?" He pointed to a small cross; the wood cracked, layers of paint peeling, even through a fresh coat of paint. Thin black letters, fractured with the wood, ran along both lengths of the cross. "It reads, 'L. Boone, 1923-1927.'"

Marnie knelt down in the grass, crinkled her forehead. "Now that's strange."

"What?"

"As far as I knew, my father's family was the only Boone family here. There's no other Boone families here, right?"

"Not that I know of. Ain't common here. The name."

"Yes, I believe my father's family is from an outport called Severed Knot. Do you know it?"

"Yeah. 'Bout an hour or more up the coast. Quarter size of Cupboard Cove, maybe smaller."

She looked again at the antiqued cross. "Yes, it does say Boone. Someone's fixed it up recently. It's got a new screw in the middle there." Then, she rose abruptly, not appreciating the newfound murkiness within her. "I think I feel like leaving now. All this trekking around through wet grass my jeans are damp. I could use a hot chocolate. You want one?"

"Sure t'ing. I t'inks they sells it at the Chicken Deelicken. Me brudder, Boyd's, workin' there, might make us two for free."

"I bet I can make it better than a fast food place. My mother's got instant packets. Cadbury's, I think. We'll make it in my kitchen."

Of all the seasons, Hazel hated winter the most. After the stage had been dismantled, boats hauled up onto the land, she could not secure a moment for herself. Harvey took up roost next to the woodstove, repairing his nets, chewing tobacco, and whittling wood. Sometimes he even hummed a tune. Sprawling near his feet, the dog, Popcorn, licked her paws with such incessant regularity, Hazel had to bite her cheeks in order not to scream.

To save herself from madness, she took to walking. She walked along the main road, down by the water, at all hours of the day and night, every day of the week. The boys were sleeping when she left and if they woke up, so be it. Inside the roar of the ocean, she found a peace that was so foreign; it became deliciously dangerous, forbidden. And every ounce of her flesh savoured it.

Whenever she returned, Harvey rushed at her as though she'd be to sea and back, his smiling eyes so shiny, someone ould have jammed crystals into his head. And the smell of his nosy sister would be in the air, on the children, even though Hazel had long ago forbidden Flo Grimes to enter their home. She knew

Harvey well. He had run across the moment she left, as he didn't know which end of a child was up. There were benefits, though. Miraculously, a fish stew would be bubbling on the stove, caramel squares baking in the oven. "Where'd this come from?" Hazel might ask and Harvey would weakly reply, "Oh, just thought I'd throw somet'ing on." The food was always delicious, so Hazel let those secret intrusions go without comment.

Soon to follow, of course, were the rumours. She heard them, and so had Flo Grimes. *Where was she going? And why would a woman be out walking on her own when she had two small children and a good man to care for?*

Flo mentioned the gossip only once to Harvey and he became furious. Frothing at the mouth, he said, "She's modern, is all. Ye'd deny her a moment? Ye knows nothin' 'bout raisin' young'uns. Let alone a pair."

Aiming that sort of comment at a childless woman bit right into the very bones. But, Flo was certain it wasn't intentional. So she never mentioned it again, for fear she would lose her brother completely. Though, if she were honest with herself, the blood bond they shared mattered less and less everyday. Harvey was so entirely blinded, Hazel might just as well have slashed his eyes through with a sword.

Hazel's walking continued, and increased in frequency, if anything. And it was innocent, at the start. It was nothing more than an hour away from her responsibilities, a release from those child-weights around her thin ankles. She had never meant to bump into him. It was not her intention. She walked merely for the sake of walking. *That was not a lie*. She would swear to it. Instead, she would blame what came to pass on the bored hand of chance. In search of torment, it had simply placed him in her way.

It began during a snowstorm. Harvey had cautioned her to stay at home, wait it out. But snow made little difference to Hazel. She had never once felt snow on her skin, never a flake landing on her eyelashes or drifting across her lips. Whatever the nature of inclement weather, she always moved in rain. Flakes melted within a foot of her, transformed into fat drops with the heat that radiated out through her clothes. She was a hot coal, and could not be cooled.

When she bumped into him, she was near the water's edge listening to the lapping tongue that never froze, no matter how low the temperature dropped. She was surprised, yes, not expecting another soul to be out in a storm that left her nearly sightless. Disguised as a Yeti, he had needed to scrape the layer of frost from his beard before she recognised him. So terribly thin he looked, so tremendously hungry. Why did he possess this sallow expression even though he still lived with his mother?

"Lyle?" she said as he stepped into her rain, and he began to thaw.

"Hazel," he replied, shoving his hands into the coat his good mother had shaped with recycled strips of fabric, old buttons, needle and thread. "I've missed ye, maid."

She giggled and a wave of refreshment rippled over her skin when she recognised a welcome return of youthfulness in her voice. "I can surely tell," she said, seizing his arm. "It ain't tough to see."

She could not have predicted their next steps, quick and furious, to the vegetable cellar behind his house. She wondered had she been pulling, or was she only following along? Though she did not consider that question for long, it never really mattered.

She moved between bins of dusty potatoes and carrots, ran her hands over the braided stalks of onions. In the dampness everything was so familiar, but new again. Hazel sighed. God, how she felt like a fistful of oats in the hand of a farmer, one flick of his strong wrist and let the sowing begin. Then she began rushing, falling, tumbling, forgetting every single label that had lassoed her, bound her to home and family. And it was in those moments of exhilaration, utter abandon, when the very roots of her addiction were unearthed.

After that, her jaunts were no longer the trivial wanderings of a hapless woman. When her feet set out on the gravel roads, they already had a very specific destination in mind.

Late on a Friday afternoon in the middle of April, Tilley strolled down the hallway of Cupboard Collegiate, stopped in front of his locker, and dug the tiny key out of the leather wallet he kept lodged in his back pocket. Mr. Collins had assigned Steinbeck's *The Pearl*, and Tilley had forgotten it in his locker. As he opened the dented metal door, a neatly folded leaf of pink notepaper drifted out, fluttered lazily towards the floor. As he bent to retrieve it, he glanced up and down the hallway to see if anyone was watching. The school was practically empty so he unfolded the note and read.

Marnie. Wanting to meet him in the woods. A lipstick print in the lower corner by her printed name, a fat heart above the letter 'i' in Marnie's name.

All corny, he knew, but his mind nearly burst with the image of her writing to him. Hunched over her clean white desk, touching the tip of her pencil off her bottom lip. Mini-explosions went off inside his body, lashed across his chest, and his smile could not be restrained. He pressed the note to his nose, sucked in a sweetness that was like cherry blossoms. Then he folded it neatly, tucked it inside the covers of *The Pearl* for safekeeping. Between the pages of the story where a scorpion stings the fisherman's son, and the father discovers one of the greatest treasures in the world.

twenty-five

After Cupboard Cove's public library closed, Marnie Boone decided to walk home with her armload of books even though the evening had slithered in, eclipsing the day. She knew her father would have picked her up, but these small communities were perfectly safe, she told herself, and besides there was a night sky worthy of poetry.

Along the gravel road, potholes brimmed with slushy water and the air was laced with the sweet stench of uncovered garbage, months of frozen dog droppings that had thawed. In the dim space between street lights, Marnie strained to see the assortment of junk that had been abandoned in the gutters over the snowy months—pop cans and chip bags, a broken stereo, a dirt-encrusted Kotex pad, a kitchen chair with mangled metal legs.

As she strolled along reflecting on the overall pleasantness of her first year in Cupboard Cove, she heard a car slowing behind her, the grunt of a heavy door.

"Hey Marnie!"

She turned toward the car, already smiling. It was a congenial voice. A boy's. Similar to Tilley's.

In the darkness, she could not see the face but she leaned in foolishly where the backseat had been bent forward and chirped, "That's my name. Don't wear it out."

An innocent grin froze onto her face as a masked head appeared and two colossal hands jumped forward, clutched her shoulders. She was too startled to resist, and was hauled into the hot car's dark wide mouth. Her stunned arms opened and her load of modern classics tumbled to the muddy ground. Four hands were gripping her now, tugging at her pant legs, feet barely in before the creaky door slammed.

"Go! Go!" The tone, a wild boar's, blended with spinning tires, flying dirt.

Her heart hammered her ribcage, whole body pulsating, but she did not struggle. At first. It had to be a joke, a surprise maybe, and the details of this simple possibility came rushing at her instantly. Any moment, the medium-sized masked boy would reveal himself, explain everything. "Geez, sorry to have been so rough on ye," he might say. "'Tis just yer fadder planned this mind-bogglin' birthday bash for ye and he paid us to deliver ye in jig time." Yes, her father just might have done that. She could picture him now, *needed* to picture him in order to calm herself. He would be standing on the covered porch with a wrapped copy of Robert Frost's best verse in his arms. She had asked him for that not because she adored the poetry, but because her father would adore that aspect of her, if only she could cultivate it.

But after several sharp turns with no such disclosure from the boy, panic gelled within her. Nipped between a pair of legs in grease-stained jeans, she squirmed frantically, cried, "Let me—"

A hand clamped over her mouth, voice growled, "Shut the fuck up!"

Then everything melted into a haze.

Her shock screamed out through his hand and she bit down, tasted the soiled fingers that wrestled with her face. A high-pitched wail behind the black ski mask, and she heard him spit, "Ye little bitch," right before he began to strike her.

It all happened so quickly.

Each time she flailed or kicked on the backseat of the car, he squeezed tighter, pounded into her ribs, her chin, her face. Writhing away, she pressed herself down behind the passenger seat, onto mildewed carpet, managed to cover herself with her forearms. But she wasn't strong enough. He gripped her bangs, whipped back her head, and delivered two sharp punches between her dazed eyes. After that, she no longer felt anything. Though she continued to hear with eerie clarity, wails, muffled bawls, tearful sucks of air through a stuffy nose. Were they all her sounds? She wasn't certain.

Tires chafing the pavement, a door groaning, and she was pitched from the car, assisted by a heavy boot to her tender abdomen. Body limp, she never extended her arms for protection. Her left temple struck the ditch first, her crumpled body following, and muddy water immediately filled her ear. Metal and dirt mixed in her mouth, and she imagined her mind spreading out like turpentine on water, coating the garbage, merging with the skinny stream that threaded its way down the gutter. Sleep, now. All she wanted to do was sleep.

As she slipped into satisfying unconsciousness, she envisioned a delicate hand continuously folding a bowl of soft-peaking egg whites. She grimaced once. A spectator might have attributed the expression to pain, but that was not the case. In that second before she tumbled into a black animal trap, she was worried where her books had fallen. Miss Knotts at the library inspected each and every text and did not take kindly to soiled returns.

"Ye can come on out," Scotty Power said as he peeled the ski mask off his head. "We's done."

A mound of plaid blanket underneath the front dash began to tremble, and slowly Ida Payne emerged, crawled up onto the seat.

"Yee-haw. Fried-Egg-Ida-Side-Order-o'-Ham," Wayne Power said, smacking his lips. "We wants to squeeze yer yolks."

Scotty and Wayne Power were brothers, and first cousins of Blackie Tripe from McGinty's Gut. During an evening promenade along the railroad tracks, Ida had happened upon the merry couple. They were smoking joints, drinking beer, and in the midst of a pissing contest to determine who could squirt the farthest. They welcomed Ida's smooth distraction. Wayne and Scotty were attracted to her smart mouth and her tiny backside, while she found their shiny car and who-gives-a-shit attitude appealing. She always felt safe cavorting with the boys in that fashion for two reasons. One because she was within shouting distance of a dozen well-lit homes, and two because she had never ventured inside the heavy doors of their monster sedan.

So, for five nights, she met them on the tracks, let them take turns bruising her lips with inexperienced kisses, but nothing else. Not until they had done her a good turn involving another girl. She never told them the whole truth, of course, what the girl had actually done, but offered them a version of events they could handle. And having a sense of fair play, the two brutish boys were game.

Scotty cawed like a gull at a dump, rubbed his wet paws together, and then said in a low groan, "Ah. Payment time."

"Don't ye t'ink ye overdone it?" Ida grumbled, frowning. "I didn't want ye to kill her, just knock the shit out of her a tiny bit."

"Doubts she got much shit in her now," Wayne said, his cigarette jerking with each word spoken.

"Uh," Scotty said, jaw slack. He hadn't meant to use so much force, but once he'd started, it was such an awesome release he couldn't rein in what was reeling out. "Uh, fuck it now, b'y."

Wayne tore off the main road, rocks crackling underneath them, then he eased the car towards the hefty log that was positioned just two feet in front of the cliff's edge. When Ida peered over the dashboard, the car's wide nose appeared at the brink, almost dangled.

"Ye t'inks she's alright?" Ida swallowed a rock lump in her throat and chewed dried skin off her bottom lip.

"Who gives a fat fuck?" Scotty said, irritated. "We done what ye asked."

After dimming the headlights, Wayne shut off the ignition. "And now a deal's a deal, Fried-Egg. Me first."

"No, ye fucker, me first," Scotty yelped, bouncing up and down in the back seat. "I don't want yer clammy mitts all over her before I gets a go."

"Alright, alright, me son," Wayne said. "Same time, one hand each, either side. Happy now, shit-for-brains?"

Ida's pupils were wide and she held her breath as she unzipped her jacket hesitantly. "C'mon with ye then, ye losers," she said as tugged out the bottom of her jersey shirt. She clamped her eyes shut as Wayne slid away from the steering wheel and Scotty lurched in from the back. Throaty groans echoed inside the enormous car as their cold sweaty hands slowly slid up over her skinny abdomen, rippled over rack ribs. Ida jerked backwards when they reached inside her beige cotton bra. Each brother had clutched a handful of rose-colored tissue.

Scotty slammed himself against the backseat, threw his find in Ida's face. "What the fuck is this," he squealed like a famished pig. "What the fuck is this, I said. Just as well I rubs me baby sister." To Wayne, "She got shit all for tits."

At first Ida said nothing, glanced from Scotty to Wayne, Wayne to Scotty, and crept backwards along the seat towards the passenger side door. Then she drew in a mouthful of air, shouted, "What the fuck do ye t'ink? I's only twelve."

Wayne was breathing so fiercely through his bull-flared nose, Ida thought she could see the stream of vapour.

"Ye t'ink ye can fuck us 'round? Cock teasin' us for a goddamned week for a go at a carpenter's dream?"

"Well, ye ain't gettin' nothin' else." Ida crossed her arms across her slender chest, her forearms sensing the empty cups of her bra.

"C'mon Ida." Scotty softened into pleading. "Me dick is hurtin'. Achin' like ye wouldn't believe, missus. Ye gone and give me blue balls, ye did. That'd damage a feller. Ruin him. Honest to Jaysus. It ain't good."

"Fuck yer balls, arsewipe. Go jerk yerself off."

Wayne grapped Ida's wrist, forced her hand down towards his crotch. "See what ye done, ye slut? We's goin' to fix this proper."

Jabbing the key in the ignition, he twisted hard and the car snarled to life. He skidded backwards blindly, ripped over the roads. "We's going' to the Gut to make this right. Cupboard Cove's only for pricks and pussies."

As Wayne screeched around a sharp turn, Ida reached behind her, coiled her fingers around the handle and pulled hard. The door fell open and she was flung from the car, rolled onto a shoulder of soft grass. Underneath a street lamp the car slowed, and Ida could see Scotty climbing over the backseat. He leaned out, hollered, "Whore," and dragged the door closed. Ida flipped up her middle finger, shook it in the air, and shouted, "Dick-wads".

As the great boat of a car scuttled around the corner, a sigh shuddered out from her lungs releasing the stifling air she'd been holding in. Her face, with all those child-sized features, contorted with soundless bawling. For several minutes, she crouched on the grass, hugging her knees, shoulders shaking. She wondered if she should walk back along the road, find Marnie, pluck her out of the ditch. But if she did, everyone would know she'd been involved. Then everyone would hate her. More than they already did.

After vomiting the remains of her scant dinner, she wiped her mouth in the knees of her jeans. No, she would never think about it again. She did what she had to do; nobody was going to hand her what she wanted. Ida Payne had to fight for everything.

Ida stood tall, swabbed her eyes in the elastic cuff of her jacket. Then after smelling the clean salt ocean air, she started the two-mile trek back to Aunt Penny's.

That evening when Marnie awoke between the stiff sheets of a hospital bed, a female police office questioned her. No, she said, she could not remember the colour of the car, the gender of the driver, or anything distinguishing about her assailant. There was little to offer: it all happened too fast. Although she did recall the vinyl seats were dark red, but that might have been smears from the blood gushing from her nose or her split lip. She also remembered smells, cigarettes, garlic, damp leather, and something fruity, maybe cherries. She looked for encouragement in the officer's eyes. But when the woman with the buzz cut flipped her notepad closed, Marnie understood those scant memories were useless, and the person who beat her, who loosened her top front tooth, would never be identified.

twenty-six

As though she was a pair of hands that were weary from knitting, Hazel Boone had laid her mothering aside. No matter how hard she struggled during those early years, she just couldn't tap into her maternal instinct and began to question whether it was there at all. Of course she tried, washed and fed them, and sewed identical miniature sets of clothing. On occasion, she even told them bedtime stories, though had to force herself to maintain innocence in her yarns, resist the sultry twists and turns her mind ached to take. But in the end, no matter what she did, tenderness still eluded her.

Often, she snapped at the younger one, couldn't tolerate the pervasive weakness he wore like a sheen on his skin. And the more she punished him, the more she pushed him away, the more needy he became, trying to obtain something from her she was unable to offer. Retaliation came through his runny nose, an enduring whine, and wet weepy eyes. Though these few efforts only served to escalate Hazel's wrath to new heights where she could literally feel hoary hairs sprouting from her scalp and wrinkles coursing out from every corner of her face in a fleshy mess of tributaries.

Many mornings Hazel screamed at the twins as the three of them stepped through the same conversation. Shaking a damp sheet in her hand, she would holler, "Which one of ye's wet the bed?"

"'Twas me." Three-year-old David always stepped forth first, chin up.

"Don't ye get smart with me, ye crackie. I knows 'twasn't."

"Popcorn, then. I seen her on the bed." Insignificant fists clenched at his sides.

"Never!" Hazel had gradually grown ever so fond of the tiny dog that adored her, waited for hours by the back door until she returned from her strolling. "Do ye t'ink I can't tell the difference?" Waving a handful of evidence before her nose, she hissed, "Smell of this would cut ye."

Then waggling it at Levi, she leaned over him until his knees nearly buckled. "See what ye've gone and done? Do ye t'ink I was put on this earth to wash up after ye, day in, day out? Skin on me hands is chapped beyond. I got half a mind to rub yer nose in it."

Levi quivered in his bare feet, so afraid of his mother, his bladder threatened to loosen again. He couldn't stop himself and she only made things worse. Her threats didn't cure him, and neither did the sharp smacks across his scrawny backside with metal knitting needles she delivered regularly. Inevitably, they only served to increase the frequency of his accidents.

"I swears if ye can't hold it, I'll tie in knot in it so tight, ye won't pass yer water 'til yer growed." She whipped the sheet into the washing bucket, plunked her hands on her now hefty hips. "And where's yer nightshirt?"

Reluctantly, Levi crept into their bedroom, lay down onto his belly, and reached deep under the bed. He retrieved a solid ball of soiled fabric, held it towards his mother. She snatched it from him and tore out of the room as though her mind was on fire with fury. She always seemed to be smouldering whenever she was close to Levi, no matter how David tried to draw her attention away.

And often it took much less than a drenched sheet to ignite her—dirty hands or knotted shoelaces would do the trick. So Levi adapted. He evolved an uncanny ability to predict her moods, forecast eruptions of temper. Over time, he became especially adept at hiding, tucking his small self away in the most unlikely of places, the linen closet, the bathroom cupboard, or underneath the basement stairs. This way he could avoid the funnel of Hazel's rage. As long as he lived, he would never understand why it needed to touch down on him.

"I don't like her one bit, Davey. She's awful mean, and she smells like rotten rhubarb." Levi rolled onto his side in the bed, mattress and sheets damp from springtime breezes, gaping windows.

"I don't like her neither. Let's grow up right fast, alright? Be men."

"We could run away. Over to Auntie's."

"Yeah. She'd stuff us with squares and peppermint knobs."

"Mudder would cry, though." Levi sighed, curled his body.

"Don't be cracked. No she wouldn't."

Levi became quiet, and David listened to the rhythm of his brother's shallow breathing. Gradually, it began to lull him to sleep. Then, as David was drifting toward a stream, bent-pin hook, nibbling on his line, Levi called to him from the shoreline, "Draw on me back, Davey."

"Whatd'ye want?"

"Fish," he said, as though sharing David's first dream of the evening. "All kinds of fish, swimming up and down me bones."

David lifted the soft fabric of his brother's clean nightshirt and pushed his fingers across Levi's clammy skin, sketching wavy fins, loops of fat bellies, and dots for eyes.

Several moments passed without a word, until Levi spoke. "I loves ye, Davey."

"I loves ye too, Levi."

"Why?" Closer to a breath than a word.

"Cause yer me little brudder."

Silence for a dozen sleepy blinks. "Yes. I is."

And like two spoons, they finally drifted off together to share another dream, this time their united minds spinning a hopeful future. The rising and falling of big men dreams. Dories brimming with a writhing catch. Perfectly painted matching clapboard homes seated side by side on a strong, sharp cliff.

twenty-seven

When the day finally arrived, Tilley never stepped outside his home until he was ready to meet Marnie in the woods. He spent the entire morning grooming. Showering and shaving the delicate fuzz that graced his chin and upper lip, dousing his stinging skin with a bottle of peppery scents Boyd had left behind. While he waited for sludgy time to pass, he drew Marnie's profile in his sketchpad over and over again. Frustration hardened within him when his memory skipped, and he couldn't capture her perfectly.

Anxious and eager, he finally wound his way through the woods, tried to amble without making a sound, stepping ball first, heel last. Following her instructions, he rounded the bend in the path that led to the hermit's shack; found the clearing where that rancid mattress had been tossed. And it was still there, threadbare, rusting springs exposed, holes torn in the sides where small animals had nested during the bitter winter.

"Marnie? Is ye here?" He spoke quietly, scanned the surroundings.

Then, from inside the shadow of a clump of spruce, Tilley heard snapping twigs. He took a full step back when he noticed Ida Payne prowling through the brush. Stopping a few feet in front of him, her hands caressed the mossy strands of Old Man's Beard that dangled from the tree trunks.

"'Tis me, Tilley." Ida was a pale bluish in the forest gloom even though her body was painted in pink pants, zippered sweater, and a silly pair of patent leather pumps with lacy socks. Underneath her arm she clutched a rolled up tattered beach towel.

"What're ye doin' here?" Tilley's gaze skittered in all directions, hoping to catch sight of Marnie approaching.

"She ain't comin'."

"How do ye know that?"

"'Cause she don't know yer here."

"Course she do." Tilley's mouth spoke, even though his mind had already realised the truth. That scented note he had taken such care to hide away from the prying eyes of his mother was a forgery. He felt a wave of guilt over not having realised it immediately, the pudgy writing, that juvenile drawing of a heart. "Whatd'ye want, Ida?"

She stepped into a ray of sunlight that had found its way through the tangle of tree branches and prickly needles. "To see ye, is all. Somet'ing wrong with that?" With an exaggerated bend in her hips, she unfurled the ratty towel on the damp mattress, then sat, knees primly bent. "Got a smoke?"

Tilley walked closer, handed her a cigarette, and puffed nervously on his own. "Whatd'ye want to see me for?"

"I don't know. Talk to ye, I s'pose."

"'Bout what?"

"I don't know." Ida picked at a hangnail. "Nothin' really.

Have a seat. Yer makin' me nervous just standin' there."

Tilley sat reluctantly. Out of the corner of his eye, he watched Ida tug a strand of peach-coloured bubble gum from her mouth and coil it like a noose around the middle of her tongue.

"I ought to get goin'," he murmured. "Mudder's goin' to be wonderin' where I is."

"Can't ye stay for anudder minute?"

"Look Ida," Tilley began, but before he could finish, Ida cut into his words, dug her heels into the fertile mulch of the forest floor.

"No 'look Ida' shit." She threw down her cigarette and scrunched it. "Don't start with that. What's wrong with ye?"

"What?"

"Why don't ye open yer eyes, Tilley?"

"Whatd'ye mean?"

"I's right here, b'y," she implored. "Ye don't need to be chasin' after no girl. I's right here for ye. Right now. Can't ye see that?"

"I's sorry, Ida. I don't like ye like that." Tilley's voice cracked, and he blushed.

At once, Ida sprung to her feet, began to holler, and pounded her skinny thighs to punctuate every phrase. Her high pitched squelching ricocheted off every surface, dead leaves, awakening branches, damp earth, and returned again and again to Tilley's ears. "What's wrong with me? What's the matter with me? Tell me that. Do me an enormous favour and tell me now. Put me out of me misery. Tell me just what the hell is wrong with me?"

"Nothin's wrong with ye. What is ye talkin' 'bout."

"Then why is ye tryin' to leave. To go find yer precious Marnie? Is that it? Why not me, hey? Why not me?" Her arms flailed as she twisted about, and Tilley leaned away before she struck him. "What's so wrong with me? Why can't nobody love me? Answer me that, Tilley. Why can't nobody love me?"

Ida stared at him hard before he stammered, "I—. I don't know."

"I knows," she said as dropped back to the mattress, and her voice was suddenly low, wobbly in her throat. "I's no better than a scrap of ol' garbage. Useless dirt. Trod upon gutter trash."

"Yer not dirt, Ida." He wrapped his arm loosely around her shoulders, felt her sharp bones through the fabric of her clothes.

"I is, then." She began to whimper. "That's what me Mudder always said."

"Don't say that," he crooned as she snuggled into the safety of his neck. "Yer alright, me dear. Don't let no one tell ye otherwise."

"She's not gone modellin'. Me mudder. No, she ain't. I lied."

"That's alright. No big deal."

"She took off on me. She did. Got a better offer."

"Yer not a bad offer, Ida. Yer not."

"Oh, Tilley."

Ida wove her thin arms around his chest. Tilley slid closer. He wasn't sure who eased whom backwards, but in a moment, they were lying side by side on the mouldy mattress. One of her willowy legs was lifted over his and her shiny shoe dangled on the tip of her toe. She feathered his neck with baby kisses, and against his will, he felt his skin getting peppery hot.

Then as she clung to him, nuzzling him behind his ear and running her eager hands over his back, his mind teetered. Marnie washed out; her absence replaced with the awesome watery freedom of what harm could it do? And he kissed her back, tasted her earlobes, rolled over onto her, and fumbled with zippers, buttons, snaps. Glorious handfuls of newness, shapes underneath his palms he had only ever imagined. Limbs knotted, sliding and shifting, the stenches of rot and rust from the mattress evaporated from consciousness.

At first, tantalising giggles filled his ears, but when they converted into protest, the objection was so distant and the resistance so feeble, Tilley hardly recognised it. And so he pressed on. Ida shoved into him, but it was as though Tilley had slipped over into a place where he was strong, driven, and unwilling to roll back. Impatience wheedled him forward. Just a little bit more. Just a little further and he could exhale.

Suddenly, a hoarse growl shocked Tilley's ears, an animal alarm waking him. Lifting his head, he saw a massive mound of dirty white fur, black eyes, and paws the size of salt meat buckets. As he stared, a massive polar bear reared up onto its hind legs, exposed an underside of fur, pale brown and matted. Tilley lay frozen on the mattress, forgetting every urge that had wracked his body only seconds earlier. Shoop-shooping through the air around his head, the sound of helicopter propellers was deafening. His heart choked him, as the beast dropped to all fours, lumbered several feet closer. Then it moaned as a tranquilliser pierced its upper left shoulder, and brought it to the ground.

Ida squeezed out from under Tilley, got to her feet, and shook herself. Then, with clothes in disarray, she tore out of the woods without glancing back. Only when she reached the backyard of Penny Payne's did she realise her patent leather pumps were still stuck in the muck beside the mattress. She reached down, peeled off the lace-trimmed socks, and clutched them in her fist. Just that morning she had purchased them in the children's section of Snook's Drugs with her last bit of allowance, and now they were sullied beyond repair.

When Tilley stumbled out of the woods, his head felt woozy. He was overwhelmed with the sudden openness of the Cove. Walking along the road he felt increasingly exposed, drivers leering as they passed, nosy housewives glaring out from their boxy little homes that lined the bay. Only an instant earlier, it seemed, Tilley was cocooned within some other world. And now he wondered if he was wearing his confusion on the outside, his missteps with Ida displayed across his chest for everyone to see.

Jamming his sneakers into blackened streaks of oil that lined the dusty road, he felt a distinct hollow sensation in his gut. His throat went dry when he realised he was not exactly the person he imagined himself to be. *How was this possible? How could he still be himself when such a shadowy subdivision existed within him?*

The gummy oil on the roads didn't help keep the dust in place. When Boyd zoomed past Tilley, skidded to a stop and reversed, powdery dirt erupted to cloud the air. With relief, Tilley climbed in the passenger door, thankful for the enclosure. Boyd reached across, gripped a length of rope coiled around the door handle, and wrenched the door closed with the sound of scraping metal.

"Hold this, or yer arse'll be kissin' the pavement when we goes 'round a turn."

Tilley grabbed the rope from Boyd and held it tightly across his lap. With windows sealed, the air in the Chevy Nova was heavy and sweet. He could smell Boyd's clothes, the permanent reek from spending hours next to a deep fat fryer. And in the cigarette tray on the dash, Tilley noticed the twisted remains of a joint.

Boyd snapped off the radio.

"Do ye like peanut butter?" he said with tremendous gusto.

"What?"

"Peanut butter, me son. Do ye like it?"

"I likes it well enough." Tilley stared out the window at the empty scar where a rear-view mirror once existed.

"There's a whack of it to me house. Come on up, buddy, and I'll make ye a sandwich."

Boyd had settled nicely into his basement closet, and had successfully managed to make payments and avoid eviction for several weeks now. "We don't want no trouble, now Boyd," Roland Roberts had said. "But as long as ye acts like the man that ye is, ye can stay on. Either whiff of either t'ing off—and I knows ye knows what I means—yer out on yer ear. Do ye hear me?"

"I got Mammie's Bread too," Boyd continued. "Peanut butter. Yeah. That stuff's right on."

Tilley watched as Boyd lifted a package of Fun Dip to his mouth, tore it open with his teeth, and let his tongue dart in and out of the envelope of lime-flavoured crystals.

With his chin sparkling green, he said, "How's yer lips?"

"Me lips?"

"Yeah, yer lips. How is they?"

"Alright, I s'pose."

"No. I means is they dry? I got tons of Chapstick up to the house. If they's dry, that is. That'll fix ye right up."

"No," Tilley managed as warmth rose up along his collar. "Me lips is alright. They's good."

"Sounds like yer on top of t'ings, then." Boyd said. "Right on the tippety top top of t'ings." A shot of laughter, a noise like ignorant fingers banging a piano, bounced about inside the small space. Boyd's clover tongue licking his mouth, and he tossed the empty candy wrapper to the floor of his car.

Tilley coughed, then cleared his throat. "How's Teena doin'?"

"Who? Teena from next door?"

"Yeah. Ye know, the one with the baby comin'?"

"Sure, ye shit. I knows. We's fightin' like usual. She can be a real bitch sometimes, always at me. Gets right under me skin it do. 'Bout me havin' a puff or two. Tell me, what's wrong with a pastime? A bit of recreation. Not like I's into anyt'ing hard. Not really."

"That's alright, I s'pose."

"That's alright is right. I's goin' to quit though. Soon as the baby gets here. She don't believe me."

"I guess ye'll show her."

"Ye got that. Women, b'y. Christ almighty. They's bad enough. But ye never met nothin' worse than one that's knocked up. I tell ye. If I ever gets any sort of schoolin', I'll tell ye what I's goin' to do. Breed 'em."

"What? I don't get ye."

"Girls, me son. Girls. There's got to be some way to breed the bitch right out of 'em. I tell ye, I's surprised no one ain't done it yet. I was just t'inkin' 'bout it 'fore I saw ye traipsin' along the road. Startin' me own breedin' program. There's got to be a way. I betcha there's government fundin' for a smart-arse idea like that. I's goin' to talk to Art Knuckle 'bout it, he knows the ins and outs of that sort of t'ing. I'll be bloody fuckin' rich, I will. Hire on me b'y when he's old enough and we'll wipe our backsides with two-dollar bills."

"'Tis a b'y then? How do ye know?"

"Have ye been listenin' to me or what? Didn't ye hear what I was sayin' 'bout girls? Better be a b'y is all I can say."

"Hope so then."

Scrawny thigh taking the wheel, Boyd clutched a KooKoo bar from the pile between his legs and peeled it from the clingy wrapper. Slipping one end between his lips, he let the tri-coloured taffy dangle like a foot-long tongue, and started earnestly retracting inch after inch with a sturdy chew.

Mouth full, he mumbled, "No b'y, though. Teena ain't all that bad as it sounds. Crooked as sin, but she's alright. I tell ye, she's real handy. That's one t'ing. Hung me up some curtains the udder day with nothin' but a pair of thumbtacks and some dental floss. I hates her guts sometimes, I tell ye. Wants to shoot her brains right out of her head half the time, but I loves her too."

"Well, that's alright."

"Course 'tis." Boyd turned sharply up the drive, halted within inches of Earl's truck, then reached over and smacked Tilley on the chest with the back of his fingers. "Hey, arsewipe."

"Yeah?" Tilley said, staring down at the oil stains on his sneakers.

"If Mudder and Fadder is ridin' ye too hard, come on up to the house. I'll make ye that peanut butter sandwich."

Tilley inhaled deeply, hoping to catch the sweet indifference that perfumed the air. He was sweating; the car heater locked permanently on high, though his skin felt cold. When Boyd pulled up to the back step, Tilley released his grip on the rope and banged his shoulder against the door. It was stuck tight.

"Out of the way, Brudder," Boyd said. He lifted his right foot up from behind the dash and with a swift kick over Tilley's lap, knocked the passenger door wide open. "I got to be gettin' that fixed," he continued between wet chews. "Teena ain't goin' to be too happy if I got to hoist her in through the window. Now is I right or is I bloody well right?"

Tilley shrugged, as he stepped out onto the driveway. "Yeah, yer right."

Boyd gripped the rope again, was about to yank when he said, "What? I don't get no thanks?"

"Thanks, Boyd. Good luck with yer breedin' program."

"That's better, me son." Boyd sprayed sugary spittle as he spoke, mounds of melting candy nestled in his cheeks. "World sure is a lot nicer with a few manners."

twenty-eight

Looking back over the past several months, David recalled how he had ached over his decision. *When was the best time to go? What would he say when he got there? Would he be recognised at once, or would he have to explain his presence?* And oh, that would be most painful. Having to put it all into words, why he had waited so long.

But since that thin wisp of smoke had ceased to twist its way up among the trees, David understood with certainty that agonising made little difference. He knew the scene he would find when he arrived. No one surviving without any amenities would let a fire die willingly. Not when the cutting dampness of a Newfoundland spring could rust every joint in an otherwise healthy frame.

Now walking through the woods, he did not rush, but moved at his body's natural pace. Along the path he noticed every sign of burgeoning life. Soft fresh needles emerged from the tips of spruce branches. Pale green blades of grass bravely had shot up through the dried brown and yellow mat. An occasional cloud of tiny flies swayed in the breeze like a sprinkling of pepper. And mud, of course. The entire path was soggy, sucking onto his boots, beckoning him to slow down. Or not to go at all.

The clearing was not difficult to find, it lay at the end of a well-trodden path. David moved towards the door and let his hand rest on the cool metal latch. He sensed an emptiness surrounding the entire place, and knew there was little left inside the walls.

Still, he continued the motions, lifting the latch, squinting with the dimness inside the tiny cabin. On the floor beside the woodstove, he found the crumbled body, coated in what looked like congealed blood, but was instead sticky and sweet smelling. In his fingers, the old man was clutching a crumpled newspaper.

David knelt on the plank floor, lifted the cold stiff hand, and cupped it in his own. His eyes welled up, tears balanced on the rims, teetered. The drips arose not just from sadness, but also from shame. Shame for the cowardice that had taken hold of him since he had become an adult. Shame for having broken his promise. But more than anything, shame from the overwhelming relief that filled his every crevice. An iron bond that fastened him to his past had finally dissolved.

Twenty-four hours earlier, the hermit reached his long arm into his dried goods cupboard and withdrew the last bottle of jam that Maureen Gover had dropped on his doorstep the previous fall. At least he hoped it was jam, he adored jam, and the bottle was still wrapped in a casing of newsprint.

The hermit balanced the weighty bottle in his hand and considered how he had managed to survive on the goodwill of others. Most of the people who knew him as a young man had already died. Or else their memories had softened. But still, week after week, like a ritual pilgrimage, members of Cupboard Cove trekked out to his dilapidated old shack, and deposited every kind of item imaginable on his porch. Cured fish, blueberry pie, new potatoes, loaves of still-warm bread, Purity syrup. Oh, of course, there was the occasional prank. Once he had heard teenagers hollering, "Delivery," and when he cracked open his door, a dead cat lay on his stoop, alongside a bottle of apple juice that contained something altogether different.

He would never forget when through his window he saw a mother and daughter moving up along the trail. The girl wore a yellow summery dress tied at sunburnt shoulders, and she carried a bulbous glass bowl that sloshed water as she stepped delicately over roots and twigs. At the edge of the clearing, the girl hesitated, and her mother urged her on, saying, "Ye dragged me out here, now lassie, ye can take the last few steps yerself."

He watched from behind his tattered curtain until the girl had approached, retreated, and they were well down the path again. Then he opened the door and peered out onto his stoop. There, laid precisely in the middle was a fish bowl, a single bright orange goldfish, circling idly around infinity. And a note was taped to the side of the bowl, printed in fat all-caps. His throat tightened as he read the words, "FOR HER MITE LOVE SARA".

He bent down, joints crackling, picked up his gift and carried it inside. That night, when he knelt down beside his daybed, he stared at his new watery companion, and whispered two prayers. The first was that little Sara would get everything her heart desired, and the second, that she would get absolutely none of it.

For three days, the fish swam in neat figure eights, at first vigorously, then gradually slower and slower. On the third morning, the hermit found his pet belly up, floating on the still surface of the water. He buried it underneath his stoop so that every time he placed a foot there he would remember both the charity and the folly. Though the child had offered it up with an open and generous heart, she had forgotten to bring its food.

He unrolled the jar in front of the fireplace. Ah, squashberry, his favourite. Using the side of his dented metal spoon, he snapped off the lid, then scooped out a taste. It melted on his tongue as he smoothed the page from the *Full Bucket*, reading the headlines by the light of the fire. Sweetness trickled back over his near-perfect teeth, down his throat, and into his stomach. The flavour of the squashberries was so intensely earthy, it tickled the back of his nose. When he opened his eyes after several brisk sneezes, it was then that he saw her. Staring out from a wrinkled page on the planed wooden floor before him. A grainy photo of his wife. Hazel Boone. Alongside it was a second photo of his son David, grown up into a handsome man.

Only two words, "Famous" and "Return", jumped out at Harvey Boone. Then, his heart ruptured inside his chest. Lightening shot down his left arm and sweat burst from his pores. Such a mesh of emotion throttled him and he could not begin to untangle it. Within moments, it overwhelmed him. Brought him down. And he thumped to the floor of his shack. Dead. Locked within his frozen fist was the youthful image of his wife, and inside his soul, pearly scars from the love for his children were torn wide open.

twenty-nine

Maureen had finally greased the screen door, so when Tilley pulled it open, it never made a sound. He stepped into the porch, removed his shoes, and placed them next to a pair of ladies ankle boots that rested neatly on the mat. His stomach growled, and he decided upon a snack of leftovers, cold roast and potato salad. A tall glass of icy milk, only a degree or two above freezing would serve to settle his mind.

But as Tilley came through the door to the kitchen, his foot halted mid-step. He stood stock-still, powerless while the lurid scene unravelling upon the kitchen table streamed through widened pupils and burned onto his retinas.

His father. Hunched over the table, tan trousers crumbled around his ankles, fat bloodless backside, fissure of skin like a plucked goose, body shuddering. Two legs, laced with green-blue veins, stuck out on either side of Earl. A large pair of khaki underwear, ring of pantyhose, dangled on one toe, threatening to tumble off with each test of the table's strength. Near Earl's head, a bright flash of orange hair bobbed, like a police siren blinking in the night.

Tilley never spoke, never breathed.

The first fractured words came from a mouth just underneath that mop of hair.

"Holy Mudder of Christ." Uttered Penny Payne.

"Oh, baby," Earl moaned. "I's givin' her."

"No, ye arsehole," she squeaked, shoving at his hulking frame. "'Tis bloody Tilley."

Earl glared over his shoulder, then sprung backwards with trouser-bound ankles, stumbled. The sound of sweaty skin smacking the linoleum, and Earl shuffled to his feet, hauled up his pants so swiftly, the fabric was likely obliged to deliver abrasions.

"Christ. Fuck. Christ. Fuck." Seesawing between fury and embarrassment.

With her face twisted in pain, Penny skidded off the table, grabbed her skirt from the floor, and dashed out of the kitchen with her reddened behind jiggling. One leg of the tan hose trailed nonchalantly behind her.

"Don't ye ever knock?" Earl roared.

From a distance of several feet, Tilley could smell deceitfulness on his breath. Like soaking bread, dissolved sugar.

Tilley thought he might cry, jammed his fingernails into his palms.

"Well?" Earl's hands were shaking as he clasped the band of his trousers. "Whatd'ye got to say for yerself?"

"I lives here," Tilley finally said, voice catching in a sandy throat. "Fadder. Oh Fadder. This is our home." And he sprinted out the screen door, into an uncertain air, body cavity warmth strangely marbled with strands of ice.

Thaw

⚜

Ida lingered in the back yard, roosting on the edge of an old-tire that her aunt had laid flat on the ground and revamped into a flowerpot. Over the next hour, she smoked the three cigarettes she had managed to steal from Tilley's back pocket before the tussle started.

Yes. The tussle.

How innocent it had all been at the beginning. When she initially slipped the note through the slats of his locker at school, she wasn't sure what she expected, where she thought it would lead. Not there. Really. Not even close.

Ida plunged her cigarette butt into the loose dirt of the pot, licked a finger, and wiped blood from a scratch near her ankle. No. She rolled her eyes towards heaven. Let's be honest here. She knew what she wanted to happen, that business, she knew all about it. *Hadn't she broken the spine on several of her Aunt Penny's romance novels?* She wanted the connection, the commitment that always came with it during the last two chapters of the book.

And now, with the way things unfolded, she felt more the fool than ever. Not a chance she could ever tell. *Who would believe her?* They would only say she'd brought it all on herself, and they were likely right.

Ida leaned her chin onto her bent knees and blew hot breath through the fabric of her pants. When she inhaled, a chill crawled up her spine, wanted to shake her and she didn't stop it.

Then coming from the kitchen window at the rear of the house, Ida heard a slamming door, raised voices. It must be Aunt Penny. Ida knew that Aunt Penny rarely arrived anywhere without an uproar. So when Ida went inside, trying to hide her dirt-stained feet and tousled hair, she snuck though the patio door into the family room. But even though she didn't make a sound,

Aunt Penny still hollered, "Ida Payne. Get yerself in here." With no escape, Ida slunk into the kitchen.

"Well hello, hunny. Looks like ye just had a nice roll in the hay for yerself."

Ida stopped, stared at the woman seated on the countertop beside the breadbasket. "Mudder? What're ye doin' here?"

Fay-Anne Payne had recently arrived at her brother's home with the intention of collecting her daughter. After rifling through the fridge for a bottle of beer, she had hoisted her portly backside onto Penny's countertop and waited for Ida to return. Perched there with dangling ankles crossed, her snug outfit had peeled up with the additional stress of bending, revealing folds of dimpled pinkish skin.

"That all ye got to say to yer Mummy?" Fay-Anne ran a thick finger underneath her nose, then turned to a substantial man who had chosen a seat at the kitchen table. "Told ye she got an attitude."

The man raised his bushy eyebrows, shook his head. "Now Fay-Anne, me duck. She's just surprised is all." When he spoke, his lips parted like a beak, fit for crushing eggs or nuts, but not well suited to conversation.

"Well Ida, girl. Me and Russell has come to get ye."

"Russie?" Ida was suddenly light-headed from shifting her gaze between the two intruders.

"Yeah. That's Russell. Me Russie. I told him all 'bout ye when we was on his business trips. He thought 'twas a shame to have ye wastin' away here, wanted to come get ye right off. Some man, he is." A smirk dripped off her sweaty jowls, and her chunky ankles, twitchy feet that would not lie still. "He's wants to be yer new daddy."

Russell's beak opened once again, and he said in a pacifying voice, "Now, now, Fay-Anne." Then his ferret eyes widened as they settled on shrinking Ida, and he purred, "Don't go worryin', me little lovey. I ain't got no thoughts to be yer new fadder. How's 'bout callin' me Uncle Russ for starts?"

"Umm." Ida put her hand to her mouth, started sucking the tip of her index finger.

"Come on over," he hummed, patting his knee. "Come sit on yer Uncle Russie's lap. Try it out for size."

Ida stared into each face in the room. Newly appointed Uncle Russie smoothing the caramel-coloured pant leg of his polyester suit. Then over to Official Uncle Winse, T-shirt straining around his gut, hands lifting to rub his leathery face with open palms. Her prodigal mother, jerky head, shiny apple cheeks, and upturned nose, tugging at a mess of stringy hair so black it appeared blue in daylight. Cousin Missy (who had recently discovered a taste for turmoil) was leaning against the grease-spattered wall by the stove, crumbling a cellophane bag, and biting cheesy debris off her thumbs. And finally Aunt Penny, chin scoured from Earl's beard, backing herself into the corner where two sections of countertop met.

As Ida stared, Penny wavered slightly on her feet, then steadied herself, and smoothed her blouse. The buttons were fastened askew and one doughy knee gaped out from a substantial hole in her pantyhose. But it was her glazed expression that held Ida's attention. Somehow, she thought, there was something different about Penny. Or perhaps it was simply due to the company. While Ida had always considered Penny to be a mean, bitchy woman, now, standing beside overblown Fay-Anne, Penny appeared stripped down, modest, uncontaminated.

"Pack yer few t'ings, Ida. We's got to get on the road. Don't give me no lip, lassie. Russ got a business to run, ye knows."

"To where?"

"So many damn questions." To Russ, "See, I told ye. She don't shut up. Can't do nothin' without a fuss." Back to Ida, "Come on with ye, ye little shit. Shut yer trap and get a wiggle on."

"Ye'll be real comfortable, Miss Ida," Russell crooned. "Real comfortable with me." He sniffed hard. "I means us."

Ida hung her head, and was starting to turn when she heard her Aunt Penny's voice strong and clear. With Penny's select words, Fay-Anne slid down from her post, and Winse removed his fists from his eyes, and let his mouth loll open. Ida saw the glow in Russell's eyes evaporating as though the waitress en route to his table let his much-wanted hamburger slide off the plate onto a grimy diner floor.

"Stop right now," Penny had said. "Ye ain't takin' her nowhere."

"Now, Penny. Gettin' awful big for yer britches, ain't ye?"

Penny took two steps forwards, coming nose to nose with bulbous Fay-Anne.

"Do ye t'ink ye can waltz in here and make off with her like she's some sort of gadget? If that's the case, well no, maid, yer sorely mistaken. She'll stay put. That's what. Right here. Where's she's wanted."

Fay-Anne slid her fingers through her hair and flicked out a few greasy locks as her head jutted ever closer to Penny's. "I got rights, ye knows."

"Rights, me arse. We can talk 'bout rights. Yes, by Jaysus. Call Constable Johnson. Ye can use me phone there on the wall. Let's get he over. I knows now he wouldn't love to talk to ye 'bout ye rights. And while he's at it, he can get the inside story on yer friend's sales."

"Well, I'll be damned." Fay-Anne sniffed, rubbed her nose again, then reached over and tugged at Russell's jacket sleeve. "Come on, ye idiot."

"But-," Russell interjected. He slurped as drool threatened to slide down his chin. "I likes her."

"I said come on with ye," she crowed, nearly hauling him off the chair. "Sure as hell don't need to be talkin' to the law."

"And stay gone, ye, ye, ye, ye tramp," Penny called out when the door had slammed.

After a full minute of absolute silence from every witness in the kitchen, Penny glanced around, relieved that the guilt over being caught with Earl had thinned slightly. Then she spoke to herself with an air of determination, as though coming to grips with a choice she had made. "She's here for the long haul. Yes, she is. And I don't give a fiddler's fat fart if the Good Lard hisself comes down here this instant and says otherwise."

Earl instantly regretted his stance, ran after Tilley. But in those few moments, Tilley had already disappeared into the thick dusky woods. Jumping into his truck, Earl spun down the drive, never flinched as stones arched upwards, chipped paint from the underbelly of his beloved truck. Along the highroad he sped as he scanned the trees, the gaps between. He was uncertain of what he would do if he found Tilley, what he wanted to say. Something. There was something he wanted to tell his young son. He would try to speak, without reservation. Some heartfelt words about the complexities of love. Explain to Tilley how Maureen had long ago stopped being a wife, opting instead to be purely a mother. Tell him how real love was a childish, next to impossible premise. There was no such thing as love that was solely pure. A good love did not exist.

Remarks formed in his mind, and Earl spoke them aloud inside the cab of his truck. Homily prepared, mind beginning to rehearse, when he saw a rush of movement in the woods. He craned his neck to see if it were his small boy. Turning his attention back towards the road, he faced a black shadow, two beady eyes blocking his view. When his head smashed though the windshield, Earl had two thoughts, fresh and simultaneous: *'That's some size of a fuckin' moose,'* and *'It serves me right.'*

Lungs burning, Tilley finally slowed when he reached a clearing in the woods. Staring at the blackened clouds that lingered above him, he whispered an innocent question, "What is this shit?" In cynical response, the sky opened up and spat out a chunk of hail the size of a hen's egg. It descended, almost driven, with great speed and struck Tilley square in the forehead.

He crumbled to the ground just as a shower of crystals began to coat him, filling his shirt pocket, the shallow dip behind his ear, and the crevice underneath his bent arm. The air surrounding him was filled with fairy tinkling as the crystals bounced off every surface, weighted branches, and bent the scattered strands of tender grass. Watery ice fell next, layer upon layer gradually building its way up over Tilley's back, encasing him in a glassy shell. When the storm finally ended, Tilley's small frame was well encrusted. And inside his casing, the heavy heart welcomed its new pace, the lazy rhythm of hibernation.

thirty

Within two hours of the freak storm, sanders and salters had blasted the road clear of all traces of ice. Even though there was no need for such a leisurely pace, Annette's car still crawled along the highroad. Several vehicles pulled out into the adjacent lane, whizzed past, horns blaring, a middle finger wagging. She did not mind. In fact, she barely noticed. All afternoon, her mind had been occupied with thoughts of her battered daughter lying on a stiff mattress at Good Hopes, and thoughts of her hapless husband who was painfully absent during this his family's time of need.

When she had told David about Marnie's accident, she thought he hadn't heard her. She repeated herself. Once. Twice. Then he only stared, as though he was gulping down the information, like tough bites of steak on an already full stomach. "Okay, okay, honey," he had finally said, a sharp edge to his voice. "I'll get to it."

Annette leaned forward and turned up the radio. George Jones was whining, rolling out his hit, "He Stopped Loving Her Today." As she sang along with the lyrics, she snorted suddenly, and came within a breath of laughing. What a farce he had written. A romantic's dream. He must have composed that ridiculous song at the onset of infatuation. Those first three months when the soul floats away and the potential for collapse is immense. And, of course, it will cave in. Either at once or with a gradual decay, like sand sliding down the walls, occasional pebbles falling. Then comes the grieving. No matter if it's shocking or subtle. Over time, love always ripens into colourless tedium.

She remembered those very instants when she fell in love with David. At that time, she was so deliciously young and naïve. How quickly her expectations careened into reality. With a marriage to David, she had conjured a life, dizzyingly rich, laden with a constant whirlwind of adventure. But instead, her ability to entice him fizzled on the third morning of their honeymoon. She had never wanted to admit it, but that was the plain truth. Breakfast turned from pastries and freshly squeezed juice into soggy cereal and margarine-coated toast. A newspaper was erected between them and velvet slippers changed into yesterday's socks. And though it made her chest ache, she now knew with conviction, even when George Jones claimed otherwise, if a man as gifted and passionate as her husband was incapable of such great depths of love, then no one was.

Annette drove on. The sun beamed in through the passenger side window and shone a soft warmth across her waist and hips. She sank deeper into the burgundy velour seats and felt the car move smoothly over mounds of pavement. Then without warning, her mind began to call forth images of Seymour, the fishmonger from the Salty Shack. Pictures flashing, teasing her willing retinas. Rough hands delving into a bucket of fillets, rubber-gloved fingers sliding among the scallops, and chunky knuckles clinking through the mussels. As these thoughts settled on her, she blushed. Even though she despised most of Cupboard Cove, there was something in the way Seymour winked at her, flicked his pink tongue across his bottom lip that made the vast emptiness within her almost tolerable.

An agitated honeybee, Maureen Gover buzzed around the windowless third floor waiting lounge, wanting to leave but trapped by nature's obligations. The room was painted bile green and decorated with a muddle of framed images; cartoon teddy bears to a breaching humpback whale. Chemical cleansers clung to the air, threatening to bleach her hair, her skin, her lungs.

She had been there all night, wondering about Earl's fate, and was beside herself over Tilley. He was not answering the phone, and she had never left him alone before. *Could her child open a can? Could he fry his breakfast egg without burning his fingers?* She ran her swollen tongue over her teeth. After seventeen cups of sour tea and hours of sighing, her entire mouth felt like gritty chalk. She groaned, lit another cigarette, acknowledged a sprig of relief. The nicotine calmed her body, steam-rollered and spring-coiled her all at once.

After sucking one last drag from the wet end of her cigarette, she crumbled the butt into a bucket of sand and flumped into one of the beige leatherette chairs.

"Maureen?"

She looked towards the doorway to see Annette Boone in an ironed periwinkle lounging suit, with a polka-dotted scarf knotted neatly at her throat. In her hand, Annette held a Styrofoam cup, edges nibbled and smeared with burnt apricot lipstick.

"Why are you here?"

"'Tis Earl," Maureen replied, fingers fumbling for another cigarette. "Struck a moose on the highroad."

"Serious?"

"Don't know. They says he cracked his head somet'ing awful on the windshield."

"Terrible luck." Sauntering into the room, Annette's perfume overrode the chemical stench, replacing it with heavier honeysuckle and orange blossoms. "And I had the silly notion you came to see Marnie."

"Marnie?" Squelching noises announced the slightest shift Maureen made in her seat. "Well, seems 'tis an out-and-out gatherin' here at Good Hopes."

"Yes, she was brought in last night. Beaten up by some of the scum that lives in this godforsaken place. She'll be fine, of course. She's tough like her mother." Annette paused. "I've spoken to her even. Just a terrible concussion. That's all, though that's plenty. I swear this Cove is burdened with a population of riffraff and pilferers."

"There is some good people here, Annette." Maureen was solemn.

"Well, I'd like to meet them." She selected a seat in the corner, alit on the very edge, and crossed her pristine runners. "I haven't told you the best of it yet. Can you believe I lost an entire load of washing?"

"Yer wash?"

"That's exactly what I said. Last week I had hung it out on the line to dry, but gale force winds tearing in off that bay made short work of that. When I went to bring them in, the line was entirely empty."

"That can happen to anyone who got their home near the ocean. And as far as I's aware, no one in Cupboard Cove controls the wind, Missus Boone." Maureen was suddenly aware of how her fingers held her cigarette, and she wished she could twist time back ten minutes, run a comb through her snarled hair.

"Yes, but they certainly control what they retrieve from their lawns, I'll hasten to conclude. Would you believe me if I told you that as I drove to the hospital this very day, nearly every home I passed had a piece or two of my good quality clothing dangling on their lines?"

"That's awful hard to believe."

"Well, that is the truth of it. Found my articles scattered about, and without the slightest thought of ownership, people started putting them to use."

"Whose to know who owns what if it comes driftin' 'cross yer lawn?"

"Anyone with the sense of a goat knows those garments haven't been bought locally. They are much too fine."

Maureen stubbed out another cigarette, then ran her empty hands over her worn pants, feeling the pills that riddled the abric. "Best t'ing to do is go and ask, and yer stuff'll be handed over, fresh and ironed too, I 'llows."

Annette's sharp pale jaw gaped slightly. "Like a beggar woman? Going door to door. I would never partake in something so, so——."

"If yer too proud, then 'tis on yer own head. Nobody wants to be squanderin' a good piece of clothin'. 'Tis not in us crowd to be that way. What ye can take an ounce of comfort in is the thought that yer few bits of t'ings won't be wasted. They'll be put to good use, and when they's worn out, yer apt to be seein' a scrap of yer shirt sewed into someone's coat, or used to mend the backside of a pair of jeans. That's the way we is here, where people struggles."

"Ah," Annette said, and emitted a short sardonic laugh. Checkmate. "You paint a lovely picture, Maureen, but it doesn't hold much water. Put to good use, I think not. For didn't I pass by the Jenkins' house and see my designer dress flapping in the wind. Was it on Frieda Jenkins? No, certainly not. I'm sure you're familiar with those absurd storefront manikins Mr. Jenkins uses to decorate his front lawn? Well, the middle one, with the better half of her face peeled off, was wearing none other than that very dress."

Maureen was about to retort, state that the wife of a painter should have some kindliness toward a fellow's artistic ventures, but her mental phrasing was cut short when Dr. Hunt entered the room. He parted his lips and Maureen sprung from her seat.

"We don't have a prognosis at this time, Mrs. Gover," he said sternly through the incision that was his mouth. Dr. Hunt worked in the Intensive Care Unit, wheedled patients back from death on a weekly basis, and eventually perfected a Godlike attitude he deemed appropriate to such feats. "We won't know until he wakes up."

Maureen over-nodded and bit at her stump fingernails. "What's the worst?"

"I really can't predict," he said, even though he knew his predictions were consistently correct. "It would be unprofessional."

"Tell me. Please, Doctor. Please. What's the worst that can happen to him?"

Dr. Hunt scratched his stubbly chin, his face bloated from lack of sleep, and let his gaze rove all over Maureen's body as though assessing its firmness. "Here at Good Hopes, we try to focus on the positive unless otherwise necessary. But-"

"But?" Maureen's voice had escalated to desperate proportions, and she tightened her damp grip on the back of the chair.

He paused for effect, then allowed his words to dribble out. "With head injuries like your husband's, it is possible he could be...well, incapacitated. Perhaps entirely dependent."

Maureen stepped backwards, put her ageing hands to her throat. "Whatd'ye mean? He'll be some kinda vegetable?"

"Now, now, Mrs. Gover. Calm yourself." The slightest hint of a smile tickled the corners of his lips, twinkled in his eyes. "We tend not to use that term. It's sounds quite—well, harsh. And it's not as though Mr. Gover, in his very bed, is going to transform into a two-hundred pound turnip." He chuckled gently, opened his holy-man hands. "Nothing of the sort."

"Oh," Maureen said as her hands slackened. She was not beyond some level of performance herself. "Whatd'ye t'ink, then? Honestly, Doctor. Will he come 'round?"

"In time, I estimate yes. And then we will know much more. It is possible that his faculties may be completely diminished. He may require full time care. But take heart, Mrs. Gover, we do have various resources to assist you in these matters. Homes and such. Our staff can walk you through the procedures, if need be. With some level of government assistance, they are entirely affordable."

Maureen waved her hands in the air, then began to stride around the room. "No, no, Doctor. That won't be necessary. Whatever God wills, we'll work through this tragedy as a family."

"Very well, then. At any rate, we have gotten quite ahead of ourselves, haven't we? Such prophesising is unhealthy at best. Good thoughts, Mrs. Gover." He stepped into the line of her pacing, clasped her swinging hand in his own, his palms supple and nearly printless. "We like to say 'Good thoughts at Good Hopes', ma'am. Can you remember that?"

"Oh yes, Doctor. I surely can. Good thoughts I got. Nothin' but good thoughts roamin' 'round inside this ol' head of mine."

As Dr. Hunt ambled out of the windowless room, Maureen's mind was brimming with images of a sedated Earl, soft and pliant under her charge. In sickness and in health. She recalled

thirty-one

azel considered herself a vibrant woman, though she spent much of her days exceptionally frustrated. Her only release came during her frequent walks to meet Lyle. Regardless of weather, she left her saltbox home either bundled in woolly winter layers or unbound in a printed cotton dress. But the liberation she found was temporary, a childish tease, never reaching the point of satiation she had experienced that first afternoon in the root cellar. It wasn't because her lover and her husband never tried. Both Lyle and Harvey told her daily that she was lovely, but she felt they were lying. She was fading fast, struggling to bite off mouthfuls of life with starvation greed.

And naturally, with that sort of bottomless pit to feed, she began to take grander risks. She opened the door to her home, permitting Lyle entrance during those few stolen moments when she found herself alone.

In mid-July, Harvey got word that his mother had died. She was found slumped over her largest mixing bowl, liver-spotted hands mid-knead, and seven loaves worth of dough rising up around her arms, pressing against her chest in an effort to dislodge her. With four-year old David in tow, Harvey travelled to Severed Knot for the funeral, leaving Hazel on her own with Levi.

"Ye be a good little man now, me son," Harvey had said, gripping Levi's dollop of a chin gently. "Yer mudder don't want to come, so ye'll have to take care of her. Like Daddy's b'y."

Sensitive through and through, Levi could not tolerate being separated from David and he whined and wept at every turn. Softly, of course, but just enough to pluck Hazel's sore nerves. She wrung her hands constantly, bunched her apron, and growled at the child through fused teeth. But still, he bleated behind the sheer curtains of the front window, while he turned Hazel's minutes into painful centuries.

When Levi knocked over the jar of fresh milk the following morning at breakfast, the weak strand stabilising Hazel snapped. Tugging him up from the table by a stretching ear, she dropped his squirming body straight into the expanding pool of warm milk.

"Clean it up," she said, as she marched to a pail of water, fished out the floating cloth, and threw it towards his head. Her tone was dangerously low, even. She felt her heart beating between her temples, and did not trust the strength building in her palms. "Clean. That. Up."

Levi lifted an arm to avoid being slapped by the cloth, and milk flicked from the fabric of his nightshirt across a clean stretch of floor. "I's sorry," he said in a weak voice, head hanging. "'Twas an accident."

"Accident? Oh, me sonny." Hazel shook her head, thinking momentarily about the devious nature of accidents and her guest who would arrive in only hours. What a stench he would meet if the milk were allowed to sit, sour. She dropped to her knees, snatched back the rag, and gripped it with both hands until it threatened to tear. As she ground her teeth, she imagined the roots that had sprouted out from her legs, her body, binding her unwillingly to the house, the children, the husband. Her eyes rolled back, lids dipping as though floating on a calm sea. And she considered what a sinful pleasure it would be if she could only float through an afternoon, absolved from the boundless responsibilities.

Levi's moan scraped inside her ears and snatched her back from her vapourish fantasy. "If ye don't get clear of me, ye'll see what an accident's all 'bout, ye little beggar."

"I can clean," he protested, reaching for the cloth.

"Is ye deaf? Go away with ye." She whipped the rag at him, leaving a red welt on his neck. "Get on. I don't want to see hide nor hair of ye this day. And if I does, I'll trounce ye like ye've never been trounced." She scrubbed and scrubbed, wrung the rag in a bucket, and slapped it back down onto the floor. "Blessed Saviour," she muttered. "How dumb can ye get?"

Barefooted, soaked nightshirt, Levi tore out of the kitchen, into the porch. He dashed out the screen door. His face contorted with crying, but his mouth was soundless. Pressing his cold body against the sun-warmed clapboard, he scanned the landscape for cubbyholes where he could hide. *Could he stay out all night?* The very thought made him shudder, and ever so quietly, he snuck back into the porch, past the shoes and shelves, coats hung on hooks, and a tin of cherry squares. Behind the door, his father had tossed a dusty sack filled with last year's potatoes. He eased in behind them, curled down. And as he thought about what to do, he sucked the sweet flecks of cream from his cuffs, and nibbled and swallowed the black sandy dirt from underneath his unkempt fingernails.

When Lyle O'Leary arrived at her back door, something about his demeanour punctured, then flattened the air balloon that was present inside powdered and perfumed Hazel. Lyle did not enter with trepidation, as he used to do, but strolled in as though he belonged, as though he owned the very house itself. Exactly what she didn't want. That cockiness. Some level of fear over the forbidden nature of their relationship made it all the more mouth-watering, but now, his confidence, his arrogance, was a blanket, damp and smothering.

"Where's the b'ys?" he said, wiping his nose with the back of his hand.

"Gone off."

"Gone off?"

"Yes, that's what I said." Such comfortable ordinary conversation reserved for the best of friends. For the first time since they were children, Hazel found herself unable, or perhaps unwilling, to look at Lyle. "David's gone off with his fadder. The udder one's gone off by hisself, over to his Aunt's, like usual. Ye'd t'ink that woman was his mudder way he's clung onto her. Good riddance, though, if ye asks me. He'd test the patience of Job."

"That's alright. He's a grand little feller, sure. And b'ys'll be b'ys, right?"

"Ye'd know," she said under her breath. "Is that why ye come over? To talk about me b'ys?"

He smirked and slid into a chair. He wanted tea. *Wanted tea!* Hazel shuddered at the very request for service. Somehow in the course of events, she had been too eager. He must have sensed her neediness, her void, and that had prompted the reversal in character. She refused him tea and he seemed delighted by her sauciness. Surely this would not do, would not do at all. Control had to be hers. It always was.

With that in mind, she skulked towards him like a hungry lioness, did exactly as she pleased for the next three hours. Orchestrating every move, she mauled him, stole what she wanted in the kitchen, the family room, her marriage bed, entirely unconcerned for the desires of her lover. When she finished, his appetite remained colossal, while Hazel felt relaxed, inwardly sedate, but her muscles were bursting with a blistering energy.

"Goodbye, Lyle," she said as she tugged on her stockings, drew her slip on over her head.

"Goodbye?" Lyle rightly sensed finality, and was confused. "I can see ye again, right?'

"Of course, ye silly creature." She smiled demurely as she buttoned up her dress. "'Tis only the size of a thimble, our Cupboard Cove."

Lyle nodded, then dressed quietly, and stumbled out the back door, head and shoulders weighted with bewilderment.

When she heard the screen door ease back into position, she counted to three and rushed out behind him. Glancing this way and that, she shook her loose hair, flaming in the sunlight. She was not searching for her lover. Had no notion to ask him back. Those hours of illicit frolicking had lost much of their charm by the end. During the afternoon, she realised she'd been taking all the risks. Men would clap Lyle on the back, while she would be disgraced. And for what? Absurd, really. Hazel decided she was much more potent as a single person. Certainly her family was not negotiable, but Lyle was incidental, festive trimming.

With the speed of purpose, she walked. More than anything she craved space, to be free in an open empty field, where a razor-sharp sickle had felled all the grass, and tended mounds lay in perfect rows. She took the most direct route. The wooded path was striped heavily with gnarled roots, and she never missed a single one.

All so peculiar, she thought. For years, there had never been such a yearning. And now, she was bound and determined to yank every weed from her mother's overgrown grave. No matter if it took her hours.

Levi did not watch Hazel through the crack in the door. At first, he tried, but his hands clasped across his eyes and would not let go. When he heard feet moving through the pantry and outside, his hands released, and he crawled out from his hiding spot, looked around. His skin tingled with fear; he did not know when Hazel would return. As swiftly as he could, he climbed into a tight box, shivered, and took a deep breath. Using his fingernails, he dragged the door closed, and heard the decisive thump of a falling latch. Good, he thought in pitch darkness, *I's safe now. I hopes she don't never find me.* And after some time had passed, even though Levi was chilled down to his very bone, he relaxed, yawned, and settled in for a nap.

David was shivering on the daybed in the shack, but did not dare to light the fire. He did not feel right about putting the body outside to prevent the onset of decay, and instead endured the terrible cold that crept in through floorboards and leaky window casings. Anyway, he figured the door was caked in ice, so he might have to kick it open.

David closed his eyes, put his hands to his weary head. *How could he even fathom putting his father outside in such a storm?*

But then again, just what had he been thinking lately? All he had made were mistakes, poor choices. Coming to Cupboard Cove was not the first; it was rather closer to the last in a long chain of many. He had arrived here with the sensation of hope, though the exact object of his hope he could not identify. *Was it to find peace with everything that happened so many years ago?* Yes, he was only thinking of himself. Like a hormonal teenager, chasing resolution. A notion so flimsy, so vague. All this when his priorities should have been elsewhere. He should now be with his ailing daughter. *His only child.*

With that thought, David bolted upright. His life became startlingly clear. For years, he'd been fixated on that one afternoon when he made a discovery that destroyed him. That single instant when too much knowledge of human nature had exploded within such a young brain. Since then, he had placed that moment above all else. It had directed him, driven him. Almost over the edge.

At once David understood—he was much more like his father than he'd ever guessed. Both were suffering from peripheral blindness. Hairs prickled up on the back of his neck and radiated outwards from his spine. And for the first time in his life, he wanted no part of it, that past. What he craved now, more than anything else, was a fresh start. A new beginning. *Could he claim a personal springtime?*

David sighed, watched the crumbled form on the floor as though he were expecting it to twitch. God, they looked so much alike. It was eerie. He would manage until morning, then he would trek out and call Constable Johnson. He anticipated a mild interrogation. Why was he there, at the hermit's? Just happened by, he would reply. Mere curiosity. No need for any further explanation. *And if someone noticed the resemblance?*

David got off the damp bed and with his thumb and forefinger closed the old man's gaping eyes. There. Now the similarity wasn't so pronounced. Just an eccentric hermit who died of a heart attack.

As he kneeled beside his father and glanced around the one-room, he wondered how such an enclosure, such a life, could be honest and humble, yet at the same time, so utterly self-centred.

Scotty and Wayne Power were still boiling inside over the stunt Fried-Egg Ida had pulled. But even though the trio had fought in the car, the boys still liked her, actually found her blameless. Instead they figured her fickle disposition had everything to do with her father. Ida had told them the whole story—about the grand house where she lived, how her father was a rich and famous painter, and how he liked to diddle her every night. All not so serious, Ida had confided with a hearty wink to Wayne and Scotty, but what burned the most was the way her mother hated her. She knew all, of course, about every visit in the dark. Spent a near fortune on Ida's sheets, as they were always marked with the telltale streaks of oil paints.

Ida was a convincing liar, and the boys believed every creative word. The craving for retribution curdled their spit, and they hawked frequently as they picked their way up the icy slope that led towards the backyard of the Boone family home. Ida had told them about the shed, about her boyfriend who sometimes visited the shed to paint there, and her fears that her father would diddle him too. The boyfriend. That was an itch. But Wayne and Scotty reasoned there was more than enough Fried-Egg to go around.

When they reached the shed, they busted their way in, tearing metal attachments for the combination lock out of the wall by its nails. Wayne was first through the door, he always was, and started by smashing jars, squeezing large tubes of paint over the floor, the shelves. Scotty darted in, and after an initial appraisal of the task, took a moment to dunk a fat brush into a tub of burnt umber, and scribble "FAGGIT" on the north wall of the enclosure.

"That's Fag-GOT, ye dipshit." Wayne giggled as he stole another huff from a container of mineral spirits. Newly invigorated, he then hauled a pocket knife from the backside of jeans and began slashing painting after painting.

Throwing down the brush, Scotty followed suit. There were so many, piles of canvases, some finished, some recently stretched. They were layered deep, and the Power boys mowed through them with gusto.

Scotty ploughed towards an easel that was wedged into a corner of the shed. He slid behind it, faced the canvas, and stopped. Nipping his blade between his teeth, he removed the painting from its perch and held it at arm's length. Moonlight drifted in through the window and cast an unnatural glow across the image David Boone had recently created. The same image he painted under every single image he had ever produced, his continual undercoat.

"Take a gander at this," Scotty mumbled from behind the knife.

He turned the image for his brother to see. On the canvas, David had painted what appeared to be an enormous ice cube. Trapped within the centre was a small boy, like a fly caught in resin. The child wore only a diaphanous shirt, though the clothing was closer to a wrapping of phantoms that reached out through the ice. He craned his neck, squinted in the moonlight, and Scotty could see the curve of the child's backside, tracks of veins, bulging eyes. The body was curled tightly, but the head was turned. And he stared straight at Scotty, almost timidly, and Scotty sensed he was never meant to stare back.

"Like Ida told us," Wayne said, as he pressed in on his left nostril, shot snot from his right. "He's some sick fuck, wah?"

Scotty nodded in reply and extended the painting to his side, cautiously, like a bullfighter's cape. He didn't like the uneasiness that was growing inside him. And in order to eliminate it, he lifted his wet boot in an impressive arc, smashed his heel though the canvas. The child tore into four fragments.

"Holy shit, man, " Wayne sputtered. His hand flicked towards a bay window on the second floor of the main house. "Up there."

Scotty glanced up. "Shit. Shit. Ol' bitch is watchin' us," he yelled.

Clothes coated in paints, threads, and cleaners, Wayne and Scotty scuttled out of the shed, slipping over the ice. "Like a bloody ghost," Wayne whispered as he cruised into the shadows of towering pine trees lining the driveway.

"Boo-oo-oo," Scotty howled as he hurried after his brother.

"I loves it, I loves it," Wayne screamed.

"Loves what?"

"The rush, man," he hollered at they skidded down the slick hill, clutching branches and trees as they went. "The rush. Ye can't beat the fuckin' rush."

Hazel had seen everything that evening, though she never alerted anyone. It had played out before her eyes with the fluffy reality of a television program. Most nights she discovered something interesting, lights travelling in the sky, lacy snowflakes flirting with the windows, or a forlorn moose at sunrise. But this had been the boldest vision to date, the most engaging of her recent evenings in Cupboard Cove. And she needed a little of it, the drama. So many years ago, insomnia had set in. Rest, peace, puffing up her eyelids like black humour. So cruel. The release of sleep settling well within her sight, but just beyond her grasp.

✤

Of course Annette heard nothing of the commotion in her backyard. She was tucked deep into her 300 thread-count sheets, under a down-filled comforter, earplugs driven in, hot pink ye-mask lowered. In an attempt to block out her mother-in-law's meandering and doorknob rattling, Annette followed this routine nightly. Sometimes when David was missing, as he was tonight, she even bit off a quarter of a sleeping pill. It did little harm, and she awoke rested. Smiling. Ready to face a brand new day.

thirty-two

*E*arly the next morning, David awoke to two distinct sounds—chirping and cracking. In the tree just outside the window, a robin was exclaiming her delight over a find of crab apples shrivelled from the previous winter. Bobbing from gnarled branch to gnarled branch, she gulped thawing fruit, pausing after each morsel to say, "thank you." Among the notes of her youthful song, David detected soft determined snaps, wet ice splintering apart. He knew this was springtime, prying its way back in, and reclaiming its rightful status.

David hesitated before stirring as he lay on the daybed, the blushing morning wafting though a glistening window and warming his cheeks. In the small cabin, he sensed Death was lingering, savouring the gratifying success of having claimed his father. But David wondered if that was the only reason. Perhaps just now, fervent Death was raking its sore pink eyes over David's face, assessing the sparse grey eyebrows and drooping features; his mouth like a broken fishhook. And if Death came, asked politely, would David be able to resist? So little holding him here. So very little. David shuddered at his own morbidity, his second nature, and listened harder to the activity outside his window. Such murky imaginings made those subtle sounds of ripening, of progress, all the more dear.

As he concentrated, David marvelled over how he heard the noises, so clear and crisp in his ears. Had the turbulence he felt over greeting his father seeped out during the night, leaving roominess he had never known before? In the past, when David was fully awake, he was deaf to the delicate fibres that strung life together. Incessant white noise humming inside his mind made short work of that. But this morning, everything seemed new. So why not steal a moment? Tuck it away before the fickle instant was up, when the full-bellied robin fled, and the ice dissolved into a memory already laden with previous storms.

Rising reluctantly, he did not yawn or dare to stretch. These gestures he deemed far too familiar for the circumstances. Instead he moved calmly, aware of the posture of his shoulders and the slight bend in his knees. And even though his spirit felt disgracefully refreshed, his skeleton still ached. Inside, brittle bones and cold muscles were unyielding, rejecting change, asking him to remain motionless. David ignored their request, trod across the room, and threw open the door. Staring down at the thinly coated stoop, he noticed a significant fissure in the ice, one deeper and sharper than any if the others. He decided it must be the original crack, the single fracture that started it all.

Out into the sweet morning air, his steps were confident. At first he worried about the sole of his left shoe, treads worn from slight dragging. But he soon realised that walking was effortless. The ice had begun to decay, and the surface had adopted a gritty pitted texture that made slipping unlikely. So, on a whim, David meandered, pursuing that original crack, as it cut across the junkyard and wound among dripping trees and shrubs in the very forest where he had played as a child.

Surrounding him was evidence of the considerable damage from last night's gale force winds, frozen branches snapped like Popsicle sticks, pale new growth shocked and stunted. It seemed miraculous to David that something so solid would soften under heavy pressure from the sun, saturate the earth and eventually offer nourishment.

As he followed along, his original crack remained true, never splitting, never ending. Similar to glass and broken bone, he could see where other cracks rammed into it, but the original merely absorbed the force and obliged relocation. On occasion, another crack would join, and together they would veer off in a united direction, but the original always dominated. Adjusting slightly, but staying its course. That was the nature of ice.

Then, before he even realised it, he was upon the boy. At first, what he saw was just a lump, an anomaly on the landscape, perhaps an oddly shaped rock, or a ball of discarded plaid fabric. Only when David was standing directly beside him, did he grasp that the fabric contained a child, and that child was fourteen-year old Tilley Gover.

Much of Tilley's body was exposed as the morning sun had forced the ice to retreat, crawl down his sides. His clothes were damp, clinging, and brown diluted blood sponged his brow. Around his head, his hair formed a shiny helmet, as though he had just arrived at the surface of a pool of still water.

"Tilford. Tilford." David knelt down and touched a shoulder. "Are you okay?"

Tilley did not budge. David slid his hand slowly down Tilley's wet back waiting to feel the gentle ebb and flow of breathing. But there was nothing. Just shocking flatness.

"Tilford," he said again. "You'll be alright, Tilford."

Without ears to hear them, David's words were suspended in

the air and wove mischievously in and out of his own consciousness. Memories rushed at him, made each square inch of his skin prickle, but this time, this time, David was on his own. And every decision was his.

He peeled off his sweater and threw it over Tilley's back. Reaching under the boy's slender arms, David yanked. He could hear Tilley's clothes peeling away from the ice, like tape torn from a dry piece of paper. With Tilley released, David could see the impression where the boy had slept in his icy womb. Gathering Tilley in his arms, David's sluggishness vanished. And he ran, slid, and skittered over the path. Fate seemed so terribly uncreative, blatant even, but here it was, offering a second chance.

When Harvey arrived home after his mother's funeral, he was sombre, and thirsty for hot tea, something sweet, like a thick slab of dark fruitcake. But when he entered the kitchen, there was no kettle simmering on the stove, and his home was damp, messy, with empty plates and crumbs scattered on the table. No sign of his wife.

Harvey sat down, let the carpetbag plop to the floor, then ground his eyes with his knuckles. Behind him, he heard the dog shake as she roused herself from sleep.

Then he heard David say softly, "Good Popcorn. I brought ye back a treat. A slab of Aunt Lizzy's pound cake. Heavy as lead."

Harvey looked up just in time to see Hazel sidling down the hallway, yawning and stretching like a lazy cat. Her face was sallow with too much sleep, and her clothes were in disarray. There was a streak of jelly on either cheek as though she had been overly hasty in gobbling her bread.

"Yer back," she said as she drew her elbows back, ran her hands over her ribs. "How was it?"

"'Twas a funeral, maid. Whatd'ye t'ink?"

"Must've been some pleasantness to it," she said, licking the corners of her mouth. "Seein' yer ol' friends, all that good food."

Harvey leaned back in his chair, scratched his stubble with eight fingernails. "What's wrong with ye, maid? Ye looks like a streel."

"Is that so? And here now, I's never felt better?" She reached to the back of the counter and pulled out a tin half-filled with cookies. "Bit of time to meself to catch me breath. Done me right good, I tell ye."

"To yerself, ye says. Where's Levi to?"

"Where else? Over to yer bloody sister's like he always is. He was underfoot from the second ye left. Blatherin' on with his whinin' and bawlin' and -"

"Me sister's? Who, Flo?"

"How many sisters do ye got livin' in Cupboard Cove." She tucked her nails underneath the lip of the lid. "Last time I checked, it weren't a boatload."

"Christ Jaysus woman."

Hazel sucked in air, decided against opening the tin, even though she was craving sugar. Something was happening. Harvey had never sworn at her before, and she uncertain whether it was disgrace or excitement that stirred so quickly and flip-flopped in her abdomen. Not sure what to do, she smiled.

But Harvey did not smile back. Something popped inside him as he stared at his wife, barely able to recognise the vulgar woman who stood before him. He felt like a drunken sponge squeezed painfully sober. And when he finally spoke, his face paled. "But Flossie come with us, Hazel. Me sister come with us to Severed Knot."

Young David Boone leaned against the doorframe as his parents spoke, their voices harsh and angry at first, then tempered, worried. As they continued to converse, he turned towards the porch. There was no visual hint, no verbal clue, no reedy voice whispering instructions, but David knew where to go. His instinct carried him towards the icebox his father had constructed for a Christmas gift for his mother several years earlier. And when he placed both palms on the cool sides of the wooden structure, his heart scraped the ground inside the hammock of his chest. Somehow touch confirmed it. He knew what was hiding inside.

David fumbled with the latch, cleverly designed to secure perishable items inside the dark closet. The handle was lifted, and in that second when the door was ajar, David felt the weight of something behind it. Then, the door burst open, and David was knocked to the floor. On top of him lay his little brother, younger by only ten short minutes. His limbs stiff were like rough planks of wood, blue veins streaking the translucent skin of his hands and face. David screamed out, then scrambled on top of Levi, started to shake him, rub his flesh. "Ye'll be alright, Levi," he cried, as the smell of spilled milk filled his nostrils. "Ye'll be alright. Yer me baby brudder. Yer me baby brudder."

"Oh sweet Jaysus," Hazel whispered, jelly-stained fingers to her lips. "The icebox. He was in the icebox. And I even changed the water."

"Did ye shove him in there?" Harvey hollered as he sprung up, displacing the table and knocking over his chair. "Is that what happened? Have him out of the way so ye could do yer, yer, yer dirty, dirty business?"

Harvey hurled himself towards the twins, clutched Levi with all the force that he might have used if he were dragging a drowning man from the sea.

"I don't know what I done. I don't-," she whimpered. Her mind blurred as she tried to piece together her hours, her long leisurely days, the absences pinching her until her skin was scalding. "Let me have him."

"Don't ye dare," he spoke through clenched teeth.

"Fadder, give him," David shouted. He ran towards Harvey, hugged his arm, willing his father to grasp what his four-year old mind understood without question. Hazel was both the cause and the solution. "She'll fix him. I knows."

"Yes, Harve. Please Harve." Hazel was crying now, and struggled towards Harvey, zombie arms outstretched. "I never meant to."

"Not anudder step." His voice shimmied and shook in his throat. "Ye and yer garbage tears. When all I tried to do was love ye. Love ye. And this-." Words arrested, swapped with gagging, tears. Face contorted, he barred his teeth, and his animal eyes shone.

But she continued towards him, and when she was in arm's reach, Harvey lashed out at her. Fists sightless. He held Levi against his torso with one arm, while the other arm flailed as though it were on fire, striking her down gradually, beating her crown of red hair, head beneath, bruising her shoulders and back. "I's sorry. I'll be good, Harve," she shrieked between blows. "No more. From now on. I'll be good." But he didn't stop until she collapsed onto the floor, soundless, blood streaming from her nose. Not once had she raised her arms in defence.

"What's all this screamin'?" Flo Grimes said as she burst through the door, ready for a fight. "Lardie, Lardie, ye'll wake the dead."

The room was silent now. David, crouched on the floor, murmured through chattering teeth. "'Tis Levi, Auntie. 'Tis Levi."

Then Harvey tumbled down beside his wife, and Flo moved swiftly to his side, pried the rigid child from his arms.

"Our blessed Saviour. Mercy, mercy," she whispered, tearing the blanket off the daybed, wrapping the body. "Mercy. Mercy."

Neil Grimes had followed close behind his wife. Within seconds of stepping through the door, he assessed the situation, and began to crumple pages torn from an old book, toss them in the stove.

"David. Fetch me a yaffle of splits."

"No." Flo walked to her husband, seized his tanned forearm with her free hand, and shook her head. "'Twould be fruitless," she said, and rolled Levi into the crook of her elbows. Then she gathered David off the floor, whispered, "Come now, me lover." He wrapped his skinny appendages around her well-fed trunk, while her mind willed tentacles to sprout so she could clasp him eight times over. "Don't ye worry none 'bout Levi, little sugar-man," she murmured. "Where's he's gone to, he's surely wanted. Surely to God. Ye sees, I knows without doubt the very hairs on his head was numbered."

As she walked out the door, she heard Harvey's grief, severing the air inside the home, outside in the yard, and far across the harbour.

"Awww," Harvey moaned as he lay on the floor, his mouth gaping, his teeth pressed into the back of his hand. "Awwww. Heavenly Fadder. Heavenly Fadder. How can I ever forgive me foolish, foolish heart?"

With his head nuzzled in the fabric between his Aunt's breasts, David breathed in her faint scent of cinnamon toast. His eyes were closed, and her movement over the rocks and grass should have lulled him, but he was too angry. With Levi stolen away, the world seemed quiet to him, void of common comfort. He suddenly felt quite alone.

Confusion foamed up in his bowels, binding his lower body into knots, and he thought diarrhea would overtake him.

He lifted his head from its warm nest, whispered in his Aunt's ear. "I needs the outhouse."

"Almost there, darlin'," she whispered back. "Ye can use the bucket."

Moments later David was squatting in the corner of the porch, nervous belly spattering the sides of a white enamel pail. He laid his head against his bare legs, but did not cry. Instead his mind retrieved a conversation he'd overheard between his Father and Aunt. And now, he decided to collect every single syllable, store it away, until he was old enough to understand it.

"I loves her, I does," Harvey had said as he used his long scythe to shear a stretch of overgrown grass. "With every ounce of me. Some days I don't even t'ink she's real."

"Well, that's the trouble," Flo had replied. She stooped to grab a load of grass that she would dump into the pit at the edge of their property. Though when her arms were full, she lingered, continued talking. "If ye asks me, yer walkin' a fine line, me son. Mark me words. One day yer eyes'll open. And they'll be mighty startled, I 'llows. Cause I knows darn well, there's only a bony shred of difference between yer blind love and its almighty other."

With Tilley folded in his arms, David rushed in the front door of his home, and found Hazel. She was bent over in her rocking chair, huffing and grunting as she struggled to haul a pair of knee-high sport socks on over her slippers. When she glanced towards her panting son, she sat upright and the puffy clouds in her eyes cleared. She did not ask what had happened, it was as though she already knew.

"Give him here," Hazel said, as she got out of the rocker, one sock on, one sock off. She moved smoothly, ignoring the arthritis in her left hip, the swollen ankles, the bony stalagmites that decorated each joint in her lower back. Cradling him so gently, she paced the floors. Her core heat oozed from her hot-oven body, gradually thawing the boy. "Come on now, me son." She spoke firmly to Tilley as he began to limber up. "Don't be like that. Come on."

And sure enough, within ten minutes, Tilley coughed, sputtered, and sneezed. Spittle landed on Hazel's wrinkly neck, but she did not wipe it away. She stepped backwards, and dropped into the rocking chair, sighed. "Ye've been gone some spell," she said. She stroked Tilley's damp head, bloody hair. "'Twas right awful. The wait. Near drove me off me head." Then they both began to tremble.

"Blankets," she hollered at her son, who was circling in the two-foot width of doorframe. For the first time in her life, a thin line of sweat trickled down the back of Hazel's neck. "I wants enough for the both of us."

thirty-three

"Come in, come in," Annette said with a flourish of ample sleeves. "You're looking wonderfully well, Tilford. Considering."

"I feels alright, though I looks a bit like a moltin' snake." Frostbite had burned Tilley's entire epidermis, and he was gradually peeling from head to toe.

"Yes," she smiled. "A genuine King Cobra."

"Ye t'inks?" Tilley stammered.

"That I do, Tilford." She stepped closer and patted his shoulder.

He drove the toe of his worn sneaker into the wool rug, made a conscious effort not to look at Annette Boone's chest. Her sweater displayed a grand array of jewels and miniature mirrors, glued in a dizzy pattern that Tilley found captivating. Tilley's could feel heat creeping up the back of his neck.

After a weighty moment, she said, "Maureen is just in the living room, tending to Mother Boone."

"Uh. I was lookin' for Marnie. Actually."

"Oh my. Yes. Of course you were." Annette's layered bangles jingled as she pointed down the hallway. Paintings lined the walls. Not David's art, but another's, innocent and pleasant. "Well you surely haven't come to see me, and I would imagine you see quite enough of your mother at home." Another glossy smile. "And your father. Any word?"

"Nothin' yet, Missus Gover."

"Dear me. Quite the circumstances, I've heard."

"Huh?"

"Oh nothing. It's a terrible tragedy. We're praying for his healthy recovery."

"Yeah. Thanks. We all is too." And Tilley started down the hallway, his back moving away from Annette's poised hand that lingered in the air and dropped slowly.

What an adorable young man, she thought, as her eyes moved over Tilley's sturdy shoulders, square hips, pinchable bottom. Then she admonished herself, tugged down her shirt, and double-checked the buckle on her thin belt. "I would never even think about that," she whispered. "Good intentions only."

But as she strolled down the hall, humming, she recalled her sister's words one Christmas. They were sitting by the fire in their long flannel nightgowns and talking about men. Judy was peeling oranges, while Annette was squirting oil from the peel into the flames and revelling at the flare-ups.

"Oh those dastardly good intentions," Judy had said. "You know what that means."

"No, I don't. Though I'm sure you're going to tell me." Her sister was always asking questions solely for the pleasure of providing the answer.

"Of course I am," she said as she squelched two juicy segments between her teeth. "Whenever a person is riddled with good intentions, it's a sure sign they're on the road to hell."

Thaw

Tilley did not look back, but could tell by the absence of tinkling that Annette was still standing by the door with her hand in the air. Watching him. He moved quickly down the hallway, and tapped at Marnie's door. The door edged open with his knocking. He gulped when he saw her. It had been a week and a half since her accident, and she was lying in bed.

"You don't need to stare, Tilley," she said as she sat up, adjusted her pillows. "It's not as bad as it looks."

"Uh. Sorry."

"Mother won't let me get out of bed. Though I feel fine."

"Well, that's good news, then." Tilley kept his eyes away from her, staring at the cluster of birthday balloons once bursting with helium, now hovering just above the floor.

"Are you coming in? Or did you climb the hill just to hold up my doorframe?"

Tilley glanced at her.

"I'm only joking," she said with a smirk, and patted her bed.

He walked over, perched himself on the very edge.

"It's nice to see a fresh face, Tilley."

"Yeah. Yers too."

"Though I must say, you're looking rather snake-like, don't you think?"

"That's funny. I just said that very t'ing to yer mudder."

"Yeah, I heard you come in. Though I'd peg you more as a Garter Snake I think, than a King Cobra. Leave it to Mother."

"And here now, I was t'inkin' I was closer to a Python." Tilley straightened his back, wiggled his rib cage.

Marnie laughed, and Tilley smiled. Joy swelled within him. And he wondered how it could be that half of him wanted to dash out the door while the other half wanted this time with Marnie to drag on and on forever.

"You know, it's funny," Marnie said.

"What?"

"They made me stay in the hospital for three days to make sure my brain was fine. While I was lying there, staring out the window, crows and gulls used to come up and land on the sill, make a mess, and then fly off. And I started thinking: those birds are still going about their business. In fact, everything is still going on outside these walls. What happened to me hasn't changed anything. My mother is still bouncing about like one of those yappy little dogs. My father still looks at me in that sad way, like he misses me even though I'm right in front of his face. And my grandmother is still muttering to herself, wandering around sometimes wearing only polyester pants, nothing more." Then she giggled, leaned forward, and smacked Tilley's hand lightly. "I can tell you, it's not a pretty sight."

"Ugh," he said, scowling. "I don't want to imagine."

"Guess I'm being a bit of a downer, hey?"

"That's alright."

"It's just, I thought something would change. With all the bad stuff that happened to you, me, your father. Still, time keeps moving forward without the slightest glitch. Without any revelations. You'd think there'd be at least one."

Tilley looked down at the bedspread, and saw that Marnie's hand was resting beside his. Though he wanted to squeeze his eyes closed, he kept them open, and as his stomach coiled within him, he gently eased his hand over and managed to hold hers. Her skin was pale and cool, and Tilley coughed involuntarily when he realised how clammy his own hand was, even underneath the peeling skin. But she never flinched, and Tilley mustered up the courage to tighten his grip.

"Am I being silly?" she asked.

"No, no. Yer not. People don't change. Everyt'ing's just the same as it always was." He had a difficult time staring into her face, still stained with shiny blotches of olive and mustard yellow. But it was not the bruises that made it awkward for him to meet her eyes. It was because he was lying. Since that night in the woods, everything had changed. Life had taken on new meaning, as though he had just woken up from years of dreariness. He swore the colours that he saw were brighter, crisper, and he could hardly tolerate waiting until his hands were healed to begin drawing. No longer just charcoal, the full spectrum was his.

How could he describe to Marnie what he didn't fully understand himself? That somehow, every inch of his little world was expanding. And his body too. There had been a queer ache lingering deep inside his tiny skeleton since the moment he'd awoken, snug in the polyester wrap of Hazel Boone's arms.

Instead of trying to explain, Tilley kissed her. He tried to be suave, but he pitched forward with too much speed, clanked his teeth against hers.

"Oh," he said, somewhat surprised at his failed approach.

But the results were soon in.

"Not bad for your first time, little man," Marnie said as she reached for his shoulders. "Though I think perhaps we should try again."

Maureen rolled once, back supported by the wall, and clutched her hands over her heart. What had she just spied through a door left ajar? How could it be her Tilley? Her little Tilley.

Without breathing, she fled down the hallway towards the bathroom and locked the door. She had only meant to go straight there anyway and wash her hands. Hazel's toenails, like thick beige seashells, had started to curl, and Annette insisted they be trimmed, feet cleaned thoroughly. Of course, the gruesome task was left for Maureen who arrived at the Boone household

Monday morning with her tail tucked slightly between her thighs. Annette didn't bat an eyelash, welcomed Maureen in. Dickie Price had fired her from the bingo hall when he found someone younger, someone who appreciated palm prints on her backside. So Maureen needed the job, even if it meant sawing through nails, massaging bunions, and scraping away the multilayered calluses. Someone had to do it. Besides, it was too soon to tell with Earl, and their need for groceries, for electricity didn't just evaporate into thin air.

But on her way, Maureen had heard her son's voice and hesitated just outside Marnie's door. She couldn't help her eyes or her ears, where they roamed, what they heard. Her stubborn feet refused to move. At least not until she saw the first kiss, then the leisurely second, and the shock of it moved through her as though she'd just jammed a metal-handled butter knife into a plugged-in toaster.

She paced the floor in the small bathroom, to the frosted glass window and back to the heavy wooden door. She would sit down, use the facilities, at least make her journey to the bathroom authentic. In the past few days, she'd had more than enough of questionable intentions, suspect actions, and pretending to use a washroom while leaning against the lip of the sink seemed unconscionable.

Maureen hoisted up her skirt, slid her white cotton underwear to her knees, and plopped down. She tugged a long strip of baby blue toilet paper, blew her nose.

Everything. And now Tilley.

Poking the paper through the gap of her legs and into the toilet, she remembered that fleeting moment of all-consuming bliss when her child was born. That instant where Tilley was a fully whole person, but still attached to her. One snip, and there began the process of slow decay, that cancerous adoration. She remembered how she used to nip him ever so gently, never wanting him to sleep, never wanting his tender expression to close. All in vain, she knew. Holding on with such tight fists, her grip only caused him to spring away with greater force, greater intensity. Memories would have to carry her now.

Maureen started gasping. "Ah God," she whispered. "I don't remember. I don't remember nothin'." His first word, the exact date he took his first step, where she had tucked away that stolen lock of baby hair, the colour shirt he wore on his first day of kindergarten. Tilley had vanished from her waking mind, leaving Boyd crawling all over her surface. 'Hubba-hubba,' fourteen months, eleven days, navy plaid flannelette, top shelf in her bedroom, back right corner. *Why Boyd and not Tilley?* Lost. All lost. Each precious second woven so deeply into her fabric, there was no way to draw them out. A sharp pain made her shiver. *Can a heart actually quiver inside a chest?*

While she wept silently into her mask of the blue toilet paper, eyelids transforming into kitchen sponge, Maureen felt disgrace rinse over her. *Doesn't every good mother want to shield her child from sadness?* If yes, then why when she had caught him in a moment of joy, did she feel so profoundly betrayed? As though part of her was dying? Was dead.

Then she sensed an involuntary wetness between her legs, and she wiped. On the tissue, she found bright evidence of her emptiness, a timely reminder from her spiteful body. And it occurred to her, getting married, having children, all she had really done was trade. One kind of unhappiness, dull and reliable. For this searing other.

thirty-four

"'Tis a slow death yer after, then," Flo Grimes said, her shrill voice landing on Harvey's back like pelting nails. "No good ye've done 'til now, and no good ye'll do if ye cuts yerself off altogether."

"It don't matter none," Harvey replied softly. He was leaning against the cool stove in his sister's kitchen. His skin was sallow, his eyes hollow inside his head.

"'Tis not normal, livin' on yer own like that. Ye'll be puffin' life right into it all, never be able to move past it. No one's askin' ye to forget, Harvey."

"Ye don't understand. I can't move, maid. I can't move. I can't breathe." He pressed his bone-dry palms into his chest.

"Ye don't got to move or breathe, 'tall. Ye needs to air out that place, make a life for yerself where ye belongs."

"There's nothin' here. There's nothin' there."

"Have ye forgotten all 'bout that wee child waitin' for ye on the stoop?"

"No. But I won't do him no good."

"Ye would, then."

"No, maid. Me mind is set."

"I knows ye, Harvey Boone, like the back of me hand. And if yer mind is set like that, Neil and I'll—"

"Won't hear of it." His voice was barely a breath. "The b'y needs a fresh start too. And yerselves, finally startin' a family. Ye don't want the taint hangin' over ye."

"The taint? Is ye gone mad? 'Twasn't yer fault. And certainly not David's."

Harvey accordioned his body down beside the woodstove. "How could I not've seen her? How could I have been that blind?"

"The Devil wears many outfits, me son. Some days he wears trousers. Some days he dons a dress."

"The Devil." He cupped his hands over his eyes, and a tinny laugh climbed the scales, descended. "I swears Flo, I'll never be able to see her face again. Never. I knows it'll kill me. She'll kill me. Strike me dead." Standing slowly, unfolding each limb, he whispered, "Now I got to be goin', maid. I needs to be goin'."

"For the love of Jaysus, Harvey. Re-t'ink it all." She paced the floors of her kitchen, hands jammed into the folds that were her waist. "Time heals. Yes, it do, but ye got to be present."

Harvey shook his head, he'd had already made up his mind. His little world seemed far too full of trickery, and he felt he could not trust his own eyes, his own hands, his own impressions. He simply wanted his world to be still, quiet. Yes, quiet. Never having to hear another useless word, another worthless lie. He moved across the room, kissed his sister dryly on the corner of her pursed lips, and walked out her door. His young son, his solitary son, was waiting.

"'Tis the heights of selfishness, Harvey Boone," she hollered after him. "The very heights. Ye figures ye hates yerself, when if ye asks me, yer the only livin' soul ye ever gave either thought to."

❧

David stood under the wooden awning on the front stoop of his Aunt Flo's home watching the drizzle pool on the windows and trickle down in a mass of intricate branches. The glass was dark, as every curtain had been drawn, and he could see his watery reflection, portions of it divided, then slipping away. He was wearing the same itchy wool trousers he'd worn to his grandmother's funeral, the same cotton shirt and navy cardigan sweater with the three wooden buttons. If his brother were to walk up the lane, take his place beside David on the stoop, they would have been identical. But with legs pleated slightly inside a smooth pine box, layer upon layer of sandy dirt upon him, David knew his brother wouldn't be walking anywhere.

When his father arrived, David shuffled aside, squeezed back against the wooden handrail where fat drops of rain tumbled off the roof, and divined the most sensitive path down his neck. "Hello, Fadder," he whispered.

"Ye got to be a little man now, David." Harvey knelt down on one knee, stared not at David's eyes, but the uneven bangs that zigzagged across the child's forehead. "A little man."

"What if I don't want to be no little man?" David whimpered and his bottom lip shook. Even though he thought of crying, he couldn't. He was already cried out. A sapless tree.

"Ye got no say." Tone ironed flat.

"Where's me mudder?"

"She's gone, David. She needed some place to rest."

"Like Levi?" A fresh well behind his eyes tempted.

"No. No." Harvey looked down now, counted the folds of fabric bunched underneath his knee. "Not like Levi. To a place where someone'll look after her."

"And when she's better, we'll go fetch her?"

"No, me son. No." Harvey shoulders began to heave, and he choked.

"Fadder." David sprung forward, curled his arms around the bristly neck. "Don't cry, Fadder."

"I ain't."

"Big men don't cry."

"Little men don't neither, David."

"Yes, Fadder."

Harvey cleared his throat, blew his nose into the mint green handkerchief Flo had given him at the funeral. "Ye got to promise me, David. Promise me that when ye's all big, ye'll come find me. Show me that ye growed up good. So that I knows. Give me some peace."

"Yes, F-F-Fadder." David put his hand over his shaking chest. "I promises."

But that wasn't all. Inside the small locket of his heart, he tucked not one, but two promises before clicking it closed. The first to fulfil his father's request, and the second to find his mother, bring her home from her earthly place of rest.

"Good," Harvey said as he stood. "Now go on then. Yer Uncle'll be along for ye."

"Uncle?"

"Me brudder. Yer Uncle Archie."

"Oh." Warm air lightness entered David's head, and it threatened to separate from his body as his future path was piled upon his slender shoulders.

"And David," Harvey said, placing a smooth hand on his son's cold cheek and staring directly into his eyes. "Don't look back." The artificial advice quavered in his throat, wanted to stick, but he forced it out. "No good ever come from lookin' back."

But David never answered, barely even heard. Pieces of him had already floated upwards, cloud high, and he wished he'd awaken from this ridiculous dream.

Stepping down over the slippery stairs, David trudged to the end of the drive, dragging the near-empty carpetbag through the mud behind him. The drizzle had let up and a thin fog was descending, veiling his small corner of Cupboard Cove in a gauzy mask. Only once did he disobey and glance back. And he noticed the home where he had lived appeared to be winking at him. The locked wooden door became a stately nose, flanked by a set of window eyes on either side. One eye had two boards nailed as an eyelid. In a day, those boards would blind his home completely, squash the nose and suffocate the entire works.

He stood in a patch of wet three-leaf clovers, and stared up and down the lane. His entire left side felt cold, he was so accustomed to Levi standing beside him, at once brother and windbreaker. His knees crumpled as he waited, and he crouched down, felt leftover rainwater pass through his trousers, goose-pimple his skin. And he took some comfort in the cold that so easily claimed his body.

Time slowed to a trickle. No one yet walked towards him, no person strolled by, no nod of a head, no sorrowful hand reached out. Nothing.

He lay down in the clover and closed his tired eyes. Rubbing his hands over the wooden buttons of his sweater, he began to think about the sharpness jabbing at his heart. *Could that be the feeling of love?* Or, perhaps it was anger. He was unable to distinguish. But he was certain of one thing. That trivial point of confusion was going to thrive within him forever.

Thaw

After Hazel was sent away and the boy buried, Lyle O'Leary spent seven damp days in the root cellar behind his mother's house. During the long hours of those summer days, he was whittling what his father had called a fairy flute, a long thin instrument that produced a charmed song. His father only fashioned fairy flutes for children, as he claimed that only sweet breath would make them sing.

In light of everything that had happened, he couldn't ask for help, couldn't ask for insight. He needed to create his own true test in order to discover if the air that filled his wheezing lungs was pure or putrid. The fairy flute would be his answer.

He drilled a smooth hole down the centre of a length of hardwood, and began to meticulously shave off fragments the thickness of a woman's hair. Hands bleeding and bubbled with blisters, he winced occasionally, but persevered. Often he would stop and stare at his work, for minutes, for hours, considering the angle of his hand, the sharpness of his blade.

"Takes a skilled 'and, b'y," his father would say, as Lyle watched him select a dry piece of wood. "Too t'in, and 'tis shrill. Too t'ick, and 'tis dismal. Yar, a skilled 'and, ye needs."

On the seventh night, Lyle finished shaping and sanding. He clutched the fairy flute in one hand and picked up his kerosene lantern with the other. Walking out to the cliff, he stopped momentarily beside the flakes of dried, split fish. The air was thick with the odour of salt and Lyle inhaled deeply. It was so wholesome, honest, the smell of sweat and hard work, and Lyle found himself holding his breath and hoping.

On the very edge of the cliff he sat, his feet dangling. Beneath him, he could see the hungry ocean churning and frothing as it chided the smooth rock. Leaning his elbows on his knees, he brought the flute to his dried lips and blew a thin stream of air. The tune was blissful, but Lyle heard nothing. A mean-spirited wind, clapping a blustery paw over the base of the instrument, filched the song before it reached his ears. Lyle perceived his private experiment as a soundless failure and hunched with the crushing weight of responsibility that came with it.

He let the flute drop, watched it splinter and disappear. Pinching back tears, he could no longer pretend or discount his role in everything that had happened. As he picked his way along the grassy path, he thought about Hazel and the thirst he had discovered that day in the root cellar. A devilish unquenchable thirst he had never known before. Something she had done to him, he was certain. That would be just like her. Inventing an affliction, only to make herself the cure.

The front of the stage where he paused was shiny and worn from the scuff of workers, the traffic of dripping fish. He stomped his feet, then climbed down the slippery wooden planks and into his dory, painted turquoise because that was Hazel's favourite colour. His stomach rolled with both the waves and the realisation of how dim he'd been to think that no one would notice. Prancing around with flushed cheeks and a cocky attitude draped across his square shoulders. Moving so eagerly through each day at the whim of his craving. Oh, if only he hadn't been there when the boy was dying. Perhaps she would accept him again. But he was there. Playing his part.

And now not a single pair of eyes would lift to greet him on the road, no cordial tap of a hat's brim to say, "Hello." He understood that he no longer blended, could no longer stay. *But what was the alternative?* He had only ever known these good people, this crumbly earth, the rich sea, and fickle sky. Beyond? He smiled wanly as he felt the sea pressing up around his boat, balancing his weight. Beyond did not exist.

Lyle rowed out into the harbour until the land became a shadow marred by only a handful of flickering lights. He bent over, hauled off his boots, patiently rolled down and removed the thin socks his mother had knit. He put his hand to his lantern, puckered his lips to puff, but stopped. And then without hesitation, he slipped backwards into the sea like a hand in a generous glove.

As he swam with sure strong strokes, he drank great gulps of black water, relieved himself with a flush of warmth, and drank again. Cutting through the infinite waves, his arms soon stiffened. Eyes blinded by salt, cheeks stinging, he began to choke. His feet were tempted downwards by an impassioned current, shuttling him along in what he felt was a most wondrous rush. Thoughts came like a twirling kaleidoscope, and in those final moments, his own awareness soothed him. So close, she was. In her watery disguise. She was never ending. Surrounding him, pushing herself down his throat, up his nose, making his bitter skin shrink against his body. Hazel Keeping once. Then Hazel Boone. He could drink her and drink her and take such pleasure in the drinking. But in the end, he could not be satiated, and he knew the drink would kill him.

※

From the ragged shoreline, Neil Grimes and his grief-stricken wife watched the glow from the lantern, bobbing and weaving on the black mass that was the sea.

"Oh, me dear Flossie," Neil said as he stopped and reached out to take her arm. "I believes 'tis a lost soul."

"No shortage. Seems." She patted his hand.

"No."

"Not much to do now."

"No. Storms a comin'. Caps comin' up on the water."

"And the boat?"

"Mornin' will tell." He squinted towards the water, placed a palm on his scalp as wind bullied his comb-over. "Though I suspects ye'll see her with the others. All good boats, when they don't know where to go, always drift back towards home."

thirty-five

Tilley awoke early, his alarm wailing like a cat in heat, just two inches from his ear. Flying fist, one pound on snooze, and the cat darted away. A second wail, and he sat upright, swung his gangly legs over the side of his bed, feet planted firmly on the carpet. As he yawned, his hands slid up and down his lower back, and counted the deep grooves in his skin. Stretch marks. Within a few months, Tilley's lithe body had lengthened a whole six inches.

From the kitchen, he could hear his mother humming, dishes clanking, and squeals from a five-month old. Since three weeks after the birth, Maureen had been taking care of Boyd and Teena's baby. Stitches not even healed, Maureen had said, and Teena had taken a full time job working nights at Nips-n-Bites. Then, the following day, Boyd decided to take an hour off from Tubby Gould's and "locate hisself." Two months later he called Maureen to tell her he'd met a decent girl in Bolter's Bay, and was staying.

"They meant well," was all Maureen had said as she got down to business, dug out old cotton diapers, safety pins, bought pink terrycloth sleepers, and a hat like a plump raspberry.

Tilley hauled on a snug t-shirt, tucked it into his octagon-patterned pyjama bottoms, and dragged himself into the kitchen.

"Mornin' Mudder."

"Mornin'," Maureen said, as she spooned milky hot cereal into Earl's eager mouth. "Fresh bread in the basket."

Even though a whole season had passed, and his father's face had healed into a criss-cross of scars, shaved head now stubbly, Tilley could not get used to the expression. Since he'd awoken in his hospital bed, Earl Gover wore a near-constant smile. The only time he scowled was whenever Penny Payne paid a visit to Maureen. At first Penny's eyes were down turned, demeanour timid, but after a few sips of tea at the kitchen table, she transformed into her gossipy self. All the while Earl's face twitched and cringed as though Maureen had just forced him to consume a spoonful of jam bitterly spiked with crushed aspirin. But Maureen seemed not to notice the shift in her husband, and Tilley wasn't about to explain the reasons why.

"He's better," Maureen said to anyone who asked. "He's much better now."

Tilley rummaged through the basket, grabbed a slice of bread, and tore off a bite. "Mornin' Fadder." Mouth full.

Earl looked up, beamed, and repeated the same few words he said every morning, "He's some man, Maureen. Some man."

And Maureen responded in similar fashion, "That he is, Earl. That he is."

Tilley glanced over at the baby. She was propped against the wooden slats of a playpen gnawing at a scrap of filthy fabric. Brown juice dribbled down over her chin, staining the single gift Boyd had ever given the child—a bib stating, "Spit Happens".

"What's she eatin', Mudder?"

"'Tis a fig tit. Handful of raisins tied up in some cloth."

"Man." Tilley scowled. "Looks some disgustin'."

"Ah sure, ye says that now, me son. But ye loved yer fig tit like nothin' else when ye was that age." Maureen leaned into the playpen, pinched the baby's dime-sized chin, shook it slightly, and cooed, "Yer Nanny's doll, aren't ye, me lovey. Yes, ye is too."

Without turning towards Tilley, she said, "Is ye goin' out tonight?"

"Yes, I t'inks so. Got me costume ready."

"Seen ye traipsin' 'round the backyard. Yer apt to destroy yerself tied up in that contraption."

"They's only stilts, Mudder. I ain't tied, and I can jump off."

"Well, then. Yer old enough to make yer own choices, I reckons. Just don't come to me if ye breaks either bone."

"Yes, Mudder," Tilley said as he sat at the table in the seat opposite Earl. His mother, dressed in a white smock, brilliant white cup towel tucked inside the string of her apron, returned to her humming. The fat baby gurgled and rasped between sucks, which made joyful Earl smile harder, spreading the worm-like scars on his face even wider.

Staring from one to the other, Tilley shuddered with the eerie feeling that every element of the scene in his mother's kitchen was completely wrong. *Where was the uproar, the acidic words, the chronic chips on shoulders?* Then, for a moment, he imagined the four of them frozen, sketched, painted, and hung on the wall above a blazing fireplace. Mind's eye retreating, he stepped back to appraise his work. Tilley adjusted his opinion. It was a lovely scene. A happy scene. And perhaps it all felt so terribly strange, because for once, everything was just fine.

❧

Later that evening, Tilley donned an eight-foot long black-and-white striped gown and hoisted himself up onto his stilts.

While Maureen had stitched the robe, he had built the stilts himself; wooden footrests, handles, and hooks that curved around his shoulders for support. For a month he had practised in the backyard, traipsing left and right across fallen leaves and soggy grass, until he was as comfortable at rooftop level as he was on the ground.

Halloween had arrived clear and calm. Chimneys pumped smoke that drifted unfettered through the sky, and on the horizon, the sun-graced ocean was smooth like an untouched cup of black tea. With modelled legs, Tilley moved swiftly down the lane to meet Walter at the base of Main Road. Walter wore a green garbage bag, banana skins and empty tin cans fastened to his front and back with packing tape.

"What is ye s'posed to be?" Tilley asked as he looked down at his best friend.

"Bag of garbage," Walter replied. "Figures Mudder's always tellin' me that's what I is, so may as well dress the part, right?"

"Whatd'ye use as stuffin'?"

"Stuffin'?" Walter patted his belly. "Whatd'ye mean?"

"Ah, nothin'. Thought ye was goin' as a jester."

"Me to. Bustin' the arse right out of me costume changed me mind on that. Still got me stick though." As though it were a wise man's staff, Walter clutched a janitor's broomstick in his hand. On the bottom, he had fixed a worn shoe, and then after piercing a collection of beer caps, he threaded them onto nails, and attached them to the length. "'Tis a regular homemade instrument," Walter said as he banged the shoe upon the road to jiggle the beer caps. "Done it for me art class."

"Not bad, b'y," Tilley said.

When Tilley started walking, Walter had to scamper three steps to his one in order to keep up. Each boy, now fifteen years old, never carried sacks to collect candy. Instead, they roamed the streets, played innocent jokes, and occasionally visited a home and devoured whatever they were given—molasses taffies, one-bite chocolate bars, tiny paper bags stuffed with salted popcorn.

Along the muddy roads, they passed clusters of miniature trick-or-treaters, ghosts, goblins, green-faced witches, lions, and fairy princesses. The throngs of excited children all stopped to stare at Tilley. Mouths agape as they gripped their sagging pillowcases, and when Tilley glowered down upon them without speaking, they turned quickly and skittered up the next drive.

"Someone's got to spook them a bit," Tilley said, laughing. "What's Halloween without either fright or two."

Loitering just outside Boyle's Billiards, Tilley spied Ida dressed as Little Bo Peep, a loyal woolly lamb as her sidekick. He kept walking, eyes locked forward. Tilley had not spoken to Ida since that day in the woods, and she had made no attempt to speak with him.

"Better not get yerself into trouble, Ida," Walter hollered.

"Shut yer trap, blubber-arse," Ida screamed back as the lamb twittered.

"I'll tell Mudder. She'll skin ye, ye knows. Knock ye into next week."

"Puh." Ida spat on the ground, but still, she lumbered away.

"Yer headin' in the wrong direction, loser," the lamb piped up as it stood on lengthy hind legs, followed Ida. "Dump's that way."

"Geez," Walter whispered. "Girls are for nothin', what?"

Tilley blinked frequently, but never responded. He knew Walter had just broken up with Christina Wong, and had been sour ever since. The four of them, Walter and Christina, Tilley and Marnie, had spent their entire summer together, racing through the woods, rowing out into the harbour, hiding in tall grass. The foursome first came undone mid-August when David and Marnie returned home to St. John's. According to Marnie,

David had walked into his kitchen, discovered Seymour from the Fish Shack sporting nothing more than a modest frilly apron and jamming toothpicks into bacon wrapped scallops. Marnie had wept on Tilley's shoulder after her father had offered her the choice of homes. She moved away, but pledged her affection for Tilley. And for two months their devotion had remained intact.

At Vickers farm, they stopped and Tilley jumped down off his stilts, gathered his gown in his fist, and leaned against the shale fence.

"I heard he keeps the sheep in his house when the chill comes on," Walter whispered. "Cozies up, I dare say."

Tilley glanced over his shoulder at the farmhouse with glowing golden windows, the gravel gardens, and the barren sledding hill beyond.

"Dare ye to go in."

"Dare me?" Tilley replied. "Go on yerself, b'y."

"Two of us, then. Alright?"

Tilley dragged his stilts up the long pot-holed drive, and dropped them beside Mr. Vickers's rusty pick-up. On the back stoop, Tilley and Walter nudged each other until Walter finally gripped Tilley's hand and made him knock. Three loud bangs before they heard shuffling within the house.

"Well now," Mr. Vickers said when he came to the door. "I's surprised to see ye b'ys all the way down here. Don't get many trick-or-treaters these past years. Maybe some spoilt eggs, a bag of dog dung plastered across me front door. Yar. But no trick-or-treaters."

"Didn't mean to bother ye, Mr. Vickers," Tilley said, coughing.

"Oh, no bother, b'ys. I got treats for ye's. Always do. But don't want no tricks though, ye hear? Come on in."

When they stood in the porch, heavily scented with boiled turnip and logs of damp spruce, Mr. Vickers waggled his finger at the banana peel taped to Walter's garbage bag smock. "What's wrong with ye, me son? Never heard of compost? Wunnerful stuff, ye knows."

"Mudder don't believe in compost," Walter said, his hand darting up to touch the white moth imprint in his hair.

"Don't believe, hey? Well, come in, come in, fellers. I loves a bit of company, but I ain't heatin' the harbour." He disappeared around a corner, called, "Bottle of drink, b'ys? Kids yer age loves pop, right?"

"Sure," Tilley said as he entered the kitchen.

"Right on." Walter followed.

Mr. Vickers bent over with a groan and opened a bottom cupboard, one hand on his knee, the other groping in the darkness. After retrieving two bottles of Coca-Cola, he clunked them onto the counter and straightened his back with considerable effort. Then, he withdrew the metal ice cube tray from the freezer, strained to tug the handle, and dropped two cubes each into three glasses. When he poured the warm Coke, it foamed and fizzed into a caramel mound, threatened to topple out, but receded.

"Spilled not a drop, b'ys. There ye go." Mr. Vickers eased himself into a chair at the kitchen table. "Don't gulp it now, else ye'll lose the girl."

On each glass was the image of a tall nude woman, and when Tilley sipped and stared again, he noticed the straps of her bathing suit appearing as the level of the Coke descended.

"Thought ye fellers would get a kick out of these," Mr. Vickers said, chortling. "Me niece sent them last year for Christmas. First time I's used them." He lifted his glass. "A drink strips them right down. Don't know how it works, but truth be told, I don't care for them meself. I's long past that."

Walter snickered as he barely wet his lips with his drink and stole glimpses of balloon breasts on a skinny hourglass.

They sat in silence, and Tilley glanced around the room. Everything was neat and clean, not a single tuft of wool in sight. A worn plaid chair was pushed in by the woodstove, and a basket held chunky brown yarn, plastic knitting needles—a project in progress. On the wall above, an owl clock counted out the seconds with shady shifts of its wide eyes.

"Me udder niece likes to go off to all those crazy places," Mr. Vickers said, nodding towards the fridge. It was covered in postcards, some shiny, others faded. There was a variety of beaches, towers, stained church windows, a plate of knotted rolls, a busy marketplace. "Don't know where she got that from. I always liked it right here. Mary's always on me to sell the farm and see some sights, but I tells her there's no way I's leavin' me sheep. Who'd care for them?"

"Ye could sell them," Walter offered.

"Bite yer tongue, me son. Like me babies, they is."

Walter kicked Tilley under the table, snickered again.

Mr. Vickers plucked an O'Henry from a plate centre-table, peeled back the wrapper with shaky hands. "I's goin' to be up all night eatin' this sort of t'ing." Taking a generous bite, he mumbled, "Some show tonight fellers," and pointed a fat finger, like a dirty wrinkled parsnip, towards the bay window.

Tilley and Walter peered out to see two bright yellow lights glowing out over the water. Headlights climbing out of the inky sea.

"'Tis a clear night, I s'pose," Mr. Vickers said as he worked the chocolate bar with his tongue. Then he grabbed his throat and hacked. "Lard, this t'ing is right packed with nuts. And me now, nar tooth. For the life of me, I don't know why God forgot to give us ol' folks gizzards."

"I heard the tale on it," Walter said, nodding towards the ocean. "But why is there two of them?"

"One's the light," Mr. Vickers' said, then paused to spit nuts into his hand. "And one's the reflection."

"O'Leary's Lantern," Tilley mumbled.

"No doubt. We knows it. Though others likes to doubt. Sure, I had fellers out from the University just three days ago, askin' all kinds of questions 'bout it. Rigged out with the most pricey sort of gear, measuring sticks, and metal gadgets. And I says to them, is this what we's payin' all those taxes for? So the likes of ye's can come 'round here with all yer fancy crap, wasting me time and me money? Well, I says, if this is the way 'tis, ye can hand me over the few dollars ye gone and stole from me."

Tilley leaned forward in his seat, stared out the window at the lonely lights twinkling on the black water. "What did they say to that?"

"Ye can be sure they had somet'ing to say. Crowd from St. John's ain't got no shortage of tongue to flap. They goes on to tell me that those lights is a honest to goodness scientific mystery that has confused the scientific community for decades. They t'inks 'tis some sort of bafflin' gases or somet'ing burnin' out on the water. Gases, me arse. I says, well b'ys, they ain't never confused this community, and we ain't no crowd of scientists. Ye fellers should get yer heads out of yer backsides, and just enjoy the show. Some t'ings is better left a mystery. I always thought, the more ye knows, the less ye believes."

"Hmmm," Tilley said. "I—"

"What's the real story on it, anyways, Mr. Vickers?" Walter said, interrupting.

"The real story? Yer askin' for the real story on it? Now who says 'tis any of yer business?"

"I was just curious, is all." Cheeks suddenly flushed, Walter took two huge gulps of his Coke to clothe his woman.

"Well, there's neither story. There's nar need to be dredgin' up the past." Mr. Vickers said, closing his fist around a handful of sticky nuts. "No good can ever come from it."

"Yer right, there," Walter said, as he repeatedly kicked the developing tender spot on Tilley's shin. "Right good sense."

"And whatd'ye t'ink, Tilley Gover?" Mr. Vickers said, staring straight at Tilley. "Cat got yer tongue?"

Tilley never wavered like he might have a year or two ago. He had grown used to scrutiny and intense looks after spending so many hours with David. "I don't know. Whatd'ye got without yer past? Without yer history?"

"Well, by Jaysus. Ye got the whole world right by the tail. Clean and light as can be."

"I still don't know, Mr. Vickers."

"Mudder said ye don't know nothin' when yer our age," Walter announced. "Nothin' 'tall."

"Bullshit," Mr. Vickers hollered as his fist came down on the thick wooden table, nuts bounding left and right. He leaned towards the boys, eyebrows like lengths of wire jutting out, threatening to cut. "Udder bullshit. The way I figures it, we knows all we needs to know 'bout the world by the time we's four or five. What comes after that, 'tis nothin' more than a bloody compromise. Most of us spends the rest of our lives tryin' to remember what we knowed, what we was right sure of, while the others, a few unfortunates, yes b'ys, they spends their time doin' their best to forget."

"What a kook, Till. Won't be goin' back there no time soon," Walter whispered as they hiked down the drive. "Did ye hear the baaaa in the background? Christ, he was sizin' up me head like ye wouldn't believe. Thought he was goin' to haul out his shearing clippers, have a go at me."

Tilley smirked, stopped beside his stilts. "Just as well to do somet'ing useful with ye. Ye won't have hair much longer, Walter. Even yer grandmudder's bald."

Walter knocked into Tilley playfully, and Tilley caught a whiff of Walter's costume, overripe banana skins, unwashed tins that once held cream of mushroom soup. Tilley winced.

"Well, I should get back," Walter said. "Mudder's waitin'. Ye knows, 'The Hulk' is on and all. See ye later, Till."

"Yeah. See ye later, buddy."

Tilley poised his stilts against Mr. Vickers' powder-blue Ford truck, climbed up the wheel, and perched himself on the lip of the back. He didn't immediately slip his feet into the wooden poles, but sat for a moment and breathed in the smell of engine oil and turpentine from loads of wood.

He remembered riding in the back of the truck when he was a boy. Joy rides where he squealed and tossed about, weightless, like a dried leaf in the wind. But while those many rides blended together into one, his very first remained true and separate. He had been standing on the rust-coloured vinyl seat in the cab between his mother and father, staring out the rectangular window at Boyd. Boyd was old enough to ride alone in the back, but Tilley was too young, and Maureen worried. Tilley cried and whined out the tiny window, until Boyd leaned in, said, "C'mon, Mudder."

Earl pulled the truck onto the shoulder, nodded, and after Maureen had sighed loudly, she carried Tilley to the back of the truck and hoisted him over. Tilley recalled his own unsteady steps as he tripped over the grooves towards Boyd.

"Hold tight to him now, Boyd," Maureen had said with a steely voice. "If he flips out, just as well ye tosses yerself out behind him."

Tilley nestled in between Boyd's legs. Boyd wrapped his arms around him in a vice grip. With a grand cloud of dust, Earl screeched down the gravel road, swerving left and right, honking the horn, war-whooping, and flapping his left arm out the open window.

With Earl's first shot of gas, Tilley was cast into hysterics. His face was locked in an open-mouthed smile, but there was no time for laughter to emerge. Although they bounced all over the back of the truck, grunting and giggling when they knocked against the side, the tire mounds, or the curved walls, Boyd never once let go. Two minutes into the ride and Tilley felt a rush of warmth down his legs. He'd peed his pants. When they pulled into their driveway, Earl walked around and opened the tailgate. Tilley tumbled out and began to bawl. Maureen rushed to scoop him up.

"Shush, shush, me baby." Maureen said as she cuddled him. "I knowed I shouldn't of let ye go. I knowed that."

Earl ruffled Tilley's hair, said, "C'mon now, maid. He's tough. Right tough like his fadder."

Boyd pointed at Tilley's jeans, cried, "Look Mudder. I squeezed the friggin' piss right out of him."

"Is ye alright?" Maureen whispered, touching every bump, every bone. "Is ye alright, me lovey?"

But Tilley could not speak; a jagged snivel had taken hold and was nearly strangling him. And even if he had, he would not have been able to explain. In those moments of hot, leaking urine, wild collision, and body contortions as he was crushed against floor and walls, while safely fused to his older brother, he was overwhelmed with adoration for his entire imperfect family.

"I loves ye," he finally managed, wiping his nose in his sleeve. "Mudder. Fadder. Boyd. I loves ye all."

While Maureen cosseted Tilley with her doughy arms, Earl looked away and tucked a lost shirttail deep into his trousers with great sweeps of his hand. "Poor beggar," he had said. "Must've struck his noggin."

To this day, if Tilley closed his eyes he could still feel his father's strong fingers dancing over his scalp. Dancing, yes, so tenderly, as though Earl had never escaped the trepidation over

Tilley's pulsing fontanel, even though bone had long settled in.

When Tilley climbed up onto his stilts, swaying as he transferred his weight, he decided Mr. Vickers' was wrong. Some good could come out of holding onto snippets from the past, even though it was not clear-cut. Would Tilley prefer them to dissolve? The truck rides with Boyd, pinecone combat with Walter, Marnie's fluttering eyelashes on his neck. Some, of course, yes, spilled spaghetti, searing accusations, spying the mole on the back of a hand just before it struck his face. But that was simply life. Joy and sorrow were more often than not in muddy cahoots, tangled up together.

From his vantage point on his stilts, Tilley could see the edges of an abandoned bird's nest, a mess of twigs tumbling out of the eaves just above Mr. Vickers's porch. At the sight of it, he had to smile to himself. And he understood; he'd already made his decision. He would leave Cupboard Cove as soon as he could. David had promised to grease Tilley's way into the world of art, and Tilley trusted him. Plus Marnie would be there. He wasn't sure if it would last, but when he had asked his mother, she insisted, "Why not try, me son? Whatd'ye got to lose?"

Rotating gradually and balancing each step, Tilley began his steady crunch up the gravel road. Everything seemed settled. And though he did not turn to look back, the sharp flames on the water flickered once more, then died away.

On the grassy path that lined the razor-sharp cliffs of Signal Hill, David and Marnie sat inside a fold of skim milk fog. The glow of headlights spread over them as the occasional car circled the parking lot. November nipped at the air, and while David ignored the cold, Marnie turned up the collar on her wool turtleneck and zipped her jacket to the neck.

Even though she shivered, not once did Marnie wish herself back inside a warm house. These unconventional outings were the highlight of her weekend. Sometimes she thought of Tilley to warm herself, but most often she quieted her chattering teeth by sipping over-brewed tea from a thermos. And she waited patiently beside her father, while he searched the salty air for apparitions.

"Winter's 'round the corner," she said as she sat on her mittens, broke the chill that was sneaking up through the damp rock.

"I feel it too," he replied. "Though I don't dread it."

In his hand, David held a Canon camera, and occasionally he brought it to his face, adjusted the focus as he stared into the fog. Several months ago, he had set aside his brushes and paints for a new passion: photography. His initial goal was to capture pockets of life in nighttime St. John's, but somehow unexplainable tricks of light, clusters of fuzzy energy kept spoiling his film. Finally, he surrendered, accepting the baffling child-sized shadows his camera liked to snare.

"Dad?"

"Hmmm?"

Marnie could sense the ocean beyond her, a vast dark body undulating in the fog, while behind her, she knew the earth was steady, solid. She leaned back into the wall of rock, said, "I never told you this, but once Tilley and I walked through the cemetery in Cupboard Cove."

"Oh?" Camera balanced on his lap now.

"And we found something."

"Yes?"

"A child's grave. With the name Boone on it."

"Yes."

"Were you related?"

Marnie could barely see her father's face, though she heard his sigh, faint above the lapping water.

"Very much so. Yes."

"Who was it, Dad?"

David brought the camera to his face once again, eliminating every chance that his daughter might spy the wetness around his eyes or his crinkled lips. Every day David thought about his brother, Levi, and the icebox his father had built. He remembered summer mornings when a man with a nose like a decaying cherry would lug a gigantic cube of ice to the back door. His mother would begrudgingly deposit a few pennies in the man's creased palm and then grumble about the absurdity of it all. Paying for nothing, she had said. Those pennies seemed so insignificant now to David, but how it had cost them. That ice, and the heedlessness of the adults who bought it.

But still, ice melts, and the run-off is tossed away.

David slipped his camera into its case, then screwed the lid on Marnie's thermos with a vigorous twist. "C'mon," he said. "We can talk on the way home."

As they walked down the winding road, wary of the cars that braved the pungent mist, Marnie said, "Did you get any good photos?"

"I'm not sure. I won't know until I develop them."

"What do you think it is? That figure that keeps showing up on your film."

"I don't know. Most will say it's just light or maybe even something wrong with my camera. Perhaps that's the truth of it. Though, if you're asking for my honest opinion, I believe sometimes when you shake off your own ghosts, other peoples' become all the more easy to see."

In the games room of Serenity's Garden Old Age Home, Hazel Boone was biding her time. She roosted in a well-worn wingback, red plaid fabric with fraying edges. Within an hour of arriving, she had claimed the seat, never forfeiting, as it was the only piece of furniture not swaddled in crinkling plastic. She plucked loose threads from the seat, tucked them into her sleeve. Time sailed past her. And when the Christmas tree lights blurred beside her, Hazel too had the soothing sensation she was in a state of motion. Though she wasn't really. Not yet.

Everything was different now. Since that tiny angel had arrived and she had carried him across, she was calmer, cooler. Yet, her mind had grown increasingly sludgy, and she could no longer retrieve her steps, her actions. Although she could recall certain moments with absolute clarity, those distant memories felt like perpetual punishment. Hazel preferred to reside in the present, where innocent confusion was akin to pleasure.

Not identified as a wander risk by the staff, Hazel was permitted to move about the home at her leisure. She did not partake in card games, avoided all crafts, and never gaped at the blaring television for hour upon hour like other residents. Instead, she lingered by the crackling fire and waited.

Nearing midnight on Christmas, Hazel was awoken by a sound similar to claws scratching at the window. Opening her eyes, she saw flecks of snow, crystals scraped across the smudged glass by strong winds. A blizzard. She stood, zipped her floor length mint green velour bathrobe to her neck. Over her head, she draped a black scarf, tied it underneath her chin. The scarf covered a mat of hair that was almost entirely white, only a scattered strand of the brilliant orange she had inherited from her mother remained. Then, softly sliding open the patio door of the games room, she plodded out.

Eager snow whisked up inside her flannelette nightgown, dove in around the cracks in her slippers. She walked steadily until Serenity's Garden disappeared. And then she stopped. Raising her face to the bursting sky, she enjoyed the sensation of the hundreds of flakes as they fluttered and flirted with her skin. In all of her years, this was a thrill she had never known.

In the two hours that followed, Hazel's senses became increasingly acute. She smelled the snow, like wet wool in her nostrils, and sensed every prickle of ice as it crept into her fingers, toes, the tip of her nose. In the distance, she heard the forlorn howls of three dogs. Calling to her. Yes, she had tarried long enough. Finally it was time to go. Turning around in the thick drift pressing up against her bare ankles, she selected a random direction. And as she began her homeward journey through the blinding storm, she felt the pure warmth of a hand, resting comfortably on her bony shoulder and guiding her every step.

Nicole Lundrigan

grew up in Upper Gullies, Newfoundland, before receiving
an MSc in Anthropology from the University of Toronto.
She has written freelance for a variety of publications including,
Reader's Digest, *Mothering: The Natural Family Living Magazine*,
Law and Order: Police Management, and the *Halifax Daily Herald*.
Nicole's first novel, *Unraveling Arva*, was listed in the
Globe and Mail's Top Ten Crime Books for 2004.
She resides in Ontario with her husband and two daughters,
and is at work on her third novel.

Also by Nicole Lundrigan

UNRAVELING ARVA

After her eccentric mother's death, young Arva House moves to a close-knit outport in the hope of escaping the past that plagues her. But tangled rumours follow, and she soon becomes the object of speculation. Craving a sense of stability, Arva makes hasty choices and finds herself enmeshed in a net laden with deceit, infidelity, and hostility.

ISBN 1-894377-05-2 / $16.95 / 5.25 x 8.25 / PB